# The Crime Trade

www.booksattransworld.co.uk

# SIMON KERNICK

# The Crime Trade

## BANTAM PRESS

LONDON · TORONTO · SYDNEY · AUCKLAND · JOHANNESBURG

TRANSWORLD PUBLISHERS
61–63 Uxbridge Road, London W5 5SA
a division of The Random House Group Ltd

RANDOM HOUSE AUSTRALIA (PTY) LTD
20 Alfred Street, Milsons Point, Sydney,
New South Wales 2061, Australia

RANDOM HOUSE NEW ZEALAND LTD
18 Poland Road, Glenfield, Auckland 10, New Zealand

RANDOM HOUSE SOUTH AFRICA (PTY) LTD
Endulini, 5a Jubilee Road, Parktown 2193, South Africa

Published 2004 by Bantam Press
a division of Transworld Publishers

A catalogue record for this book is available from the British Library.
ISBN 0593 051351 (cased)
0593 052420 (tpb)

Typeset in 11/16 pt Times by
Falcon Oast Graphic Art Ltd

Printed in Great Britain by
Clays Ltd, Bungay, Suffolk

1 3 5 7 9 10 8 6 4 2

Papers used by Transworld Publishers are natural, recyclable products made from wood grown in
sustainable forests. The manufacturing processes conform to the environmental regulations of
the country of origin.

*For Rachel*

# Part One

## THE OPERATION

# 1

'Where's the money?'

'Where's the gear?'

'Gear?'

Stegs kept his expression neutral. 'The dope. The drugs. The stuff we're buying.'

The Colombian allowed himself a tiny smirk. It reminded Stegs of the expression Barry Growler, a notorious bully at his old school, used to pull before inflicting one of his famous punishments. 'It's close to here,' he said.

'So's the money.'

'OK. That's good.'

'I'm going to need to see the gear first, before I hand over any cash. I'll have to test it, see that the quality's right.'

'You don't trust me?' asked the Colombian, his hands raised in a gesture of jovial innocence. The smirk grew wider.

Stegs didn't like the look of it at all, but that was the thing in their game. You couldn't trust anyone, and not only that, you could never tell how they were going to behave either. This was his first time dealing with Colombians and he couldn't help thinking about the scene in that old Al Pacino film, *Scarface*, when Al and his mate, Angel, go to a Miami hotel to buy some coke from a group of Colombians, only for the sellers suddenly to pull guns on them and use a chainsaw on Angel's head in a (surprisingly futile) bid to get Scarface to reveal the whereabouts of the money. Stegs was not enjoying this meeting one little bit.

Neither was his colleague, Paul 'Vokes' Vokerman. Vokes was sitting in a chair next to Stegs, across the table from the Colombian, Fellano, and he was fidgeting big-time, like he had crabs.

Fellano, on the other hand, was oozing confidence, but then he also had three bodyguards scattered about the hotel room, and Stegs would have bet a grand no problem that they were all packing firearms. Under those circumstances, he had pretty good reason to be confident.

Now it was Stegs's turn to smile. 'It's not like that, Mr Fellano.'

'Jose, please.'

'Jose.' Jose. Typical. It had to be fucking Jose. 'It's not like that, but you have to understand my position. I have to satisfy myself, and my partners, that the goods are genuine. We've only done business once before, on a much smaller scale, and I don't want there to be any complications or misunderstandings this early in the relationship.'

'Of course. You are right. We don't want any . . . misunderstandings.'

Stegs didn't like the way Fellano emphasized the word 'misunderstandings'. In fact there wasn't anything he liked about him, and he knew Vokes felt the same way. Fellano was about forty-five, possibly a couple of years older, and well built with a large, square-shaped head and features that were berry dark and more South American Indian than Hispanic. He was dressed very smartly, but without ostentation, and he had an amiable air about him which Stegs had seen on serious criminals plenty of times before, and which he knew would disappear faster than a bun at a weightwatchers' convention the moment you got on the wrong side of him. Stegs was keen for that not to happen.

He pulled a weighing machine out of the bag and put it on the desk, hoping that it would act as a hint, which it did. Fellano turned in his chair and nodded to one of the bodyguards, who was leaning against the opposite wall, next to the kingsize bed with the silk sheets. The bodyguard, also wearing dark glasses (in fact, Fellano was the only one of them who wasn't), left his post and walked into an adjoining room, emerging a few moments later with a briefcase. He brought the briefcase over to the table and handed it to Fellano. There was a moment's pause while Fellano fiddled with the locks, then the briefcase flicked open. He put it on the table with the open part facing Stegs. There was a single kilo bag of coke in there.

Stegs stared at Fellano. 'Our deal was for twenty kilos, not for one. I was under the impression you were a major player.'

'Come on, Steve, we're wasting our time here,' said Vokes, using the codename for Stegs he always liked to stick to.

Fellano didn't even look at him. Instead, he addressed Stegs. 'You talk about trust, Steve, and I understand that, but tell me this. How can I trust you? You could be anyone. You could be a police officer for all I know.'

'I think my colleague might be right, Mr Fellano. Maybe we are wasting our time here. I thought I'd provided you with all the credentials you needed, plus twenty grand of our money for that first kilo. If you still don't think I'm kosher after all that, then there's nothing I can do about it.' Stegs started to stand up. 'Maybe you ought to look for another buyer.'

'I have the rest of the consignment nearby, but I now wish to see the money.'

'OK, but I want to see the rest of the gear at the same time.'

Fellano nodded. 'Sure, I understand that.'

'The money's not here, but it's also nearby. I'll show you it, Mr Fellano, and one of your men, but I'm not going outside with all of you. It's too risky. We'll arouse suspicion.'

'Then your partner will need to stay here.'

Vokes looked at Stegs, his expression one of concern. 'I told you this was a waste of time, Steve. We don't need to deal with people like this.' He stepped away from the table.

Stegs put his hand up. 'Hold on, Paulie. Wait a minute.'

'What's the point? We're just getting taken round the houses here.'

'Because I didn't drive all the way over here for nothing, that's why.' He turned to the Colombian. 'All right, Mr Fellano, here's what I suggest. My man stays here with two of yours, then you, me and your other guy take a walk down to wherever you've got the stuff. You show it to me, and after that, if you want, I'll take you to the money. Then we return here and make the transaction. How does that sound?'

Vokes wanted to say something, but Stegs gave him a look that said 'Come on, don't blow this,' and Vokes appeared to relent, although he didn't look too happy about it. But that was the thing about the drugs business, particularly the high end. The complete lack of trust meant that even a routine retail transaction required a half-hour debate and more than a couple of heart-stopping risks.

Fellano thought about it for a moment. 'OK,' he said, nodding slowly. 'That sounds fair.'

Stegs turned to his mate, who'd now sat down again. 'Are you all right with staying here for a few moments, Paulie?'

'No, not really. Maybe *you* should stay here.'

'We've decided,' said Fellano with some finality. 'You stay here.'

Stegs patted Vokes on the shoulder. 'I'll only be gone a few moments and I don't think Mr Fellano here is reckless enough to cause any problems in a hotel room with thin walls in the middle of Heathrow. Am I right, Mr Fellano?'

'I want this deal done as much as you do, Steve, even if your friend is not so keen.'

'He's just cautious, that's all.'

'A man can get over-cautious.'

'Not in this game,' said Stegs, with a cold smile. 'So whereabouts nearby is the other nineteen kilos you promised?'

'In the trunk of a hire car in the parking lot.'

Stegs nodded. It wasn't an ideal location, but it was wet and windy outside, so they probably weren't going to get too much attention. 'Shall we go, then?'

'Are you sure about this, Steve?' asked Vokes.

'I'll be ten minutes. No more. Then we do the deal and we walk.'

Fellano stood up and motioned for one of the bodyguards – a wiry little guy with a droopy moustache and seventies hair – to come with him. He then said something in Spanish to the other two. Vokes looked nervous, and Stegs felt a pang of guilt, having given him the worst job. The job of hostage. But he couldn't see any other way.

'Let's go,' said the Colombian, and he and Moustache walked to the door.

'Tell him to get those fucking shades off,' Stegs said to Fellano. 'He'll stick out a mile in them on a wet March day at Heathrow airport.'

Fellano gabbled something else in Spanish, and Moustache took them off, giving Stegs a dirty look as he did so. Stegs ignored him. 'I'll be back in a mo, Paulie, all right? Just stay here and keep these two company.'

Vokes looked at the two silent Colombians watching him from the far wall, then back at his partner. 'Don't be long,' he said.

'Ten minutes,' Stegs answered. 'Ten minutes max.'

No-one spoke in the lift down to the ground floor, and when the doors opened, Stegs hung back while the two Colombians walked through the busy reception area and out of the rear doors that led directly into the hotel's car park. After spending a few seconds perusing a selection of the day's newspapers and magazines that were laid out on a low mahogany table, he walked casually in the direction they'd taken.

It was raining steadily outside and the cloud cover was so grey and thick that the day was almost dark. Only a handful of people were scattered about, and they were mainly businessmen, hurrying along under umbrellas, so immersed in their working lives that not one of them even glanced up as he passed.

He walked between the rows of parked cars and made his way towards the back of the car park, keeping ten or twelve yards behind the Colombians, watching for anyone who looked out of place. A middle-aged man in jeans and a Barbour jacket getting out of his car caught his eye, but the man looked away without interest, and the moment passed.

When the two Colombians got to the last row of cars, parked against a high brick wall that marked the car park's boundary some fifty yards from the hotel, Fellano looked left and right as nonchalantly as possible, then back at Stegs. Stegs smiled like he knew them both, then quickened his pace and caught up, walking between the two of them without speaking as they approached a new metallic-blue BMW 7 Series. A typical high-end dealer's car. It made Stegs wonder whether BMW approved of the fact that so many of its customers were involved in the illicit drugs trade. Perhaps one day they'd end up sponsoring crack dens.

Fellano stopped three feet from the back of the car and de-activated the alarm.

Upstairs in the hotel room, Vokes Vokerman paced nervously, trying to ignore the two other men in the room as they watched him boredly, one by the door, the other against the opposite wall. Vokes had expected there to be the usual to-ing and fro-ing, as there always was on a big deal like this one, but he hadn't wanted to be the one left up here with the Colombians while Stegs went walkabout. It had happened before of course, them being split up on an op. More than once, since nobody ever took you at your word in the drugs game; except this time, it shouldn't have happened. They'd been told by the handlers to bring the money into the room with them, but instead had opted to keep it back, thinking it would show they were serious buyers (i.e. distrustful) if they turned up without it. Which was now looking more and more like a mistake. This meeting had been in the making for weeks, months even. The Colombians had their credentials, knew their backgrounds – their pedigree in the importation game – and there'd already been a test purchase of a kilo, for which they'd handed over twenty grand. And still they didn't seem satisfied.

Since he and Stegs had arrived more than an hour ago, they'd been thoroughly searched, before undergoing a long and repetitive sequence of questions from Fellano about deals they'd done, people they were meant to know, etc. The Colombian had been trying to read them, to probe for weakness, not so much in their accounts of themselves, but in their characters, and Vokes was beginning to convince himself that the reason for this was that he was on to them. Knew who they were and was working out what to do about it. Fellano was a ruthless man. He had a reasonably good reputation in the marketplace (as much as anyone who sells hard drugs has a reasonably good reputation), but cross him – give him any reason to doubt you – and you could expect no mercy. Vokes had heard a rumour once that Fellano had personally cut the tongue out of a police informant's mouth back in Cali, and had replaced it with the man's penis. It wasn't a thought he wanted to dwell on.

He kept pacing, telling himself that it was he who was getting too paranoid. What possible reason was there to suspect the two of them? As always, they'd played everything just right, their stories standing up even to the closest scrutiny, their demeanour that of men not to be trifled with. And with back-up just round the corner, ready to move in if anything looked like it was going to go wrong. But even bearing all this in mind, Vokes didn't like the fact that he was split up from his partner and stuck in a hotel room with two armed men who insisted on wearing sunglasses on a wet English afternoon.

The phone on the bedside table rang, shattering the heavy silence.

Vokes stopped. Dead.

Slowly, he turned and stared at it. So did the two Colombians. It rang again, a long, shrill tone that seemed far too loud for the room. Who the hell was this meant to be?

An urgent message in his head said: Run! Get out of there! In fact, it didn't just say it, it screamed it. RUN! GRAB THE DOOR HANDLE, TURN IT, AND GET YOUR ARSE OUT OF THERE!

He glanced at the two Colombians, who were looking at each other, their expressions puzzled. The phone rang a third time.

One of them strode over and picked up the receiver. At the same time, the second Colombian, perhaps reading their hostage's thoughts, produced a silver Walther PPK from inside his suit. He pointed it at Vokes and motioned him to get on the bed. 'Now, now,' he demanded impatiently.

Vokes looked over at the other Colombian, the one on the phone. He hadn't said anything since he'd picked it up but was listening to someone on the other end, at the same time staring hard at Vokes. He too removed a gun from his pocket – a Glock, Vokes reckoned. It didn't seem like he was pleased by whatever it was he was hearing.

Vokes thought of his two young children and realized then that he was too old for this game; that this was the last time he'd ever go undercover; that no more would he attend clandestine meetings in bleak hotel rooms with men who'd kill him without a second's thought because that was what life was worth where they came from – nothing. He realized too that he was beginning to panic for the first time ever on an op, an unfamiliar feeling of dread spreading through him like a poison, and that was another reason why Stegs should have been up here in this room instead of him, because he was always able to handle the pressure.

'Get on the bed, now.'

The words came from the one holding the phone, except now he wasn't holding it, he'd replaced it in its cradle, and his expression behind the glasses was angry. He walked over, gun waving, and grabbed Vokes by the arm, pushing him towards the bed. Vokes tried to sit on it, but was roughly pushed face down. He could feel the barrel of the Glock against the back of his head.

'Stay there, do not move,' said the gunman, before adding something to his colleague in Spanish.

Vokes was shaking, shaking with absolute fear, and he could

feel the sweat from his forehead sliding onto the sheets. He offered a silent prayer to the Lord, but it didn't make him feel any better. He had never been so scared in his life because he knew that this was the closest he had ever been to death. And all the time he was wondering who the hell had made that phone call, what they'd said and, most importantly of all, when the cavalry were going to show themselves.

The boot opened to reveal a leather briefcase similar to the one Fellano had shown them upstairs. He and Stegs leant in, trying to look as inconspicuous as possible, while Moustache stood back. Fellano unclipped the locks and opened the case. A quick count revealed nineteen kilo bags of white powder inside.

'Are you satisfied, my friend?' the Colombian asked with a smile.

'I'll need to test it, a sample from each bag.'

'Of course, we will do that back in the room.'

Stegs nodded, standing back up as he shut the briefcase and closed the boot. 'I'll go and get the money and catch you up,' he said. 'My car's just over there.'

Fellano raised an eyebrow to indicate that he wasn't sure about this change of plan.

'We'll look too conspicuous going over and staring in the boot of my car as well,' Stegs told him, 'and now I know you've got the stuff, plus my colleague, I've got no incentive not to bring it up to the room.'

Fellano still didn't appear convinced and gave him a hard stare in an attempt to prise out any lies from behind his eyes, but Stegs kept his business expression firmly on his face, and eventually the Colombian relented. 'All right, but I want to get this deal sorted out right now, so hurry up. I have a plane to catch.'

Stegs felt like telling him that if he hadn't messed them around so much earlier he'd have had a lot more time, but instead he turned and walked away in the direction of the parked Merc fifty yards further along the row of cars. When he'd gone about twenty yards, he turned and saw Fellano and Moustache walking back to the hotel, Fellano's ample wedge of black hair flying comically about in the high wind. He was talking on a mobile, and Stegs wondered who it was he was speaking to, and what exactly he was saying.

He reached the Merc, flicked up the boot and removed the holdall, putting it over one shoulder. Fellano and Moustache had slowed right up in the middle of the car park, waiting for him. Reluctantly, he started after them, wondering just how conspicuous they wanted to be, and why they didn't want to wait five minutes in the warmth of the hotel room for him to arrive, rather than hanging about in the rain.

When he was within about twenty yards of them, something caught his eye. Three smartly dressed men – two black, one white – in raincoats and caps were getting out of a car a few yards behind the Colombians and to their right, and one of them was watching them intently from behind a pair of glasses that looked brand new and didn't seem to fit his face.

The man didn't look right, not at all. Neither did the other two. They might have been dressed smartly but they weren't like any normal businessmen Stegs had ever met. Who on earth wears a baseball cap with a suit? Maybe the odd fashion casualty, not three together. There was something else too. They were hard bastards, you could see it immediately; it's not a look a man can hide very easily. He also noticed that the black guy with the glasses was holding something under his coat.

Straight away he knew it was a gun, most likely a shotgun, and straight away he knew that it was there to be pointed at Fellano. Instinctively, he slowed down. At the same time, Fellano turned in Stegs's direction, tapping his watch in a gesture of impatience, and then suddenly a look of shock crossed his face.

Stegs froze as he heard the sound of rapid footsteps behind him, and the next second something hard and metallic was being pressed into his back. 'Don't fucking move,' hissed his assailant, ripping the holdall from his shoulders, 'or you're dead. I'll blow your fucking spine out. Got that?'

'It's all yours,' said Stegs calmly, making no move to resist, too busy looking straight ahead of him at the scene unravelling in what felt a lot like slow motion. Moustache was reaching into his pocket for a gun while Fellano himself simply stood there, mouth open, watching Stegs, still completely unaware that the three men were making straight for him and the briefcase, weapons now appearing from under their coats. Stegs was right about the shotgun; it was a nasty-looking sawn-off pump-action, and it was pointing straight at Fellano's back.

At that moment, Fellano must have heard them, or seen something out of the corner of his eye, because he swung round in their direction. Moustache turned as well, an Uzi coming out from his jacket, and Stegs, still standing there as his assailant secured the holdall, knew then that this was going to get very very messy.

'Give us the fucking case!' screamed the man with the shotgun, now only five yards from Fellano.

At the same time, Moustache aimed the Uzi at the three robbers, pushing his boss out of the way and going for the safety at the same time. Beyond the group, Stegs could see those people in earshot turning round to see what on earth was going on, utterly transfixed by the shock of the surreal scene being played out in front of them. It was a first for Stegs as well, and difficult for him to get his head round, because even in his sort of game you didn't expect everyone suddenly to go for the guns and start shooting. That sort of thing belonged firmly in Hollywood films.

'Drop the fucking gun!' yelled the pistol-wielding white robber as he caught sight of the Uzi for the first time, but it was already too late.

Shotgun screwed his face into a snarl and, still coming at his target, pulled the trigger.

And that was when all hell broke loose. Moustache flew backwards, the force of the blast lifting him off his feet, while his Uzi suddenly kicked into life, its thirty-two rounds discharging at the sky in a shrill clatter as his grip on the handle loosened. He hit the ground hard and the shotgun roared again, the noise making Stegs's ears ring. This time, though, it missed its target and blew a gaping hole in the tyre of a people carrier opposite, immediately setting off the alarm.

Someone somewhere let out a scream. Someone somewhere else shouted: 'Armed police, drop your weapons!'

The white robber had reached Fellano now and was trying to wrestle the briefcase out of his hand, with the help of one of his colleagues. Meanwhile Shotgun was waving his weapon in the direction of the dozen or so men in casual clothes – all wearing black caps – who were now appearing from among the cars, guns drawn, closing in on the scene.

'Armed police! Drop your weapons!'

But you could see straight away that Shotgun was not going to go quietly. This was a man who had never gone quietly anywhere in his life. His face screaming defiance, he pointed the weapon at a youngish guy in jeans and a leather jacket who was just coming round the back of the people carrier, an MP5 outstretched in both hands.

The cop made the decision no-one with a conscience ever likes to make, and he made it quicker than his target. Two bullets cracked out of the MP5, hitting Shotgun in the upper body.

Another cop also fired from behind a Nissan, the same two-shot double tap, this time the rounds striking their target in the face.

Shotgun whirled round, still holding the weapon, still trying to fire, and then a third two-shot volley struck him in the side of the head, the final bloody *coup de grâce*. He died immediately, staring in Stegs's direction, the shotgun slipping out of his hands and discharging for a third time as it hit the ground in a final gesture of defiant rage, the blast setting off another car alarm.

No-one else decided to go out the hard way. Fellano's hands shot skywards, and the other two robbers made the same gesture, although far more slowly, the shock of their predicament taking a little longer to register. At the same time, two cops in caps came round from behind Stegs, and he was pushed roughly to the ground. He just managed to get a glance at the man who'd relieved him of his holdall getting the same treatment five yards away before his face was pushed into a puddle and the cuffs were unceremoniously forced on to his wrists.

The hotel room was on the fifth floor and the same side as the car park, so even with the soundproofing the shots and the general cacophony of the confrontation were clearly audible.

Vokes heard his two guards talking rapidly to each other in Spanish, and his fear grew even more intense. He was shaking violently, the dread at what might happen to him becoming almost unbearable. If I get out of this, then that's it, he told himself. I'm retired. Not just undercover, but the whole thing. They had a codeword if things went wrong but he didn't want to draw attention to himself by using it, and anyway, help should have been here by now. They were only in the next room. What was keeping them? Hurry up! he silently cursed. Get your arses moving! Let me get back to my family. Please, Father. Please, Lord. Not for me, but for them.

One of the Colombians had stopped at the end of the bed. Vokes could sense it. Then he heard the door opening, the sound of movement and shouting in the corridor outside, and he was already thanking the good Lord for listening to his prayers when the silencer spat and the bullet ripped through the back of his head and into his brain.

Paul Vokerman's executioner was twenty-eight-year-old Manuel Lopez, known as Manolo to his friends, a long-term junior member of the Cali cartel and an ex-soldier in the Colombian army, now resident in London. He was a killer by trade and, as Vokes had suspected, thought no more about ending a life than he did about taking a leak. It was, after all, just business.

Manolo fired a second round into the back of Vokes's head, just to make sure, then turned towards the open door where his colleague, twenty-six-year-old Pedro Daroda, was standing. He could hear the noise of footsteps coming from outside, then the staccato bark of orders, and he realized they'd been betrayed. Pedro stepped out into the hallway, raised his gun, and then fell backwards as shots rang out. Manolo ran over to the side of the bed furthest from the door, then crouched down gun pointed out into the hallway, thinking that he was at least going to make it difficult for them.

A black-clad figure half appeared round the door, gun outstretched, and Manolo fired twice, both rounds hitting the burgundy-coloured wall in the hallway as the cop stepped back. A moment later, a second cop appeared round the other side of the door, and started firing. Manolo let off a shot but was forced to turn away as the bullets passed over his head, the noise of them bursting in his ears. Suddenly there was a much louder bang somewhere near the foot of the bed, and he became disorientated and unable to see properly. It was as if somebody had force-fed him a bottle of whisky and dropped him on his head from a fifth-floor window, and he knew they'd used a stun grenade. But, even dazed, he still held the gun as the black-clad police in breathing apparatus came into view and, with a gesture of defiance that perfectly mirrored the expression of the man with the shotgun in the car park below, raised it in front of him, aiming at the first officer's crotch.

Sergeant Phil Winter of Scotland Yard's elite firearms squad SO19 didn't hestitate. He'd already seen the body of DC Paul Vokerman face-down on the bed, a growing bloodstain soaking the sheets around his head; now one of the suspects, hunched down in the corner of the room beside the bed, was lifting his gun. Two shots, then a step, two shots, then another step, then another two shots, every one of them finding their target. Beside him Constable Sammy Jecks opened up with his MP5, and the body of Manuel Lopez did a strange dance as the bullets ripped into his head and body and charged about his insides, ripping them and him apart.

Minimum force. The training always says only the minimum amount of force possible must be used to incapacitate a subject. Shoot him too many times, particularly when it's clear he's no longer a threat, and a police officer leaves him or herself open to charges of manslaughter, or even, in extreme cases, murder. But Winter couldn't resist pumping another two into the Colombian's guts as he continued towards him, knowing that statistically he probably wasn't going to get another opportunity to pop a bad guy. Lopez's head slumped, the Glock with silencer fell from his dead hand, and Winter stopped in front of him, before kicking him hard in the face.

Jecks rushed up to Vokerman and tried to find a pulse, but Winter could tell from the expression on his colleague's face that it was a lost cause. He turned to the door as the senior officers involved in what was supposed to have been a highly successful sting operation entered the room along with the remainder of the SO19 team. They didn't look too happy.

And that, unfortunately, is where I, DI John Gallan, join the tale, being one of those senior officers involved. The thing is, I was only meant to be there as an observer, as was my colleague, WDS Tina Boyd, but I don't think that fact made either of us feel any better. It had been our informant who had provided the details and false character references that had set up 'Stegs' Jenner and Paul 'Vokes' Vokerman, both members of Scotland Yard's specialist undercover unit, SO10, with a group of high-level Colombian drugs traffickers, so as Tina and I followed DCS Noel Flanagan and DI Asif Malik of Scotland Yard's organized crime unit, SO7, into the hotel room, I was experiencing a feeling in my insides that was a nasty combination of fear, shame and nausea. As I saw the ruined bodies of Manolo Lopez and Vokes Vokerman, one of whom I'd got to know quite well over the past few weeks, watched the frantic efforts of the medical team as they worked their futile magic, and heard DI Malik curse loudly under his breath, the question I remember I kept asking myself was a very simple one.

What the hell had gone wrong?

# 2

'What the fuck went wrong?'

The voice belonged to Detective Chief Superintendent Noel Flanagan who'd been in charge of the monumentally misnamed Operation Surgical Strike, the carefully planned sting that had resulted in the deaths of five people, one of them a decorated police officer with eighteen years' service under his belt, and the hospitalization of a witness who'd suffered a heart attack at the scene. It was a good question, and one Flanagan was going to need to get answered if there was any hope of him saving his hitherto successful, if not entirely blameless, career. Three hours had passed since the gun battle in the hotel car park and the fall-out was already beginning.

The scene of this, the first inquest into the events of that afternoon, was a specially set up incident room in one of the hotel's ground-floor conference suites. At one end of the table, sitting with his legs crossed and a cigarette in his mouth, was DC Stegs Jenner. There was a half-full cup of coffee – his third – in front of him. Facing him down at the other end of the table was the skinny, stooped frame of DCS Flanagan, whose normally dour face was now red with anger. The others in the room were DI Malik; Inspector Leon Ferman who'd been running things from the SO19 standpoint; and finally Tina Boyd and me. The atmosphere was thick with the tension and impatience of individuals who know they're going to be in the verbal firing line. What had happened that afternoon had been near enough unprecedented in post-Second World War Britain, and there was a strong feeling that the media were going to be crawling all over this bloody event, which meant that it was important to find out as soon as possible exactly where it had all gone so pear-shaped. And the best person initially to answer that question was Stegs Jenner.

I was watching Stegs carefully. Everyone was watching him carefully, waiting to hear what he had to say. We'd met three times in the run-up to today, two of those meetings over a beer, and, if truth be told, I liked the guy. He was a maverick, and a cocky one at that, with the sort of devil-may-care attitude that always makes enemies in the insular, regimented world of the Met, but he carried it well, and I couldn't help admiring the fact that he was prepared to risk his neck in some very dangerous situations, this afternoon's being a case in point. The last time we'd met up had been six days earlier at New Scotland Yard. Stegs had been sounding confident then, and when I'd told him to be careful on the op, a beaming smile had lit up his face and he'd told me not to worry, he'd done this sort of thing plenty of times before. Call me a pessimist, but I always worry when someone says that.

He looked very different now. Drawn, tired, and most of all tense, as if he knew the tidal wave of questions was only just gathering momentum and could end up sinking him. Even his startlingly bright-blue eyes appeared to have dulled. The expression invited sympathy, and I was prepared to give him some, although I'm pretty sure I was the only one in the room who was.

'So come on, Jenner,' continued Flanagan, 'tell us. What the hell went wrong?'

'I don't know,' he said wearily, taking a drag from his cigarette. 'The Colombian, Fellano, was fucking us about. He was really paranoid. I think he may even have had half a sniff we were police.'

'Then why on earth did you split up from Vokerman?'

'You know why I split up from him. Because I wasn't going to show Fellano the money until I saw the gear, and the gear wasn't there in the room. That's the way it works in these sort of things – in case you didn't know.'

'I know exactly how it fucking works, Jenner!' snapped Flanagan, his expression darkening until his face was almost puce. 'That's why I run SO7. But it wasn't in the plan for you to split up, was it? You were meant to take the money up to the room with you in the first place. Why didn't you do that?'

'I didn't want him thinking he was dealing with a couple of amateurs. If we'd gone waltzing in with the cash, that's what we would have looked like. They would have suspected something. I told you that when we were planning it. We would never have got hold of the drugs.'

'And we wouldn't have had five dead bodies strewn round the airport, dozens of petrified civilians, including one in intensive care, and half the world's media coming down on us like a pack of fucking wolves.' Flanagan's face grew redder as he spoke, something that thanks to his lanky frame gave him more than a passing resemblance to a matchstick. I thought that he'd better watch himself otherwise he was going to be joining the civilian in intensive care.

'This is the first time one of my ops has ever gone wrong,' said Stegs firmly, holding Flanagan's gaze.

'And go wrong it certainly fucking did. You only need one mistake when it's as big as that.'

'It's easy enough criticizing when you're stood watching everything from a safe distance. It's a lot harder when you're out there on your own. Ninety per cent of that cash was counterfeit. If they'd checked it carefully enough, we'd have put ourselves in even more danger.'

'Don't make excuses, Jenner. You didn't follow procedure, and because of that you put yourself, your colleague, the targets . . . the whole operation, in jeopardy. And, as a direct result, it all ended in . . .' He chewed around for the right word. 'Tragedy.'

'Bullshit! I did what I thought was right. I wanted to get evidence against the target, and that was the only way I could do it. It wasn't my fault that someone decided to rob us in the middle of it all. If they hadn't turned up, none of this would have happened.'

The two men continued to stare at each other, the tension between them growing. It had been there since the meeting had started. That's what I meant about Stegs being a maverick. He didn't follow procedure; he improvised – on this occasion, with alarming results – and it made him enemies. I could see why he'd done it, and I understood his explanation. If he and Vokes had simply gone in there with the money, they might have been rumbled on the spot as undercover police, too eager to make a purchase. And, to be fair to him, if the robbers hadn't turned up in the car park, we almost certainly would have got the result we were looking for. I doubted that this would be enough to save him, though.

Out of the corner of my eye, I saw Tina fixing him with an

expression of scepticism. She'd never liked him, one of those instinctive dislikes she hadn't got round to explaining, and it made me think that Stegs really was a one-man band, always on his own against the world. In other words, perfect scapegoat material.

Malik spoke next, his tone calm and even as always, his question one that had also been bugging me. 'Just after you split up from the two Colombians in the car park, Fellano made a call on his mobile. Do you have any idea who he might have been phoning?'

Stegs shook his head.

'The reason I ask,' Malik continued, 'is that at almost exactly the same time, one of the Colombians in the room received a call on the hotel phone. At the moment, we don't know what was said, because the individual taking the call didn't say anything to the caller, but as soon as it ended he became very irate, and, according to our translator, told his colleague that there was a serious problem. They then became far more agitated, and we believe they manhandled Vokes over to the bed.'

'I thought you had cameras in the room.'

'We had two cameras in there,' answered Malik, 'but it was a big place and they were pointed at the desk to cover the transaction. So there was a blind spot round by the bed. After the call, they heard the shots and decided to bail out, but they finished off Vokes first. Quite why, we're not sure. And for some reason he didn't give his codeword.'

'I'm surprised that when the shooting started out in the car park you lot didn't go in anyway,' said Stegs, looking first at Malik, then at Flanagan.

'SO19 were in the room within twenty seconds of the first shots being fired in the car park,' said Leon Ferman, a powerfully built black man who looked like he didn't take criticism lightly. 'And within thirty, both suspects were dead. How much faster would you have wanted it done?'

'Fast enough to have saved him,' said Stegs drily.

Ferman started to say something else but Malik put up a hand to stop him. 'It's OK, Leon,' he said, and Ferman reluctantly quietened. 'The fact remains, Stegs, that he didn't give the signal, and we had absolutely no idea they were going to shoot him. SO19 were in the rooms directly on either side, as you're fully aware, and were given the order to go in as quickly as possible. It's a tragedy that it wasn't quick enough, but there was nothing we could have done about that.'

The operation's handlers – Flanagan, Malik and Ferman – had been watching events unfold from a room some way down the corridor from the one where the meeting had been taking place. Tina and I had been in there too, along with the translator and several other technical staff, and we'd seen near enough every-thing, bar the final bloody denouement, which had taken place off camera. Because the operations room had been on the other side of the hotel from the car park, and the shooting out of immediate earshot, it had only just been picked up on the surveillance tapes. As a result, there'd been a momentary delay before the order to go in was relayed by Ferman to the SO19 team, a delay that had proved fatal. However, it was difficult to know what could have been done to prevent it. Our operational incident room had deliberately been located some distance from where the deal was going down, because having that many people so close, particularly when we had the tapes of what was being said playing in the room, would have aroused too much suspicion.

Flanagan, though, clearly knew that plenty of people were going to be hunting for mistakes, and would probably find at least some, so he was following the politician's standard philosophy of blaming someone else. 'So, you had no idea why Fellano could have made that call, or who he was calling?' he demanded, the suggestion clear that he thought Jenner must have known.

'Of course I didn't. Why would I?'

'Nothing was discussed?'

'No.' Stegs stubbed out his cigarette. 'Look, I don't know what the fuck you're trying to insinuate, but all I was trying to do was nail one of the bad guys. It fucked up, the whole thing fucked up, and I lost a good mate . . .' He paused for a moment as if that particular piece of news had only just fully arrived in his consciousness. 'But it can't be my fault that a bunch of blokes I've never seen in my life suddenly turn up out of the blue, pull shooters, and stage an armed robbery right in the middle of the op. Someone should have spotted them a mile off. Why didn't that happen? And why did they get a chance to start shooting?'

'The op was stretched,' said Ferman. 'If you hadn't decided to go walkabout with the target, then we'd have had a lot better coverage. We had to pull men from all over the place to get them into that car park.'

'You know, you're all looking at everything the wrong way.'

'What do you mean?' demanded Flanagan.

'Those blokes who turned up out of the blue were the ones who fucked this job. How did they know about the operation? That's the question.'

Which was the moment when Flanagan, Ferman and Stegs all turned and looked straight at Tina and me.

'Hold on,' said Tina, making a pre-emptive strike. 'Wait a minute here. We gave you guys a lead, and we've had nothing further to do with it, so don't start setting us up for fall-guys.'

'It's a good question, though,' said Malik. 'How did they know about the deal? Could your informant have talked?'

Our informant – the one who'd helped organize this meeting – was Robert O'Brien, better known as Slim Robbie on account of the fact that he was as fat as a house. A thirty-year-old thug and career criminal who'd only agreed to set up the Colombians to save himself from a long prison sentence, after being set up in a similar sting by undercover police. It was fair to say that Robbie O'Brien lived and breathed the illegal. Asking if he could have talked, particularly if talking resulted in a profit for him, was like asking if whores have sex or Christians believe. It was pretty much a rhetorical question. Except for one thing.

'We never told him the details of the op,' I said. 'I didn't even know them myself until a few hours ago. I set up the intro- ductions between the informant and Stegs, and I've spoken to him since then, but only about other matters, so if he knew any- thing about this meeting, he didn't hear it from us. And anyway, how would he have known that Stegs and the Colombians were going to end up in the car park with the money and the drugs?'

Eyes now returned to Stegs, who shrugged. 'Robbie O'Brien was involved in setting up today's meeting. He had to be: the Colombians were his contacts, not ours. And he was involved all along as well, at least up until a few days back. But I never told him the location, and I'm sure Vokes didn't either. Like you, John' – he nodded towards me – 'we didn't know it ourselves until a few hours back. Fellano likes to leave those sort of things to the last minute, for obvious reasons. O'Brien might have guessed, I suppose, because he knew Fellano had met people at this hotel before. And he would have been aware that Fellano was flying in in the last few days, but I haven't spoken to him since Sunday, so I can't see how he'd have known the timing.'

'We're going to have to bring O'Brien in for questioning,' said Flanagan, also looking at me.

'We're on the case, sir,' said Tina firmly, making doubly sure that Flanagan knew she was there too. 'We've already called the station and they're searching for him.'

'No joy yet?'

'Not yet, but we'll get him,' she said confidently, a tone in her voice suggesting that you wouldn't want to be Slim Robbie when she got her hands on him. Tina Boyd might have looked like the pretty, college-educated girl from a good, middle-class family that she was, but you know what they say about appearances. She was a far tougher cookie than most people gave her credit for, and I would have almost felt sorry for Robbie if he hadn't been such a scumbag.

At that moment, a mobile rang shrilly. It was Malik's. He removed it from his pocket, and I noticed with some amusement that it was a new and predictably flash little number that probably doubled as a pocket PC and digital camera. Typical. With Malik, appearances weren't deceptive. He looked like the smart, young, gadget-carrying go-getter that he was. He spoke into the minuscule mouthpiece of the phone briefly, then listened for about twenty seconds, writing something in his notebook as he did so. Finally he hung up with a curt goodbye.

'Ashley Eric Grant,' he said, reading out what he'd just written. 'Also known as – and I'm not sure if he took this as a compliment or not – "Strangleman". Fingerprints have just identified him as the dead robber.'

Flanagan, now standing, looked round the table. 'Anyone know that name?' he asked hopefully. 'Ring any bells with anyone?'

'I never saw any of those blokes before in my life,' said Stegs, lighting another cigarette.

Flanagan's gaze got round to me, and I sighed loudly, wondering how much worse this day could possibly get, then told him and the room that, yes, I knew exactly who Ashley 'Strangleman' Grant was.

# 3

Ashley Grant allegedly got the nickname Strangleman years back in the Tivoli Gardens ghetto of Kingston, Jamaica, where he'd grown up. The story went that as a drug dealer and gunman loosely affiliated to the Jamaican Labour Party, or JLP, which ran that particular area, his very individual method of disposing of rivals was to have them impaled on meathooks before disembowelling them with a large butcher's knife. He would then, it was claimed, strangle the unfortunate victims with their own entrails while they choked out their last breaths.

Nobody knew how many people he'd killed this way. Nobody even knew if the story was true or not. My feeling was that there was probably something in it, but if he'd ever murdered someone in such a messy fashion I suspected that he'd only done it the once, and the victim would probably have been long dead before his colon had been wrapped round his neck. I hoped so anyway.

But what was not in doubt was that Strangleman Grant was a dangerous man. He'd been residing in the UK for about ten years, having come over in his early twenties looking to make his fortune, and had married a local girl, thereby giving him the right to remain, even though it quickly became clear that his respect for the laws of his adopted land was near enough non-existent. Of those ten years, something like half had been spent in prison, mainly for drugs and weapons offences, but he'd been out for a while now and was settled on mine and Tina's south Islington manor, which was how I knew his background. What concerned me immediately, however, was the fact that he was hooked up with the crime organization of one Nicholas Tyndall, a new and potentially very violent player in the north London cocaine trade.

A little bit of history here. Up until a few months earlier, cocaine importation and distribution in north London, particularly Islington, had been primarily the work of the Holtzes, an extended family of gangsters who'd had a stranglehold on the area's organized crime since the late 1970s, and one of whose members had been Slim Robbie O'Brien. But the Holtzes had fallen from power in spectacular fashion, their leader and one of his sons killed, and now many of their senior associates, including the leader's deputy, Neil Vamen, were in custody, awaiting trial for a variety of offences.

I'd been involved in their downfall, as had DI Malik, which was how we knew each other, but our victory had been something of a hollow one. With the Holtzes out of the picture, a vacuum had developed, and everyone knows what they say about nature and vacuums. Plenty of other outfits, some of them distinctly amateur, had tried to grab a piece of the wealth that was there to be had in the distribution of coke to the ever-growing customer base, but one of the more organized, and by all accounts more violent of them, was the Tyndall gang.

Tyndall himself was a thirtysomething, locally born thug with an entrepreneurial streak who'd started out surrounding himself with men from his own estate, but who over the last couple of years had developed relations with Jamaican and Albanian criminals operating locally, and was, as a result, one of the bigger players coming through. Strangleman Grant was one of his top enforcers and was believed to have murdered another Jamaican who'd tried to rip Tyndall off two months earlier, blowing the back of his head off in an illegal drinking den in Dalston. There'd been at least fifty witnesses to the shooting but, as is almost always the way in these sort of violent in-your-face crimes within the black community, no-one was talking, particularly as it was well known that Nicholas Tyndall was behind it. Already he was getting a reputation for being untouchable.

This is the London of today, a vast multicultural city of consumers breeding an ever-growing array of gangs from every ethnic background imaginable, all vying for control of the city's huge and incredibly lucrative crime industry. I'd heard some-where that London's organized and semi-organized criminals were responsible for raising ten billion pounds of revenues per year; mainly from drugs, but also from prostitution (now effectively sewn up by the Albanians), people smuggling and occasionally armed robbery. When I'd mentioned that figure, the ten billion, to Malik, he'd told me it was almost certainly a conservative estimate.

What I couldn't understand, though, was why Tyndall's men would be involved in robbing Fellano. I've said it before, and I hope I can keep saying it: you should never underestimate the stupidity of criminals, and it's certainly par for the course for them to rip each other off, especially when it comes to deals involving drugs, but Tyndall was no short-term merchant. He was a man on the up, with business sense as well as ruthlessness, so it made no sense for him to be falling out with a man like Fellano who was likely to be his main supplier in the coke trade.

He would be wanting to build bridges with him, not burning them down.

I told all this to the people sitting round the table, with Malik (who also knew something about the Tyndall gang) filling in some of the gaps. We both agreed that it didn't seem the typical behaviour of a man who so far had taken his steps from petty to big-money crime carefully and with plenty of thought.

'The three we've got in custody over at Paddington Green aren't talking at the moment,' said Flanagan, 'but they're facing some very long stretches, so they've got a lot of incentive to open their mouths and start incriminating each other, and whoever may have organized it. If it is anything to do with Tyndall, we'll find out.'

He was about to say something else, but then his mobile rang, the third time it had gone off since the meeting had begun. He opened it up and examined the screen. On the first two occasions, he hadn't answered it, but this time it was obvious that whoever was calling was worth talking to. It was a short, one-sided conversation, with Flanagan doing most of the listening. He did say 'Oh fuck' at one point, then there was a thirty-second pause, then he said 'Bollocks'. Then, ten seconds later, he mumbled something about being there shortly, and hung up.

Everyone looked at him expectantly. 'That was the assistant commissioner,' he said with an actor's croak, his eyes focusing on the table in front of him. 'The lady who had the heart attack, Eileen Murdoch . . . she's died.'

'Shit,' said Ferman.

And that pretty much summed up the predicament, not only of Flanagan, but of all of us involved in the violent and wholly unexpected events of that fateful day. A death toll of six now and a tidal wave of fall-out still to break.

# 4

The meeting broke up five minutes later. I had a quick word with Malik, telling him that I'd take responsibility for tracking down Robbie O'Brien, and let him know as soon as we'd picked him up. I wanted to say a few more words but he was in a hurry. He looked more concerned than I'd ever seen him before, which I could understand. Malik was a career copper, a good man with a keen sense of right and wrong, but still someone with his eyes on promotion to the upper echelons of the Serious Crime Group, and ultimately the Met, and a catastrophe like today's could set him back years if he was found to be even partly responsible.

It could set me back years too, but I wasn't so worried about it. I'd been knocked back from a DI to a DC a couple of years before, when I was stationed south of the river, so I knew not to expect much help from above when things started to go wrong. Admittedly, that time had been my own fault. I'd seen a fellow officer strike a seventeen-year-old mugger he'd arrested and, out of loyalty (misplaced or otherwise, I'll leave it for you to decide),

I and the other two officers who'd witnessed his actions had covered up for him, denying that we'd seen any wrongdoing take place. That would have been the end of it too, but an investigative journalist had picked up the story and blown the whistle. A very public investigation had followed that had culminated not only in me transferring to another station in Islington, but with my marriage breaking up, and my wife taking up residence with the same investigative journalist who'd wrecked things for me in the first place. Now, you don't often get a run of luck that bad in a lifetime, but once you've had it once, you learn a valuable lesson: always expect the unexpected. And never get too comfortable when things are going well, because otherwise the fall'll be a lot harder. I got the feeling that Malik was beginning to realize this now, and the knowledge wouldn't do him any harm.

Tina and I were parked a mile or so away from the hotel in the Compass Centre, British Airways' Heathrow offices on the A4. We got a lift there in the back of a squad car whose driver, a local uniform with a big false-looking moustache and glasses, was desperate for information as to what had gone down that afternoon. It seemed he was just as ill informed as the members of the public who'd stood gawking over the police tape at the entrance to the car park as we'd left. I told him there'd been a series of shootings, and an officer had been killed.

'When are they going to start arming us, eh?' he asked, turning round in his seat, taxi driver style.

'I've got a feeling it's not going to be long,' I answered, hoping that the day never came when I patrolled with a gun, but knowing that it was pretty much inevitable, and that today's events were just one more nail in the coffin of an unarmed force.

When we were back in the car, with Tina driving, she shook her head and cursed. 'That O'Brien, I'm going to kill him when

I catch hold of the bastard. He must have been the source of the leak.'

'I don't know what the hell he was thinking about if he was responsible,' I said. 'Why set it up when it's always going to come back to him? If he tipped Tyndall's people off, then what would he gain from it? He'd know that they'd end up getting caught, and that suspicion would automatically fall on him.'

'But it's got to be a process of deduction, hasn't it? Who else knew?'

She had a point there. It had been a secretive operation, but it's always possible for someone to talk, and I told her as much.

'O'Brien's got to be the most likely, though,' she persisted. 'He's stupid enough to think he can get away with it. And greedy enough too. We all know the sort. Always after one more big payday.'

'But the thing is, there wouldn't have been a payday, would there?' I told her. 'And O'Brien would have known that. The robbers would never have paid him in advance for selling them the information, they'd have split the proceeds afterwards, and since he knew the robbery was always going to end in failure, it would have been pointless.'

Tina sighed, still not convinced. 'Maybe he had another reason for setting it up.'

'Maybe. Either way, he needs talking to.'

I removed the mobile from my pocket and phoned my boss, DCI Knox, who'd now been given the task of organizing O'Brien's arrest. His extension was busy so I tried my colleague and occasional partner, DC Dave Berrin.

Berrin answered on the second ring with a hushed hello.

I wasn't sure whether it was the reception on the phone or not, so I spoke loudly. 'Hello, Dave? Where are you?'

'Outside O'Brien's place,' he whispered loudly back at me. 'Me and Hunsdon are across the street from it now. He wasn't in when we called round earlier so we're staying put. Knox's orders. So what happened out there today, then?'

There was excitement in his voice as he clawed and picked for the gory details. I had a feeling I was going to get a lot of this over the next few days. Shoot-outs, particularly ones with multiple casualties, seem to engender a mood of morbid curiosity in most people, and coppers are no exception.

'I'll tell you all about it later,' I said. 'Are there any lights on in O'Brien's place?'

'Nothing, and it's almost dark now. The place is empty. Definitely.'

'Have you tried the Forked Tail, or the Slug and Lettuce on Upper Street?' I asked, thinking they'd probably be his most likely haunts for a weekday afternoon's drinking.

'We tried the Slug earlier, and Baxter and Lint were sniffing round the Forked Tail, but from what I heard, they didn't get anywhere.'

'Well, stay where you are and don't leave until he turns up. All right?'

'Of course, no problem, boss.' The words were delivered in serious tones that were meant to let me know he was fully aware of his responsibility, but he couldn't resist a final dig for information. 'It was bad then, was it? Today?'

'Yes, Dave,' I said wearily, and with a finality in my tone. 'It was bad. It's always bad when an officer gets killed, especially when it's right under the noses of his colleagues. Now make sure you get hold of O'Brien. I'm off home. I'll see you in the morning.'

I hung up and sighed, cutting him off mid-goodbye.

Tina turned away from the windscreen and looked at me. 'He hasn't put in an appearance, then?'

I shook my head, beginning to get the first pangs of concern. Like a lot of mid-table professional criminals, Slim Robbie O'Brien was fairly predictable in his habits. He was a big drinker who liked to spend his days in the bars and pubs in and around Upper Street, particularly the two I'd mentioned to Berrin. Whenever I'd met up with him, it had always been in Clerkenwell or Euston, well away from his stomping ground, and he never looked very comfortable in different surroundings. He might have had some good contacts, including those with a route into the Colombian mafia, but he was as geographically challenged as a nineteenth-century chambermaid.

I tried Knox's number again but it was still engaged, and as I sat back in my seat, staring through the windscreen at the orange-tinged darkness of a London evening, my concern about O'Brien grew.

Where was he?

# 5

Stegs Jenner's real first name was Montgomery. His dad had been a massive Second World War buff whose hero had been the field marshal of the same name and, according to Stegs's dad, the man responsible not only for the defeat of Rommel at El Alamein but also, ultimately, the vanquishing of Hitler and Nazism. Forget Stalin, Roosevelt, Eisenhower or even Churchill. Monty was the man, and Stan Jenner immortalized him by bestowing the name on his first and only son.

Monty Jenner. It had been a fucking nightmare at school. At first they'd called him 'Mont-ay' in effeminate tones to suggest that anyone bearing such a name was quite obviously queer. When he'd complained to his dad, Jenner senior had invoked 'the spirit of the Blitz', telling his son that he had to be prepared to deal with adverse circumstances, that it would make him a better person. And that he had to be prepared to fight. 'I will give up my gun when they prise my cold, dead fingers from around it,' he'd said wisely. Stegs was one of the smaller kids in his year and didn't really understand what his old man was going on about, but even so, the next time someone had called him 'Mont-ay' (it had been Barry Growler, the school bully), he'd responded with his fists, launching a full-frontal blitzkrieg-style assault that had caught the Growlster completely by surprise and had cost him a black eye and a bleeding nose. The fight had been broken up by one of the teachers before Growler had had a chance to launch a substantial counter-offensive, and Stegs had ended up the winner on points, earning a grudging respect for his actions. People still laughed at his name, but they were a little bit more careful about it, and preferred to address him as 'Mental Monty' rather than the more irritating 'Mont-ay'. Even Growler had left him alone for a while after that.

About the same time, he'd decided to call himself Stegs. Although he'd never admit it now, it was short for Stegosaurus. He'd been interested in dinosaurs as a kid, and his two favourites had been Triceratops and Stegosaurus (two even-tempered plant-eaters who preferred to be left alone, but who, like Dirty Harry, could hit back hard if attacked). He felt he could identify with that. Since neither Triks nor Trice had a very cool ring to it, he'd gone with Stegs, claiming to those who asked him about it that it was his grandmother's maiden name. He'd also changed his whole demeanour. He strutted instead of walked, he answered back to the teachers, he became a bit of a joker. For a long time, though, he couldn't get either the name or the image to stick, but he perservered, did a few detentions for his backchat, got a couple of kickings for the way he didn't get out of the way for the bigger boys, and eventually even the teachers started address-ing him as Stegs. It taught him a valuable lesson: you can be anyone if you try.

Stegs Jenner did not look like a typical police officer. At five foot eight, he only just beat the height restrictions, and his face, even at thirty-two, was chubby and boyish, topped off by a receding mop of fine gingery-blond hair that had the curious effect of making him look both his age and a dozen years younger at the same time, like one of those illusionists' acts. Blink and he was twenty; blink again and he was back to thirty-two. But Stegs Jenner talked the talk, and he walked the walk, and he wasn't afraid to put his head into the lion's mouth, which made him an invaluable asset to SO10, Scotland Yard's specialist undercover unit.

He'd been a copper since the age of nineteen, and plainclothes since twenty-four. His full-time posting was still in the area where he'd grown up, the north London suburb of Barnet, but he'd been attached to SO10 for the previous six years, and probably half his time was spent seconded to them on undercover assignments, which is the way it works in the Met. No-one's full-time undercover. You could be meeting Colombian drugs dealers one day to discuss a multi-million-pound deal, and hunting for stolen office equipment the next.

Not that Stegs was going to be doing too much of anything for the next few days, at least not work-wise. He'd been officially suspended (thankfully on full pay) until a preliminary internal investigation could take place to see whether he'd acted improperly or not. They hadn't let him go until half-nine that night, at which point a very pissed-off, newly arrived assistant commissioner of the Met had formally told him that he was not to report for duty until further notice and not to speak to anyone about what had happened, other than those directly involved. The assistant commissioner (a middle-aged accountant look-alike with silver hair, an immaculately pressed uniform and a very long nose) had then stood there for a few seconds, waiting, it seemed, for Stegs to say something, presumably along the lines of 'I'm sorry for causing you all this inconvenience'. Stegs hadn't given him the satisfaction. Instead, he'd given the bastard a look that said, 'If you think you can do better, you get in there and talk to people who'd flay you alive if they knew your true identity. Then maybe you'd actually be earning your money, instead of waltzing around passing the buck to the junior ranks.'

After they'd finished with him, he reluctantly phoned the missus. She must have seen something about the operation on the news because she'd left three increasingly worried messages on the mobile. She didn't know what role he'd been playing, of course, or where he'd been playing it, but she knew he did under-cover work, and the news that an undercover officer had been killed would probably have seeped out by now, so he felt duty-bound to let her know he was all right.

She answered on about the tenth ring, and in the background he could hear Luke screaming and crying.

'Oh, Mark, thank God you've called. I've been worried stiff. Are you all right?'

She always called him Mark. She didn't like the name Stegs, and he sure as fuck wasn't going to let her call him Monty, so they'd had to come up with something that was acceptable to both of them, and after much discussion it turned out that Mark was it. It was how he was known to all her friends. One day he was sure he was going to end up being diagnosed as a schizophrenic.

He told her he was fine but very busy, and she asked him if he'd heard about the incident at Heathrow. He said he had.

'It makes me so scared, Mark, thinking of you out there all alone. I don't want baby Luke growing up without a father.'

Stegs was touched by her concern, in spite of himself. He told her everything would be OK, but neglected to mention that he'd been suspended on full pay. He'd been advised by his superiors that no correspondence would be sent to his home address regarding what had happened, and that all contact would be made on his mobile or his encrypted email address, so there was no point mentioning it, particularly as he had no intention of hanging around the house all day with her and Luke.

'Are you coming home then?' she asked him. 'I know Luke wants to see you.'

That he seriously doubted. Luke was never pleased to see him. He always gave him the evil eye when Stegs tried to pick him up or play with him. At eight months old, he was definitely his mother's son, and treated his dad like some sort of usurper whenever he came into the room. Stegs loved the kid (of course he did, he was his flesh and blood) but, though he never liked to admit it, he didn't like him much, and was never in any doubt that the feeling was mutual.

'I've still got some paperwork to clear up here,' he told her. 'I'll be back later on but don't wait up for me, I don't know what time it'll be.'

She sighed loudly down the other end of the phone. 'I can't do this all on my own, you know. Bringing up a baby's hard enough when there's two of you, let alone one.' As if to confirm quite how hard, Luke's crying went up a couple of decibels as she brought him nearer the phone. 'Tell Daddy to come home, Lukey,' she cooed at the infant. Fat chance of that, Stegs thought. If he could speak, he'd be telling him to fuck off, no doubt about it. 'Tell him he's making Mummy miserable.' Luke had clearly been brought right up to the mouthpiece now because Stegs was forced to hold the phone away from his ear as the howling increased still further. 'Seriously, though, Mark,' she continued, coming back on the line. 'It can't carry on like this. It's too much for me.'

'I know, I know,' he said, and made his excuses, citing the usual: workload, lack of staff, etc. But it didn't sound convincing, and he knew it. She told him she understood all that but that maybe he ought to think about changing careers so that he could help a bit more, and he said he had to go, that his boss needed to see him. 'We'll talk in the morning,' he said.

She sounded down as she hung up the phone with Luke's wailing continuing in the background, and it made him wonder why she'd wanted to have kids. He'd tried his hardest to convince her that they were better off continuing as they were, childless but reasonably well off, with her nurse's and his copper's wage, but she'd been adamant, and he knew that part of the reason for her desire probably stemmed from the need for some companionship, given the fact that he was hardly ever there. You reap what you sow, and he was reaping.

He drove back to Barnet on the M25, but instead of turning off on to the East Barnet road and heading home, he carried on going until he reached a pub just off the Whetstone High Road. He found a parking spot about fifty yards away and walked through the driving rain to the battered front door. It was ten to eleven.

The One-Eyed Admiral had a one o'clock weekly licence but was one of those places that was never going to be that popular because (a) it never looked very clean, and (b) it had never been able to rid itself of its low-life clientele, probably because they were the only people who'd frequent it. It wasn't a rough place, but one look through the smoky haze at the middle-aged petty criminals clustered round the tables and the fruit machines told any self-respecting punter that it wasn't a pub he wanted to be seen in. Which was one of the reasons Stegs liked it. Because he knew he'd always get a seat at the bar, and people wouldn't pay him too much attention.

He'd been going in there for years, ever since he'd been introduced to it by a small-time gun dealer who'd been a regular. Stegs had been undercover at the time, investigating the dealer, whose name was Pete, and the One-Eyed Admiral had been their main meeting place. After Pete had got nicked, along with several of the other customers, Stegs had continued to drink there now and again (no-one had ever suspected that he'd been the one who'd put them behind bars), and it was always the place he adjourned to when he needed time to think. They knew him as Tam in here, and thought he was the son of Irish immigrants hailing from County Cork.

The pub was busier than usual and all the tables were full, although there were still seats at the bar. Stegs nodded to a couple of blokes he recognized, then took a seat at one end – his usual spot, if it was free – and waited for Patrick, the barman, to come and take his order.

'All right, Tam. Long time no see,' grunted Patrick in that less-than-charming manner of his. He'd been here for years and Stegs had never seen him smile once. 'What'll it be?'

'Pint of Stella,' said Stegs, thinking that he should be thankful for men like Patrick. A lot of barmen'll take it as an invitation to talk if you sit at their bar, and talking was something Stegs had done enough of for one day. At least he knew Patrick would leave him alone.

He took the pint when it came to him, and handed over the exact money. He gulped down at least a third of it, savouring the much-needed taste of alcohol, before putting the glass down on the bar and sparking up a Marlboro Light. The missus was always on at him to give up the fags, even though she continued to smoke three Silk Cut Ultras religiously every evening (giving her teeth a ferocious clean after each one). Stegs never smoked in the house any more; apparently the residue on his breath could potentially be harmful to an infant (hence the missus's tooth cleaning). It was the same with the booze. Next she'd be telling him not to eat curries.

He dragged on the Marlboro and looked at the clock on the wall. Two minutes to eleven. Gill Vokerman would have been told by now what had happened to her husband, and Stegs wondered how she'd be coping. Badly probably. They had two kids: Jacob and Honey (not a name Stegs would have chosen – too gooey). Jacob was six and Honey either two or three, he couldn't remember which. Gill was a committed Christian, so maybe her beliefs would help get her through it. He hoped so. She'd always struck him as a stoic sort, one who could call upon the old 'spirit of the Blitz' to help her through adversity, but losing a husband suddenly, violently and unexpectedly was as adverse as you were likely to get. He was going to have to go and see her, offer his condolences. It wasn't going to be easy, especially as she didn't like him anyway. Vokes had told him once that she looked upon him as a bad influence, although quite how he'd deserved that accolade, he didn't know. Perhaps Vokes had blamed him for the occasional night the two of them had stayed out late. That was the problem with their job. You spent so much time living on the edge, acting out roles in environments where things were always on a knife-edge, that you had to be able to unwind. That meant sinking a few beers, coming in late, sometimes not making it in at all. Whatever Gill Vokerman might have thought, there was no way round it. If you couldn't unwind with your mates, you'd go mental.

He was going to miss Vokes, who'd been a good mate to him. They'd known each other for about three years, ever since they'd been thrown together on an assignment to trap a team of luxury-car thieves. That particular case, in which the two of them had posed as potential buyers with heavyweight contacts in the Middle East, had lasted close to two months, and with its successful conclusion (four members of the team had ended up with prison time totalling twenty-three years), so their partnership had been cemented. They'd worked together wherever possible since and each had learnt to cover the other's back in even the most dangerous situations. When you're an undercover copper, everything's based on trust. If you're working with another SO10 operative you've got to know that they won't crack whatever the provocation, that they'll continue to hold on to their identity even with a gun against their head, and it takes a special kind of person to be able to handle that sort of pressure. Vokes was one of them, so was Stegs.

One time, eighteen months ago, that capability had been put to the ultimate test. The two of them had been working on an assignment to infiltrate and gather evidence on a south London-based coke and cannabis smuggling gang led by a psychotic thug named Frank Rentners. Rentners, an ex-boxer who'd served time for manslaughter, had ambitions to tie up the dope and coke market in his patch of south-east London, and he ran a sophisticated and lucrative operation in which the drugs were brought in on lorries overland from Spain among consignments of fruit and veg. At the time of the assignment, it was estimated that Rentners and his crew were turning over close to a million a year in sales, and were expanding fast thanks to their policy of undercutting (quite literally in one case) the competition.

Once again, the two of them had posed as buyers from the provinces looking to set up an ongoing business relationship with Rentners to purchase quantities of his imported gear. An informant had introduced them to a small-time player called Jack Brewster who knew someone else within the gang. This is usually how it works in the criminal world: word of mouth. Somebody knows somebody who knows somebody else. It's a good way of working because so many people get involved that by the time the bad guys are nicked they're not sure who it was who actually grassed them up. That was the theory anyway.

Brewster, who'd had no idea that the people he was representing were police officers, had been promised a commission by Stegs and Vokes if he could get his contact within the gang to set up a meeting between them and Rentners. Feelers had been put out and eventually Rentners had agreed to see Stegs, Vokes and Brewster in a pub in Streatham for an initial chat. If all went well, then they'd take it to the next step: a test purchase.

So when they'd gone to the pub, there'd been no reason to suspect that things were going to go wrong. It was just a first meeting. He and Vokes weren't even wearing wires, relying instead on the fact that officers from SO11, Scotland Yard's intelligence-gathering unit, had put a tracking device under Rentners' car, just in case they changed venues. Brewster, who'd met the two of them in a Burger King just down the road, had been laughing and chatting, and was keen to know when he could expect some money. Stegs remembered that he'd told him it wouldn't be too long and that he had nothing to worry about because he, Stegs, was a man of his word. Brewster had seemed happy enough with that.

Rentners had been in the pub with three of his men. They all looked pretty much identical: shaven-headed, powerfully built, and togged out in three-quarter-length black leather jackets, black jeans and Timberlands. Like a doormen's barbershop quartet – not that Stegs expected this lot to break out in song, not unless it was the Funeral March anyway. Rentners had been shorter than the rest, and older – probably about forty-five – but you could tell from the way he stood in the middle of the group, one elbow resting on the bar, that he was the leader. He had a black goatee beard modelled along the lines of one Satan might wear, and a similarly fiendish half-smile. All that was missing were the horns and forked tail.

He'd looked the three of them up and down slowly and

silently, trying to maximize the menace, then said straight away that they were going somewhere else. No-one had argued, this sort of welcome being par for the course, and the seven of them had left the pub through the back entrance that led out to a tiny car park. Two Mercedes, both black, were parked next to each other. Brewster was ushered into one along with two of Rentners' goons, while Stegs and Vokes were invited into the back seat of the other. Rentners sat in the front passenger seat while the fourth member of the group drove.

'Where are we heading?' asked Vokes, who on this particular occasion was acting as the senior of the two of them.

'Just for a little drive,' growled their host, with that same devilish little half-smile which was not designed to make the recipient feel any better. 'Sit back and relax.'

And with that, he pressed a button and a tinted partition came down, making further communication impossible. The two SO10 men glanced at each other, but remained calm. In the end, Frank Rentners was a businessman and they were potential customers with some serious money to spend, so neither of them expected any real problems. They'd done this sort of thing plenty of times before.

They drove through the streets of south London for close to three-quarters of an hour, losing the other car in the process. The driver kept to the quieter roads, occasionally doubling back on himself until eventually they were into the suburbs. They passed through Orpington, crossed the M25 at Swanley, and continued in a south-easterly direction. There was still no sign of the other car, and Stegs wondered whether they were going to see Brewster again that day, and whether the SO11 men were also on their tail.

An hour and five minutes into the journey by Stegs's watch, they suddenly pulled off the road they were travelling on and drove up a dirt track through woods until they came to a modern two-storey red-brick house set back on its own behind a small, neatly trimmed garden. The other Merc was already there, parked up on the driveway, along with a red Golf. They pulled up behind the Merc and the driver cut the engine.

Rentners got out along with the driver, and beckoned them to do the same. 'Are you hungry?' he asked, when they were standing on the driveway.

It was one o'clock in the afternoon and they both said they were, so Rentners, his smile a little more welcoming now, ushered them towards the house. Stegs noticed that he had his own key which he used to let them in, and he wondered briefly if this property was in Rentners' name.

The interior was surprisingly sparse. There were no pictures or ornaments in the hallway, and the unfashionable black carpet looked cheap. Rentners led them through to a large dining room that looked out on to trees. A large table took up most of the room and it was laid for seven people. Two bottles of Ty Nant mineral water were in the middle of the table along with a bottle each of red and white wine. Even eighteen months on, Stegs Jenner remembered all these little details. He remembered everything about that day.

Brewster was already sitting down at the table along with the other two. He greeted them with a slightly confused smile, as if he too wasn't a hundred per cent sure what was going on. Stegs and Vokes took seats opposite him.

'Help yourselves to drinks,' said Rentners, and disappeared out of the room.

Stegs helped himself to a glass of red. He wouldn't have drunk on duty normally but it was Châteauneuf du Pape. Whatever else could be said of Rentners, he had good taste in wine. Vokes shot him a sideways glare and poured himself some water.

'Well, this is very nice,' said Stegs, not really meaning it at all.

It wasn't nice. It was weird. He'd been working with SO10 a long time, and no-one had ever fed him at a first meeting.

'It is, isn't it?' said Brewster, an excruciatingly ingratiating smile on his face as he looked around. Stegs thought then that he really didn't like Brewster. He had the furtive air of a child molester.

Nobody else spoke.

A few minutes later, Rentners returned carrying a huge pot. A big, blonde-haired woman in a kitchen apron came in behind him. She was carrying bowls which she put down in front of everyone without speaking. Stegs thanked her but she ignored him, not even looking his way.

'Spaghetti al araba,' said Rentners, who must have thought he was John Gotti or Tony Soprano, lifting the lid off the pot. 'I hope you all like chilli.' He then doled out a portion of spaghetti in a tomatoey sauce to each and every one of them while the blonde came back several times bringing salad and garlic bread. '*Bon appetit*,' he growled when he'd finished, before sitting down at the head of the table and proceeding to stuff his demonic face.

As they ate (and Stegs would always remember that the food was excellent), Rentners asked the two of them questions. What sort of quantity of gear were they after? How were they raising the funds needed? Where'd they done time? Did they know so and so? The questions were probing but nothing unusual, and the two of them answered confidently and without hesitation. Only once did Rentners speak to Brewster, to ask him if he knew how a mutual acquaintance of theirs was doing. Brewster, between sizeable mouthfuls of spaghetti, said he hadn't seen the bloke for ages. Rentners nodded, as if accepting the answer, and carried on talking to the two SO10 men. Vokes did most of the talking, but Stegs had entered the discussion where necessary, and he remembered thinking, as he poured himself a second glass of the

Châteauneuf du Pape, that it wouldn't take more than a few meetings to reel in Rentners. He obviously rated himself very highly, and they're always the easiest to bring down because they never see it coming.

Rentners was the first to finish. As he did so, he gave his belly a satisfying rub and raised his glass. 'To crime,' he chuckled.

'To crime,' said everyone else with varying degrees of enthusiasm. Stegs even raised his glass.

Then Rentners lifted up the empty bottle of white wine and smashed it over Brewster's head. Brewster didn't even know what had hit him, he simply slid off the chair and fell to the floor. Stegs and Vokes stared at Rentners, wondering whether they'd missed something. Vokes began to speak, but their host stood up and pulled a long-barrelled Browning from the waistband of his black jeans and pointed it at him.

'Shut the fuck up, cunt!' he hissed, his face dissolving into a malevolent glare, which hadn't required much of a transformation.

At the same time, Stegs felt something warm and metallic being pushed against his temple as the bloke next to him – the one who'd driven them down there – produced his own gun. Stegs carried on chewing. When he'd finished, he turned to Rentners and glared right back. 'What the fuck is this? What are you trying to do?'

'Shut your fucking mouth, copper!' snarled Rentners, moving the gun round so it was pointed right between Stegs's eyes.

Stegs felt his heart shoot up to his mouth and he silently thanked God that he had Vokes with him because he knew his partner was experienced enough to handle this sort of situation.

'What the fuck are you talking about?' he yelled, indignant. 'Who the fuck's a copper? How do I even know you're not a fucking copper?' He stood up, flinging his serviette onto the table and ignoring the gun to his head, a picture of righteous anger.

Bluff, bluff – it's always bluff.

'Get fucking down!' roared Rentners, his gun hand shaking with rage.

'All right, Steve,' said Vokes. 'Sit down and take it easy.' Stegs slowly sat back down while Vokes turned to Rentners and spoke calmly but with barely suppressed irritation. 'What the fuck is this, Mr Rentners? We came here to do business. We don't like having weapons pointed at us, and having accusations made that are, quite frankly, fucking insulting.'

'Don't fucking try that one. You're coppers. I know you are. And him' – he motioned with the Browning towards the prone form of Brewster – 'he's a fucking grass. You're here to fucking set me up.'

'Bollocks!' yelled Stegs. 'I can't believe you're doing this to us.'

'Is this the way you treat all your customers, Frank? Because if it is—'

'SHUT THAT FUCKING MOUTH!' roared Rentners. 'NOW! BOTH OF YOU! YOU HEAR ME? NOW!'

The whole world had probably heard that. It left Stegs's ears ringing, and he knew that this was serious. Very serious. Rentners had killed before. Knifed a man in the heart over an alleged drugs debt. He'd got off on manslaughter charges because the bloke had also slept with his missus, which meant extenuating circumstances. Nineteen times he'd stabbed him, the defence barrister at his trial describing it as a passionate rage in search of an outlet, which seemed a very generous way of looking at it. Some fucking outlet. The point was, though, that this was a bad situation. Rentners was unpredictable, he was violent, and he had a gun. Stegs was as scared as he'd ever been, but he knew it would be fatal to show it. He gave Rentners a look that said that he wouldn't forget this sort of treatment.

'Get 'em in the weights room,' said Rentners, ignoring him, 'and wake that cunt up. I don't want him missing all the fun.'

Vokes started to tell him that he was making a big mistake but never finished the sentence as Rentners let fly with a wicked right hook that sent him stumbling back into the wall. Vokes was a big lad, six two and about fifteen stone, but he was left dazed by the ex-boxer's blow, and offered little resistance as Rentners grabbed his shirt and pulled him back out into the hallway. At the same time, the one with the gun against Stegs's head hauled him to his feet and led him out the same way, keeping the weapon in position. 'Make a wrong fucking move and you die,' he told Stegs helpfully.

The weights room took up the whole of the basement. It was even more sparsely furnished than the rest of the house and, being windowless, was brightly lit by strip lights on the ceiling. It was also carpetless, and consequently quite cold. At one end of the room were two racks of weights, a treadmill, and several other exercise machines. A single leather sofa was at the other end, about thirty feet away, facing this makeshift gymnasium.

Rentners shoved Vokes onto the sofa, and Stegs followed a couple of seconds later. Their hands were then forced behind their backs by one of Rentner's gunmen, and amid continued protestations they were tied with duct tape. While this was going on, Brewster was dumped unceremoniously onto the stone floor halfway between the sofa and the nearest rack of weights. For the first time Stegs noticed a steam iron plugged into one of the mains sockets a few feet away from him.

'This is fucking ridiculous,' he told Rentners, trying hard not to look at the iron. 'We're here offering you money for your merchandise, and you're treating us like shit. If I'm a fucking copper, why aren't I wearing a wire, then? Come on, search me. See if I'm fucking wearing one.'

A tiny glimmer of doubt crossed Rentners' features, then disappeared. 'Tape their fucking traps up, Tone,' he told the gunman.

Tone stuffed the gun in his waistband and took the duct tape back out of his jacket.

'He's right, Frank,' said Vokes, trying hard to keep the nerves out of his voice. 'Search us if you don't believe us. Don't fucking do business with us if you don't trust us, but tying us up and doing all this is just going to make your reputation—'

He was forced to stop when Tone pulled the tape round his mouth several times over, before biting the end off it.

'You'd better make sure you never run into me again, Tone, you cunt!' snarled Stegs, as Tone prepared to do the same thing to him. When he'd finished, he punched Stegs in the side of the head, knocking him into Vokes. Their eyes met for a second, before they were pulled apart. Stegs thought that Vokes was more nervous than he'd ever seen him.

Brewster was taking his time coming round, so one of the other men disappeared into an alcove round the corner. The sound of running water followed and then he returned with a full bucket. He chucked it over Brewster, and now Stegs realized why the room wasn't carpeted.

Brewster coughed and spluttered and tried to sit up. Rentners then stepped forward and kicked him in the face. 'Lie on your front, now!' he demanded.

Brewster appeared confused but did exactly what he was told. Tone then came over, leant down, and ripped the shirt off his back, leaving only the arms still attached to him. He chucked the material to one side, then wrapped more of his roll of tape round Brewster's wrists, binding them together. He did the same with his ankles. Brewster didn't move while any of this was going on, or say anything.

'You're a grass, aintcha, Brewster?' said Rentners gently, walking round the other man. 'You're trying to fit us up, aintcha? And these geezers, they're coppers, right?'

Brewster desperately protested his innocence, but it was no good. Stegs could see in Rentners' face that they were going to punish him whatever he said. Rentners had decided he was guilty, and now that he had that thought in his head it was going to take a miracle to budge it. Stegs didn't believe in miracles. That was more Vokes's line. He'd bet that Brewster was praying for one, though.

Rentners turned and smiled at the two undercover cops, then walked over to the iron, removing it from its base. He gently touched it with his finger, then pulled the finger away with mock suddenness, mouthing the word 'Ow!' He was still smiling, and his whole demeanour had calmed considerably. He looked like a man at peace with himself.

'Do the honours then, Tone,' he said, and Tone stepped onto the prostrate Brewster, putting a foot on each arm above the elbow, thereby severely restricting his upper body movement. Rentners stood there motionless, watching Stegs and Vokes. His expression was blank.

'Aagh!' yelped Brewster. 'Get off. I ain't done nothing. That hurts.'

'That don't hurt,' said Rentners. '*This* hurts.'

He dropped one knee onto the back of Brewster's legs, careful not to conceal the view for the two SO10 men, then pushed the iron hard against the centre of his victim's back, directly beneath the shoulder blades. Steam shot up as the iron sizzled and crackled, and Brewster unleashed a blood-curdling scream of agony that reverberated round the room. Rentners kept the iron in the same position, pressing hard, and using his weight to keep Brewster's legs from moving. Brewster kept screaming, louder and louder, and Stegs suddenly had a desperate urge to piss. It took all his self-control to stop himself. He couldn't have that. Couldn't show them how scared he was. He avoided looking at Vokes but couldn't help but catch the eye of the man holding the bucket. He blew Stegs a kiss.

All of a sudden the screaming stopped, and Rentners removed the iron, revealing a red-raw, sizzling wound. The smell of burnt skin drifted through the air.

'The cunt's passed out,' said Rentners. 'Get some more water, Alan,' he told the bucket man. 'We need to wake him up.'

Once again Alan disappeared into the alcove with the bucket. While he was gone, Rentners used a screwdriver to scrape off scraps of flesh from the iron before replacing it on its base and walking over to the sofa, stopping in front of Stegs and Vokes. He removed the gun from his waistband and put it against Vokes's head.

'You look nervous,' he said, 'and you ought to be. You're next.' He patted Vokes's shirt, manhandling him in the seat as he hunted belatedly for a wire. 'I know you're coppers,' he said when he'd finished without finding anything. 'You know how I know, because earlier on you' – he motioned towards Stegs – 'said you'd done time in Parkhurst for dealing last year, on D wing. But you can't have done. Tone was there then and he don't remember you, do you, Tone?'

Tone, who'd stepped off Brewster's arms now, shook his head slowly. 'Never seen him before in my life.' He stepped out of the way as Alan the bucket man chucked more water over Brewster's upper half.

Brewster moaned and shook his head. 'My back, my fucking back . . . What are you doing?' He tried to move but Tone stood on his arms again, and the next second Rentners had grabbed the iron and reapplied it to the same area.

The screams started again – animal-like howls of suffering – and out of the corner of his eye Stegs saw Vokes shift uncomfortably in his seat.

'PLAAAAYYYSSE!'

Stegs tried to shut out the sound but couldn't; it seemed to be coming from everywhere. Tried to concentrate on anything other than the events being played out before him, tried to tell himself that they wouldn't kill them (it'd be too much hassle). Knowing he'd made a mistake. Knowing he shouldn't have been so specific about when he'd done his supposed time. Cursing his bad luck. And bad planning. They should have done a better job of checking out Rentners' associates.

The screams stopped.

The room fell silent.

Stegs would have given both his bollocks to have got out of there then.

Don't burn me, you fucks. Please do not fucking burn me.

Alan the bucket man went to get some more water. Rentners smiled at them both. 'If you both admit to me you're coppers, and you tell me what evidence you've got, and give me details of who you are and where you live, then I'll let you walk as soon as I've checked them out. You don't fucking talk, then you're going to get the same treatment as this cunt. Understand? I've got a business to protect, and I'm going to fucking protect it. From grasses and undercover cozzers. You understand me? Yeah, I think you do now, dontcha?'

More water splashed over Brewster, and slowly he came round again. This time, Rentners lifted him up by his hair and shoved his gun against his head. Brewster's eyes were vacant. He looked drugged up.

'Are these two cozzers?' Rentners demanded, pushing him round so he was facing Stegs and Vokes. For a couple of seconds, Brewster didn't answer, his eyes struggling to focus. Rentners repeated the question, pushing the barrel harder against his head. 'Answer me or I'll blow your fucking head off.'

Stegs heard himself praying that Brewster, who could surely have no fucking idea that they were SO10, didn't simply say yes to deflect attention from himself. Don't say it. Don't fucking say it!

'No,' Brewster croaked. 'Course not.'

Once again a sudden flash of doubt crossed Rentners' features but was gone just as quickly. He let go of Brewster's hair and let him fall onto the wet floor, then he walked purposefully over to the sofa and pulled the tape from Vokes's mouth. 'Last chance not to burn,' he said. 'Just admit it, tell me what you know, and you'll be out of here inside an hour with your back in the same condition it's in now.'

Vokes was sweating profusely, but he held Rentners' gaze. 'I am not a fucking undercover copper,' he spat. 'I am a fucking businessman. I was here looking to make a deal, now I'm just looking to get the fuck out of here.'

'What about him, then? How come he fucked up about doing time in Parkhurst?'

'Fuck knows. Ask him.'

Rentners ripped off Stegs's duct tape and started to speak, but Stegs knew he was going to get only one chance to turn the tables, so he cut him off straight away. 'Is that what this is all about? Are you putting us through this just because of something I'm meant to have fucking said? Because I tell you this, I was fucking there, and I was on B wing, you deaf cunt! Not D! And if he doesn't fucking recognize me, then he obviously wasn't looking very hard! Or maybe he's the fucking undercover copper, because I'll tell you something, I don't fucking recognize him either, the cunt!'

His words spilt out so fast that Rentners didn't get even half a chance to interrupt. When he'd finished, the ex-boxer's expression had changed. He looked thoughtful now. Stegs and Vokes both glared at him, letting it be known that they were not best pleased with the way serious liberties had been taken with them.

Rentners appeared at last to realize he'd made a mistake and placed the gun back in his waistband. 'Listen, I'm sorry about that, boys,' he said. 'You just can't be too careful, though, can you? We've been hearing bad reports about Brewster for a while now, and then he gets all keen to introduce youse two to me. I put two and two together and it looks like I come up with five. Let me get you a drink.'

And that was how it had ended. The two of them had been released and given a large brandy each, which they'd drunk while Brewster lay ignored on the stone floor. Rentners had then begun acting like nothing had happened, and had even started trying to put together a test purchase. In Stegs's experience, that was how a lot of violent criminals acted. It was as if they couldn't understand what was wrong with their actions. Vokes had told him to fuck off and to watch how he treated potential customers next time, which was the attitude to take. It demonstrated how pissed off they were and bolstered their credentials as bona fide buyers. Rentners had apologized again and had got Tone to drive them back to London. On the way back, Tone had said sorry too, admitting that he'd made up the bit about being in Parkhurst as a bluff. 'The boss told me to' was his explanation. Stegs had told him that he'd better never show his face in Southampton, otherwise he'd get an axe in it. Tone had actually looked a bit worried at that, and had brought up the partition.

He'd dropped them off at Waterloo station, and as soon as he was gone they'd grabbed each other in a long and emotional bearhug that got the late-afternoon commuters giving them some very strange stares.

Not that any of those bastards would ever know the half of it.

He really was going to miss his partner. He wasn't sure if he could trust anyone else like he'd trusted him. He wasn't even sure if he could keep going with SO10 duties. It seemed one hell of a lot of risk for not very much reward. A few weeks earlier, he'd read in one of the Sunday newspapers about an investment banker in the City who was paid so well that he earned in three and a half days what Stegs made in a year, and he wasn't even the highest paid in his department. Was some fucking accountant in a suit worth so much more than him? Did he really contribute so much more to society? It seemed plenty of people thought he did. He wondered how they would react if someone like Frank Rentners came knocking on their doors with a long-barrelled Browning in one hand and a steam iron in the other.

'Do you want another one, Tam?' asked Patrick, coming over. Stegs nodded. 'Yeah, please. Same again.'

He knew he was going to end up drink-driving, but he was past caring. The last time he'd been stopped, the previous year, he'd managed to convince them to let him go, although they'd warned him that if they saw him doing it again they'd have to nick him. Fair enough. He'd take his chances.

The pint came and he paid for it with a twenty. As Patrick went over to the till, a thought struck him. Vokes had been a lot more nervous than usual today. He was usually pretty cool, but this time he'd definitely looked under pressure, even before they'd arrived at the hotel. Maybe he'd just been losing it, finally burning out under the pressure of the job. It happened. Plenty of times, particularly to undercover cops.

Or maybe it was something else.

Out of the corner of his eye, he saw that a young blonde had taken the stool next to his at the bar. She was early twenties, dressed in tight-fitting hipsters and an oldish suede jacket. She flashed him a smile, and he knew straight away she was a pro. You got them sometimes in the Admiral, usually on their nights off. They had a couple of saunas on the high street nearby and some of the girls lived on the estate opposite, so they liked to stop in for the odd drink, and were tolerated by the management as long as they kept their activities discreet. Stegs hadn't seen this one before and hadn't noticed her when he'd come in earlier. Perhaps she was new. Patrick returned with his change, gave the girl a quick once-over, then turned away again to serve someone.

'Hi,' said the girl, smiling again. 'How are you?'

Her accent was eastern European, probably Romanian or Bulgarian. She was heavily made up with bright red lipstick, and her hair, cut into a bob, was dyed. She was quite attractive in a harsh, lived-in kind of way, but her blue eyes were weary and she was too skinny for Stegs's liking. He wondered briefly whether she was on the pipe, then decided he honestly didn't care either way.

'How do I look?'

'Very nice.' The smile was now fixed on her face. 'You look very nice.'

He turned and gave her a vaguely dismissive glance. 'Really? I shouldn't do. I'm tired, pissed off, and my best mate got killed today. Some bastard blew his head off.'

The smile dropped a little at the sides even though she made a valiant effort to keep it there. Her expression suggested she didn't know whether he was joking or not. Stegs just looked at her with the same expression for a couple of seconds longer, then turned away.

Patrick came over. 'Everything all right here?' he asked. He looked at the girl. 'Do you want a drink?'

She glanced at Stegs, saw that he wasn't going to offer, and ordered a large vodka with ice. When she'd got her drink, she slipped off her stool and disappeared. Stegs took another huge gulp of his beer and lit a Marlboro Light.

'Did you hear about Pete?' asked Patrick as he poured a Murphys from the tap.

'Who?'

'Yer man, Pete. The one you used to come in here with back in the old days. Pete Moss.'

Pete the gun dealer. 'What about him?'

Patrick left the three-quarters-full pint of Murphys to settle for a moment, and looked hard at Stegs. There was something innately distrustful in his expression. Stegs didn't react. He was used to that kind of look.

'He's dead.'

Stegs dragged on his cigarette. 'Shit. How did that happen?'

'The old C. Throat cancer. Died in Ford a few weeks back. I'm surprised you didn't hear.'

'I haven't seen him for a long time. I visited him a couple of times after he got sent down, but you know what it's like. You lose touch.'

'No way to die though, is it? Behind bars. The last four years of his life ruined. Another six months and he'd have been out.'

He continued to look at Stegs as he spoke, with a greater intensity than he'd ever shown before, and Stegs wondered if he suspected him of having had something to do with it. Maybe he should have tried a bit harder to keep up with Pete's progress inside. Still, it was a bit late to worry about that now.

'That's always the way,' he said. 'There's no justice in this fucking world. Poor old Pete, I always liked him. Did you get to the funeral?'

Patrick shook his head and went back to pouring the rest of

the beer, having seemingly lost interest in the conversation. 'Nah, I didn't,' he replied eventually, and walked away with the pint.

They all fucked up in the end, thought Stegs. The small-time thieves, knifemen, the fences, the dealers, the thugs, all those who worked on the wrong side of the crime trade. They all thought they'd live for ever, breathing the ripe air of freedom, but it never worked like that. He'd always liked Pete, though. He'd been a laugh, a good bloke to be around. They'd had some good times together. Stegs tried not to picture him wasted and rasping in a prison hospital bed. Instead, he pictured a smiling Jack Brewster, the way he'd been before Frank Rentners had tattooed his back with a steam iron, and he remembered that Brewster too was now dead. Someone had garrotted him a few months back, then dumped his corpse in Mulgrave Pond in Woolwich, case unsolved.

They all fucked up in the end.

Stegs drained his drink and, catching Patrick's eye, ordered another one.

# 6

At 6.45 on the morning after the failure of Operation Surgical Strike, I was woken by the shrill bleeping of the alarm. Immediately, my thoughts went back to the events of the previous day and I wondered if we'd got hold of O'Brien. They then moved on to the woman lying next to me, which served to cheer me up a bit. Tina Boyd's a very attractive woman. I'm not bad-looking (honestly), but I can't help thinking she's a league or two above me. Still, if she wants to slum it, I'm not going to complain. I leant over and kissed the pale skin of her back; she groaned painfully, then mumbled something about me getting the kettle on. I took pity, hauled myself out of bed, and went through to the kitchen to do her bidding.

We've been together a few months now, Tina and I, even though it's always been a rule of mine not to get involved with work colleagues after a particularly bad experience a long time ago. But sometimes you've just got to make an exception. You don't get that many chances to get yourself into a decent relationship with a good-looking woman, and as the years fly by they get fewer and fewer, so one night last November when we'd been sat together in a car, staking out the home of a well-known local sex offender, I'd decided that it was now or never. I'll be straight with you, I'm one of the world's shyer people when it comes to making my feelings known to the opposite sex. Having been married for thirteen of the previous fourteen years, and involuntarily celibate for the other, I was a long way out of practice, but I'd had this feeling for a while that Tina might have some of the same feelings for me as I had for her, so it wasn't an opportunity I wanted to miss.

But how do you go about it after fourteen years? I'd said, 'Hey, look over there,' and pointed in the vague direction of the house we were watching. She looked, and I leant over and kissed her on the neck, catching her unawares.

She'd then swung round and shot me an expression of shock, the sort I would imagine her pulling if a favourite uncle had just pinched her arse, and I got the sort of terrified sinking feeling I haven't experienced since school.

'John?'

'Yes.'

'Did you just kiss me?'

'I couldn't help it,' I said, trying without success to sound casual. 'You've got a nice neck.' Not a great line, I admit, but the best I could come up with in such difficult circumstances.

'Oh, shit.' She wasn't looking at me as she said this, but rather over my shoulder in the direction of the pavement.

'What is it?' I demanded, turning my head.

Which was when she grabbed me by the short and curlies and gave them a squeeze that was halfway between affectionate and bloodthirsty.

'Now we're quits,' she said, laughing.

There then followed one of those movie silences when we both looked at each other, wondering whether a fleeting kiss and a painful grope were going to lead to anything else.

After three seconds they did, and we kissed. Properly this time. Then finally carried on with the surveillance (which, unlike the relationship, never came to anything), and so far we haven't looked back.

I came back into the bedroom with two cups of strong coffee. She was sat up in the bed now – naked, groggy and very desirable. I briefly thought about trying to get her interested in a bout of morning glory but knew that it would be a lost cause. Tina Boyd was not a morning person.

'Are you feeling a bit better today?' I asked, handing her one of the cups.

The previous night, when we'd got back to my flat in Tufnell Park, she'd talked about leaving the Force, saying she'd had enough of working so hard for so little reward, only to have everything blow up in her face. I think she felt that what had happened yesterday was partly her fault, and since it had cost the lives of six people, it had hit her pretty hard.

'Not a lot,' she answered, sipping her coffee. 'The people killed yesterday are all still dead, and one way or another we're going to have to prove that it wasn't us who messed things up.'

'Don't blame yourself. Yesterday wasn't your fault or mine. We did everything right in the build-up, and in the end we had nothing to do with setting up the final meet, so we're in the clear. Remember that.'

She sighed loudly. 'I know, but at the moment it doesn't make me feel any better.'

I sat down on the bed and gave her a supportive smile. 'You're not still thinking about leaving, are you?'

'How would you feel if I did?'

'Are you going to?'

'I'm thinking about it. I've got a degree, I could get a decent job. Something that pays more but with a lot less stress.'

'We could do with you staying. You're a good cop. We're losing too many of them as it is. Soon there'll only be me and Knox left.'

'That's the way it goes sometimes, John. It's just not working for me at the moment, that's all, and I can't see it getting any better. It might do us some good as well. It's hard work trying to keep the whole thing quiet at the station, and we do see a lot of each other. I don't want either of us to start getting bored.'

She had a point, and I was pleased to hear that she thought our relationship was going somewhere. We didn't live together yet but slept in the same bed more nights than not, and, although we never talked about the future and what it would bring, I'd already upped the ante by introducing her (fairly successfully) to my twelve-year-old daughter, Rachel. The idea of us making something of it was a nice one. I still didn't want to lose her from the job, though. I meant it when I'd said she was too much of a good copper, and I also meant it when I said that they're getting rarer.

'Just don't make any hasty decisions,' I told her. 'Yesterday was a bad day. I don't think either me or you'll see a worse one, not on the job anyway.'

'I'm thinking about it, that's all.' She took another sip of the coffee. 'In the meantime, I want to get hold of that arsehole O'Brien.'

Which was as good a place to start as any.

In the car on the way into the station we didn't speak much, letting BBC Radio 5 Live do the talking. The events at Heathrow appeared to be the hot topic of the day. By now most of the main details were in the public domain and it had become clear that a Scotland Yard sting had gone horribly wrong; that one police officer (name as yet unreleased) had been killed; and that, incredibly, the targets of the sting had themselves become a target for a group of armed robbers, one of whom had managed to shoot someone dead before he himself had been killed by armed officers. From the DJ to the breathless people phoning in, no-one could quite believe what had happened. Some of the callers bemoaned the fact that this sort of thing could take place in England, others seemed genuinely pleased that the police had finally become what Derek from Brent described as 'trigger-happy'. He claimed that it was about time the coppers started hitting the criminals. 'Normally the bastards'll do anything not to hurt them. It's pathetic. The law's a joke. All softly softly and make sure you don't upset anyone.' He'd continued on with this rant for several more minutes, veering between supporting and criticizing the police, but remaining happy that they'd managed to kill three gunmen. 'I bet they was all black as well,' he'd added, at which point the DJ had cut him off, saying that there was no need for that sort of talk.

When the eight o'clock news headlines came on, all the news-reader talked about was the shootings. She didn't even bother with an 'in other news' section. It was like a domestic September eleven story, something for them to talk about endlessly, along with all the obvious offshoots like gun control, rising crime, drugs, etc. In the end Tina announced she could take no more and leant over to switch to Capital. Celine Dion was warbling meaningfully about true love, and for once in my life I was actually pleased to hear the sound of her voice.

'I'm really beginning to get tired of this,' she said.

'They're just a bit short of a decent story at the moment. Something else'll come up soon enough.' I hoped so anyway.

Like her, I could have done without the constant reminder of our part in such a bizarre and tragic event.

We were stuck in heavy traffic on the Holloway Road on our way to her place so she could pick up her car, and it had started to rain again. The weather forecaster at the end of the news said that it was going to be mild with heavy showers and cloudy skies for the next three days, getting brighter towards the end of the weekend. I didn't believe her. I never do. Weather forecasters are like prison visitors. Nice people, but usually misguided.

I pulled out my mobile and phoned Berrin to see if there'd been any sign of O'Brien during the night, but he wasn't answering, so I called Knox's office extension. He wasn't answering either so I tried him on his mobile, and this time I struck lucky. Or unlucky, depending on your view of the news he had.

'Sir, it's Gallan.'

'John, where are you?'

'In a car on the Holloway Road moving very slowly and getting rained on.'

'We've had a development. A major one.' He sounded breathless and pissed off.

'What is it, sir?'

'Your man O'Brien. The one who started all this. Someone's only gone and topped him. And his grandma.'

'His grandma? That's a bit harsh, isn't it?'

'It's a harsh world.'

'Where did it happen?'

'Over in her apartment. She lived opposite him, in the same flats. We only got the call ten minutes ago, so I'm still at the station. We're going over to the address now. You need to get over there too. We'll need a positive ID, although we're ninety-nine point nine it's him.'

'I know where he lives. I'll meet you there. Do you want me

to try and get hold of Tina Boyd?' I glanced at her as I said this, rolling my eyes. With our relationship a secret down at the station, it wouldn't have done me any favours to let on that she was sat in the car beside me that early in the morning.

'If you can, it'll be a help. Tell her to get over there too.'

I said I would, then hung up.

'It's O'Brien, isn't it?' she said straight away.

No flies on this girl. I nodded. 'It looks that way.'

'Any details?'

'Nothing at the moment. They only found the bodies twenty minutes ago.'

'Bodies?'

'His grandma got killed as well.' I explained that she lived in the same building as O'Brien.

She sighed. 'That sounds like a professional job.'

'I can't see the timing being coincidental. Let's get over there. There's no point going to collect your car. I'll say I picked you up.'

'OK, but weren't Berrin and Hunsdon meant to be watching his place?'

I shrugged. 'That's what I thought. Maybe they just weren't paying attention.'

I indicated, pulled into the bus lane and turned down a side street, taking a short cut in the direction of Slim Robbie and his grandmother's temporary resting place, wondering just how much more complicated things were going to get.

# 7

Slim Robbie O'Brien lived in a first-floor apartment in an immense Georgian townhouse that stood regally on an upmarket residential street just north of Highbury Corner, and an area he knew well, although he'd actually been born a mile away in the less upmarket Barnsbury, one of six children of Irish immigrants from south of Dublin. His parents had died young – his father of a heart attack, his mother of cancer – and his grandmother had come over from Ireland to look after Robbie and one of his sisters, the two youngest of the brood. Robbie had been fourteen at the time and had lived with his beloved gran for four years, before finally moving out to become a violent and integral member of the Holtz crime family, who were already well established in the area. He'd never forgotten what she'd done for him, though, and when he'd bought his current place five years earlier, he'd bought the apartment opposite for her. He'd never been much interested in women, due in part to his size, and the story went that when he wasn't out drinking or on business he'd be round at her place watching the box and eating her ample helpings of traditional Irish fare. Some of the braver members of the Holtz fraternity had even taken to calling her his girlfriend, which wasn't an entirely inaccurate summary.

I'd never met her but had heard that she was a good-hearted woman who, though she'd always refused to see any bad in her undeniably sadistic grandson, had never been in trouble in her life, and was spoken of fondly by those who knew her. It seemed a pity that she'd met such an ignominious end, and I hoped that she hadn't suffered unduly.

When we pulled into Robbie's street twenty minutes later, a uniformed officer I didn't recognize in a fluorescent jacket immediately stopped us. Up ahead, the road was closed in front of the house where the murders had occurred and the houses on either side of it, scene-of-crime tape sealing it off from the public. A number of police vehicles and two ambulances were double-parked on either side, while small groups of residents watched the proceedings with rapt, nervous interest from their doorsteps.

I brought down my window and showed the uniform my warrant card. 'DI John Gallan, and DS Tina Boyd. Any idea how they died?'

'Shot, I heard,' he replied, a tone of boredom in his voice.

People get shot all the time these days, particularly in Greater London. Twenty years ago it would have been front-page news. Today, it barely raises an eyebrow.

We parked up behind one of the ambulances, whose two-man crew were leant against it, smoking cigarettes. Over by the front door of the house, I could see DCI Knox standing talking to one of the white-overalled scene-of-crime officers. Knox was looking pissed off, which wasn't surprising. When you're as busy as we were, and after a day in which our original legwork had led to a meeting that had ended in six deaths, a double murder in the heart of our patch was not what you'd call helpful.

We got out of the car and walked over. Knox saw us approach and nodded curtly. 'Morning, John, Tina. This is Sergeant Andy Davies, SOCO. They're up there now.'

We shook hands all round and I asked Davies what we'd got so far. 'Two bodies, both IC1. One female, mid to late seventies. One male, early thirties. Both shot in the head from close range. From the look of the injuries, I'd say it was a smallish-calibre weapon, probably a .38. The bodies are in separate rooms. The male appears to have been killed where he's fallen in the living room, but, from the position of her body, we think the female was moved to the bedroom after she'd been shot.' He spoke matter-of-factly, in a curiously high-pitched voice that didn't fit with the rest of him. He was a big man, late forties, with a thick beard and very brown, intelligent eyes. As far as I was concerned, his voice should have boomed.

'Were they killed at the same time, do you think?' I asked.

'Too early to say. The doctor's up there now doing tests, so we should know fairly shortly.'

I nodded, knowing we wouldn't be getting any theories out of Davies. Like a lot of scene-of-crime officers, he only liked to deal in bald facts, and it was still very early days, with the inquiry less than an hour old, so there weren't even very many of them.

'We haven't had a final positive confirmation,' said Knox, who'd also met O'Brien before. 'I haven't been up there yet. But I can't see it being anyone else, and it would certainly fit, given the events of yesterday.' Davies looked at him quizzically when he said this, but Knox didn't elaborate. 'We're going to be coming in a few minutes to ID him, if that's all right.'

'OK,' said Davies, 'but you'll need to get kitted up.'

Knox nodded, then led us over to a police van with its rear

door open. A young uniform handed all three of us sterilized overalls, hats, overshoes and hoods to put on so we didn't contaminate the scene in any way. Fully togged up, we headed back in the direction of the house.

'This is looking bad,' said the DCI, turning to us both. 'Very bad. Operation Surgical Strike, and I can't think of a more inapt name, was badly compromised, and there's going to be a huge amount of pressure to get a result. If the body in there is O'Brien, and I'd bet my mortgage that it is, then we're in a lot of trouble.'

I didn't say anything. Neither did Tina. There wasn't a lot to say. He was right. Not only did it suggest that O'Brien – our informant – was the source of the leak, but also that we'd been powerless to prevent him being eliminated from under our very noses.

Which was the crux of Knox's concern. Our station had had its fair share of negative attention over the years, most famously (or infamously) when one of Knox's men in CID, a DS Dennis Milne, was unmasked as a contract killer with at least five, and probably many more, corpses to his credit. That nasty little affair was two and a half years old now and finally sinking into the past. The last thing Knox needed was something like this to throw it back into the limelight.

An attractive blonde woman in her late twenties stood in the doorway of her apartment as we stepped inside the building. She was dressed in a smart business suit and looked worried. 'Can you tell me what's going on? I've got an important meeting in the City at half-nine, and I've been told by someone that I've got to stay here.'

Knox smiled at her, unable to stop himself from sliding his eyes down to her shapely, nylon-clad legs, and not even being very subtle about it. 'I understand you live here, is that right, miss?'

'Williams,' she answered. 'Dana Williams.'

'I'm afraid there's been a serious incident in one of the other apartments.'

'Whose?'

'I can't tell you at the moment.'

'It's Robbie O'Brien, isn't it?'

'As I say, Miss Williams, we can't tell you at the moment. If you go back into your flat, someone will be down to take a statement as soon as possible. But it might be wise to make your meeting for this afternoon. This may take some time.'

'I'm afraid time is what I haven't got a lot of. This meeting's extremely important.'

'This is also very important. So, if you'd go back inside.' Knox's tone was firm and only just the right side of annoyed, and she relented, giving him a dirty look and mumbling something less than complimentary.

The wide, thickly carpeted hallway on the next floor was busy, with a number of SOCO coming in and out of one of the doors, some carrying plastic sample bags that they placed carefully in cases lined up against the wall. We stepped gingerly through this activity and into the apartment's living room where we were immediately confronted by the ample corpse of Slim Robbie (and it was him, there was no mistake) lying on its side in an approximate fetal position, with one arm outstretched, his jowly face in profile, the thick ginger hair just touching the wall. The tell-tale thin white scar that ran for two inches along his jawline, just below his left ear, was easily visible, confirming what I already knew. It was the result, he'd told me once, of a teenage knife fight years before. 'You should have seen the other bloke,' he'd said, with his trademark leer. 'He was in hospital for a month.' And I could believe it too.

There was a lot of blood on the carpet round the head where

he'd fallen, now thick and partially dried, and a few drops had splashed onto the many family photographs lining the wall, presumably resulting from the moment he'd been shot. A murder victim never really fits in with the décor of someone's front room, particularly when he's bled a lot, but Robbie's corpse looked more out of place than most in the midst of this spacious, neatly furnished and very chintzy lounge, which, with its porcelain animals and commemorative plates, could only have belonged to an old lady. On a large, comfortable-looking armchair in the corner of the room near the entrance to the kitchen was a cream-coloured lacy cushion with an unsightly black burn on it. It too looked as out of place as Robbie. Barely visible spots of red dotted the chair.

'It's him,' I said. 'No question.'

'I think it's fair to say he had it coming,' said Tina, with only the barest hint of regret.

The two of them had never really got on, thanks to the dirty-old-man-style leers Robbie had insisted on giving her every time they were in the same room together, something he knew she didn't like. As if anyone would when they were coming from an obese thug with a sweat and attitude problem. It's never nice to speak ill of the dead, but it has to be said: Slim Robbie O'Brien was the sort of bloke only a doting granny with her blinkers fully on could have loved. And look what it had cost her.

We stopped where we were for a few seconds, each pair of eyes hunting for clues. I'm no Sherlock Holmes, but I've been in this game long enough, and seen enough corpses who've met a sticky end, to know what I'm looking for and to be confident enough to express my opinions when I've found it.

'What do you reckon, John?' asked Knox.

'I think what Tina told me earlier's right,' I said eventually. 'This was a pro job. There's no sign of struggle, no damaged ornaments, no other obvious signs of injury to the body. Robbie died quickly, and I bet he didn't even know what had hit him. Or who.' I looked around again. The corpse was about six feet from the front door, lying parallel to and directly facing it. 'I don't think he died after opening the door either, not with his body in that position, which means the killer was in here already.'

'Someone they knew,' said Tina.

'Possibly. Shall we take a look at the other victim?'

Knox nodded, and we followed him through to the bedroom in silence. It was spacious and, like the living room, traditionally furnished and immaculately tidy, the dominating feature being a kingsize bed with purple satin sheets that didn't quite fit the colour scheme. A perfectly ordinary scene, except for the powerful smell of decay. There were three more SOCO in there, inspecting every nook and cranny with patient, focused eyes, studiously ignoring the corpse of Slim Robbie's grandmother which lay face-down on the carpet like a prop in a cheap whodunnit, fully clothed in a violet sweater and check skirt, between the bed and the walk-in wardrobe near the door. The police pathologist, a youngish guy with thick-rimmed glasses whose name was Jackson, was crouched down beside her, writing something in a notebook. As we stepped inside, I checked the carpet and noticed that it was scuffed where it seemed the killer had dragged her corpse. As Davies had pointed out, she'd almost certainly died elsewhere.

We stopped in front of her body, and Jackson finished writing and looked up. 'I know what you're going to ask,' he said.

'Are you going to answer it, then?' replied Knox, with the beginnings of a smile.

'They've both been here a while, I can tell you that,' he said, sounding like he was thinking very carefully about what he was saying. 'Rigor mortis is well advanced, and the body temperatures are low enough that it's at least twelve hours, possibly as long as twenty-four. I'll be able to get a more exact time when I've conducted more tests and made the necessary calculations, but that's my first estimate.'

'Is there any significant difference between the two body temperatures?' I asked. 'That might suggest they were killed at different times?'

'This victim's is slightly lower, but I wouldn't read too much into that. Not on its own. There are a number of factors that could have contributed to it. Their size difference for a start.'

'Do you think they were killed separately then, John?' asked Knox.

'I'm not sure, but if they were killed together, I would have thought there would have been more of an obvious struggle. Robbie doted on his grandma. He would have tried to protect her, and with his size there would have been one hell of a mess.'

'The killer could have tidied up after himself,' pointed out Tina.

I nodded. 'True, but then why did he move her body, which he must have done?' I pointed out the scuffing on the carpet. 'What would have been the point? If he killed them together, why not simply leave them where they fell? And why move one without the other? On the other hand, if he killed her first, then moved the body so it was out of sight, before taking out O'Brien when he arrived, that would suit the scene we've got here.'

'There's no sign of forced entry on the door to this apartment,' said Knox, 'or the door of the building, so it's possible that he was let in. Most likely by her. Then he finishes her off, and waits for O'Brien. Yes, I quite like the sound of that one.' I had no doubt that he'd take the credit for it as well, but that was Knox for you. He hadn't got to the position of DCI on the back of his laid-back, generous approach to the job.

'Who says he was let in?' said Tina, pointing at the bedroom window, which was slightly open at one end. We hadn't spotted this before since the view had been obscured by one of the SOCO, who'd now moved. 'He could have come in through there.'

We approached the window, not touching it, and peered down into the small, neatly trimmed communal garden some fifteen feet below. There didn't appear to be any obvious means of climbing up from the garden to the window, and it would have taken a very agile killer indeed to have made it without a step ladder, and there wasn't one of those in evidence either. Nor would it have been very easy to take it away with him afterwards. Because the house we were in was terraced and its garden backed directly on to the gardens of the houses on the next street, the killer would have had to cross through a number of properties to reach its rear, a task that would have been very noisy and time-consuming if he'd been carrying a ladder with him.

Knox made exactly that point, and it was hard to argue with him. 'No,' he said, turning away. 'I think we can assume he came through the front door.'

I leant forward to take one more look outside, which was when I noticed something sticking out of the wall several feet below the window. I pushed the glass with my gloved hand and it opened further.

'What is it?' asked Tina, who was still beside me.

I craned my neck to get a better view.

It was a rusty nail. Not only that, but a rag, or piece of cloth of some kind, barely a couple of inches across, was hanging from it, drifting idly in the early-morning breeze. It could have been nothing, but it didn't look like it had been there that long, and I doubted that Robbie's grandma would have caught her clothes on it while hanging out the window.

'Take a look at that,' I said, motioning towards my find.

Tina and Knox both squeezed in beside me and looked down.

'Well, well, well,' said Tina.

'Hmm,' said Knox.

'Maybe he came *out* this way,' I ventured. 'And caught his clothing.'

'Maybe,' said Knox. 'We'll bag it up anyway. You never know.' He turned away for a second time and informed the nearest SOCO of my discovery, then walked towards the bedroom door. 'Good work, John,' he added as an aside.

Personally, I thought that it merited a bit more than that, but I could understand him not getting too excited. Even if it was connected to what had happened, it was hardly a 'smoking gun'. Still, from small seeds and all that.

We both followed Knox out of the room. 'Who alerted us this morning, then?' I asked him.

'Robbie's sister, Neve. The female victim, Mrs MacNamara, looks after her two-year-old every Tuesday and Thursday. She came round to drop him off, then, when there was no answer from inside, or from Robbie's place, she let herself in.'

'God, poor thing,' said Tina. 'Where's she now?'

'DC Hunsdon and one of the WPCs have taken her down the station. They'll get a statement from her. Luckily, she called in straight away, as soon as she saw her brother's body. She didn't take the child inside or touch anything.' He paused, then moved on swiftly, which was a long-standing habit of his. 'We need to find out who was here yesterday afternoon and evening. See if anyone let the killer in, or at least saw or heard anything. You two can take a statement from Miss Williams downstairs. As soon as we've got some more numbers down here, we'll get statements from everyone else. There's another apartment on the ground floor but I think the occupants may be away. We haven't heard anything from them this morning. There's also someone on the top floor as well. A retired widower named Carlson. I've told him to stay inside and we'll get someone up to him as soon as we can. We'd better deal with Miss Williams first, though,' he added. 'You know what these high-flyers are like.'

Tina and I spent half an hour with Dana Williams, who, it turned out, was a financial recruitment consultant for Barnes and Penney (apparently, the largest and most profitable such con-sultancy in the City of London), but didn't get a huge amount out of her, other than an idea of her company's balance sheet. She hadn't been that shocked to learn that Robbie had been murdered, having heard enough rumours of his involvement in organized crime to know that he was always going to have enemies, and had freely admitted to not liking him much anyway; but when we'd told her about his grandma, her tough exterior had cracked a little.

'She was a nice person, she didn't deserve to go like that,' she'd told us solemnly, and then, after a three-second pause for reflection, she'd launched into a diatribe about the extortionate cost of the brand-new double-lock they'd had put on the front door and how ineffective it had been, until we'd told her that the killer had been let in by someone. 'I wasn't here,' she'd told us quickly, as if we were about to accuse her of being the one. 'I didn't get back until eight o'clock last night. We're very busy at work at the moment.' She'd then taken a none-too-subtle look at her watch and begun fidgeting noisily, the shock of finding out that two of her neighbours had been murdered obviously not getting in the way of Barnes and Penney business.

It was quarter past nine by the time we finished with Dana

Williams, and she hurried out of the room after us, already jabbering into her mobile.

Knox was back out in the hallway talking to DC Berrin, who'd now arrived, and we told them what we'd found out from Miss Williams, including the time she'd returned. 'She was there all evening after that,' I said, 'and she didn't hear anything. My feeling is it must have happened before eight.'

Knox turned to Berrin. 'What time did you get here last night, Dave?'

'Ten to six, bang on. I checked my watch. And we didn't leave until midnight. Nobody came in or out in that time.'

'I've just talked to Carlson, the widower on the top floor,' said Knox. 'He was here all day yesterday, except between two and four when he went out for a walk up in Highbury Fields, which he does most days. He thought he heard a bang coming from Mrs MacNamara's apartment at some time between half-one and two. He was watching TV at the time, *Neighbours*. He said he didn't take much notice because it wasn't very loud, and could easily have been just something breaking. When he came down the stairs to go out, he said that he heard the sound of the TV coming from her apartment, so assumed everything was OK.'

'It could have been the shot that killed her, though?' said Tina.

'Davies says that, as far as he can tell, she was only shot the once, so it sounds logical. That was the killer taking her out, and then it was a matter of waiting for O'Brien to arrive. Perhaps he lured O'Brien into his grandmother's place, then surprised him, which would explain the lack of evidence of a struggle.' Having effortlessly assimilated my theory, he was now embellishing it like a true pro.

'So now we need to get an idea of what time O'Brien returned, if we're assuming they weren't killed at the same time,' I said, muscling back in. 'You went looking for him in the Slug and Lettuce yesterday, didn't you, Dave?'

Berrin nodded. 'That's right.'

'Did they say whether he'd been in or not?'

'We didn't ask, guv, to be honest. Just poked our noses round, looking for him. He wasn't there, so we left.'

Which was typical Berrin. He was a good kid, very pleasant and presentable, with a nice line in polite patter with the public, and a grad too, like Tina; but unlike her, he hadn't been blessed with much in the way of know-how or work ethic, which made the life of his superiors harder than it should have been. But this is the Met, and these days it's a case of beggars can't be choosers.

'We'll need to have a thorough check of O'Brien's movements,' said Knox. 'It's essential we find out what time he died.'

'Are we going to be taking this case then, sir?' asked Tina, and I was sure I heard a hint of enthusiasm in her voice. We had a lot on at the moment, and the events of the previous day and the subsequent investigations were only going to add to the workload, but there was a challenge here. Someone had killed two people and evidently thought he could get away with it. Most coppers worth their salt would be interested in proving him or her wrong. Whatever Tina had said about leaving, I knew she was one of them.

'I very much doubt it,' answered Knox. 'With the potential connections with yesterday, I think it's definitely going to be a Serious Crime Group investigation, but we need to do our bit, and do it well, while it's still in our jurisdiction.'

The rest of us nodded soberly, knowing that our involvement might soon be at an end. But, like Tina, I was already hoping it wouldn't be.

# Part Two

## THE INVESTIGATION

# 8

Tina and I spent close to another hour at the scene, interviewing the immediate neighbours in the houses on each side (none of whom could provide us with any leads), before leaving and heading back to the station where we both had plenty of work that needed doing. Among other things, the two of us were heading up an ongoing inquiry into local people who'd supplied their credit-card details to an internet child-porn site based in Arizona. The inquiry had been going on for weeks and there were twenty-two men in our locality who had to be checked out, arrested, questioned and, if necessary, charged by a team of four of us. So far we'd collared nine of them, including a magistrate, a children's charity worker and a doctor, but each individual case took a lot of effort and manpower, as court orders had to be obtained for credit-card checks and confirmation gained that the cards hadn't been stolen or were in false names before finally houses and computers were painstakingly searched and arrests made. Every one of the men had visited the site at least five times, most over fifty, a handful over a hundred, and the images contained on it involved the pay-per-view abuse of children, and even babies. It was horrific stuff, all of it, and no-one involved in that inquiry thought it was a waste of our time. We were currently concentrating on a fifty-five-year-old retired school teacher with no previous convictions and an exemplary employment record. He'd visited the site 110 times, on one occasion spending four hours solid on it, at considerable financial cost to himself. We were hoping to arrest him before the end of the week, but I was also due in court that afternoon to testify in a rape trial, so I was no longer sure it was going to happen. In this sort of case that can break a reputation in seconds, you have to be very careful how you tread. Either way, I was going to have a busy day, without any distractions from Operation Surgical Strike.

But if I was hoping to avoid those distractions, I was being unduly optimistic. We got back to the station at 10.40. At 10.45, I convened a meeting of the team on the arrest of the retired paedophile teacher. At 10.50, my extension rang, and the DC who answered it interrupted the meeting to tell me it was urgent. 'It's Asif Malik,' he said. 'SO7.'

Reluctantly, I got to my feet and asked Tina to chair the meeting in my absence, then left the meeting room.

'Hello, Asif. Are you all right?' I asked, picking up the phone.

'Not really, John, no. I don't like the fact that Robbie O'Brien's dead before we can get any information out of him. It makes us all look very stupid. You've seen the headlines in this morning's papers.'

'I haven't actually. I haven't had a chance.'

'Well, they don't look too clever.'

'No, I can imagine.'

'"High Noon at Heathrow", according to the *Sun*, and they're going to get a lot worse than that as more details start coming out. When they hear about O'Brien, they're going to be thinking that we're being completely outmanoeuvred, and we can't have that.'

'Who's taking the case?'

'Joint Serious Crime Group East and SO7. DCS Flanagan's going to be heading it up.'

I raised an eyebrow at that one. 'What? After yesterday?'

'He followed everything to the letter with Surgical Strike, and we're very short of available SIOs of DCS level, and this is definitely a DCS-level case. At least he knows the background.'

'If there's any assistance I can give, I'll be more than happy to help.'

'There is,' he said. 'We want you seconded to the inquiry. You and DS Boyd. Flanagan's clearing it with your chief super now. You both know the victim, you're familiar with the background, and I hate to say it, but you're also involved in what's happened.'

'Only a limited involvement,' I told him, keen not to get tarred with the wrong sort of brush.

'But you know all about it. With everything else, that makes you ideal. Plus, you're a bloody good copper, and I know you rate Tina Boyd as well.'

I didn't say anything for a moment.

'Are you still there?'

'Of course I'm still here. I'm thinking, that's all.'

'Well, that's the end of my flattery. I want you on this case – we all do. And if you refuse, you're going to have to have one hell of a good reason why.'

But there was no way I was going to refuse. I was busy, yes. Extremely so. But that was never going to change. As long as I remained in the Met I was going to be overworked – it was as good as part of the job description – but opportunities to get involved in something like this don't come along very often. Especially cases where you know the victim. I might not have liked Slim Robbie O'Brien, but I wanted to see whoever had murdered him and his grandmother punished. It takes a very dangerous, very cold individual to snuff out two lives as efficiently as the perpetrator of this had. An individual who could do that deserves to spend his days behind bars.

'If you can clear it with the chief super down here then of course I'm interested. I know Tina will be too.'

'Consider it done. We're setting up an incident room at your station, so that's nice and convenient. We've got a meeting scheduled for two p.m.'

'I can't do two. I'm in court this afternoon, giving evidence. There's no way I can get out of it.'

'Fair enough. Tina'll have to attend, though. You can get the relevant info off her. What are you doing afterwards?'

'After court? Going home and having a bite to eat probably.'

'You're going to need to talk to Stegs Jenner. Preferably today.' He gave me Stegs's address in Barnet. 'We're going to want details of all his meetings with O'Brien, what was said—'

'Haven't we already got that information? A lot of it came out in the questioning yesterday, and presumably there are records.'

'There are, and it did, but I want you to go over everything with him again. See if you can pick up anything we might have missed. I also want you to check his movements yesterday in the run-up to the operation. From when he left his house in the morning.'

I was surprised at this last part. 'He's not a suspect, is he?'

Malik sighed. 'Not as such, but there's a concern that he's not telling us everything.'

'What do you mean?'

'O'Brien had a mobile phone in his pocket when he was found

this morning. It looks like a pay-as-you-go. Stegs said yesterday that he hadn't spoken to O'Brien since Sunday, and he might not have done, but in the phone records section of the mobile it clearly states that a total of three of the last ten calls made on that phone were to a number that we've just found out is a Met mobile currently issued to Stegs. Now, it might mean nothing. We've got no idea yet when these calls were made, or how long they lasted, or even whether they were answered, but it's worth asking again whether he's spoken to O'Brien since Sunday. Can you go and see him tonight?'

'All right,' I said, wondering whether this was all they had on him. I found myself hoping so, and hoping too that there was an innocent explanation for it. I didn't want to see old Stegs get thrown even deeper into the mire.

'And take Tina if you can. We've got another meeting scheduled for nine a.m. tomorrow. You can let us know how it went then. We should also have the initial results of the post-mortem at that point, so we'll have a more exact time of death for both victims.'

Malik was a fast mover. But I was pretty sure we were all going to have to be fast movers on a case like this, one where even the politicians were interested in seeing a result.

It made me glad I hadn't made any plans for the next few days.

# 9

Stegs was writing a book about his exploits undercover in SO10. It had been done before by former officers of course, several times, but he was certain there was still a market for this kind of material: tales of derring-do amid the violent world of cops, robbers and killers. That last bit was the first sentence of the synopsis for *Undercover Cop*, the tell-it-all novel he was hoping was going to attract some serious literary attention of the financial kind once he released it into the public realm. He'd decided on the title after much thought, concluding that it was best not to try and be too subtle with the punters. Tell them straight what it was all about, no fannying around. The plan was to finish it, get an offer in from someone big, then retire from the Force and give the bastards a richly deserved two fingers.

Progress, however, had been slow. Stegs had been writing it for more than two years and was still only on page twenty-seven. He'd had a lot of trouble with the first chapter, in which he'd described his schooldays. He couldn't seem to get the right combination of tough and vulnerable and had found it particularly hard to avoid mentioning the name Monty without making the whole thing sound wrong, and in these sort of things you had to be authentic. He'd finally moved on to chapter two a few months earlier, having given himself the new name of Martin for chapter one, and was now at the training stage in Hendon. A few more pages and he'd be on to the good stuff: football riots, his first case at SO10, the sex, the drugs, the rock and roll. And any other bullshit he could think up.

On the morning after the death of Vokes, Stegs made a vow to turn adversity into opportunity and use his period of suspension to make a concerted push on *Undercover Cop*. This was at twenty to seven while he sat feeding baby Luke at the breakfast table. The missus, meanwhile, was carrying out a two-pronged pincer attack: on the one hand complaining about the fact that he hadn't got in until quarter to two the previous night; on the other bemoaning the Jenner family's lack of money. The latest Visa bill received the previous day, which was being waved like a piece of evidence, showed that they owed £2,311. And sixty-eight pence, if you wanted to be exact. This was on top of the latest bank statement brandished three days earlier, which carried the grim news that the joint account was £240 in the red with a week still to go before Stegs received his pay.

'We can't carry on like this,' she said in a voice that was a mixture of angry and pained, a tone peculiar to her that he always thought would have been better suited to someone who'd been constipated for a week and wanted to blame someone else for it.

Money had been becoming more and more of an issue recently. The missus's sister was married to an insurance broker in the city called Clive who liked to flash the cash, and it was making the missus jealous. They also had a kid a couple of months older than Luke, a real ugly bruiser called Harry who had a flat, bashed-in face that looked like it had been used as a hammer by Mike Tyson, but who was always dressed up in the latest designer clothes. Clive, the missus's sister and young Frankenstein were off to a villa in the south of France for three weeks in August, and had invited the Jenner family along. The missus wanted to go but Stegs wasn't keen on the idea. He'd said it was because they couldn't afford it, but in reality it was much more to do with the fact that he couldn't stick Clive, who was about as full of life as the Unknown Soldier. But since then the missus had got it into her head that Stegs was going to have to change jobs in order to solve their financial woes and put them in a position where they could go on fancy holidays and dress Luke up in the manner he deserved. Not that the little bugger appeared too bothered about his sartorial elegance as he sat there drooling lumpy porridge all over his romper suit.

Stegs decided to use the nuclear option and nip this broadside in the bud by telling her that Vokes had been the officer killed yesterday, and that he himself had been present only minutes before it had happened. It had the desired effect. Her hand went to her mouth, and her eyes widened. 'Oh God, Mark. It could have been you. Are you all right, baby?' She grabbed him in an intense hug, crumpling the Visa bill against his dressing gown, and causing a burst of jealous displeasure from Luke who started screaming and spraying bits of porridge everywhere. The missus was not a big woman – in fact, her mother thought she was too thin (mind you, the mother was pushing fifteen stone) – but on that morning she had a grip of steel, and Stegs felt himself losing breath.

'It's all right, love,' he gasped. 'I'm fine. It's going to be OK.' Not if you don't fucking let go of me, it won't.

She sobbed silently into his shoulder, unlike Luke who sobbed loudly into his ear, occasionally hitting it with pieces of half-eaten shrapnel. Stegs felt bad that he'd broken it to her like he had, and not for the first time he cursed himself for being so thoughtless. She didn't have the most comfortable of lives at the moment and he ought to go a bit easier on her.

She pulled away from him and turned her attention instead to Luke. 'It's all right, Lukey, Lukey, Lukey. It's OK, babe. Mama's here now.' Like a wild animal who'd met his match, Luke calmed down and his screams became the occasional hiccoughing sob. The missus took the porridge spoon from Stegs and began refilling her son's face. He gave Stegs a nasty look out of the corner of his eye, as if to say, 'Watch it, she's mine.' Stegs, to his shame, gave him one in return. That kid was going to have to learn a bit of respect.

The missus turned to him, still feeding Luke. She'd recovered now, but there were still tears in her eyes. She'd only met Vokes twice – once when they'd gone round there for dinner, and another time for a meal in the West End (neither occasion had been very successful, in part due to Gill's rampant Christianity, which meant you had to be careful what you said) – but she was aware that Stegs had worked with him for a while, and that they were close. 'Have you spoken to Gill?' she asked.

'Not yet. I will do, though.'

'Poor thing. It's going to be awful for her.' She shook her head in disbelief. 'Imagine losing your husband like that. And with kids as well. You're going to go round and see her, aren't you?'

He didn't feel any better about doing it than he had the previous night, but he knew he didn't really have much choice. 'I'll go and see her later today. She'll probably have her family and the police round this morning.'

'It's just so . . . so awful, Mark. What happened?'

Stegs didn't like talking about his job with the missus. He

never had. To be fair, she'd never been that interested, and on those occasions when she had asked, he'd always cited security reasons for not saying too much. This time, though, he knew he wasn't going to get away without at least telling her something, not least because she was going to be able to get most of the details from the news and the papers, so he gave her as brief a rundown as possible of what had happened, making no mention of his suspension. In his story, he'd been at the scene in one of the other rooms, but at no time had he been in any danger. Vokes had been the one taking the risks (Stegs explained that he didn't get directly involved in the more dangerous situations, describing his responsibility as back-up, which she seemed to buy) and, unfortunately, things had gone wrong. 'He was just unlucky, you know. It's very, very rare that these jobs go tits-up.'

'Don't swear in front of Lukey, Mark.'

'Why not? He can't understand what I'm saying.'

'It's just not nice, OK? Please.'

Stegs took a slurp from his cup of tea. It was going cold. 'Yeah, whatever.'

'Are you sure you're all right?'

'I'm fine. Tired, that's all.' And hung over, he thought. He'd sunk four in the Admiral, then two cans of Stella when he'd got home. He was amazed he hadn't been up pissing all night, but then he'd always had a strong bladder.

The missus sighed and gave him her trademark calm-but-serious look. This was always a sign that she was going to nag him about something. And he knew straight away what it was. 'I want you to think very seriously about changing jobs, Mark. Really. Linda was saying the other day that Clive could get you a job as head of office security at Warner Tomkins and Nash Associates. The current incumbent's not doing a very good job and they want to make him redundant and replace him.'

Stegs thought that his missus was probably the only person he knew who actually used the word 'incumbent' in conversation. 'Look, can we not talk about this now? It's a bad time at the moment.'

'When can we talk about it, then?'

'Not today,' he said, getting up from the kitchen chair and looking around for his cigarettes. 'Please not today.'

'The pay's good,' she called after him as he found the pack and retreated out the back door and into the cold for his first smoke of the day.

He locked himself in his study with the PC for most of the morning, explaining to the missus that he was doing some work from home. Instead he made a valiant effort to get *Undercover Cop* flowing, and after much scratching of head, he managed to get it to midway down page thirty. To spice up the otherwise boring details of his training, he put in the bit on his graduation night when he'd slept with a Scottish prostitute with a prosthetic leg. Stegs remembered how shocked he'd been when he'd bumped into it during sex and jarred his knee (it had been covered with a black stocking at the time, so wasn't that obvious), but he didn't mention how he'd got her to remove it for the remainder of their bout to see what it would be like, not wanting to come across like some sort of pervert. Having wound up Hendon, he was now on to chapter three where he was a probationer pounding the beat of Barnet (or driving round in a squad car, anyway). Soon he'd be getting on to the good stuff, having already decided to slap in a fictitious murder for him to help solve in chapter four. Then it would really start to flow.

But even the most hardy of scribes needs a rest, so at 11.30 Stegs emerged from the cramped little room which was the only one in the house he could truly call his own (no-one else could fit in it while he was in there) and told his missus that he had to go to a debriefing session at Scotland Yard.

'Are you sure you're OK to go?' she asked him. 'Maybe it'd be better if you stayed here for the afternoon. They really ought to give you a couple of days off after something as traumatic as what's happened.'

'I've got a duty to the people who need me,' he told her piously. 'And I'm fine, honestly.'

'Are you going to call in on Gill and the kids?'

He nodded. 'Afterwards.'

'Give them my love. And my condolences. Maybe you should pick up some flowers on the way.'

'Course I will.' He gave her a quick kiss on the cheek, then picked up Luke who was playing at her feet. The boy gave him a hostile look at first, then slowly his face broke into a smile. Stegs smiled back, suddenly feeling all soppy. 'Hey, my little man, I'm going to miss you today. Kiss for Dada, eh?'

As he leant forward to give him a big slobbery one on the lips, he was suddenly assailed by a ferocious smell, so powerful that it could probably have stripped paint off walls. He swallowed hard, trying not to gag. An old man couldn't have produced worse. No wonder the little bugger had been smiling. That one must have been brewing up for hours.

Swiftly he handed him back to the missus, having given him only a cursory lip-scrape across the cheek. 'I think he needs changing, babes. I'd love to stop and help but the meeting starts in an hour. I've got to run.'

He was out of there like lightning, the smell fair chasing him out of the door, a noxious cloud warning him not to return. No chance of that, he thought. Not for a few hours anyway.

For a while he just drove around, not really sure what to do with himself. He knew he had to go and visit Gill but was desperate to put off the inevitable. Seeing her was going to be a nightmare. It was bad enough on a normal day. God knows what she was going to say to him. He couldn't help thinking that he was going to get the blame for what had happened, even though there was nothing he could have done. He hoped Vokes hadn't been too scared in the last few seconds before he died, and he hoped too that death had come quickly. It felt strange knowing he was never going to see his colleague again, that this was it: the end of their relationship. Vokes had always claimed to have believed in God, but Stegs was never a hundred per cent sure whether he really did or not. More likely he was trying to keep the missus happy and hedge his bets at the same time. In a job like theirs you never knew when your card might be marked. Better to be on the right side of the Good Lord if he did exist. Maybe it had given him some comfort in those last frantic moments. Stegs hoped so, and wished at the same time that he'd had a chance to say goodbye, so that he could have let him know that he'd always been a good mate. It upset him that his last words had been to tell him not to worry, that he'd be back in a few minutes, but that of course was the injustice of sudden death. It deprived you of the opportunity to tie up all the loose ends and finally close the book.

Vokes's family lived in Ealing, a few miles down the road from the station in Acton where he'd been based for the past ten years. By the time Stegs had meandered his way down there, it was one o'clock and time to eat. Hungry, tired and still vaguely hung over, he had a rank taste of old beer in his mouth and the best way to get rid of it was to sup a bit of hair of the dog. The pub beckoned.

He parked on a backstreet near Ealing Common and made his way down on to the Broadway, keeping an eye out for a decent boozer as he strolled along the crowded shopping street. He and Vokes had never really drunk round here so he didn't know the watering holes and wanted to make sure he found a good one. Stegs was a traditionalist where pubs were concerned. He didn't want a wine bar serving tapas or somewhere where they only flogged bottled beer at £2.50 a pop. He wanted carpets with fag burns on them, the smell of beer and smoke; the noise of loud, rasping, unhealthy laughter. Pork scratchings; a dartboard; food with big chips on the side; barmen who look like barmen, not fucking students.

He eventually found a place near Ealing Broadway Tube that at least had some of what he was looking for. It was a bit big, and there were a few too many businessmen and estate agent types, but they did do steak and kidney pie and chips and they had a good variety of beers on tap. He asked the barman, who unfortunately did look like a student, whether the chips were chunky or those little thin ones like you got in McDonald's. The barman, who said he was new, had to go and check with the kitchen, and when he came back he said that they did bakers' chips, which were apparently in between.

'That's not a bad marketing idea,' said Stegs, and ordered a pint of Stella and steak and kidney pie with bakers' chips, before taking a seat at the bar.

The grub, when it came, was good and he finished the lot. There are very few men in the world who can have just one pint and leave it at that, and in Stegs's opinion those who can have something wrong with them. He wasn't going to be driving for an hour or two so he ordered another Stella and drank it swiftly with two smokes. That was the point when he should have stopped – he could usually last just about on two – but the knowledge that stopping meant heading round to Gill's place made him think that perhaps one more would be in order.

He shouted for another pint, paid for it, then made his way to the toilets, taking the drink with him. They were clean enough for pub bogs, but they still had that stale, pissy smell you always get in such places, and the sight of a cockroach floundering on its back in a pool of water by the sinks did little to add to the ambience. There was no-one else in there so he went to the nearest cubicle, stepped inside and locked the door. He then fished a small, transparent packet filled with white powder from the inside of his jacket, opened it, and chucked half of its contents into the new pint. The beer fizzed up angrily, then settled again as the speed began to dissolve, the chunkier bits sinking towards the bottom. Stegs didn't consider himself an addict by any means, but more and more these days he needed the speed as a pick-me-up for when he was feeling knackered or hung over – or in this case both. He'd been introduced to it by Pete the gun dealer, had liked it (particularly the fact that it was cheap) and, given his excellent and varied contacts within the criminal classes, had never had a problem getting hold of it. He never took it more than two or three times a week though, and considered his usage firmly under control.

With one hand, he flipped himself out of his jeans and opened fire directly into the bowl, while using the other hand to guzzle the drug-fuelled lager in a classic example of recycling. One minute later he'd given his dick and the half-full glass a good shake, and was feeling better already. He went back out, his heart thumping and teeth grinding, a grin already erupting on his face, knowing that now he was ready for anything. A vision of Vokes marched unwelcome into his mind, and he pushed it aside with a survivor's laugh that had a group of businessmen standing near the door to thc gents giving him the resigned, moderately contemptuous look that so many Londoners aim at the mentally unstable. Stegs ignored them.

His seat at the bar had been taken by a young woman with a pudgy face and a big arse who was sitting talking to a spotty teenager in a cheap suit. The teenager was making a pretty lame attempt to appear interested in what the girl was saying, but he perked up noticeably when she put a flabby arm on his and leant forward, giggling, to tell him something. Stegs imagined the two of them naked and on the job, and it made him feel a bit sick, so he turned away and found some space by a pillar in the middle of the floor. He leant against it and took another huge swig of his pint, wondering whether he had time for just one more.

At that moment, his private mobile rang. He instantly recognized the tone: *Mission Impossible*. This was the phone used by family, friends, work and informants who knew his real identity. He had another purely for undercover work. The ringtone on that one was *The Magnificent Seven*.

He removed it from the pocket of his jacket and checked the number, not immediately recognizing it. 'Hello,' he said, putting it to his ear. The bar was crowded now with office workers on their lunchbreak, and he had to speak up.

'All right, Stegsy?'

Only one man called Stegs 'Stegsy', and that was Trevor Murk, a petty criminal and informant whose activities matched his name, and who occasionally provided him with tidbits of information about the activities of small-time crims operating out of his Barnet locale. Stegs hadn't heard from Murk for a while, which was why he hadn't recognized the number.

'Hello, Trevor. What can I do for you today?'

'I think it's more a matter of what I can do for you, me old mate. Got a little bit of info that might be of great use. Great use indeed.'

Murk spoke like Michael Caine did in *Get Carter*. Loud enough to stop a conversation, yet taking care to enunciate every word individually with an air of cheery cockney menace. It was all an act, though. He'd actually been brought up in St Albans.

'Oh yeah?' said Stegs, not sure whether it was worth mentioning that he was suspended. 'What's that, then?'

'Behave, sweetboy. Not over the blower. This sort of thing requires some alcoholic lubrication. Are you in the boozer at the moment?'

'I am, but nowhere local. I'm in Ealing.'

'What the fuck are you doing there?' asked Murk in a tone that suggested he might as well have been in Kathmandu.

'I'm having a drink,' said Stegs, who was already beginning to get tired of this conversation. Murk wasn't bad company as informants go, but he did rate himself highly and could therefore become severely irritating on occasion.

'Well, I can give it to someone else, Stegsy, but I reckon you'll regret it if I do. This'll be a nice little collar, and I reckon you'll have a laugh doing it as well.'

'What do you mean?'

'Exactly what I said. I'll tell you more if we meet up. And I'm going to need a nice little drink for my troubles.'

In spite of himself, Stegs was intrigued. He took another gulp from his pint, leaving nothing but a powdery mouthful in the bottom. He could hear his heart pounding but knew it was the gear. 'There'll be no money until I hear what you've got to say, all right?'

'Fair do's, but you'll like it, I promise you that.'

'We'll see. I can meet you tomorrow lunchtime. Soon enough.'

'That'll do. Usual place?'

'I'll be there at one o'clock.'

'Are you pissed?'

'Eh?'

'You sound a bit pissed down there. How many have you had?'

'What are you? My fucking mother? I'm fine. See you tomorrow.'

He hung up, hoping he didn't sound too inebriated. He'd been thinking about having another, but decided he'd better knock it on the head for now.

He didn't know why he'd agreed to meet up with Murk. Even if it was an easy collar, in the end it was none of his business now that he was suspended, his future in the Force looking shaky to say the least. No-one likes a copper involved in controversy, least of all the politically sensitive Brass. But regardless of all that, that's what Stegs Jenner still was. A copper. And a copper likes getting collars. Plus, it would give him something to do to-morrow. If Murk wasn't being too cocky, it might even be quite a good afternoon.

He finished the last bit of his drink and put the glass on a shelf on the pillar he'd been leaning against, then headed out the door, trying to compose a few fitting sentences of commiseration for the recently bereaved widow.

It took Stegs close to half an hour to find the Vokerman house-hold. He'd only ever been there once before, and this time had forgotten to bring the address or the directions with him. Or the flowers, come to that. He knew the number, and the rough location, but couldn't think of the street name, so he'd had to tramp around the whole area until he'd come across it, quite by chance. A quiet residential road made up of bland but spacious 1940s semis in view of the Thames Valley University campus.

He walked along until he came to the house where his friend had lived for more than ten years. He stopped for a moment at the gate, recognizing the familiar yellow paint, then steadied him-self before walking the three yards through the tiny but well-kept front garden up to the front door. A bunch of flowers wrapped in black paper had been placed in the porch. He knocked hard on the door.

A few seconds later he heard footsteps, and then it opened to reveal a tall, bespectacled gentleman with a kindly smile, a dog collar and not much hair. 'Good afternoon,' he said. 'Can I help you?'

Stegs's heart banged hard in his chest and he had to fight back a sudden urge to shriek loudly. 'Yes,' he said, as sombrely as possible. 'I'm here to see Mrs Vokerman. I worked very closely with her husband.'

The vicar nodded slowly and wisely. Stegs doubted if he was more than a couple of years older than him, but he had the demeanour of a fifty-year-old. It probably went with the territory. He opened the door wider. 'Please come in.'

'My son.'

'I'm sorry?'

'My son. Sorry, I thought you were going to say "my son". You know, "Please come in, my son."'

'I think that's Catholics, Mr . . . ?'

'Jenner. Mark Jenner.' He had to think about that last one.

'Come in, Mark. I am sure it'll be a comfort for Gill to see you.' He looked like he meant it too. Whatever you say about these Christians, they do try hard.

Stegs followed him through the hall and into the lounge, cursing himself for not being able to keep his mouth shut. Gill was in there, sitting in an armchair sipping a cup of tea. An older lady, with her grey hair tied into two huge buns like giant headphones round each ear, held onto Gill's arm. She also had a cup of tea. On the wall was a large framed photo of Vokes, Gill and the two kids, all looking very happy as they smiled into the camera. Other photos of his former colleague and family adorned the walls and mantelpieces of the room. It was half past two.

This time the previous afternoon the man of the house had been alive and well. Stegs almost burst into tears. Thank God he hadn't had that fourth pint.

'Hello, Gill,' he said, stopping enough distance away from her so she wouldn't smell the booze and fags. 'I came round to say how sorry I am about your loss. He was a good man.'

'Thank you, Mark,' she said quietly, fixing him with a moderately disapproving look.

Stegs couldn't help wondering what Vokes had ever seen in her. She was a very plain woman to look at and did nothing to try to minimize it. She wore no make-up, dressed very conservatively and had a shrewish personality. Vokes wouldn't have won any good looks contests (he had a beard for a start), but he could have done a lot better than this.

'Please take a seat. This is my mother.'

The mother nodded menacingly.

The vicar plonked himself next to the woman Stegs would only ever know as Mother, while he himself took a seat at the other end of the room, furthest away from Gill.

'The police came round this morning,' Gill said wearily, staring up towards the ceiling. 'They talked for a long time but were unable to give me any details of how Paul died. Were you there?'

They all looked at him. The vicar was still smiling, or maybe that was just his normal expression. Stegs suddenly had a terrible desire to masturbate, to rush out of this room, lock himself in the toilet and pull one off at the wrist. It was a reaction he often got to speed, he wasn't sure why. It was ironic, really, because amphetamines made it very difficult to get a hard-on, something that at that moment was proving quite useful. A tentpeg stiffy in a room like this would have been a disaster.

For a couple of seconds he didn't answer as his thoughts shot off here and there, so she repeated the question.

'Are you finding it difficult to talk about what happened, Mark?' asked the vicar.

'No, I'm fine. Really.' He turned to Gill, putting on his most earnest expression. 'I'm not allowed to make any comment about it either, I'm afraid, Gill,' he said, trying to stop his teeth grinding. 'All I can say is that I was part of the same operation, and that his death would have been very quick. Very quick indeed.'

The mother gasped. 'The name of the Lord is a strong tower the righteous run into and are safe,' she said stiffly. Whatever that was meant to mean.

The vicar nodded slowly. 'These are very trying times,' he said, which was a bit of a statement of the obvious. 'We must all be strong.'

'How are the children taking it?' asked Stegs, unable to think of anything else to say.

'Jacob is very upset, as you can imagine. Honey's still too young to understand.'

'Where are they at the moment?'

'My dad's looking after them.'

'Kids are very resilient. Very, very resilient. They can get through this sort of thing. Yup, definitely. No problem.'

There was a long silence. Stegs felt himself sweating. The room was stifling.

'I am the living bread which came down from heaven,' said Mother. 'If any man eat of this bread, he shall live for ever.'

No thanks, thought Stegs, with an inner shudder.

'Amen,' said Gill quietly, and he saw tears form in her eyes.

He had to get out of there, he couldn't handle it. There was a pressure building in his head that for some reason seemed far more intense than any of the situations he'd found himself in during his undercover activities. With the exception of Frank Rentners and the steam iron, of course.

'You must be traumatized yourself, Mark,' said the vicar gently. 'You've lost a friend.'

'We've all lost a friend,' said Gill, and this time the floodgates opened. Mother squeezed her arm tightly before leaning over and giving her another encouraging quote from the Bible.

Stegs and the vicar exchanged sympathetic looks. 'I'm sure I'll be OK,' he said.

'These are trying times,' the vicar repeated, 'but with the help of the Lord we will get through them. Are you a Christian, Mark?'

'I like to keep an open mind,' said Stegs, thinking that this would be the easiest answer. It was yes, no and maybe all rolled into one, and hopefully strangled any further debate on the issue.

'Mark's a biblical name. Mark was, as I'm sure you know, one of Jesus's apostles.'

'My real name's Ken,' said Stegs, who always liked to lie when he'd had a few.

'Ah, Ken,' mused the vicar wisely. 'It's a name I always associate with hard work.

'My dad was a dustman.'

'Tell me about Paul,' said the vicar breezily, changing the subject. 'I knew him from the congregation at the church, and from my work in the parish, but it would be nice to hear something from one of his colleagues.'

Stegs was beginning to go off the vicar. That idiot grin just didn't want to leave his face, like it was squatting there waiting for the bailiffs, defying court order after court order. Perhaps he was retarded.

Stegs saw that Gill had brought herself back under control now, and she and Mother were also waiting for him to say something. He wished he hadn't had that speed. It was making sitting still next to impossible. 'He was a lovely guy,' he blurted out.

'Absolutely lovely. Hard-working, hard-playing, hard-everything ... a real team player. Great to be around, and very conscientious. Always on the look-out for his mates. A real copper's copper. I loved that bloke, I really did.' He shook his head to signify his sense of loss but did it a little bit too vigorously and saw a bead of sweat fly off onto the carpet.

They all stared at it for a moment, then at him, no-one saying anything, and he thought that, no, this was worse than any undercover op. Even Rentners. His left leg was going up and down like the clappers.

'Are you all right, Mark?' asked Gill.

He nodded, just as vigorously. 'I'm fine, honestly. Just a bit shocked, that's all. The whole thing's taken it out of me. Do you mind if I go to the toilet?'

'Of course not. You remember where it is, don't you?'

He stood up. 'Yeah, I do. Straight down the hall, through the kitchen, and right to the end.'

He exited quickly, wiping his brow as soon as he was out of the lounge door. He walked down the hall, through the kitchen and into the room where they kept the washing machine and the tumble-drier. This part of the house was the extension, tacked on a couple of years back. A door opposite him led to the toilet. There was also a door to his right, and this was the one that Stegs opened before stepping into Vokes's study. It was small, but still getting on for twice the size of Stegs's, and was a lot more orderly. Photos adorned the walls: of family, of Vokes in uniform, on graduation day, all that sort of stuff. At the end of the room facing the window were his desk and PC.

Stegs walked over to the desk, had a quick check through the neat stack of papers in his former colleague's in-tray, then opened the top drawer as quietly as he could. There was a transparent box containing floppy disks in there, plus a dog-eared Len

Deighton novel (*SS-GB*, one of Stegs's childhood favourites) and a black address book. He pocketed the address book straight away, then went to open the box of disks, but it was locked. The lock didn't look too strong so he took it out and tried to force it open, but it wouldn't go. He scanned about inside the drawer for a key but there wasn't one in there. He tried again, pulling harder this time, amazed that a piece of plastic could be so stubborn.

Just then, he heard footsteps coming through the kitchen. His teeth clenched reflexively and he chucked the box back in the drawer, shutting it at the same time.

'What are you doing, Mark?'

It was Gill's voice. He turned round from his position staring out of the window into the Vokerman back garden and organic vegetable patch, and gave her a whimsical smile. 'I was just thinking about Paul. I miss him, Gill. Already. I wish I could have done something, anything . . .' He picked up a photo of Vokes in a ridiculous Hawaiian shirt from the desk and stared at it for a moment, shaking his head as slowly as he could, but with close to a gram of uncut amphetamines soaring through his bloodstream it was never going to be slowly enough.

His words and actions seemed to have the desired effect, however, and the beginnings of a smile appeared on Gill's face. 'It's going to be hard for all of us,' she said. 'Paul was a good Christian husband and father.'

'He was,' said Stegs, putting the photo back down and walking slowly towards the door. He suddenly had an urge to take a leak for real. 'It all just seems so . . . so permanent.' She gave his arm a supportive squeeze and he shot her a grim smile. 'And do you know what? I've been thinking about him so much, I haven't even been to the toilet yet.'

'Would you like a cup of tea, Mark?'

'No, thanks,' he sighed. He couldn't think of anything worse than another twenty minutes in that lounge. 'I'd better be going.' He started to move past her but, like the worst kind of doorman, she blocked his way.

She smiled her grim, worthy smile that Stegs presumed was meant to make him feel part of the flock but came out more like the expression a movie killer pulls just before he knifes his victim. 'You've come a long way to see me,' she said. 'Stay for a quick cup. It'll do you good to talk about things.'

There was something in her voice that said she really didn't want him to argue, and would take it badly if he did. He knew then that she could smell the drink, and he wondered whether they were going to make an attempt to convert him. For the life of him he couldn't work out what Vokes had ever seen in her. She was only a small woman, but there was no doubt she had the ability to frighten even the most hardy of men.

'OK, I'll stop for a quick cup, but it really will have to be quick. I've got a number of important things I have to do this afternoon. I only came to pay my respects.'

'That's very kind of you. We all appreciate it. Paul always found you a very capable colleague.'

Damned with faint praise, thought Stegs. Briefly, she looked past him towards the desk and he wondered whether she had any suspicions about what he'd been doing. She then looked back at him, gave him that smile again, and turned away. 'He was a good man,' she said, going back into the kitchen, and then repeated it. 'A very good man.' He decided she hadn't.

After he'd finished in the toilet, he went back into the lounge where he was handed a cup of watery tea and then spent a very long fifteen minutes talking about and listening to all the good things Paul Vokerman had done in his life, and how much he was going to be missed. The problem with tragedies is that all the conversations relating to them go round in circles, so not a lot was actually said, but it was said in a different way many, many times. Stegs lost count of the number of occasions he heard the phrases 'good man', 'committed Christian', 'sense of justice' and 'sadly missed', but one thing was for sure, it would be a long time before he wanted to hear any of them again. Vokes had definitely been a good bloke, no question, but Stegs didn't want to share his views on him with a bunch of people like this, so it was with a sense of real satisfaction that he finished his tea and got up to leave, with goodbyes all round.

The vicar stood up, shook hands firmly, and told him that if he ever needed to talk to anyone to please feel free to give him a call or drop him an email. 'My name's Brian and I'm always available.' He handed Stegs a card. It seemed even the servants of the Lord had gone twenty-first century.

Stegs thanked him and told Mother that it was nice to meet her. She nodded severely and said that the Lord always welcomed sinners back into the flock. It wasn't quite the same as a good-bye but, under the circumstances, it would do. She added that she hoped she might see him again. Not if I catch sight of you first, he thought.

Gill saw him to the door and thanked him once again for coming round.

'It's no trouble at all,' he told her. 'I only wish the circum-stances could be happier.'

'How well *did* you know Paul?' she asked.

He already had one foot outside the door but stopped and looked at her, taken aback by this sudden question. She was staring at him intently as if trying to hunt down lies. It wasn't the sort of expression he'd seen on her face before.

'Well enough, I think,' he said cautiously. 'Why do you ask?'

She continued to stare intently and he felt himself sweating under her gaze. 'I don't know,' she said, choosing her words care-fully. 'He didn't seem his usual self recently. I felt that he was concerned about something. That there was a weight on his shoulders of some sort.'

'He never said anything to me about it, Gill. It's a very difficult job that he did. Perhaps it was the pressure of that.'

Her expression relaxed and she managed a surprisingly pleasant smile. 'Perhaps it was,' she said. 'It's a very difficult job that you both do.'

'Someone's got to do it,' said Stegs, trying hard not to sound too much like Clint Eastwood.

She pursed her lips, the conversation at an end. 'I hope I see you again soon, Mark. I don't know when the funeral will be. It could be a while.'

'I'm sure they'll do their best to wrap everything up as soon as they can,' he said, before turning away and walking down the footpath in the direction of the street.

It had started to rain again and the sky was an iron grey. He was still speeding but the urge to drink had gone. He needed to walk. To walk and to think. What exactly had Gill meant back there? How well had he known Vokes? Very well, he'd always thought. But like anything in life, you can never quite tell. People you know always have the ability to shock you. But Vokes? No, he'd always had the run of Vokes. I knew him well enough, Gill.

Definitely well enough.

It was four o'clock when he eventually got back to the car. The rain had stopped but the clouds remained, thick and foreboding. He'd walked for a while, but his thoughts had been a jumble: mainly memories of old Vokes interspersed with concerns about his own future now that he was suspended, until finally he'd found himself with a strong desire to go home and have a cup of tea. He hoped the missus wasn't in nagging mode, and that Luke was either asleep or in good cheer.

But he'd picked a bad time to drive back and he got caught in an almighty jam on the North Circular. He tuned into Capital and found that there'd been an accident further up at Staples Corner (according to the Flying Eye, it was a four-car pile-up), so he was stuck in it, wondering how on earth four cars could have actually got up to the sort of speeds necessary for a collision like that. Usually, you never got to more than thirty miles an hour tops on either of the circulars during the day.

At five to five, when he was stationary again, with the beginnings of a headache and the flashlights of the emergency services visible a few hundred yards ahead, he got a call on the private mobile. He picked it up off the front passenger seat and for the second time that day didn't recognize the number.

'Jenner.'

'Stegs, it's John Gallan. There's a few things I need to speak to you about, and I need to do it sooner rather than later.'

'Do you want to meet somewhere?'

'It's official business. Can you come down here?'

'Where? Islington? To be honest, I've been out all day and I'm on my way home. Can we do it tomorrow?'

He heard Gallan sigh down the other end of the phone, but he was in no mood to be helpful. A black Mercedes in the next lane tried to nudge in front of him and Stegs inched forward, blocking his way.

'Tomorrow's a bit late.'

'Is it urgent?'

Gallan paused. 'It's important,' he said eventually.

Now it was Stegs's turn to sigh. He was tired, but he knew from experience he wasn't going to get out of it. 'Listen, if it's that important, come up to my house. I'm nearly there now.' He gave Gallan the address.

'We'll try to make it as quick and painless as possible.'

'We?'

'WDS Boyd and me. We'll be with you in an hour or so, traffic permitting.'

'The traffic in this town never permits,' said Stegs, and hung up.

At the same time, the driver of the Mercedes – a stressed young commuter who appeared to have gone prematurely bald, probably in this traffic jam – snarled at him, actually baring teeth. Stegs pulled out his warrant card and pushed it against the window, at the same time mouthing 'fuck off' and inching forward still more. The Mercedes driver backed off.

He wondered if he was going to make it home in an hour himself.

# 10

Stegs Jenner lived on an estate consisting mainly of 1950s and 1960s semi-detached houses off Cat Hill in east Barnet. Some were quite substantial, and attractive for post-war housing, but Stegs's semi was one of the smaller and newer ones and looked a little forlorn opposite its bigger neighbours.

A thick, oppressive layer of cloud hung over Barnet that evening, and a light rain spat weakly as Tina Boyd and I got out of the car. I looked at my watch. It was quarter past six, and I was getting hungry. It had been a long day and a draining one. I'd been on the stand for more than two hours in court that afternoon tesifying in the rape trial, much of it under detailed and laborious cross-examination from the defence barrister, who was doing his utmost to get his client off on a technicality now that it was becoming patently obvious to all concerned that he was guilty. I think I did OK, but sometimes it's difficult to tell. Particularly when you're tired, and I was as tired as hell.

Tina had filled me in on the details of the earlier murder squad meeting – not that there were many of them. So far there'd been no sightings of O'Brien on the day of his murder, and we were still waiting for further tests on the bodies to determine more specific times of death. SOCO hadn't reported any obvious clues left by the killer, and no-one among those interviewed in the surrounding area had seen anything suspicious. Perfect. As for the three phone calls made on the mobile in O'Brien's possession to Stegs's mobile, all had been made since Sunday, the last on the previous morning, but none had lasted more than a minute, so it was possible he was simply leaving messages. Either way, it was inconclusive.

Stegs's wife, Julie, answered the door, a very miserable-looking baby under one arm. The baby eyed me belligerently. Julie, meanwhile, tried to appear welcoming, but it was clear the day was getting on top of her. She was an attractive woman, taller I think than Stegs, with big brown eyes and full lips, but exhaustion and stress had given her a tense, almost haunted look.

Tina spoke first. 'Good evening, Mrs Jenner,' she said with a smile, 'we're here to see your husband.'

'Oh yes, he said something about that. Come in, come in. He's in his study.' She opened the door and we followed her inside into a tiny entrance hall. 'It's opposite you at the top of the stairs. You'll have to excuse me, I'm feeding Luke.'

I told her that was fine and followed as Tina led the way up the almost unfeasibly steep staircase which was about as child-friendly as an unattended pond.

Stegs was waiting for us at the top, wearing a cautious grin, as if he was letting us know that he wanted to be friendly but it was up to us whether we allowed him to be. 'Evening all,' he said. 'Come on through.'

He led us into a tiny room, half of which was taken up by a single bed. A PC running a screensaver featuring brightly coloured fish swimming around was perched on a desk at the end by the window. The desk took up about another quarter of the room, which didn't leave room for much else.

'You'll have to sit on the bed, I'm afraid,' said Stegs, taking the seat at the desk and manoeuvring himself round so he was just about facing the spot where he wanted us to sit. 'I don't really want the missus hearing any of this. Can you shut the door please, John?'

I did as he asked and then the two of us sat down side by side on the bed facing him. It was all very cosy.

'What can I do for you then?' he asked.

'We've got some bad news, Stegs,' said Tina.

He raised his eyebrows. 'Oh yeah? What's that?'

'Slim Robbie O'Brien's dead.'

He looked shocked. 'How did that happen, then? And when?'

'He was shot. We don't have a time of death yet.'

We let it sink in for a few moments, watching him. He rubbed a hand across his brow, the other hand drumming a rapid tattoo on the side of the chair. I thought he looked stressed. His face had taken on a reddish tinge and he appeared pumped up, making me think that he might be suffering from some sort of delayed shock. I wondered briefly whether he'd been offered counselling. If not, he should have been.

'Christ,' he muttered, wiping the hand back across his forehead. 'That's not going to make things any easier.'

'No,' I agreed. 'Quite the reverse.'

'Who do you think could have done it?' he asked.

'Slim Robbie O'Brien? I imagine the list of suspects is going to be pretty long. When did you last see him?'

'I said all this yesterday evening.'

'Humour us, Stegs. We wouldn't ask unless we had to.'

'Last Sunday night at a pub called the Shakespeare near

Barbican Tube. Me and Vokes met up with him.'

'You said yesterday O'Brien was involved in setting up the final meeting,' said Tina in formal tones, looking up from her note-taking. Stegs eyed her suspiciously as she continued. 'What part did he play exactly?'

Stegs sighed. 'Quite a few of SO10 got involved in setting up yesterday, but Fellano was suspicious of blokes he didn't know so he wanted to keep O'Brien in the loop because he trusted him. That meant O'Brien was the main man who kept in contact with him between the test-buy we did at the end of Feb and the final meeting. Me and Vokes also had a couple of conversations with Fellano as well – you know, just to show that we were keen – and I know that he was using contacts in this country to check the two of us out. But he still liked to talk to O'Brien, which is what me and Vokes were meeting him about in the pub. O'Brien was getting worried that when the op went down and Fellano got nicked it was going to be pretty bloody obvious who was behind it. In fact, he wasn't just worried, he was scared shitless. He was talking about pulling out.'

'But you managed to reassure him?' said Tina.

He nodded. 'Well, yeah, obviously. But he still wasn't very happy about it. He started harping on about us having to get him a new identity with all the trimmings if it all went wrong. I told him we'd see what we could do, but we weren't going to promise anything.'

I cleared my throat, thinking that I was very thirsty and could do with a cup of tea. Somehow, though, I didn't think one would be forthcoming. I got the distinct impression Stegs didn't like our presence in his house, though I suppose you could hardly blame him. No-one likes being questioned by the police, particularly the police. 'But you said last night he didn't know the actual location of the meet itself.'

'He didn't. He knew roughly when Fellano was going to be flying in . . .'

'And that was?'

'I think he came in Tuesday night. Late.'

'So who set up the actual location for the rendezvous?'

'Fellano did. He spoke to me on Tuesday night. I phoned Vokes afterwards.'

'And Fellano said that the meeting was going to be at the Donmar Hotel?'

Stegs shook his head. 'No. He told me that the meeting was going to go ahead on the Wednesday, yesterday, but he didn't say where, because they like to leave that sort of thing until the last minute. It's safer that way. But SO11 had a tap on my phone and they used it to trace his call to the vicinity of the Donmar, so we concluded it was almost certainly going to be there. And at that point it became common knowledge among everyone on the op, which was what? Ten o'clock Tuesday night. That gave it eighteen hours to leak.'

'Well, not really,' I said. 'You and Vokes knew because the information on the location of Fellano's mobile was relayed to you by DCS Flanagan. He knew, obviously, as did the operator who actually pinpointed the call, and Malik, I believe, because he was with Flanagan at the time. But they were the only ones. We weren't made aware of it' – I pointed to myself and to Tina – 'until we arrived at New Scotland Yard yesterday morning for the briefing. Neither was anyone else on the team. It was a very secretive operation, as you for one ought to appreciate.'

'So you didn't speak to O'Brien at all at any point after you found out the location of the meeting?' asked Tina.

The big question.

'No.' There was the first sign of annoyance in his voice. Then his expression changed. 'Hold on, tell a lie, I had a quick twenty-second conversation with him on the way into work yesterday morning. He rang me on my private mobile, the one I give to people who know my real identity. He was hassling me about what we were going to do to protect him when everything was over. I told him it was out of my hands, but that he'd definitely get protection. I hung up on him. That was it. As far as I know, Vokes didn't speak to him either. There'd have been no point.'

'Where were you when you made the call to Vokes on Tuesday night?' I asked.

'I was here, at home. In this very room, in fact, and I stayed at home for the rest of the night. You can ask the missus if you want. Or SO11. They'd have a record of the call and where it was made from. I'm not hiding anything, you know.'

I put up a hand to calm him. 'Listen, Stegs, we're not here to interrogate you or pick holes in any of your answers, we're just trying to find out what, if anything, O'Brien knew which might have acted as a motive for someone killing him. You have to admit, the timing of his death is worryingly coincidental.'

Stegs sighed loudly. 'Yeah, all right. Fair enough.'

He fidgeted in his seat, trying to get comfortable, and I noticed he was still sweating even though the room was cool.

'Can you give us your movements for yesterday morning, Stegs?' asked Tina, trying to sound as casual as possible. 'Starting from when you left the house.'

'Hold on, am I a suspect for something?' he demanded, trying hard to keep his voice calm. 'Are you making out I murdered him? Because if you are, or you think I might possibly have done it, then I want to stop this right now until I've got a federation rep here, or even a lawyer.'

'No-one's saying any of that,' Tina reassured him. 'But you know the score. We wouldn't be doing our duty if we didn't eliminate everyone involved from our enquiries. It's just routine.'

He didn't look convinced but gave her a detailed rundown of his movements anyway, including the times. There was nothing untoward or inconsistent in anything he said. While Tina wrote it all down, he stood up, opened the window as wide as it would go, and lit a Marlboro Light, blowing a lungful of smoke into the drizzling dusk.

'Whose idea was it to leave the money behind in the car when you went into the meeting, Stegs?' asked Tina when she'd finished.

He took a long drag on the cigarette before he answered, then fixed her with an expression only just this side of contemptuous. 'Both of ours,' he answered simply, daring her to disagree.

He continued smoking while we continued questioning him as carefully and as diplomatically as possible about aspects of his testimony the previous evening, trying our best not to rile him, but I think it was too late for that. He answered the questions without pause and didn't appear to be lying, but of course you wouldn't have been able to tell with a man like him anyway. His whole job was one long lie after another, so there weren't going to be many people out there better at it than him.

After a further ten minutes, however, we ran out of things to ask, and thanked him for his co-operation and patience. 'We're sorry to intrude on you at a time like this,' I told him. 'We both know how difficult it is for you, having lost a mate and colleague, but I hope you understand we've got to ask.'

Tina said pretty much the same thing, and he nodded in acknowledgement, replying that he knew it wasn't our fault but that he'd only done his job and now felt that he was being penalized for it.

'That goes with the territory, Stegs,' I said. 'A policeman's lot is rarely a happy one. Especially these days.'

He grunted something in reply and showed us down the highly dangerous staircase and to the front door. His wife called out a goodbye from the kitchen where she was feeding the baby, and admonished Stegs for not offering us a drink. 'I would have done it but I've got this one here to deal with,' she added as we stepped out into the rain and headed back to the car.

As we were driving back down the Finchley Road in the direction of my place, Tina asked me what I thought of Stegs Jenner's overall demeanour.

'He was looking stressed. I think he needs to talk to someone.'

'Do you think they think he did it? Flanagan and Malik? I don't mean pull the trigger, but that he was involved somewhere?'

'In Robbie's murder?'

'In the whole thing. The robbery at the hotel, Robbie's death. All of it.'

'I don't know,' I said. 'The thing is, what would he gain by setting up the robbery? Not only did it leave his partner dead, but it could easily have left him dead too. And if he did set it up, what part did O'Brien play in the whole thing, and who then actually had him killed? And why? No, I think the problem is that Stegs rubs people up the wrong way. They don't like him, and they don't like the way he doesn't follow the rules. So when something goes wrong it becomes very easy for them to think that at the very least his big mouth was responsible for the leak. My opinion is they think he might have spoken out of turn, and might have let slip something to O'Brien, but that's the sum of it. What about you?'

She sighed. 'There's something about him, you know?'

'That's what I mean. People don't like him. They think he's a rule-breaker, someone you can't trust.'

'He *is* a rule-breaker. If he'd taken the money with him into the hotel room like he was meant to have done then he wouldn't have split with Vokes, the robbery wouldn't have occurred and six people wouldn't have died.'

'A fair point, but it doesn't mean he was involved in setting the whole thing up.'

'True, but I didn't like the way he suddenly changed his story about when he last spoke to O'Brien. I got the impression he realized we were aware the call had been made to his mobile, and that's why he suddenly conveniently remembered it.' She shook her head. 'Either way, I think he knows more than he's letting on. That's my gut feeling. Call it female instinct. I'd like to dig into his background a little bit. See what comes up. What's the time?'

'It's just gone seven. Why?'

'I want to go and see Joey Cloud,' she answered, referring to the man who, more than anyone else, had started all this.

It had been small-time informer Joey Cloud who'd come to Tina three months earlier, telling her that Robbie O'Brien was trying to set up a coke importation deal with a group of Colombians and was looking for partners to help him finance it. Using that information we'd got two SO10 operatives (one of whom was Stegs Jenner) to set him up, and having been caught bang-to-rights he'd turned informer and had then been used by SO7 to set up the meeting at Heathrow. Cloud's involvement, however, had ended right at the beginning of everything, making him irrelevant to what had gone on since, and I told Tina as much.

'I just want to find out if he's heard anything,' she answered.

'About what?'

'About anything. About O'Brien.'

'Now?'

'It's as good a time as any. He'll probably be in at the moment.'

'And this is the woman who just over twelve hours ago was announcing she'd had enough of her job.'

'A day's a long time in police work,' she told me.

'Does that mean you're staying?'

'The jury's still out,' she said, weaving through the last of the rush-hour traffic.

I was tired, but I knew from the tone of her voice that she wasn't going to be swayed. There was therefore no point arguing. Instead, I closed my eyes and tried to get a few minutes' shut-eye before our next port of call.

# 11

After they'd gone, Stegs helped put Luke to bed before cooking himself and the missus a pretty bland spaghetti bolognese out of a tin. The label said it was 'just like Mama used to cook', but if that was the case then Mama had obviously long since been banned from the kitchen. While they were eating, the missus asked him what the police had wanted to see him about, and he told her that it was just clarifying some issues about what had happened with Vokes. She seemed to buy it and started on again about him switching jobs, but he made it clear that tonight was really not a good night to talk about it, and once again she let it go, although she didn't look too pleased.

They ate at the kitchen table, then washed up in silence before retiring to the lounge. The missus insisted on watching *Scream Team* on one of the Sky channels, a weekly programme in which a select team of photogenic young members of the public visit some of Britain's most haunted places and, as far as Stegs could see, simply run around yelling and screaming, jumping at the slightest noise, and generally making tits of themselves without actually seeing anything vaguely ghostly.

While the missus sat staring raptly at the screen and occasionally making comments like 'Did you see that, Mark?' or, more typically, 'There's got to be something in it, there was definitely a face there' – even though if there had actually been a face there it would have been the lead story on the BBC news, not cast adrift on some crappy backwoods satellite channel – Stegs thought about the visit he'd received from Boyd and Gallan. It concerned him. They were definitely suspicious that he'd had something to do with the leak on the op, and maybe even the death of O'Brien, a man he was not too upset to see in the ground. Stegs didn't consider himself to be that much of a crusading cop, trying to right society's many wrongs, but he did look down on O'Brien, a man who'd have sold his children to cannibals and even skinned and gutted them himself if the price had been right.

He had the feeling that Boyd, particularly, thought he was the villain in all this – it was the way she'd looked at him as she'd taken her notes, with no attempt to hide the suspicion in her dark eyes. Gallan, he reckoned, was keeping a more open mind, but he knew he'd still have to be careful. He'd heard enough about the other man to appreciate the fact that he was a good copper, with a nose for sniffing out the truth, as well as the sort of perseverance you don't get so much in the Force these days.

Suspicion. He'd been under suspicion almost since the day he'd started working with SO10. It was the place for mavericks – for people who were prepared to bend the rules, to walk the fine line between infiltration and involvement in the criminal enterprises they were investigating – and mavericks in a police force are always mistrusted. But he also knew how to cover his tracks. He'd had plenty of practice of that, and was prepared for any detailed probing into his affairs.

He wondered briefly whether Boyd and Gallan were sleeping together. There was something about the way they looked at each other, the messages that seemed to pass between them, that made him think they were more than just clued-in partners. They didn't come across much like an ideal couple. She was good-looking but in a vaguely untouchable way, and with an air of authority that he didn't much like the look of. Gallan seemed a lot friendlier and more laid-back. They'd had a couple of beers together just after they'd first met, and Stegs remembered that Gallan had been good company. Come to think of it, Boyd had been quite a laugh on that occasion too, and he remembered that he'd quite liked the look of her, as had Vokes. Maybe her attitude had changed as her suspicions had grown. If so, she'd made a mistake. Never let your quarry know you're on to them.

It was one of the first things he'd learnt in SO10, and it was why he'd survived this long.

# 12

Joey Cloud lived in a bedsit above a row of shops on the Caledonian Road between King's Cross and Islington. Access was via a set of metal steps round the back that led up to a cramped walkway where the bedsits were all lined up in a row. Darkness had fallen by the time we arrived and there was a light on in number 3.

'I thought you said he was strictly small-time,' I said, dodging a pile of rubbish bags as I started up the steps with her behind me, not entirely happy to be there. I consider myself a pretty dedicated copper, but I'd definitely had my fill for the day. 'What's he going to know?'

'He's been reliable down the years, and occasionally he gets a gem. I'm hoping he's got one this time.'

I'd met Joey Cloud once, when we'd been setting up the sting on O'Brien, and I'd taken an instant and very natural dislike to him. He looked exactly like you'd expect someone who informs on people for financial gain to look. Late twenties, with the furtive air of a man who's always on the hunt for the next fix of cash but who also knows what it might cost him, he was also a long-term pipehead and occasional smack user who suffered from the same ailments that many chronic adddicts do: rapid and premature ageing coupled with an inability to wash properly or look anything other than scruffy and unkempt. I remember having to turn my head away on our first meeting to get out of range of the stench of piss and sweat that seemed to come off him in nauseous waves, and it made me think then that I couldn't understand how he ever got near enough to other people to hear their secrets. In fact, it still amazed me that he'd somehow heard about O'Brien's efforts to set up a major coke importation ring with the Colombians. I could only put it down to the sort of sheer luck that in the life of a pipehead, even a cunning one, is rarely, if ever, repeated.

'When was the last time you spoke to him?' I asked Tina, as I climbed the steps.

'Months back. Not since the O'Brien sting. He hasn't had anything for us.'

Which, I thought, went some way to proving my point, although I didn't say anything.

We walked along the balcony until we got to his front door. It had been painted navy blue, probably when the block was first built, but was now peeling badly to reveal the wood beneath. The outline of a 3 could be made out, but the sign itself had long since fallen off. I could already smell the interior, even from here. It wasn't pleasant.

There was no doorbell, so I rapped hard on the door. There were the faint strains of music coming from inside so he was probably at home, although what state he was in was another matter.

I gave it ten seconds, then knocked again, harder this time. We hadn't come all this way on a shitty wet evening for nothing.

I was just about to knock for a third time when I heard the shuffling of feet coming towards the door.

'Who is it?' The voice was slurred a little and I wondered if he'd been on the smack, or had just woken up.

'Police,' I called through the letterbox. 'Can you let us in, please.'

'I've got nothing to say to the police, and I ain't done nothing wrong, so fuck off.'

Tina leant forward so her lips were almost touching the door. 'This is very important, Mr Cloud,' she said, hoping that he'd recognize her voice, but not letting on that she knew him, in case anyone else was listening. 'Can you please let us in? Otherwise we'll come back with a warrant.'

'I ain't done nothing,' he whined, sounding like a snot-nosed kid. 'Leave me alone.'

'Mr Cloud,' I told him, again speaking through the letterbox. 'We need to speak to you and we're not going to go away until we do.'

I heard him curse and then the door was opened a few inches. There was a chain on the latch preventing us from entering. Joey Cloud's gaunt, unshaven features appeared in the gap looking like the 'before' picture in an Alka Seltzer advert. The smell arrived at exactly the same time. Maybe it was a good thing he didn't want to speak to us after all.

'This is fucking harassment. I told you, I ain't done nothing. I can't say fairer than that, can I?' His eyes were slightly glazed but he appeared reasonably compos mentis. For him, anyway. He stared hard at Tina. 'I got nothing to say to you. Nothing. You understand? Now, get the fuck out of here or I'll call my brief.'

'You haven't got a brief,' I told him. 'With your funds and

habits, you wouldn't be able to retain one for more than ten minutes.'

He turned to me, his face still squeezed in the gap, but this time his defiance had evaporated and been replaced by a pleading expression. 'Listen,' he said, his voice dropping to a whisper. 'Leave me alone, please. I'm not in the info game any more. I just want to be left alone. Please.'

I tried to give him a reassuring smile but, amid the BO, I think it must have come out more like a grimace. 'This won't take long, I promise.'

His face cracked into a hideous broken-toothed grin, utterly devoid of any humour. 'Yeah,' he said, the grin twisting into a sneer, 'that's exactly what they told me when they come round before.'

Tina pulled a face. 'They? Who's they?'

'They,' he answered, the sneer now transforming into a look of anger. 'They are the people who did this.'

He shifted his weight, moving his head back from the door, then slowly raised his right arm so that it was level with his face.

Straight away, I saw the bandage wrapped round the hand.

'God almighty,' hissed Tina, her eyes fixed on the blood-flecked dressing where Cloud's little and index fingers used to be. 'Who did that to you?'

For two, maybe three, seconds, he didn't speak, simply kept the mutilated hand in front of his face for us to see. Finally, he let it drop to his side and out of sight. When he spoke, the words were slow and addressed to both of us.

'People who told me I shouldn't be speaking to you,' he said simply.

Then, with his good hand, he shut the door on us.

*

When we were back down on the street, standing in the glow of the street lamps and watching the cars drift past in both directions, Tina let out a deep sigh. 'It feels like someone's always one step ahead of us.'

I stopped beside her and put an arm on her shoulder. 'It could be anything, Tina. He might have just upset one of his dealers, or maybe someone found out he was a grass.'

'Then why did he say the people who'd done it didn't want him speaking to us?'

'Because I expect they don't. If he knows who they are, which he almost certainly does, then they don't want him going to the police, do they? It doesn't mean it's got anything to do with O'Brien and Heathrow.'

Tina shook her head, staring into the evening drizzle. 'There are too many coincidences, John. He was the one who put us on to O'Brien, and I think someone's got to him to make sure he keeps his mouth shut. What's worrying me, though, is the fact that hardly anyone was aware of his existence, let alone his role in setting up Robbie.'

I thought about this for a moment, because I knew what she was going to say next.

'But one of those people was Stegs Jenner.'

We stood in silence for a few moments, contemplating that particular thought.

'Come on,' I said eventually, taking her by the arm. 'Let's go get a drink. I think we've earned one.'

# 13

I awoke the next morning with a dry mouth and a desire to get going on the case. Tina and I had driven back to my place in Tufnell Park, then gone to the pub round the corner for a bite to eat and a few much-needed drinks. We'd talked about the case a little and I'd encouraged Tina not to read too much into Joey Cloud's missing fingers. Violence among addicts and dealers, even violence that extreme, was endemic. Back when I'd been south of the river, there'd been a small-time thief and coke addict called Fredo Wanari who'd had a habit of not paying his suppliers and running up huge debts. One time, he'd gotten on the wrong side of the wrong person, a bigshot dealer who didn't like to be messed around, and when Fredo couldn't pay what he owed him he was given an ultimatum: find the money in forty-eight hours or, as the dealer allegedly put it, pay the interest in pain. Fredo had more chance of sprouting a second head than finding the cash, so when the forty-eight hours was up the dealer paid him a personal visit and removed the little finger of his left hand with a meat cleaver, while his men held him down. He then promised to remove another finger for every day he wasn't paid. Sadly, Wanari never did find the money and these days he goes by the name of Fingerless Freddie, but it shows you that criminals can do some pretty gruesome things to each other in the name of cash.

I'd told Tina this story as we sat drinking, but again, I don't think she was convinced. Eventually, though, tired of clawing about in the dark with theories and half theories that weren't really leading us anywhere, we'd moved on to other, easier subjects. Sometimes you've just got to let go, although maybe we'd let go a little bit too much the previous night. At least that was what my hangover was now telling me.

But I was still feeling ready for the fray as I came into the O'Brien/MacNamara incident room on the third floor of the station at quarter to nine that Friday morning, Tina following a gossip-quelling two or three minutes behind. The room was crowded with getting close to two dozen mainly unfamiliar faces, some of whom were already working at computer terminals, while in the middle of the room stood DCS Flanagan, talking animatedly to Malik and one of the other detectives. He still looked tense, but less so than he had when I'd last seen him, the natural confidence he'd exuded in our earlier meetings already beginning to make a reappearance. He'd done extremely well to land this high-profile role so soon after his involvement in the disaster of Operation Surgical Strike, and I think he knew that. The Met might have been very short of senior officers capable of running a major inquiry, but that on its own didn't explain why he was in charge of the O'Brien/MacNamara murder squad. A cynic might have said he was there because he knew the right sort of people, and that he was almost certainly a freemason, so had plenty of senior colleagues watching his back and making sure that the mud never stuck to him.

And you know what? I think the cynic might have had a point.

From what I knew about Flanagan (and it wasn't a lot, I admit), he was something of a Teflon man. He'd made mistakes in the upward trajectory of his career – there'd even been the faint rumour of corruption, though no direct accusation was ever made – and he wasn't so talented that you'd make excuses for him. He wasn't even that popular, his manner considered too haughty and self-important by many of those who worked for him, myself included. I didn't like him because he didn't strike me as being a true copper, more an aspiring technocrat with his eye firmly fixed on building a power-base, and he always seemed pissed off about something, which is a trait I've never associated with success. But he'd made it all the way up to being the head of SO7, and it was possible that he was looking even higher. Assistant Commissioner Flanagan. Six people might have just been killed on his watch, eight if you include O'Brien and his grandmother, but he wasn't going to be the scapegoat for Operation Surgical Strike. They already had Stegs for that, and I was pretty damn certain that the SO10 man wasn't a regular down at the local Masonic Lodge.

Seeing me, Flanagan excused himself from his conversation and strode over, a small smile forming like a crease at the corners of his mouth. It wasn't replicated in the thin blue eyes that remained as serious and businesslike as ever. 'Hello, John,' he said, putting out a hand. 'Glad you could join us for this one.'

'Glad to be here, sir,' I replied, shaking it. 'Any new developments?'

'Some interesting ones,' he said, the half-smile melting back into lines on his face. 'Very interesting. But nothing that's a real case-breaker. I've got a news conference at Scotland Yard at eleven o'clock, and I wouldn't have minded a bit more to give them. Still, this one was never going to be easy. How did it go with Jenner last night? Did you get to speak to him?'

'We did, but he didn't tell us anything we don't already know.'

'What about the calls to his mobile from O'Brien?'

'He says he remembers getting one on Wednesday morning. He claimed O'Brien was just demanding protection again.'

'Did you believe him?'

Flanagan, who must have been six feet three, and a good four inches taller than me, leant his long head forward like a praying mantis as he asked the question, his beady eyes locking into mine. I had the feeling it was a pose he'd learnt to strike in interrogations, and I could see that it would be disconcerting if you were a criminal, but I thought it was a bit much for nine o'clock in the morning. Especially as I hadn't done anything wrong.

I told him I didn't see why Stegs would bother lying.

'I worked with him once,' he said thoughtfully, moving his head back out of my field of vision. 'He's a slippery character.'

I think he was about to add something more, but he saw Tina coming into the room. 'All right, we're all here. Let's get this meeting started. Right, everyone,' he announced loudly, his thinly veiled attack on Stegs's reputation forgotten as he clapped his hands together like an impatient headmaster, 'let's get underway.'

He went over to a whiteboard with a table next to it on the far side of the room, facing the door, and those people not at their desks went back to them. Malik nodded at me and I gave him a wink as I took a seat next to Tina.

'Not present at the meeting yesterday for reasons outside of his control but joining us for the duration of this inquiry will be DI John Gallan, who, like his colleague from this station Tina Boyd, was acquainted with the victim, and who also had some involvement with the op on Wednesday that we all keep reading about and seeing on telly.'

Everyone turned round, making various grunts and casual gestures of welcome, and I gave a slightly embarrassed smile in return, keen to get on with things. I thought that Flanagan would give some justification as to why it wasn't his fault that Surgical Strike had gone wrong, but he didn't. Maybe he'd already done that yesterday.

'Right,' he continued, 'so where are we so far? Let's recap. Robert O'Brien and Katherine, or Kitty, MacNamara were shot dead two days ago in what appears to be a highly professional hit. I have the preliminary autopsy reports here, hot off the press this morning' – he tapped a thin pile of A4 sheets on the table – 'and they tell us that the two of them died at different times, possibly as long as six hours apart, with Kitty the first to go.' At least I was right so far. 'She was killed with a single shot from a .38 calibre weapon, possibly an old Smith and Wesson, delivered at point-blank range to the side of her head, half an inch above the right ear. A cushion was used to muffle the sound of the bullet, and it happened at some point between nine o'clock in the morning and three o'clock in the afternoon, but given that a neighbour heard a sound that could have been a shot during *Neighbours*, which runs from one-forty to two o'clock, it's quite possible that it was then.'

He then explained his theory (or Knox's theory, or even my theory, depending which way you wanted to look at it) that MacNamara's murder had been opportunistic in so far as the killer had disposed of her purely so that he could use her apartment to ambush Robbie. According to Flanagan, the killer had almost certainly been let into the building and the apartment by Mrs MacNamara, since there were no signs of forced entry and no-one else in the building had let anyone in. That meant she'd either known him or he'd somehow tricked his way into her confidence. Flanagan said that we were going to need to interview all of Robbie's known criminal associates who were still on the outside in case it had been one of them, and he assigned several of those present to the task, before revealing his first useful lead of the day.

'The killer was in that apartment for three or four hours at least, and he was extremely careful not to touch anything or contaminate the scene in any way. Very professional, as you'd expect from someone who could execute two human beings, including a hardened killer, with the minimum of fuss. But he did, we think, make one mistake.'

There was a pregnant pause as those who weren't in the know waited to hear what that mistake was. I already had a good idea.

'We don't think he went out the same way he came in, instead opting to go out the back way through a window in Mrs MacNamara's bedroom. We think this firstly because the window was slightly open whereas Mrs MacNamara, who according to her granddaughter hated the cold, always tended to keep hers locked in the winter, and secondly because of the timing. From what we've built up so far on Robbie's movements on the day of his death, we think he arrived home at some point between five and five forty-five that afternoon, if witness reports are correct.' He turned and addressed a middle-aged detective in the front row. 'Isn't that right, Joe?'

Joe, who was wearing a frighteningly retro purple shirt with black tie, cleared his throat and picked up his notebook. 'That's right, guv. We've been down to every known haunt O'Brien used in the Islington area. He had lunch on his own in the Sacre Coeur in Theberton Street. They reckon he left about two-fifteen, and was acting normally. We don't know where he went after that, but he did turn up in the Half Moon on Essex Road later on that afternoon. The barman said Robbie told him he was on his way home. He was in there for about fifteen minutes and just had a pint and a couple of packs of crisps. He left approximately five o'clock, give or take fifteen minutes, according to the barman, and from there it's about a ten-minute walk to the murder scene, probably fifteen or twenty when you're his size. So it would have been some time around five-thirty.'

'And, according to Islington CID, O'Brien's building was under police surveillance by ten to six, at the request of SO7. No-one emerged after that, and a neighbour who was parking his car opposite at twenty to, and who stopped for a short conversation with a passer-by he knew, didn't see anyone come out the front either, so the back route looks like his most likely exit.'

'What was his mistake then, guv?' asked one of the younger detectives.

'We think he might have caught the jacket he was wearing on a nail sticking out of the wall as he climbed out the window, leaving a piece of it behind. It might not be his, of course, but it hasn't been there long, and I can't see who else's it would be. I have to tell you, there's not much left of it, and it's wet, but it's a clue and, given how careful he was in every other aspect of the murders, it may well be the best we're going to get from the actual scene itself. It's being analysed now and hopefully we'll get an idea of the type of jacket it came from within the next few days. I'm hurrying things along as fast as I can.

'And also, if he did go out through the back window, then he still would have had to cross a number of gardens to get back to the road, and he might have been seen. It's therefore especially important that we talk to everyone in the surrounding streets. A Portakabin's going up at the scene this morning, and it's going to be manned by DCs Holby and Birch' – he pointed at two young officers sitting near the back – 'and a couple of uniforms, and we've also managed to get hold of a further twenty uniforms to conduct house-to-house enquiries. I can't see the killer hanging around in the flat with the two bodies, so it's probably safe to assume that he killed Robbie as soon as he arrived back at the building, and made his escape immediately afterwards.'

He paused for a moment before continuing.

'Which leaves an important question. Why, after he'd killed O'Brien, did the killer choose to exit the building through the back window, which was surely a lot less convenient and potentially more risky than going out the way I believe he came in, i.e. the front door? It's a question we're going to need to answer. Was he disturbed? I don't think so, otherwise we probably would have had a third corpse. Or did he think it was too risky going out the front because the police might be looking for Robbie O'Brien? In other words, did the killer know about the op at the hotel? Because if he did, that means he was somehow connected with it. Which brings me on to motive. Why was O'Brien killed? We didn't cover the "why" so much in the meeting yesterday because I wanted us to get moving on the basics of what actually happened, but now we need to look at his murder in relation to the events of Wednesday, because I believe it's in there that we'll find our solution. Not only is it highly coincidental, Robbie dying like that on the day of Operation Surgical Strike when he'd had so much input in setting it up, but it's clear that a lot of planning went into his and his grandmother's murder. O'Brien undoubtedly had a lot of enemies, but I'm not sure how many of them could have organized this.

'And that's not all.'

Everyone in the room waited expectantly. Flanagan gave another dramatic pause lasting at least five seconds, and I decided that this was how he'd risen as high as he had. The bloke loved the centre stage, basking in the glow of self-importance. He was an actor, and I bet he could have kissed ass with the best of them when it suited.

However, even I had to admit that what he had to say *was* dramatic.

'As you know, we recovered a mobile phone from the body of Robbie O'Brien on which a number of calls had been made to Stegs Jenner's police mobile. There were also several other unidentified numbers on there, the most recent of which, according to the phone company, was phoned on Wednesday afternoon at three thirty-five p.m.' His suspicious little eyes scanned the whole room as he paused yet again, before continuing. 'We've just identified that number as the Donmar Hotel. It looks very much like it was Slim Robbie who made the call that got Vokes Vokerman killed.'

Now this was an interesting one, but it was also a revelation that we could all have done without, mainly because it made no sense whatsoever. Why on earth had Robbie made that phone call? Had he had a sudden fit of nerves and made a last-ditch attempt to save himself from the Colombians' wrath by warning them about what was going to happen? It was possible, but highly unlikely, because at that point, with the police next door, the Colombians were doomed anyway and would hardly have turned round and forgiven him.

For the next ten minutes we debated this apparent paradox, not really getting anywhere. The closest we came to a theory was that Robbie O'Brien had somehow managed to find out about the location of the meeting and had set up the robbery with Tyndall, knowing full well that when the robbery went down Tyndall's men would be caught. The theory went that he'd done this because he was setting up Tyndall in order to remove him as a potential rival in the north London coke trade. The phone call, then, was a deliberate attempt by O'Brien to ingratiate himself with the Colombians by warning them about what was going to happen and therefore making things even worse for Tyndall, while at the same time hopefully removing all suspicion that it was in fact he, Robbie, who'd been the source of the set-up in the first place.

If so, it was a clever plot. Unfortunately, as a theory, it was also one with a hell of a lot of holes in it. First and foremost, why would Tyndall have got involved in the robbery in the first place? As I've said before, he was no fool or short-timer, and would have known that he'd become number one on the Cali cartel's hitlist as a result of his actions. Why too did Slim Robbie end up dead if he'd masterminded the whole thing, and who'd killed him? And, of course, how had he been so sure of the location of the meeting that he'd made that phone call?

Tina asked this last question, adding in the same breath that Stegs hadn't been a hundred per cent convincing in explaining away the calls made to his mobile by O'Brien in the days leading up to Operation Surgical Strike – a none-too-subtle hint of the possible involvement of the SO10 man. Thankfully, she didn't mention Joey Cloud and his disappearing fingers. I think that, on that day at least, it would have been a complication too far. It was hard enough as it was getting our heads round the possibilities on offer for O'Brien's death and the car park robbery without putting in yet another angle.

Flanagan nodded sombrely to show he was taking WDS Boyd's comments on board. 'How did you think Jenner came across last night?' he asked her, studiously avoiding my gaze.

'He seemed uptight.'

'Did you go through all his movements on Wednesday?'

She nodded, opening up her notebook and reeling out what

Stegs had told us the previous night. When she'd finished, the room was silent for a few moments.

'Is Stegs a suspect, sir?' I asked Flanagan, deciding to get it out into the open. 'Because I can't see what he'd be gaining from it.'

'No, I don't believe he's involved,' he answered, choosing his words carefully, 'but it is important that he's fully eliminated from the inquiry. We wouldn't want doubts to remain.' He let the last words hang in the air for a couple of seconds, and it made me think that he was more than happy for any doubts to stay put. Poor old Stegs. He really did have enemies.

Finally, Flanagan continued. 'I am, however, getting the feeling that the solution to this crime is not going to stand up and smack us right in the face. It's going to take a lot of legwork. What we've got to do is keep digging. Keep asking around. See what clues, what physical evidence, we can turn up. If we can get O'Brien's shooter, then we're going to be able to crack the whole thing. At the same time, Tina, you have raised an important point, so I want you and John to look into the backgrounds of Stegs and Vokerman and see what, if anything, crops up. As I've said, it's important that everyone involved in Wednesday's operation is eliminated from the inquiry.' I noticed he didn't include himself in this. 'And the pressure for a result is going to be massive. More intense than any case I can remember for a long, long time.'

Final pep talk over, he then brought the meeting to a close, checking with each pair of detectives what their tasks were for the day, and making sure that every angle was covered. When he got round to Tina and me, he gave us both a grim smile. 'Nicholas Tyndall, Strangleman Grant's boss. He operates off your manor, so I want you two to pay him a visit and rattle him a bit, make out that we know a bit more than we do. Get him down here to make a statement and see what you can get out of him.'

'He probably won't talk,' I said. 'We've never got anything out of him before.' Which is the case with a lot of the more serious criminals. They don't build up their little empires and stay out of nick by being co-operative. I guessed that Tyndall would do nothing more than point us at his lawyer.

'Well, see what you can do. This is important.'

He gave me a look that suggested he didn't think my attitude was positive enough, but I looked away, deciding that I didn't like DCS Noel Flanagan. I'd met his sort before. Ones who think they're born to lead and everyone else is born to be led.

The annoying thing is they're often right, but what they tend to forget is that it doesn't actually mean they're going to be any good at it, and Flanagan was a case in point. In Vietnam, he'd have been shot by his own men.

And would probably have deserved it.

# 14

Trevor Murk was annoyingly good-looking. He had finely chiselled features, unblemished olive skin that hinted at summers spent in warmer climes and ancestors from the mysterious south, naturally tousled jet-black hair and deep-brown eyes that twinkled with mischief and easy charm. He was six feet two and he always dressed in clothes that fitted him perfectly and flattered him to just the right degree. It was annoying not only because his first name was Trevor rather than Enrique or Antonio and his last name Murk rather than something exotic, but because, for all his physical advantages, coupled with no small measure of intelligence, he would never amount to anything more than a petty criminal and grass. Put bluntly, he was too fucking lazy. Trevor Murk wouldn't get off his arse if it was sat on a nest of fire ants, and it was well known that he'd never completed a morning's work in his life, let alone a full day's, and, moreover, was proud of the fact. He wasn't work-shy, he was work-allergic.

However, it was still difficult not to like him (although Stegs tried hard enough) because in the end he was a good laugh, and his cheerily amoral demeanour was somehow infectious. Spend too long in his company and even a Godsquadder like Brian the vicar or Vokes's missus would have probably ended up mugging old ladies or sacrificing chickens as an offering to the Dark One.

The place where he and Stegs met on those occasions when they had business to discuss was the quaintly named Cherry Tree Inn, a huge, hellish place of fruit machines, loud carpets and all the atmosphere of your local job centre, situated in Enfield, a short drive from Barnet. It suited their purpose because it was big and soulless with plenty of space between the tables, making eavesdropping or even accidentally picking up snippets of conversation a near impossibility. It also had eleven different lagers and a similar number of bitters on tap, and served big chips with the food, so it at least had a few things going for it. Not that Stegs was hungry as he pitched in there at five past one that afternoon, waiting to hear what interesting tip Murk had for him. He'd already had a McDonald's Big Mac happy meal down the road and it had just started to repeat on him. That was the thing he hated about Big Macs: they took about ten seconds to eat and about ten hours to get rid of.

He ordered a pint of Kronenberg in the front bar, then made his way round to the much larger lounge bar and dining room, which was roughly the size of a provincial bingo hall but, today at least, was a lot less crowded, with only about a third of the tables occupied. He was disappointed but not surprised that Murk was nowhere to be seen. He'd once told Stegs that he never rose before eleven and, if entertaining, often didn't make it out before the early afternoon, depending on the lucky lady's looks and stamina.

Stegs found himself a seat in the corner next to a window

overlooking the Cherry Tree's beer garden: a hunched, cobbled backyard containing a handful of forlorn-looking plastic chairs and tables that was surrounded on every side by a high wall and had probably not seen the sun since some time in the nineteenth century. Then he lit a cigarette and waited, trying not to think of what Murk might be up to at this very moment in time because it would only make him jealous.

Five minutes later, just as he was putting out the smoke and thinking about whether or not it was worth lighting up another one, he saw Murk emerge from the front bar, carrying a pint of his own. Stegs acknowledged him with a cursory nod and a tapped finger on his watch, and Murk gave him a rueful grin in return. He looked about as guilty as the Guildford Four. A girl at one of the tables with her boyfriend eyed Murk subtly but admiringly as he passed and he gave her a cheeky little grin in return before sidling over to where Stegs was sitting and clumping himself down in the seat opposite.

'Long time no see, Stegsy,' he said, putting out a hand.

'That's right,' said Stegs, taking it reluctantly, 'about fifteen minutes longer than I thought it was going to be.'

'You know me, my man, I don't like to be shackled by the chains of time. You got a spare fag?'

Stegs pulled one out for himself, then slid the pack along the table. Murk teased one out and smoothed it between his lips, accepting a light from Stegs. It was amazing. The bloke didn't hurry anything.

'So, you had something I might be interested in.' Stegs was keen to get down to business.

Murk tried without success to stifle a chuckle. 'That's right, I have.'

'What's so funny, Trevor?'

'All right, all right, cool it a mo, sweetboy. Don't get peeved.

I've got a very tasty morsel for you. It's just that every time I think about it, it makes me laugh.'

Stegs took a drag from his cigarette, and noticed with annoyance that the girl who'd been looking at Murk earlier was watching him again. There was no justice in this world.

'Go on.'

Murk leant forward. 'I've told you before I've been in a few pornos over the years, haven't I? You know, support roles, so to speak?' He was trying hard to look serious but it wasn't working. Stegs didn't bother replying, he simply sat glaring at Murk, wondering what the fuck sort of tip it was that he was offering. 'Well, I did one once called *Ass Lovers in London*.'

'Am I meant to be impressed?'

'Not particularly, but the point was it was quite a big film by porno standards. You know, a big budget and all that. And the star of it was a bloke called Tino Movali, better known as Tino Ten Inch. You might have heard of him.'

'Why would I have heard of a bloke called Tino Ten Inch?'

'Because he's been in loads of them. As porn stars go, he's like A-list. Anyway, during the making of *Ass Lovers* we got quite matey.'

'I'm not sure I want to hear about that.'

'No, no, no, no. Not like that.' He shuddered theatrically. 'What I'm saying is, when filming was over, we went and had a few drinks together, got friendly – you know, in a having a grin together sort of way, and all that. He even offered me some work over in Amsterdam. He's Dutch, by the way. I didn't take it because I had something else on at the time, but I sort of kept in touch with him, and when I was in the Dam a few months back spending some taxpayers' on a much-needed weekend R and R, we met up for a few drinks. So we're like mates.' He paused to take a drag from his fag. 'Anyway, we went our separate ways, and I hadn't heard hide nor hair from him since then, until suddenly out of the blue he gives me a bell the other night, and do you know what he's saying?'

'Go on, surprise me.'

'He's saying,' whispered Murk, leaning forward, 'that he's got gear to sell, and he's looking for a UK buyer, and would I be interested.'

'What sort of gear?'

'Es. He's got five thousand pills he wants to sell, and if the price is right he can get hold of a regular supply. As much as five thousand a week. Apparently, the first batch is already in the country, waiting to be flogged.'

Stegs looked at him sceptically. 'If he's as big a star as you say he is, how come he's getting involved in something this risky?'

'He's a victim of market forces,' answered Murk in a voice that suggested he was imparting some great wisdom. He took another leisurely drag on his Marlboro Light and sat back in his seat, nodding sagely through a cloud of smoke. 'You see, the thing is, these days porn stars ain't meant to look like porn stars. It's all like amateur stuff now; the girls and the boys are meant to look like everyday, normal people, not like beautiful models with plastic tits or giant wangers. Tino's a handsome bloke with ten inches' worth of prime sirloin, an all-over tan and a funny accent, and nowadays that's just no good. You'd have more chance than him at the moment, Stegsy. It's just the way it's going.'

'I'll take that as some sort of back-handed compliment.'

'You might want to think about it, you know. It's an easy way to make a few quid. It's not hard work and you get to fuck some very attractive young fillies. As long as you don't mind being watched and you can get it up on demand, then you're laughing.'

For one terrifying moment, Stegs actually did think that it might be quite a nice little career move. It would certainly solve his ongoing problem of not getting a great deal of action domestically on the bedroom front. The passionometer *chez* Jenner had been stuck round the zero mark ever since the missus had got pregnant, close to a year and a half back now. But he quickly scotched that one as he pictured himself stark bollock naked and freezing cold in someone's front room with a balding director in a medallion who thought he was Martin Scorsese telling him what position to get in while a camera crew prodded around his nether regions trying to get close-ups of areas best seen from long distance and on panoramic. In Stegs's experience, there was no such thing as easy money. Unless, of course, you were Trevor the Murky one.

'So he's out of work then, is he? Your mate?'

'Yeah, things ain't going so good for him at the moment. There's been a bit of a scandal as well. He's only a young lad, our Tino, and a bit over-enthusiastic where the chicks are concerned.'

'And?'

'And, he got caught fucking a fourteen-year-old.'

'Christ! The dirty dog.'

'It wasn't like that really. I mean, they're a bit more liberal about these sort of things over in Holland. The age of consent's like twelve or something, so it's not frowned on like it is here.'

'Perverts.'

'No, no, come on now, Stegsy. When in Rome, and all that.'

'I'm not in Rome.'

'You know what I'm saying. Anyway, as it happens, the porn fraternity share your concern at such unwelcome actions. They don't like that sort of thing – the shagging of chicks so young by their up-and-coming stars. It's not good for the export business. So they've sort of frozen him out. And then there was his accident.'

'His what?'

'His accident. He was doing a film a few months back fucking this bird in the wheelbarrow position – you know, holding her up in a semi-handstand while doing her from behind.'

Stegs was horrified. 'What? That's a real position?'

'Come on, Stegsy, get with the Kama Sutra. Of course it is. Provides just the sort of deep penetration a young woman requires. Plus it's very useful exercise. Builds up your biceps and triceps.'

'Sounds fucking knackering.'

'Ah, well, there's the problem. Tino's perhaps not as fit as he thinks he is. Too many late nights, and all that. Anyway, there he is, doing this bird at ten to the dozen, just building up a head of steam for the money shot, when he gets a sudden attack of the cramp, mid-thrust. He yelps in pain, stiffens up, so to speak, and can't fucking move. The director's going mental, the bird on the receiving end wants to know what the fuck's going on because obviously she's a little uncomfortable, and Tino's just stuck there, legs bent, rooted to the spot, with all the lower-body flexibility of a breezeblock.'

Murk stopped to savour the moment, chuckling heartily. Stegs joined in, unable to help himself.

'What the fuck happened?' he asked.

'Apparently, he was stuck like that for three hours. They had to take him to Casualty in the back of an ambulance with both of them stark bollock naked and him still inside her.'

'Ah, fuck this, you're making it up.'

Murk nodded, still chuckling. 'I am, as it happens. That last bit, anyway. Still, I have heard it's happened before. And on a porno as well. The rest of it's true, though. Tino's not having it easy getting hold of money, and one of his contacts within the industry is this director who's also fallen on hard times.

Apparently, the fourteen-year-old Tino shagged was this bloke's girlfriend, and he's like fifty or something. Anyway, he's the one who's the source of the gear. Him and Tino have gone into partnership. The director's producing the goods and Tino's job's to find a buyer and transport the stuff to where the transaction's going to take place. Which is where I come in. I think I must have mentioned to him at some point that I liked to indulge in tablets of a recreational nature, and so he thinks maybe I'd be a useful business partner as well. He was offering the whole batch at six grand.'

'What did you say?'

'I said I wasn't in the market – cashflow problems, and all that – but I knew a bloke who might be.' He grinned happily. 'My mate, Stegsy. As reliable as he is trustworthy. Though I did say you'd probably only pay five for that sort of bulk.'

Stegs nodded. 'A wise move. I don't like to fork out too much for my pills.'

'Exactly. Anyway, I told him I'd try to make contact with you and set up some sort of meeting. What do you think?'

Stegs thought it incredible that informants like Trevor Murk could be quite so blasé about double-crossing and thereby ruining the lives of people they were meant to like, and, since he was suspended, he said as much. 'Doesn't it bother you that your actions are going to send that poor bastard down for two, even three, years, minimum?'

Murk looked genuinely upset by the question, as if Stegs had just accused him of something heinous he hadn't done. Like shagging his best friend's missus in the wheelbarrow position. 'I can't fucking believe you're getting like that. You lot survive on the sort of info people like me are good enough to provide – at considerable danger to ourselves, I might add. I didn't ask him to come offering me gear, did I? If he's stupid enough to try and flog five thousand tabs to someone he once starred in a porn film with, he's got to accept the, you know, consequences, hasn't he? It's dog eat dog out there, Stegsy. You know that. You don't bite, you don't fucking survive. Anyway, you were the one who called him a pervert. Why are you suddenly getting all moralistic about it? Found God or something?'

Stegs stubbed out his cigarette and took a drink from his beer. 'No,' he said eventually. 'If I found God, Trevor, I'd put him back. No place for someone like him in my life.'

He smiled from behind his near-empty pint glass, pleased that he'd riled Murk. It was a small victory, but it still felt good. He had an urge then to tell him to fuck off. To tell him that he could go and peddle his nasty little tales to some other mug, that he didn't want anything to do with it. He thought it might even be quite a hoot to print up some posters of Murk with that smug fucking grin of his, and plaster them all over Barnet with the message in bold black letters that here was a grass who made money out of putting fellow scumbags behind bars. Then maybe someone would end up wiping that smile off his face for ever.

But if there was one thing Stegs had learnt over the years, it was never to cut off your nose in order to spite the rest of your face, and already an idea was beginning to form itself in his mind. An idea for a nice little piece of payback. He'd always been good at improvising.

'Tell him I'm interested,' he said, 'and let's set up an initial meet. As soon as possible.'

Murk grinned, Stegs's alleged defamation of his character forgotten in the desire to make a bit of cash. 'That won't be hard. He's flying in tomorrow.'

'Good. Like I say, as soon as possible.'

Murk licked his lips. 'And, er . . . how much are we talking for this? Gonna be a nice little collar, innit? Nasty Class A peddler, ex-porn star to boot, foreign. That'd look sweet on your record, wouldn't it?'

He spoke the words coaxingly, like a lustful adult to a child, and another truly unpleasant smile spread like gangrene across his face. The love of money. It really is the root of evil. And all for five hundred-odd quid, which would be the maximum he'd get for a collar like this, courtesy of the taxpayer. Not that, sadly for him, he was going to be seeing any of it. The germ of Stegs's idea was growing fast. It had potential, real potential. And best of all, it didn't involve Murk.

'You'll be nicely reimbursed, Trevor, should it end in a result and conviction. As befits a grass of your quality.' Like fuck you will. 'Fancy another pint?'

# 15

There's a story about Nicholas Tyndall that's long been doing the rounds. For a while a couple of years back he was running a crack den out of a semi-detached house in Stepney which belonged to a retired panel beater of West Indian descent. Or perhaps it would be more accurate to say allegedly, because Tyndall always denied that he had anything to do with that particular house.

The retired panel beater's name was Tony Lackman, and he was in his early sixties. He had no criminal record, had lived a pretty blameless life, and lived alone, having been married and divorced many years earlier. There were no children. Unfortunately for Mr Lackman, the fact that he was the sole occupant of his property and without close family made him an ideal victim for what's becoming a fast-growing problem in London: the forced colonization of an individual's home by a crack gang who then use it as a front for their business. It happens a lot more than people think, but because there's usually very little publicity (the victims, often elderly, tend to comply under threat of violence), people don't tend to hear about it. Lackman, however, was different. He wasn't prepared to give up his home that easily and, though understandably terrified of his unwanted guests, committed the cardinal sin of complaining to the police. A few days later a team of armed officers raided the property, made several arrests and recovered a small quantity of crack cocaine. One of those arrested was a close associate of Nicholas Tyndall, but because he hadn't been in the same room as the drugs, had later tested negative for being under their influence and had denied all knowledge of them (claiming he'd been round there for a party), he'd been released without charge.

Two days later the dealers were back, and everything carried on like it had done before, only this time Lackman received a severe beating for his troubles and was forced to retreat to his bedroom on a permanent basis while the dealers lorded over the rest.

Finally, Lackman could take no more and complained to the police again. The same story then played out. A few days later armed officers raided the place (although this time they were delayed by a series of deadbolts screwed into the front and back doors, giving the dealers time to get rid of some of the contraband) and further arrests were made. This time, Tyndall's associate wasn't in the house, having decided that he would let a guy below him run things there. That guy, way down the criminal food chain, was the only one to face charges relating to the crack cocaine found, and because the quantities recovered were so small he escaped with a fine and a suspended sentence.

Tony Lackman wasn't so lucky. Three weeks later his naked body was found on wasteground a few hundred yards from his home. His hands and feet were tied and he'd been shot in the back of the head. The police, in an effort to gain public co-operation, stated that he'd been tortured before his death. What was never made public, however, was the fact that he'd also been castrated and that his eyes had been gouged out.

It had been a warning from Nicholas Tyndall to the whole community: do not defy me. And it had worked as well. Nobody was ever convicted of the crime, even though the names of the killers were widely known, and Tyndall continued to control a number of crackhouses in the area (albeit in a hands-off capacity) until he moved on to bigger, more lucrative crimes, safe in the knowledge that his reputation for violence had been suitably enhanced and that no-one would ever be daft enough to testify against him.

I don't like men like Nicholas Tyndall. Their very existence offends me, and one of the reasons I'm a copper is so that I can do my bit to bring them down.

But for the moment, Tyndall remained scot-free, wealthy and powerful, living in a palatial semi-detached villa on a quiet, leafy Islington avenue just off the Canonbury Road, no more than half a mile from where Slim Robbie O'Brien had been murdered. It had originally been three spacious flats, but when Tyndall moved in he'd decided that he wanted a bit more privacy and had made it known in no uncertain terms to the owners of the other two apartments that it was about time they moved, in the process selling their properties to him. The young couple living on the ground floor did exactly that; the Asian family in the basement needed a bit more persuading, but after having a brick thrown through their window, followed seconds later by the freshly severed head of somebody else's pet labrador, they'd come to the conclusion that discretion was the better part of valour and had sold at a heavily discounted price.

The problem these days is that gangsters, whether they be small-time drug dealers with guns and attitude or wannabe urban godfathers like Nicholas Tyndall, have no qualms about using serious violence and the threat of it to get what they want, because they know that neither the judicial system nor the police service have the wherewithal or the powers to protect those who speak out against them. It's something the Met and the government are supposedly trying to address, but sometimes, when you're operating at the coalface, it's difficult to get too optimistic. In the meantime, the advantage lies with the bad guys, and they didn't come much badder than Tyndall.

I was a little nervous about going to see him, and I got the impression Tina was too, although she wasn't the sort to admit as much. Although neither of us had met him before, we'd heard from reliable sources that he was canny enough not to pick fights with the Law. It's a lot harder (although not impossible) to intimidate police officers, so I felt reasonably confident that we weren't walking straight into the lion's mouth. However, with someone who can order the castration and blinding of an innocent householder for the sin of wanting to be left in peace, you can never be too sure.

It was 11.20 a.m. and cloudy when we walked up the steps to the imposing front door of Tyndall's house and banged on the knocker. Two separate CCTV cameras stared down on us from either side of the entrance portal and there were steel joins on the door's hinges that looked like they'd been added recently to reinforce it from attack. There were also bars on all the ground-floor and basement windows, which made me wonder what the neighbours must have thought – not that I could picture any of them complaining. A sign on the door said 'No Salesmen or Beggars' in big black writing.

'Who are you?' said a belligerent male voice over the intercom.

'Police,' I said, holding my warrant card up to one of the cameras. Tina did the same with the other one. 'We're here to see Nicholas Tyndall.'

'You got an appointment?' grunted the bloke on the other end, in a way that told us he knew we hadn't.

'We don't need an appointment,' I told him. 'Let us in, please.'

'He's not here.'

'Well, have a look round and make sure, because if he isn't we'll swamp this whole borough looking for him, and if we can't find him then we'll assume he's hiding from us and we'll come back here with territorial support officers, knock down this nice big door, issue you with a search warrant and rip this place apart from top to bottom. All right?'

The intercom clicked, and we were left standing there for what felt like a long time. Neither of us spoke, not when it was probable that whatever we said would be listened to. We didn't even look at each other. Simply stood there.

After about two minutes, I went to press the intercom again when I heard the sound of feet clumping heavily down stairs. We stepped back from the door, and I experienced a momentary spurt of adrenalin as someone on the other side released the locks and pulled back the bolts. Then the door came open quickly and I was looking up at the smiling face of Nicholas Tyndall: six feet four and sixteen stone of murderous charm.

'Let's go for a walk,' he said in a booming but not unfriendly voice, pulling on a black puffa jacket and stepping outside.

Before I had time to reply, he shut the door, slid between us and started down the steps. Tina and I looked at each other. She raised her eyebrows and I shrugged, turning to follow him.

'Slow down, Mr Tyndall,' I said as we got to the bottom of the steps. 'Anyone would think you were running away from something.'

He stopped and waited for us, the smile sitting easily on his face. Tyndall looked like a man who smiled a lot. He wasn't a bad-looking guy really: early thirties, tall, well built, with clearly defined patrician features and smooth coffee skin. He was completely bald, but the style fitted him so well that it was obvious he was hairless by choice rather than fate. Today, he was dressed casually in Levi's, khaki Timberlands and a white T-shirt under the jacket. He could have been a clothes model for a company like Gap. Everything looked brand new, including him.

'What can I do for you, then?' he asked.

'I think you know why we're here,' said Tina sharply, keen to show she wasn't intimidated by Tyndall's reputation.

The grin grew wider as he sized her up. 'Do I look like Mystic Meg? I can't read minds, otherwise I'd have been outside waiting for you when you turned up. You're going to have to give me a clue.'

'We need you to come down to the station and make a statement,' I told him.

As we caught him up, he turned and began walking steadily down the road, careful to avoid a young mother pushing her two young kids in a twin buggy. She smiled at him and glared at us.

'About what?'

'About what you know regarding the events at Heathrow on Wednesday.'

'I don't know nothing about them.'

'We'll be the judges of that,' I said, grabbing him by the arm and slowing him up. It was quite an effort, and probably not the safest move in the world, but it had to be done. You start kow-towing to the big boys and you never stop. 'We need you to accompany us down the station.'

His eyes fell to where my hand was on his jacket, and then came back to me. The expression in them was dark and cold, and even if I hadn't known his reputation I would have been able to tell that, for all his smiles and friendly greetings, this was a very dangerous and ruthless man. 'I don't like people I don't know trying to manhandle me,' he said, his tone threatening.

I held his gaze, but let my hand drop. 'I want you to take this conversation seriously, Mr Tyndall. We're not going to chase round after you begging for your co-operation, we're demanding it. Three close associates of yours were involved in trying to rob a drug deal that ended in six deaths, and since it's well known that they don't even so much as breathe without your say-so, it's a fair bet to assume you organized it.'

'Prove it.' The classic career thug's riposte.

'We intend to, but first we want you to come down the station.'

'I ain't got time at the moment. You want to talk to me, you talk here. Otherwise, contact my lawyer.'

'All right, then. When was the last time you saw Ashley Grant? Otherwise known as Strangleman.'

Tyndall looked as if he was going to answer me with a wise-crack, then obviously thought better of it. 'A few days back. Monday, I think it was.'

'Whereabouts did you see him?'

'At the Turnham social club,' he answered, referring to his organization's unofficial HQ off the Holloway Road. 'I play pool down there sometimes.'

'Yes, we know,' said Tina, pulling out her notebook. 'Quite a lot, apparently.'

'Listen, I don't think I want to carry on with this conversation any more. I don't like your attitude. Either of you. You want to speak to me, I want my lawyer present.'

'Hold on,' I said. 'If you really have got nothing to do with this, then it'll look a lot better if you co-operate, won't it? And lawyers and co-operation aren't two words that normally go together. So talk to us now.'

'I've got nothing to say. I saw Strangleman Monday. I know him and so I spoke to him about this and that, but he's not that close to me no more, whatever you lot might think. I don't trust him, and I think he feels the same way about me. We used to do a bit of work together but not any more.

He never mentioned nothing about a robbery.'

'Where do you think he could have got the information from?'

Tyndall gave an exaggerated shrug. 'Fuck knows. I ain't got a clue, and that's the truth.'

'Do you know a Robert O'Brien?' asked Tina.

'I know of him, yeah. Most people round these parts do.'

'Have you ever met with him for any reason?'

He shook his head with a humourless smile. 'Somehow I don't think so.'

'What do you mean?'

'I mean, he's the last bloke in the world I'd want to meet up with.'

'Why?'

Tyndall sighed loudly, again stepping aside as an older lady in her sixties walked past on the pavement with a collie. She didn't give him quite such a pleasant look as the young mother, but hurried past head down, as if fearful he'd catch her eye. Perhaps she'd been the owner of the labrador whose head had ended up in the Asian family's kitchen.

'Why? I'll tell you why. Because when he used to hang round with that fucking nutter Krys Holtz they had a run-in with one of my cousins. Rene Phillips. Remember him?' We both shook our heads. 'He was a doorman at a club in Holborn. One night he kicked out Danny Fitzgerald, another member of Krys Holtz's little crew, because Fitzgerald was being pissed and lairy and upsetting some of the clientele. But the thing is, Fitzgerald didn't want to go, so him and Rene had a bit of a tear-up, and Rene won. None of the other doormen would get involved because they knew who Fitzgerald was, but Rene didn't scare easy. None of my family do.' He gave us both a look as he said this, and once again I forced myself to hold his gaze. 'Anyway, a couple of days later, Rene was leaving his flat when he got a tap on his head with an iron bar. The next thing he knows he's woken up bound hand and foot in Krys Holtz's workshop. You must have heard of that?' I nodded. So did Tina. All the area's coppers had heard of Krys Holtz's infamous workshop. 'They were all there. Krys, Fitzgerald, Mick Noble and Slim Robbie O'Brien. And by the time they'd finished with him he was walking with a permanent limp, had all his fingers broken and part of his ear missing, and needed plastic surgery to get rid of the burns on his face.

'I never did nothing about it. At the time, the Holtzes were just about untouchable, and anyway, I'm not my cousin's babysitter. If he wants to get involved with people like that, that's his look-out, but I'll tell you this for nothing. Both of you. There is no fucking way I'd ever have anything to do with a prick like O'Brien. He's nothing. And now that he's out on his own, and without his mates to back him up, he's lucky I ain't fucking killed him.'

'Well, someone has,' I told him. 'He was murdered two days ago. I'm surprised that a man with your contacts hasn't heard all about it.'

Tyndall looked neither surprised nor unsurprised. 'I've been out of town the last few days,' he said. 'Down in Marbella. I've got a villa there. You can check my plane ticket if you want. So, someone killed him, did they?' His face broke into a wide, beaming smile. 'I'm glad. I hope it was slow. He was one geezer who definitely deserved it.'

'When did you leave for Marbella?'

He furrowed his brow in thought. 'Must have been Monday night. Yeah, Monday,' he repeated, nodding. 'I got the eight-thirty out of Stansted. Came back late last night and went straight to bed. That's why I ain't heard nothing about poor old Fat Robbie.' He looked at his watch. 'Anyway, I've got to go. I've got a meeting.' He turned and started walking back in the direction of the Canonbury Road.

We walked alongside him. 'We haven't finished asking you questions,' snapped Tina. This time it was she who put a hand on his arm, and this time he brushed it away, only stopping to glare at us each in turn.

'Well, I've finished answering them. Whoever's done over Robbie O'Brien, good luck to them. But it definitely ain't me. Now, you want to ask me anything else, you contact my lawyer.' He gave us the name of someone I hadn't heard of, and once again turned on his heel.

We continued after him, firing off questions that were invariably delivered to the back of his head while he remained tight-lipped, right up to his front door, which he slammed in our faces.

'What do you think?' asked Tina when we were back on the street. 'Would Strangleman really have carried out the robbery without his boss's knowledge?'

'I doubt it,' I answered, watching his front door. 'I can't see anything happening within Tyndall's crew that he doesn't know about, or authorize. He's not the sort of boss who lets his workers freelance.'

'But that story about his cousin. If it's true, would he really have set something up with O'Brien?'

'O'Brien's dead, isn't he? It's not that unlikely that Tyndall would have organized the whole thing with him and had him killed afterwards. It would have been a good form of revenge. I expect we'll find that the story about his cousin's true, which, like Tyndall's alibi, would be very convenient for a defence lawyer. The problem is, we're dealing with people who are good at covering their tracks.' I shook my head slowly. 'I think Flanagan's right. Our best hope's going to be finding the shooter.'

'A lot easier said than done.'

I allowed myself a thin smile. 'Isn't everything?'

# 16

It was near enough lunchtime so Tina and I decided that, for
once, we'd go Continental and actually sit down and eat. Life's
too fast in London. It's always go go go, and when your job
involves go go going through the heavy tide of human
corruption, then occasionally you need to sit back and take a
break. We went to a cheap French restaurant I knew near
Islington Green where they served moules marinière with french
fries and crusty bread, a meal that always brings back happy
memories of childhood family camping trips to the coast of
Brittany. And they only charged £4.95 for it as well, so, being
overworked and underpaid, I felt doubly rewarded.

When we'd eaten and broken all the rules by washing it down
with a glass of white wine each, we left and headed our separate
ways: she to talk to Stegs's boss at SO10, me to interview his
guvnor at Barnet nick.

On the way, I got a call from a Mr Naresh Patel of the Police
Complaints Authority, telling me that he'd like to speak to me as

soon as possible in relation to the shootings at Heathrow. Knowing there was no point putting off the inevitable, I agreed to meet him later that day. He wanted to do it at their head-quarters in Great George Street over in Westminster, and though I tried manfully to get him to come to the station instead, he insisted. So we set it for four-thirty, and I phoned through to Flanagan and told him that I wouldn't be able to make the five o'clock murder squad meeting. Since it was routine anyway, he didn't mind, but told me to call him beforehand with any relevant information I'd picked up that day. I told him about our meeting with Tyndall and the fact that he'd been out of the country for the last three days.

'Setting himself up with an alibi suggests to me that he was more involved than not involved,' said Flanagan, which were my thoughts exactly. 'But, as I said this morning, it's facts we need. We've got plenty of theories.'

I told him I'd see what I could come up with.

Stegs's overall boss at Barnet, DCI Tom Clay, was overweight and looked like he'd had it with policework. It's not an un-common trait in coppers who've been in the job too long, but Clay had it more than most. He was genuinely concerned about Stegs, though, and hoped that he'd be back on duty before too long.

'I could do with him back here,' he told me as we sat in his office on the building's third floor, overlooking the high street. Outside it was drizzling, and I wondered when we were next going to see the sun. 'He spends three-quarters of his time on SO10 business – not that it's ever done him any good.'

'What do you mean?' I asked.

'I mean, he gets involved in all these dangerous activities, risks his neck constantly, and it never helps his chances of promotion, doesn't get him paid any more, and the first opportunity, they hang him out to dry.'

'I wouldn't put it quite like that.'

'Wouldn't you? I would.' He sat back in his seat and it creaked under his weight. 'He's suspended from duty; you're here asking questions about him; and he's got that arsehole Flanagan to look out for.'

'What do you mean?' I asked, taking a sip from the tepid station coffee Clay had provided me with, and remembering the atmosphere between the two men during the meeting after the hotel shootings. 'Why would Flanagan have it in for him?'

'Stegs and Flanagan haven't seen eye to eye for a long time. Flanagan was the DCI in overall charge of an op him and Vokes Vokerman did once for SO10. The two of them almost got killed. I don't think it was entirely Flanagan's fault that things went wrong, but Stegs took a different view and told him that he was an incompetent arsehole who couldn't do his job properly. I don't think either of them have ever forgotten the set-to they had, and I doubt if Flanagan'd lose any sleep if Stegs took the rap for what happened Wednesday.' He took a crumpled pack of Embassy No. 1s out of his pocket and stuck one in his mouth. 'Don't tell me you're one of those new breed who can't stand the smell of smoke.'

'Do I look like I'm new breed?'

He managed a smile, his first since we'd shaken hands at the front desk ten minutes earlier. 'No, not really.'

'Then please feel free. It's your office.'

'They're trying to ban it everywhere,' he said defiantly. 'It makes me wonder why I joined up sometimes. They give the criminals a slap on the wrist, but if you're law-abiding they're on to you like a shot. So, where did you say you're from?'

'I don't think I said I was from anywhere, but since you ask,

I'm based out of Islington. I've been seconded to the inquiry into the murder of Robbie O'Brien, the guy they found dead alongside his grandma yesterday.'

Clay's eyes narrowed. 'What's that got to do with Stegs?' he demanded through a haze of smoke.

'He knew the victim, and the victim had links with what happened on Wednesday. We've been trying to keep that part out of the papers, but I don't suppose it'll be too long before someone leaks it.'

'I saw a mention about it on *London Tonight*, but I haven't had a chance to read the papers for weeks, so I'd probably miss it if it was leaked. There's no time, that's the problem. No time for anything when you're a copper. Apart from policework, that is.' He took another drag on the cigarette, and eyed me as if he was somehow laying down a challenge. I got the feeling then that Clay didn't trust me much. 'Well, let me tell you this, Stegs Jenner's a good copper. One of the best. He's had the occasional run-ins, and his career's not entirely unblemished, but I'd take him back here full-time tomorrow if I could. And I sincerely fucking hope that he doesn't end up getting hounded out of the Force, because he doesn't deserve it.'

I nodded. 'Look, I've met him a few times myself and, for what it's worth, I tend to agree with what you're saying. Now, this incident when him and Flanagan fell out. What was it all about?'

'Why do you want to know?'

The question bordered on hostile. I was going to have to tread carefully on this one. Tom Clay obviously had a lot of time for Stegs and was not going to want to say anything that made his situation worse.

'I want to know because I'm trying to build up a picture. Personally I like him, but at the moment there's questions being raised about his integrity, and I just want to make sure that I've got all the information I can.'

Clay continued to watch me like a hawk. Then he cleared his throat with a rattling cough that did not bode well for his long-term health and began. 'It was when Flanagan was running CID at Greenwich. There was a drug importer and thug down there called Frank Rentners who was looking to expand his business, and Flanagan was interested in making sure he didn't. So he brought in Stegs and Vokerman. The first meeting was in a pub and neither of them were wearing wires, but SO11 had a tracking device under Rentners' car just in case they changed venues, so the handlers could intervene if anything went wrong.'

He then told me the whole story about how the two SO10 men had ended up having to watch another man being tortured while being told that they'd be next, and how they'd only just managed to persuade Rentners that they were kosher dealers, and therefore escape relatively unscathed. The way the operation had been controlled had been slapdash. According to Clay, Flanagan had only put a couple of DCs in as back-up since the risk of things going wrong on a first meeting was considered small. The DCs had followed the two Mercedes carrying Rentners and his entourage but had lost them quickly, and had then called the control room to alert them to this fact. However, it seemed that Flanagan had still considered the SO10 men a low priority because, by the time the car was tracked to the house and officers had arrived there, more than two hours had passed since they'd left the pub. The officers on the scene had been unaware of what was going on inside and had even seen Stegs and Vokes leave. By the time the police had finally approached the house and knocked on the door at ten to three, Rentners and the rest of his men had also left, along with an injured Brewster. Brewster had declined to press charges and had immediately disappeared from view.

Put bluntly, it had been a fuck-up of the first order, and afterwards Stegs had blown his top on Flanagan. 'He called him a lot of names,' said Clay. 'Some real choice ones. Told him in no uncertain terms that he should have known that Brewster, the guy who was their contact, had been under suspicion, and made sure that they had proper back-up. I assume you know Flanagan?'

I nodded. 'Yeah, I know him,' I said with the right degree of ambivalence.

'Well, you know what a wanker he is, then.' I didn't say anything so he continued. 'Instead of holding his hands up and admitting he'd made a mistake, he reported Stegs to his bosses at SO10 and here and accused him of gross insubordination. Stegs ended up being disciplined, and almost got put back in uniform. I think if I hadn't stood up for him, he would have been too.' He lit a new cigarette with the butt of the old one. 'And Flanagan ends up being promoted, even though the bloke he's meant to have been sorting out, Frank Rentners, is still in business down there and doing very fucking nicely thank you. Now there's justice for you.'

So that explained a few things. No wonder the two of them hadn't got on. No wonder, too, that Flanagan hadn't exactly been effusive in defence of Stegs's character and innocence in the meeting this morning.

I didn't say anything to Clay about any of this. Instead, I asked about Stegs's disciplinary record aside from the Flanagan incident and was told, with some reluctance, that he'd been cited twice in the past: once for assaulting a prisoner nine years previously when he'd still been in uniform, and the other time for embellishing his expenses. That had been three years ago. I asked what had happened.

'He just added a few things in that maybe he shouldn't. The amounts involved weren't a lot – a few quid here and there, that's all. It happens, you know that.' His look told me that if I thought that fiddling the expenses was a big deal, then I wasn't living in the real world.

I told him I knew it happened, and after a few more minutes the meeting drew to a close without me uncovering anything else of any note about Stegs Jenner, other than confirming the fact that his boss liked him, which I suppose was one thing, although I wasn't sure that a character reference from someone so jaded and tired as DCI Tom Clay was that much of a recommendation of innocence.

I stopped off back at the nick on the way to my meeting with Naresh Patel to go on the system and check Stegs's record within the Force. It was pretty much what Clay had said: a not exactly spotless disciplinary record, which was probably why he'd never risen above DC level, but nothing too untoward or crooked, and nothing that Clay hadn't mentioned. On the expense fiddles there were no details of the money involved, and I decided to take Clay's word for it and assume the amounts weren't a lot, since his penalty had only been a fine, not a demotion.

I arrived for the interview five minutes late (problems on the Victoria Line), and Patel, who I suspected worked to office hours, was keen to get started. However, if I thought that this would make him keep it short, I was very much mistaken. A bookish young man you'd probably avoid going to the pub with, he was a real stickler for detail and made me go over, step by excruciating step, what I'd seen, when I'd seen it and whether or not any of it could have been avoided. Were adequate warnings given to the suspects? Was it a life-threatening situation? I know he was only doing his job but I felt like grabbing him by the collar and telling him that when criminals are brandishing guns – particularly when they're already in the process of using them, as they had been on that day – then it's always a life-threatening situation; and if you're the copper who's unlucky enough to have your finger on the trigger then maybe you might pull it a couple more times than regulations insist. It's easy to stand back at a safe distance and raise doubts about whether the SO19 officers had acted beyond their remit; it's a lot harder to decide when you're on the spot. And that's the problem we have as coppers. Not only are we up against the criminals, we're also up against the establishment as well. They might be trying to be fair and impartial, but, ultimately, the only people who end up benefiting from their actions are the ones who least deserve it. You know what they say. The road to hell and all that . . .

As it was, I stated categorically at every available opportunity that I hadn't seen a single officer do anything wrong. 'It was a botched operation,' I concluded, 'in so far as unforseen elements compromised it and caused the shooting to start, but it was ended as professionally as possible by the people on the ground.' I'd practised that phrase on the way over there and it came out just right.

'And do you have any idea what caused the arrival of these unforseen elements?' Patel asked in slow, careful tones tinged with natural distrust, as if he half expected my reply to be a lie. 'How they could have known this alleged drug deal was happening?'

'At the moment,' I said, 'none whatsoever.'

His nod of acknowledgement had something of the sceptical about it. 'Thank you,' he said, after a supremely long pause, switching off the tape recorder. 'I may need to speak with you again.'

It was six o'clock by the time I left and a wet, and unseasonably cold, drizzle was falling over the cacophony of central London's dirt-fumed rush hour. Even Big Ben and the Houses of Parliament, those grand bastions of the city's tourist trade, looked forlorn. Definitely a good night to be getting home.

When I got back to the nick to collect my car, it was half-six and the murder squad meeting had broken up. Apparently, they were round the Roving Wolf with members of the station's CID, enjoying a few end-of-week drinks – a loose tradition not harmed by the fact that the start of the weekend usually heralded another two days' work for most of us. On another night I would have stopped by and joined them for a couple, but tonight tiredness got the better of me and I drove straight home.

It was five to seven when I shut the front door of my flat behind me for the last time that night. The first thing I did was try Tina's mobile, but she wasn't answering. When I'd spoken to Flanagan earlier, he'd told me that she'd called to say that she wasn't going to make the meeting either, and I wondered whether she'd picked up a lead. If so, I'd find out soon enough. I was expecting her round later, as I did most nights these days.

I pulled a beer from the fridge, then sat down in front of the TV, trying to push the thoughts of the day out of my head. A copper can work too hard, and sometimes I felt I was almost living my cases and that, aside from Tina, and perhaps my daughter, they were the only things governing my existence. I needed a holiday. We both did. I hadn't had a trip abroad for two and a half years, when I'd spent two weeks in Barbados with my ex-wife and daughter. It had been a good time – good food, good weather, a little bit of scuba diving – but it also felt like a long time ago. I wondered how to broach the subject of going away together to Tina. Something like that would make our relationship official at the station since there was no way we could both take time off at the same time without it being commented upon, particularly when we'd be coming back with suntans. But I didn't much fancy going on my own, so something was going to have to give.

Tina came back at seven-thirty, looking tired, but still as gorgeous as ever. The drizzle outside had turned into a downpour and her hair was tousled and wet, curling up around the smooth, pale skin of her face. I immediately got a surge of lust that knocked the cobwebs off my exhaustion straight away. She came over and gave me a kiss on the lips. I could smell the scent of her skin, and the lust went into overdrive. A tubful of Viagra wouldn't have had a more positive effect.

'Let me just get out of these clothes,' she said. 'Then we'll talk.' An invitation, if ever I'd heard one.

'Talking wasn't what I had in mind,' I said as I followed her into the bedroom.

I wasn't sure whether she was up for it or not, but it was either that or she was feeling sorry for me, because she took me in her arms and nature took its all-too-swift course. I'm not the world's greatest lover, nor does the mood take me every waking hour like it does some men, but when I put my mind to the task I can be pretty successful, if I say so myself. Dogged rather than devastating, but Tina seemed to enjoy it which, as she would tell you, was the main thing.

'Well, that wasn't exactly romantic,' she said after we'd finished and were lying naked on the bed, she smoking the obligatory cigarette, 'but it did the trick.'

'We aim to please,' I told her, thinking that there weren't many things better than sex with someone you care about. 'Do you fancy something to eat?' Though good food was probably a close second.

'Are you cooking?'

'I've even bought the wine.'

She smiled, ruffling my hair. 'I could get used to this.'

'Fine by me. I'm hoping you do.'

We looked at each other for a moment and I suddenly felt awkward, as if I'd just been caught putting pressure on her. These last few weeks I'd been finding it harder to keep the pace of our relationship casual, but I was also keen not to scare her away, knowing that she wanted to take things one step at a time.

'I'll go and rustle something up for us.' I kissed her on the cheek, threw on my dressing gown and headed into the kitchen to attempt to produce some home-made chicken fried rice.

While the rice boiled and the chicken browned in the wok, I cracked open the bottle of white wine and poured half the contents into two large glasses. A few minutes later, Tina followed me in, dressed in a white dressing gown and slippers, her hair wet from the shower, and it occurred to me, not for the first time since we'd got together, that I was a very lucky man.

'Smells nice,' she said, coming over and giving me a kiss on the cheek.

'So do you.'

She stepped away, picked up her wine, then asked me what I'd found out that afternoon. Whatever she said about leaving the Force and doing something a bit more in line with her background and education, she lived the job just as much as me. I was sure she wouldn't last five minutes in an office, dealing with customer enquiries or adding numbers to balance sheets. Our job was a bad one, whatever the recruitment ads might say. Underpaid and under-supported, over-stressed and increasingly over-dangerous. But it was still addictive to the right sort of person, and Tina, like me, was the right sort of person. Maybe it was one of the reasons I liked her so much. Because she knew the pressures, and unlike a lot of the wives and girlfriends of coppers, she could tolerate them.

I gave her a brief rundown of my interview with Clay, and she raised her eyebrows when I told her about Stegs's previous run-in with Flanagan.

'That's an interesting one,' she said, lighting another cigarette and taking a decent-sized gulp of the wine. 'I thought there was some tension between them on Wednesday. I found out something as well.'

'What?'

'Stegs used to partner up with a guy called Jeff Benson at SO10, before he worked with Vokes. I spoke to Benson today. He left the Force three years ago, very suddenly. Just before he slung his hook, he got inside the Holtzes, posing as a doorman who was also a drug dealer and enforcer. He was well inside too, not just on the periphery. It took him months, but he got to the point where they trusted him, and he even got introduced to the big boss, Stefan Holtz.'

I chucked some Chinese vegetables in with the chicken and gave the whole lot a good stir. 'Go on.'

'It was a top-secret op. Only his controller was meant to know about it, but Benson made a mistake. He let slip what he was doing to Stegs one night when they were out drinking, against all the rules. He told me it was because the pressure was getting to him and he wanted to talk to someone about it. Since he couldn't say a word to his family, he chose someone he felt he could confide in. Three weeks later his wife and child got a visit from a group of Holtz thugs. No-one was hurt, but she was given a letter containing photos of her going in and out of the shop where she worked, plus the nursery where she dropped her baby off every day. And then, the very same night, Benson, who knew nothing about the visit, was getting into his car outside a pub when a man with a scarf round his face leant in the window and stuck a gun against his head. The shooter said, "This is a message from the Holtzes to their favourite copper," and pulled the trigger. Thankfully the gun was empty, but Benson knew they were serious. When he saw the photos, that was it. He resigned on the spot.'

'I remember Malik telling me something about that when I first met up with him,' I said, emptying the rice into a colander before adding it to the mix in the wok, and giving it another stir. I was getting hungry now. 'I didn't know the guy had had anything to do with Stegs, though. Not that it necessarily means anything.'

'Except that Benson's certain Stegs was the leak. He said that within days of him telling Stegs, his contacts within the Holtzes began to shut him out of things. Meetings were postponed, the information he was gathering seemed to dry up. Then obviously all this other stuff happened, and that was it. Another career beckoned. He left within days and refused point-blank to tell his controller what he'd found out. The Holtzes knew what they were doing. He's still scared now, even though they're no longer a threat. I visited him at home today. He's moved south of the river and become head of security for an investment company in Kent. A lot less money, but at least he sleeps at night. The thing is, he blames Stegs for what happened, without a doubt. They've never spoken since, and they were good friends.'

I thought about that for a moment. 'There's never been any evidence that Stegs had anything to do with the Holtzes, though, has there?'

'I asked Benson about that and he said no, not that he was aware of. That's why the controller didn't buy it. But he's sure, John. Benson's sure Stegs set him up, and let's face it, Stegs is not exactly whiter than white, is he?' She took another long drag on the cigarette.

'But if he did work for the Holtzes, then how come when we first used Stegs to set up Slim Robbie, Robbie didn't recognize him?'

Tina shrugged. 'I don't know. Perhaps Stegs was only known to a handful of people in the organization, and Slim Robbie wasn't one of them. It still doesn't seem right, whatever you might think.'

I could hardly disagree with that. 'We'll need to keep our ears to the ground, but we'll also have to be careful. He's going to know we're asking questions, but it's important we make him believe that it's only routine, and we don't rattle him.'

I dished up and we ate at the kitchen table while steadily draining the bottle of wine. The conversation remained on the case for a few minutes but, with some prompting on my part, finally moved on to other things, and after we'd finished eating I brought up the idea of a holiday together.

'It sounds nice,' she said carefully, 'but it means everything's going to end up out in the open, doesn't it?'

'It's going to have to come out eventually. And anyway, I think most people in CID have got a pretty good idea of what's going on. They are detectives, after all. I'd be a bit concerned if they hadn't.'

'But at least they're keeping quiet about it at the moment. If we come right out with it, then people are going to be asking all sorts of questions. Let's leave it a few weeks, eh? See how it goes.' She put her hand on mine. 'I don't want it to sound like I don't want to – I do – but I want to play things slowly where work colleagues are concerned. You understand what I'm saying, don't you?'

I wasn't going to push things, thinking that gentle persuasion would be far more effective, so I told her that, yes, I did understand. 'But if you ever did decide to go, where would you fancy?'

She thought about it for a few moments. 'I think I'd like a week on safari, and then maybe a week somewhere in the Indian Ocean. The Seychelles, or Mauritius. That way you get a good combination.'

'A good combination and a bad bank balance.'

She lit another cigarette and poured the last few drops of the wine fairly evenly into our two glasses. 'Don't be boring, Mr Gallan. You can't take it with you when you go, and you can't put a price on memories. You know, the days when I travelled after uni are still the best of my life, even though all I have to show for them are boxloads of photos and a massive overdraft that I'm still paying off now, seven years on. But so what? I wouldn't have changed those days for anything. That's the attitude you've got to take, John. We've only got the one life.'

I didn't like it when Tina mentioned her travelling days because, if I'm honest, it made me jealous. I often look back – too often – and wish that I'd gone off and seen something of the world and experienced what it had to offer while I was still young and free enough to be able to do it. Instead, I'd left school and joined the Force straight away; got engaged at twenty; was married at twenty-two; and became a dad at twenty-four, rendering such thoughts utterly redundant. But now and again I still imagined myself stretched out on a far-off palm-fringed beach, drinking a rum punch while some gorgeous local girl rubbed suncream on my back. I'd just got used to the fact that it wasn't going to happen.

Maybe now was the time to live a little and stop feeling sorry for myself, something I'd been doing far too much these past couple of years. 'You're dead right,' I told her. 'You can't take it with you. Safari and the Seychelles it is. If, of course, you change your mind.'

She smiled at me through the smoke, and I got the impression that she was tempted. 'Let's see how we go, eh?'

I took a gulp of the wine. 'Sure.'

At that moment, her mobile rang. I'd switched mine off, having done more than enough work on the taxpayers' behalf that day. She stood up, saying she'd better take the call, and picked the phone up off the kitchen sideboard. The conversation was short, with her doing most of the listening, but I could tell that whatever she was hearing was significant. I could read it in her animated expression. Something, it seemed, had happened on the case.

When she put the phone down she turned to me, smiling. 'That was Flanagan. It seems our killer wasn't so clever after all.'

I felt an immediate surge of excitement. 'Go on.'

'A witness approached the officers manning the Portakabin down at the scene a couple of hours ago, while the meeting was still in progress. Apparently, she saw someone come through her garden and then climb over her wall and into someone else's at about half-five on Wednesday afternoon. Her garden backs on to the one next door to Slim Robbie's building. She thought it was odd because the guy was dressed in a suit and didn't look much like your typical burglar. He'd disappeared before she could challenge him, but she did manage to give a description. White, twenty-five to thirty, with dark, curly hair. Looking agitated. It's got to be our man. No-one else is going to be clambering over back gardens at that time in the afternoon. It's too much of a coincidence.'

I grinned. What we had didn't sound like much, but it was a start. Now we could concentrate on asking potential witnesses who lived in the surrounding streets if they'd seen the same guy. From there, we might get a better physical description, or even a description of a car he got into. I remember a case I worked on once south of the river where a rapist had gained entry into a house through an open back window in broad daylight and violently sexually assaulted a nineteen-year-old student who'd been in there on her own. The student, who'd been made to wear a blindfold for most of the ordeal, had only managed to give the most basic of descriptions: skin colour and a rough age (twenty-five to forty if memory serves me correctly), but a retired lady who lived three streets away always made it a habit to write down the registrations of cars she didn't recognize, and to note down the descriptions of any suspicious-looking strangers. Obviously the rapist fitted that last criterion, and he'd also made the unfortunate mistake of parking his car in her street. She saw him get into it, tagged the number, and when we publicized what had happened shortly afterwards she supplied us with the details we'd needed. The rapist had been driving his brother-in-law's motor but he had a couple of prior convictions and was quickly apprehended as a result of her information.

There might not be many people around like our amateur detective, but there were enough to make me hopeful that from this first step on the trail of our killer we could take some larger ones.

And I couldn't help wondering whether the trail would eventually lead all the way back to Stegs Jenner.

# 17

The first time Stegs Jenner ever clapped eyes on Tino 'Ten Inch' Movali was on the porn film *Ass Lovers in London*. Stegs hadn't wanted to admit it to Murk when they'd spoken, but nowadays he was something of a porn aficionado, particularly since the missus had concluded, some five years into their relationship, that sex (at least with Stegs) was only really satisfactory if the end result was pregnancy, thereby relegating it to a couple of times a month, with him on top doing all the work, whenever the moon or whatever was in the right position, and rendering it completely redundant when she'd finally got up the duff. As a result, porn films had become an integral part of Stegs's solo sex life, to be watched whenever those rare moments occurred when the missus and Luke decamped from the house.

One such occasion had been a couple of months earlier when she'd gone off to see her parents in Colchester for the weekend, taking Luke with her. On the Saturday night Stegs had settled down to watch *Ass Lovers*, a purchase from a porn shop on the

Charing Cross Road, with a takeaway ruby and a hefty supply of canned Stella. What passed for the plot was as follows. An individual, known only as 'Ass Lover', appeared to be walking round London with a video camera, filming passers-by, especially attractive women, and their arses in particular, with Tino in tow. Tino, Stegs had to grudgingly admit, was a good-looking, if slightly vacant, young bloke but his dress sense wasn't up to much. He was wearing a checked sports jacket with brown leather patches on the elbows which would have fitted in perfectly in an early 1980s Essex golf club, but which wasn't exactly going to pull the punters in turn-of-the-century supposedly swinging London. He also had a rather unpleasant blue jeans and sandy-coloured cowboy boots combo *à la* Bon Jovi, which at least provided Stegs with a few laughs, as did Tino's English – fluent enough, but delivered in a comedy Continental accent that veered between French, German, Italian and back again, complete with hackneyed medallion-man chat-up lines such as 'You're looking good, baby' and 'Man, nice tits.' Still, this didn't appear to put off the two local girls Tino and 'Ass Lover' got talking to in Hyde Park by the Serpentine. Both were young and pretty, and none too bright either, and when Ass Lover asked them to come back to his hotel room with him and Tino to do some modelling, both accepted eagerly, giving Tino admiring glances that looked worryingly genuine.

All laughs stopped, however, when, back in the hotel room, Tino produced his startlingly impressive ten-inch appendage and began to service the girls in a variety of positions and in places where, to put it bluntly, the sun don't shine. In fact, Stegs was masturbating furiously and having a particularly enjoyable time of it, all thoughts of Tino's clothes sense forgotten as the Dutch dickmaster got to work doing what he obviously did best, when on the screen there was a loud knock on the hotel-room door. It then opened to reveal the hotel's manager – a smartly clad Trevor Murk, dressed in a suit for possibly the first time in his life outside of a crematorium, who strolled in to complain about the noise. Stegs had had to do an alarmed double-take, penis already wilting in hand, but it was Murk all right. One of the girls immediately knelt down in front of him, unzipped his fly and popped his dick out. Though less impressive than Tino's, it still wasn't a bad size and was standing to attention in double-quick time as the girl proceeded to administer a very professional-looking blowjob while Murk stood there looking very unmanagerial, smirking at the camera and making the odd grunt of encouragement.

Stegs had lost all interest at this point, unable to watch a spawny git like the Murky one have it away with an attractive young filly and get paid for it while he, Stegs, was reduced to wanking at home on a Saturday night. The contrast was simply too great and too tragic, and he'd switched off.

The second time he clapped eyes on Tino Movali was in the Cherry Tree Inn on the Saturday evening following his suspension. He was sitting at a corner table alongside Trevor Murk. The two of them were talking and laughing like old friends, oblivious to the fact that more than one woman in the place was looking their way. Stegs bought a pint and made his way over. The room was busy, with most of the tables taken, but thankfully it didn't feel oppressively crowded.

As Stegs approached, Murk saw him and stood up with a welcoming smile. 'Hello, Mark,' he said, using the name they'd agreed. He put out his hand and Stegs shook it reluctantly, affecting a deliberate air of indifference. Tonight, Matthew, I'm a shifty dope dealer with little in the way of patience or morality.

'All right, Trevor,' he grunted.

'This is Tino,' said Murk, and the youthful Tino stood up with a big grin.

They shook hands and Tino said that he was very pleased to meet him. 'I have heard from my friend Trevor here that you are the sort of man that is, how you say, good to know.'

'That depends,' said Stegs enigmatically, giving Tino a careful once-over. Tonight, the Dutchman was dressed in a paisley shirt and black jeans. There was a suspect-looking bulge in the groin area that Stegs would have thought was a deli-style salami sausage if he hadn't known better. 'You look familiar,' he added, sitting down with his pint. The others followed suit. 'Do I know you from somewhere?'

'Do you enjoy erotica?'

'None of your fucking business,' replied Stegs, lighting a fag.

'I'm sorry, man, I didn't mean it like that. What I'm saying is, I've made appearances in porno films. If you watch them regularly, you may have seen me.'

'I normally only look at the girls.'

'Well, in the films that I am in, they are usually on the end of my cock.' He gave a nervous laugh.

'Anyway,' said Murk, butting in, 'Tino's here with a business proposition. We thought you might be interested in what he had to sell. We've already talked about quantities, now we need to sort out a price. That's if you still want to go ahead.'

'I may want to,' said Stegs, thinking that Murk really was a treacherous back-stabbing dog, so impatient to betray his friend that he didn't even allow for a bit of small-talk. 'But first I've got to satisfy myself about a number of things.'

'And what are they, my friend?' asked Tino, leaning forward.

Strangely enough, he had a very innocent-looking, cherubic face that didn't really fit with the jaded expressions so many in the porn industry wore, that hound Murk included. Stegs put him at early twenties tops, and reckoned he'd probably make quite a good salesman. He had the sort of face you can't imagine ever having the gumption to deceive you. It seemed a pity that he'd been wasting his life in skinflicks, and was now about to waste it still more in the short-term, fast-burn-out world of small-time dope dealing.

'First of all, I want to make sure of the quality. I need to acquire a sample of what you've got in order to check how pure it is. If it's satisfactory, then we'll take things further. Also, I want to make sure that you're kosher. That is, who you say you are. I don't like dealing with people I don't know, even if Trevor here does speak highly of you.'

'He's hardly likely to be dodgy, is he?' said Murk, keen to get things moving. 'He's a porn star, for fuck's sake. He wouldn't exactly make good undercover.'

'Not so loud, Trevor. I don't much want the whole pub to know of our business dealings.'

'He's right, though, my friend. I've never spoken to a police-man in my life. I'm not, how you say, dodgy. And me and Trevor have known each other a long time. Is that not right, Trevor?'

'Too right, Tino.' Murk gave him a comradely pat on the back, then turned to Stegs, flashing him a quick wink. Bastard. 'I can vouch for this man, Mark. He's straight. I've told you that already. Now, if you're not interested, we can always go some-where else.'

Stegs ignored him. 'Have you got a sample of the goods?' he asked Tino.

Tino nodded. 'Sure, man.'

'All right, give it to me outside when we leave. But in principle, I'm interested. Trevor says you've got five thousand to sell, and you could be able to get as much as five thousand a week. Is that right?'

Tino sipped his drink. It looked like a scotch and soda. 'Yes, that's right.'

'And it's E, yeah? Ecstasy?'

'That's also right.'

'I usually deal with bigger quantities than that. Do you think you'll be able to get more?'

'I don't know, man,' he answered. 'I might be able to, but I cannot say for sure.'

'Fair enough. Well, five'll do for now. We'll have to play it by ear.'

'Excuse me?'

'See how it goes.'

'Sure.'

'I can pay you five cash for the first consignment, as long as it's you who gets it into the country.'

'It's already here.'

'Fine. That's my price. Take it or leave it.'

'I was hoping for six, man. You know, I've got expenses.'

'We've all got expenses, Tino.'

'How about five five, Mark?' said Murk. 'A nice clean compromise.'

Stegs sat back and took a drink of his pint. Murk was breaking the cardinal rule of informants everywhere – the rule being, never get too involved in the sting. A grass should sell his information, make an introduction if he has to, then slip into the background and try to put as much distance as possible between himself and the arresting officers. That way he tended to stay alive and healthy a lot longer. But Murk was playing it different. He was acting as Tino's partner, even though he knew the porn star was going down, involving himself in the whole thing for no obvious benefit. After all, he'd done his bit so, in essence, there was absolutely no point in him hanging around, which made the

194

fact that he was very suspicious. Perhaps he simply thought Tino was too stupid to make the connection. Either way, Stegs decided to cut him out.

'Five on the first. As I've said, that's my final offer. If the stuff's good, and I sell it on easy enough, I'll go up to five five for any subsequent purchase. Trevor'll tell you I'm a reliable bloke. Isn't that right, Trevor?'

'I've known Mark years, Tino,' bullshitted Murk. 'He's kosher.'

Tino nodded. 'All right, man,' he said. 'Five it is.'

'If, of course, I'm satisfied with the quality of the sample.'

'Sure.' Tino didn't seem too happy, his face slipping into a boyish hangdog look, but that wasn't Stegs's problem. He was going to be even less happy in a few minutes.

'I only like to deal with one person when I'm setting something up, Trevor, as you well know.' Murk opened his mouth to say something, but Stegs continued without pause. 'So, if you'll excuse us, I'll go through the details alone with Tino. You can catch up with him later.'

'I was hoping to advise him. He's a bit new to all this, Mark.'

'I'm sure he'll learn.'

Tino looked at Murk, not a hundred per cent sure whether he wanted to be left alone with Stegs. Murk shrugged in return. 'If that's how you want to play it,' he said to Stegs.

'It is. Thanks, Trevor, I'll see you later.'

Murk finished his drink and said his goodbyes.

'I'll catch up with you later, man,' said Tino.

Stegs didn't say anything. He waited until Murk was out of earshot, then turned back to the Dutchman with a hawkish smile. Tino returned the smile, but it lacked confidence. He was wary of Stegs, and Stegs knew it, enjoying the fact that he was intimidating the other man.

'You know, Tino, you seem like a nice guy. Amiable. I like that. You don't often get it in this industry.'

'That's kind of you to say so, man. Thanks.'

'But you've got a slight problem.'

Tino's forehead creased into barely visible worry-lines. 'What's that?'

'I'm an undercover copper and your mate Trevor – and I use the term most fucking loosely – is a police informer, or grass as we sometimes prefer to call them here in the UK.'

'Oh no,' said Tino, looking like he was about to burst into tears. 'No way, man. Did Trevor – did he, how you say – set me up?'

Stegs's smile grew wider. 'He did, I'm afraid. That's the thing you ought to know about Trevor. He's a Class A cunt. He always does this.'

Tino put his head in his hands, slumping in the seat. 'Stupid, stupid, stupid,' he said to himself angrily, sounding not unlike one of those mental people you sometimes get on the Tube.

'Well, whatever. The point is, I have you, how you say, bang to rights. That's my warrant card, just in case you're in any doubt.' Stegs placed it, open, on the table in front of Tino, who slowly removed his hands from his eyes and gave it a cursory glance before groaning loudly. 'But luckily for you,' Stegs continued, replacing it in his pocket, 'I'm not a heartless man. There may be a way out of this.'

'What?'

'Well, for a start, I'm not necessarily going to turn you in. I mean, you're an idiot, and a criminal too, obviously, but I'm thinking that I may give you a second chance.'

'Oh man, please, please. I'm not a criminal, I promise. If it hadn't been for the way the industry treated me, I would never have got involved in this drug dealing, I promise you.'

'All right, Tino, not quite so loud. I get the picture.'

'I can't go to prison, man. Sorry, what is your name again?'

'Mark.'

'I can't go to prison, Mark. It would tear me into pieces. Please. I would die.' He tried desperately to get his eyes to well up, but failed miserably. He was, Stegs thought, a fucking terrible actor. Thank God he'd got a big cock. 'And I know you would not want that, Mark,' he went on, 'because I can see that underneath the steel you are a good and decent man who would not want my death on your mind. Which is what would happen. It would be the end of me, the end. Do you understand what I'm saying, my friend?'

'Well, it's a bit mangled, but I think I get the gist of it. And you're right, I am a decent man. So maybe we can help each other here.'

'I'll do anything, man. Anything at all.'

'I understand that, Tino, and it's a good thing too, because I can tell you this: English prisons are roughly on a par with English traffic, English weather and English hospitals. In other words, fucking terrible. And on this little tape recorder in here' – he opened his jacket slightly to show the edge of the portable tape recorder he'd strapped to his chest – 'I have evidence that will indict you on charges of conspiracy to sell Class A substances, a most heinous crime in this neck of the woods, and one which will result in you spending several years in exactly such an establishment, and for once being on the receiving end of a rampant penis, like so many of your unfortunate female co-stars, rather than dishing out the punishment. Then maybe you'll appreciate why some of them scream so loudly when you shove your dick up their arses.'

'I thought you didn't watch my films, Mark.'

'Trevor told me. Apparently, it's your speciality.'

Tino shrugged. 'They seem to like it. And they get paid well.'

'I'm glad to hear it.'

'Excuse me.' Stegs and Tino both looked up. A young man in his early twenties with glasses and the last remnants of a powerful attack of teenage acne was standing by their table. 'Are you Tino "Ten Inch" Movali?'

'I am, my man,' Tino said with a smile, suddenly perking up.

'Would you mind signing this?' asked the young man, handing Tino a beermat and a pen.

'Sure, of course.'

'Can you make it out to Pete?'

'Pete. Sure, no problemo.'

'I'm a big fan of yours, Tino. I've seen loads of your stuff.'

'Be careful, sonny,' said Stegs belligerently, annoyed at this unwelcome interruption, 'it'll make you go blind.'

The young man turned to Stegs. 'Who are you? One of the money men?'

'Don't be cheeky. I'm his co-star, Charlie "The Chopper" Flanagan. I'm new to the scene. You'll be seeing a lot more of me.'

'Can I have your autograph as well, then?'

'Sure. Have you got another beermat?'

The young man picked up one from another table and handed it to Stegs. Tino finished his signature with a flourish and passed the pen over to Stegs, who wrote the name Charlie Flanagan and drew an erect penis complete with hairy testicles alongside it.

'So, are you in anything at the moment, Charlie?'

'We've just completed my first film, *Urban FuckFest*,' replied Stegs. 'It's due for release later this year.'

'That's fantastic. Look, I've always wanted to be in porn films. Do you mind if I join you?'

Stegs gave him a rueful smile. 'I'm afraid not, son, we're

198

discussing something very important. However, I appreciate your desire to get into the industry, and we're always on the look-out for new blood, so I'm going to give you the number of an agent I know.' Underneath the signature, he wrote down his brother-in-law's name and number. 'When you ring, you'll get either him or his secretary. Just tell them Charlie the Chopper said for you to call, and make sure you say too that you've heard there's a vacancy in one of Ben Dover's new productions, and that you're interested. And don't forget to give them your cock size – that's always at the top of their list of questions. And make sure you add an extra inch.'

'Are you sure that's a good idea?'

'Don't worry. Everyone does it.'

He smiled. 'Thanks, Charlie. Thanks a lot. I really appreciate it.'

'Good luck, son.'

The young man called Pete thanked them both, deposited the beermats in the pocket of his anorak, then did the honourable thing and left them alone.

'What number did you give him?' asked Tino. Stegs told him, and a smile cracked the Dutchman's features. 'Man, you are one hell of a good actor, Mark. Just like that dolt Trevor.' He shook his head, the smile disappearing as he remembered the position he was in. 'I cannot believe that he did this to me. Did you put pressure on him to make him betray me?'

Stegs shook his head. 'He rang me up and volunteered the information. He makes money out of betraying people. We pay him when his information secures us a conviction.'

'The bastard! I show him kindness and this is how he pays me. By being a, what is it you call it?'

'A grass.'

'A grass, yes. It doesn't seem right.'

'And it isn't right. And I think you might get the opportunity to pay him back in kind.'

For the first time, Tino eyed Stegs with something akin to suspicion. 'What do you get out of all this, Mark? You are a policeman, no? So why help me?'

'Because you're going to do something for me, Tino.'

'What am I going to do?'

Stegs pulled a photograph of a girl of about twenty from the pocket of his jacket. In the photo, she was standing in what looked like a central London street with high buildings on either side, dressed in winter clothing and smiling at the camera. Judy Flanagan wasn't particularly pretty, but there was something natural in her expression that gave her a certain attractiveness. Her cheeks were rosy, her smile genuine, and her whole demeanour that of a young, well-educated, middle-class girl who was almost certainly kind to animals and fellow human beings in equal measure, and who probably bought the *Big Issue* from one of the homeless with a smile and a thank you. Her hooter was a bit of a let-down, though. Wide and flattened, with splayed nostrils, just like her old man's.

'Who is this chick?' asked Tino, inspecting the photo carefully like he was searching for the hidden prize. 'She has a strange nose.'

'She's someone I want you to get to know. And when you get to know her, which is going to happen very quickly, I want you to take her away for a couple of days.'

Tino gave him a confused look. 'Why, my man?'

There was silence for a few moments as Stegs finished his pint. Then, taking his time, he lit a cigarette and explained.

# 18

Saturday began just like any other working day for those of us on the O'Brien case.

The Met's detection rate for murders has come under a lot of criticism in recent years, with clear-up rates of a little over seventy per cent lagging far behind those of the rest of the country, mainly because there are too many murders and, given the trend among CID for early retirement, not enough senior detectives. So when you had an increasingly high-profile double-killing (the papers that morning had finally picked up on the fact that Robbie O'Brien was linked to the botched operation at Heathrow), those officers involved were expected to pull out all the stops.

At the murder squad meeting that morning, Flanagan informed us that he had another news conference set for eleven a.m. to try to, as he said, play down the connection between Slim Robbie and the events of Wednesday. On the one hand, such a connection raised the profile of the case and therefore made it easier to appeal to potential witnesses, but this was outweighed by the fear that those witnesses might well end up keeping quiet if they thought there was some strong 'organized crime' element to what had been going on. No-one wants to make themselves a target or end up lost in a witness protection programme, and Flanagan was as aware of this as anyone, and was acting accordingly. I also don't suppose he was vastly keen on the idea of an intrepid reporter finding out that the man who'd led and planned Operation Surgical Strike was also the one leading the O'Brien murder inquiry, but his demeanour (tenser and more strained than it had been the previous day) suggested that he didn't discount it as a possibility.

However, he was also excited about our new and potentially ground-breaking lead: the first description of the killer. At last we had something to go on. 'We're going to bring the witness in this morning to see if we can get some sort of e-fit together,' he explained. 'I don't know how good a likeness we're going to get, she didn't see him for long, but you never know. As soon as we've got something, we'll knock on every door within a quarter-mile radius and see if the face rings any bells. I've been promised the use of thirty uniforms, but even so it's going to take a while. There's a lot of houses in that part of Islington.'

Next, Flanagan moved on to the material I'd spotted hanging from the rusty nail. Apparently, there wasn't much of it, but tests at the Forensic Science Laboratory in Lambeth were still continuing to see if there was any way of identifying the make, and therefore where it might have been sold. 'They haven't been able to pinpoint it yet,' he told us, 'and even the forensics guys aren't miracle workers. It was only about an inch of cloth, and that's not a lot to go on, but it is top priority down there.'

Flanagan was right, it wasn't a lot to go on, but at least on this case the resources were going to be there.

The meeting continued with members of the squad bandying about ideas for widening the search and trying to see if there was any angle we hadn't covered yet. I mentioned the weapon used. 'Is it possible it was used before? Has anyone checked HOLMES to see if it might have been?'

As yet, no-one had, though Flanagan wasn't especially confident that it was going to turn up anything, particularly as we'd yet to recover the gun itself. 'He was a pro, the man who did this, as much as anyone who kills people is a pro. But the point is, he's been careful all the way down the line so I can't see him using a dirty weapon. It will need to be checked out, though, just in case the bullets used can be matched with any that have been fired in separate incidents. I know that the Forensic Science Service did ballistics tests at the crime scene. Speak to Roy Catherwood down at Lambeth, can you? He's the one who'll be in charge of documenting all the results.'

I said I would.

'Also, sir,' said Tina, 'if he is a pro, then he's going to have done something like this before, isn't he?'

Flanagan nodded severely, not even looking at her. 'Good thinking,' he said, which, with him, was about the best compliment you were going to get. 'Take a look through HOLMES, see if there's any other killings with the same MO in London in the past three years, and if any of them throw up a description of the killer.'

Tina said she would, then brought up what she'd found out about Stegs Jenner's partnership with Jeff Benson, his former colleague in SO10, and how it had ended with the latter's cover being blown. 'It's possible he betrayed a colleague once, so he could easily have done it again. Which means he's got be worth considering as a suspect for leaking the details of Operation Surgical Strike.'

Flanagan nodded, not looking too displeased with what Tina had said, which wasn't surprising. 'Mr Jenner still has some questions to answer, but at the moment we haven't got an adequate motive for him, or any real evidence. Keep digging, though, and something might come up. And that goes for all of you. Keep digging. We're unearthing clues. They might be few and far between, but the harder we work at it, the more we'll turn up.'

So dig we did. I didn't see much of Tina that weekend. We were like ships passing in the night. When she wasn't on HOLMES, the police major inquiries database, going through old cases, she was involved in tracking down local Islington-based informants to see if they could throw any light on a possible relationship between Robbie O'Brien and Nicholas Tyndall and his associates – not that she had a great deal of success.

Meanwhile, the internal investigation into what had happened at Heathrow was also gathering pace, and I was contacted by DCS8, Scotland Yard's successor to the Complaints Investigation Bureau, or CIB, to set up a meeting, which was arranged for Monday. I'd heard from Malik that they'd pretty much exonerated Flanagan already, since it seemed he'd done every-thing he could to ensure that the op had run smoothly, and it made me wonder whether they were going to end up concluding that somehow O'Brien had found out the venue and had simply sold that information on, which seemed just a little bit convenient for me.

By late Saturday afternoon there was a further breakthrough in the case. The material left behind on the rusty nail had yielded results. It turned out that it contained a tiny portion of the jacket's inner label, and an eagle-eyed employee had identified it as belonging to Louis Desmarches, a suit manufacturer whose clothing was only sold through a fairly small and supposedly exclusive number of retail outlets. After further tests to determine the dyes and materials used in the manufacture of the suit, the FSS had contacted Desmarches to see if they could identify the batch from which it had come. Although there wasn't enough evidence to specify the exact batch, it was possible, the company's representative explained, to state categorically that the material recovered from the crime scene belonged to a Desmarches charcoal-grey suit jacket (it could have been either single- or double-breasted) manufactured between March 2001 and December 2002. A list of outlets that sold such suits in the Greater London area was immediately despatched from Desmarches to the FSS, and then from the FSS to us.

You always need a little luck in any murder investigation, and it seemed we'd got some here. Not a huge amount, granted, but no copper worth his or her salt minds putting in the hours when you're actually heading in the right direction.

For my part, then, much of the weekend entailed working with a number of other officers from the team contacting those outlets (many of which, being London-based, were open on Sundays) and getting hold of the records of sales made of those particular suits, and the names of the purchasers. At the same time, I was chasing Roy Catherwood, one of the FSS's senior firearms consultants at Lambeth, for anything he could give me on the bullets found at the scene of the murder. Not surprisingly, given that he was dealing with the use of guns in the commission of crime throughout Greater London, he was extremely busy, plus he liked to have a bit of time off now and again, so progress in that quarter was slower than I would have liked.

By ten o'clock on Monday morning it had been confirmed that 104 suits matching the description given by the Desmarches representative had been sold in Greater London since they'd first gone on sale in March 2001, and now the task of tracking down the purchasers began. Like I said earlier, there's a lot of legwork, and no shortage of dead-ends either. I was spared getting involved in this last lot, however, by my interview with DCS8, which took place at Scotland Yard that morning, and by what happened immediately afterwards.

It was half-twelve when I got back to the station, and I was hungry. I phoned Tina to see if she was in the vicinity and wanted to meet up for lunch, but she wasn't answering, so I made my way up to the incident room. It was nearly empty, with only a handful of detectives and support staff in front of their PCs, but I spotted Malik among them and was just about to ask if he fancied popping out for a pie and a pint when my desk extension rang.

'Good timing,' I said, striding over and picking it up.

I recognized the voice at the other end straight away. I'd never met Roy Catherwood but could tell from the shortness of breath and the gravel in his voice that he was both a heavy smoker and a big eater, and probably not destined for a hundredth-birthday telegram from the Queen. He was a nice enough guy, though, and engagingly jovial, as is more common than people think among those who work in the science of violent death.

'Hello, Roy,' I said, crossing my fingers, though more in hope than in expectation. 'Have you got anything for me?'

'Do you know what?' he rasped in reply. 'I think I actually do.'

He sounded as surprised as me. He hadn't been all that hopeful that without the gun itself it would be possible to tell whether it had actually been used before, particularly as all three slugs recovered from the murder scene had been badly damaged by the impact of being fired point-blank through human bone and tissue.

'Well, go on.'

'I've been checking through our database of .38 bullets fired in the commission of crimes for the past year, and there's a case – a recent one at that – that stands out.' I didn't say anything so he continued. 'A domestic incident over in Paddington a couple of weeks back. Someone – it says here, a man – fired a shot into the ceiling of a flat while in dispute with its tenant, a woman he'd apparently been having a relationship with. I've checked the striation marks between our bullets and the bullet that was recovered from the ceiling and they're remarkably similar – so similar, in fact, that I'm convinced they came from the same gun.'

The striation marks on a bullet are the microscopic scratches caused by imperfections on the surface of the interior of a gun's barrel that are unique to each individual firearm, and act as its calling card. The same striation marks will appear on a bullet every time a particular gun is fired.

'If the incident had been months ago, I don't know if I'd have spotted it,' he continued. 'At least not for a while anyway. It's because I was working backwards, and it was so recent, that I did.'

'How sure are you?' I asked, thinking that this didn't quite sound right. A hitman using his weapon in a domestic dispute?

'Very,' he answered with a wheeze and a huff. 'All the cartridges involved are badly damaged, but there's no mistaking it. I'd say that the match is ninety-nine per cent. Not good enough for some courts of law, unfortunately, but it ought to be something to be going along with. I've got the name of the DI involved in the case if you want it.'

'That'd be great. Thanks, Roy.'

He gave me the number and I thanked him again, saying I'd be back in touch shortly.

'Yeah, I bet,' he snorted. 'That's what they all say.'

I got straight through to DI Seamus Daly at Paddington Green nick and he gave me a rundown of what had happened. 'The name of the shooter, or alleged shooter as he'll have you believe, is Robert Panner. He's a small-time pimp – a bit of an Ali G type, a white man who thinks he's black – who operates round Paddington station. He'd been in a relationship of sorts with the tenant of the flat, a Miss Fiona Ragdale, and had her on the streets earning for him. Apparently, she'd been trying to quit, there'd been some arguments, and then one night a couple of weeks back he turned up and put a bullet in the ceiling. She called us, but he went AWOL and we didn't catch up with him until last week. He was nicked, but any sulphur traces from the gun on his fingers had disappeared. He's on bail at the moment, pending further enquiries.'

'What about the gun itself?'

'Couldn't find it, and Panner denied everything. Said it must have been someone else, and I don't know how easy it's going to be to get charges to stick. It's his word against hers, and she's been on the pipe and got a few convictions of her own, so she's not exactly reliable.'

I told Daly the nature of the case we were investigating and asked him if he thought Panner could possibly be the shooter.

'Well, the description fits roughly. He's about the right age, he's got black hair and he's definitely a nasty bit of work. He's got a record for theft, drugs, and ABH and GBH, so he's definitely capable of some serious violence.'

'But?'

'But he's small-time, and a bit of a dopehead to boot. In the end, I can't see anyone hiring him for an important murder. He might have the right temperament, but I can't see him shooting dead two people, then being savvy enough to tidy up for himself afterwards. He's a typical criminal really. Not very bright, and fairly predictable.'

'Fair enough,' I said, then asked him a few more questions and arranged to fax over the e-fit of our suspect for comparison, before ringing off.

Malik had come over and was leaning against my desk. 'What have you got?' he asked.

'A lead, but I'm not sure where it's going to take us.' I told him briefly what I'd heard while he listened in silence.

He looked pleased. 'Well, let's have a look at him. Bring his details up on the system and see how well he matches the e-fit.'

I logged on to the PNC database, fed in the relevant details Daly had given me and, after a few seconds, the black and white mugshot of a young man with a thin, pallid face, defiant eyes and unkempt, greasy black hair stared back at me. At first glance it looked as if he was snarling at the camera, but on closer inspection I could see that he had a harelip. A wispy, untidy moustache did little to conceal it.

'Nice-looking lad.' Malik chuckled.

'It's amazing,' I said. 'He couldn't be anything but a criminal. Whoever said you should never judge a book by its cover should come here and take a look at this guy.'

'But is he our man?'

'I don't remember the e-fit of the suspect being this ugly.'

Malik stepped across to his desk, picked up a hardcopy of the suspect e-fit and put it up next to Panner on the screen. It wasn't exactly a close match, but the hair colour, age and facial features were similar, although the hairstyle (if you could call Panner's dishevelled mop a style) was markedly different. The e-fit suspect's hair was curlier and shorter.

We both stared at the two pictures for a moment. 'Inconclusive,' said Malik eventually. 'It says here that Panner's five feet nine inches, which fits within the witness's height range, but it's difficult to tell.'

'If they are one and the same then she was being very flattering in her description.'

'We don't know how good her eyesight is. Are you and Tina going to check this lead out?'

'I can't get hold of her at the moment. I know she's got a lot on. How about you coming with me?'

'I've got a lot on myself.'

'Come on. We could do with some quality time together.'

'The last time I spent quality time with you was Heathrow last week, and five people ended up shot.'

'Well, it can only be an improvement, then.' I stood up. 'Let's grab a bite first. I'm starving.'

'All right,' he said, putting the hardcopy back on his desk. 'It's a good enough lead to warrant some effort, I suppose.'

We took a bit of a stroll and went to a pub called the Dragon which served good food all day, according to the sign outside the door. I bought Malik an orange juice and, trusting him not to give me any trouble over it, a pint of Greene Man for myself. We also ordered our food, going Dutch this time (I don't get paid enough to be too generous), then found ourselves a table by the door. I plumped for the lasagne, with a green salad; Malik, the home-made steak and kidney pie with veg and mash.

'So,' he said, watching me take a healthy mouthful of beer, 'have you got an address for Panner?'

I nodded. 'If he's no longer there, he'll be in breach of his probation. I've got the victim's, Ragdale's, address on there too. Perhaps she could throw some light on whether or not he's a hitman on the side.'

'If he is, he's not a very good one.'

'That's my concern, because I'm sure our man is. But three

weeks ago Panner was in possession of that gun. So at the very least he can point us in the right direction.'

Malik nodded. 'Tell me something,' he said, sitting back in his seat and giving me a smile. 'Are you and Tina Boyd an item?'

His question caught me completely off guard, which I suppose it was designed to, and I made the mistake of hesitating for a second. 'No, course not,' I said lamely. 'What makes you say that?'

'There's something in the way you look at each other. It's very subtle, but it's there for definite. Either you're an item, or you definitely fancy her like mad. It's one or the other.' He sipped his orange knowingly.

'I fancy her,' I said with a smile. 'But as far as I know, the feeling's not mutual.'

'It is, I think.'

'Christ, who are you? Dr Ruth? Our relationship is purely platonic, I promise you. I always keep my working relationships above board, it's a long-standing habit of mine.' I felt bad lying to him, because we got on well and I'd come to count on him as a friend in the time since we'd met on the Holtz case, but I knew it would be more than my life's worth for Tina to find out I'd let the cat out of the bag.

'It's a pity,' he said. 'I think you'd make a good couple. You look right together.'

'Thank you, Cupid.'

'I'm serious. You do. Maybe you should think about it. A relationship'd do you good.'

'What do you mean?'

He was about to answer and give me another piece of domestic advice when his mobile rang. He pulled it out and started talking, getting up from the table at the same time and walking out the door. I watched him go, taking another drink of my beer and thinking that usually I didn't like being lectured by anyone, particularly colleagues, but with Malik I was prepared to make an exception. Mainly because I could tell he genuinely meant what he said, and was motivated by all the right reasons. In fact, I'd wanted to come right out and tell him that Tina and I were together and were very happy too, because I knew it would please him, but the moment was gone, and maybe that was for the best. I wasn't sure I liked the comment that a relationship would do me good, though. Especially as I was in one.

'Anything interesting?' I asked him when he came back a couple of minutes later.

He sat down and put the phone away. 'Your friend and mine, Mr Jack Merriweather. Apparently, he wants conjugal visits.'

Jack Merriweather. Now there was someone I hadn't thought about in a while. Thanks to Malik's and my efforts, he was currently behind bars in London's maximum-security Belmarsh prison, and was to be the main prosecution witness in the upcoming trial of a number of associates of the Holtz crime family, including its most senior surviving member, Neil Vamen. Merriweather had been a Holtz man through and through, and had only escaped a very long prison sentence because he'd agreed to testify against his old friends and bosses.

'He wants conjugal visits? Who from?'

'His mistress, apparently. A hatchet-faced blonde called Cheryl who's older than he is and about as attractive as our man Panner.'

'Christ, that's saying something.'

'Believe me, it's true. Apparently, he's been seeing her for years, and she hasn't been put off by his latest predicament.'

'He's not going to get visits just like that, is he? That really would damage what's left of my faith in the criminal justice system.'

Malik shook his head. 'Apart from anything else, it'd be too much of a security risk.'

'What do you mean?'

He leant forward, lowering his voice. 'Between you and me, Merriweather's no longer in Belmarsh. He's in a safe house. Has been for the past two weeks. Ever since someone tried to kill him.'

'So Vamen hasn't thrown in the towel just yet?'

'Did you think he would? Men like him are survivors, John. They don't give up until they're underground. Vamen wants Merriweather out of the way, and he's going to keep trying until he's succeeded.'

'Is Merriweather all right?'

He nodded. 'He was lucky, though. It was a very near miss. A paedophile on the same segregation wing attacked him with a sharpened lamb chop bone, of all things. Tried to jam it in his neck while they were out in the exercise yard. He managed to slash him but Merriweather's quite handy with his fists and he managed to fight the guy off until the warders broke it up.'

'A lamb chop?' That was certainly a new one.

'If the attacker had got a clean shot, and some power behind it, it could easily have killed him. It was solid bone.'

'It's not exactly hi-tech. Was it definitely an organized hit?'

'The assailant's not saying anything, but it was a completely unprovoked attack, and there was no history at all between the two of them. And that's not the end of it. While Merriweather was recovering in the prison hospital someone put ground glass in his food. Luckily for him his appetite had been affected by what had happened, and the stuff they were feeding him wasn't exactly gourmet, so he only had a couple of bites. He didn't like the taste, said there was something wrong with it, and spat the stuff out. That's when someone put two and two together and checked it. They found enough in there to have ripped his insides to shreds. And it was professionally ground down as well, almost into dust. He could have eaten a fair bit without realizing what was wrong. Whoever was behind it took a lot of trouble getting it ready.'

I sighed, concerned by what I was hearing. You think that when you've nicked someone and built a decent case against them, then that's pretty much that. But in reality all we had against Vamen was the testimony of Jack Merriweather and those handful of witnesses prepared to follow his example and point their fingers at him for past crimes. If Merriweather was silenced, then so would they be, you could bank on it. And without them there was nothing like enough evidence to secure a conviction.

'So, he's not got any second thoughts about testifying?'

'He's doing fine now we've got him out of Belmarsh and into a nice little pad in the country. He's moaning that he wants every creature comfort going, and even Cheryl to come and play happy families, but he's holding up, and that's the main thing. This is classified information, though, John. Only a handful of people know about it, and even fewer are aware of the location. Don't mention any of it to anyone. Not even Tina.'

'I won't. I promise.'

A plump girl carrying two plates of steaming food came out from behind the bar and shouted out our number. I lifted my hand to acknowledge her and she came over and dumped them down in front of us.

We ate largely in silence, both of us hungry, but as I finished, a thought suddenly struck me. 'Do you think what's happening with Merriweather's got anything to do with our case?' I pushed my empty plate to one side. 'I mean, there's what Tina found out about Stegs Jenner and his possible involvement with the

Holtzes. If he was somehow involved in the leaking of the Heathrow op . . .'

Malik didn't look convinced. 'There's no evidence against Jenner, nothing at all, and he seems to be co-operating fully. Plus, as Flanagan points out, there is the problem of motive.'

I nodded slowly, thinking. I'd been doing a lot of thinking these past few days. 'But there could be a motive if we assume that Stegs is still working for the Holtzes, or at least for Neil Vamen.'

Malik's eyes narrowed. 'Explain.'

'Well, say, Stegs uses O'Brien to set up the robbery at the airport hotel, knowing full well the robbers'll get caught, thus implicating their boss, Nicholas Tyndall, and causing him no end of trouble – that would be a very nice outcome for Neil Vamen, wouldn't it? A potentially very serious rival in the shit, which is effectively what's happened, and if he can get rid of Merriweather at the same time, a chance to be back out on the streets and in complete charge of his old manor.'

Malik thought about it for a few moments, taking the odd pensive sip of his orange juice, which seemed to be lasting an unfeasibly long time. 'Part of it fits, but there are still unanswered questions,' he said eventually. 'Such as, why would Stegs put himself in such a dangerous position, which he undoubtedly did, for someone like Vamen? Also, we're assuming that Vamen's positive he's going to get out of jail, otherwise why would he bother trying to set up Tyndall? And why put his old friends, the Colombians, out of business?'

I finished my pint and placed the glass carefully on the table. 'Something's going down, though, Asif. I'm sure of it.'

# 19

Fiona Ragdale was pale and skinny, with bottle-blonde hair show-ing dark roots. She looked older than the twenty-three years she claimed to be, and tired too, but then she did have a hyperactive three-year-old boy jumping all over her. 'Leave it, Jack,' she said, swatting him away with an arm that was dotted with bruises. 'I'm talking to these men. Go and play with your train set.'

She turned back to us as Jack ran off towards the other side of the room. 'I ain't seen him since that night,' she said. 'And I hope I never see him again. Not after what he did to us.'

We were sitting opposite her in the lounge of her cramped tenth-floor flat on the Warwick estate, a collection of monolithic 1960s council-owned tower blocks overlooking the A40 flyover, just west of Paddington station. Malik and I were hunched together on the tiny semi-collapsed sofa, trying desperately to stay upright, while she was hunched forward in a matching chair that looked like it had been savaged by a dog. The room itself was tidy but cold, and it badly needed a new coat of paint. The hole in the ceiling where Panner had fired the all-important round was still clearly visible, surrounded by long spider's-web cracks in the plaster.

Malik made a manful attempt to lean forward in his rapidly sinking seat. 'He hasn't attempted to make contact at all since?'

She shook her head. 'No. I thought he would. Usually when he threatens something, he comes back to finish it off. Maybe he reckoned he'd gone too far, what with the gun an' all.'

'Gun!' shouted Jack happily, coming back over and standing in front of Malik and me. 'Gun! Gun! Gun!' I gave him a brief smile and he continued his running round the room. I thought it was tough on the little kid, being cooped up high above the ground when he should have been outside playing.

'I'm not working the streets no more, all that stuff's behind me. And I'm clean too. I ain't touched a thing since January.' She looked us both in the eye as she said this, and there was an unmistakable pride in her voice. 'That's why he was so pissed off with me.'

'You're doing the right thing,' I told her, hoping she'd be able to keep it up.

Malik pulled the e-fit of our suspect from his jacket and passed it over to her. 'Can you tell us if Mr Panner looks anything like this?'

She checked the picture out for a couple of seconds, then her face lit up with a surprisingly pleasant smile. 'Nah, it don't look nothing like him. This bloke might not be real but he's a lot better looking. And his hair's shorter.'

I asked her if she was sure.

'Ain't you got a photo of Pretty Boy?'

'Who?'

'Panner. That's his street name. Pretty Boy. I think someone was taking the piss.'

'I think you're right. Yes, I have seen a photo of him. I was just double-checking.'

It had been the answer we'd been anticipating. On the way over here we'd checked with the incident room to see if Panner's name appeared on the list of Desmarches suit owners, and it hadn't. It still wasn't conclusive proof that Panner and our killer weren't one and the same, but it was getting close to it.

Malik took back the e-fit, and now it was his turn to speak again. 'You said just now that you thought he might have gone too far by coming here and firing a gun. Was that the first time you'd ever seen him with a firearm, then?'

She gave a barely perceptible nod. 'Yeah, it was.'

'But he'd hit you before?'

'Oh yeah,' she said matter-of-factly, as if this was par for the course in her life. 'He used to knock me about quite a lot, especially if I wasn't making enough money for him, or I was threatening to quit. But this was different.'

'I can imagine.'

'No, not like that. It's just that normally he works himself up before he does it. You know, shouts about, smashes a couple of things. But this time he was only in here two minutes before he pulled the gun. He waved it in my face, then fired it into the ceiling.' She shuddered. 'I couldn't believe it. And in front of Jack as well, poor kid. Scared him shitless. He was crying all night.'

'What happened at that point?' asked Malik. 'After he'd fired the gun.'

'Well, that was it. He told me not to say anything to anyone about what he'd just done, then he turned round and walked out. Didn't say another word. It was weird.'

Malik and I glanced at each other. She was right. It was weird, and just more confirmation that Panner wasn't our man. He was just too much of an amateur. But then, if he wasn't, who the hell was?

'He didn't say anything about you going back to work for him, then?' I asked.

Jack was shouting again – something unintelligible but loud, in a futile bid to get attention – and I had to repeat the question. She told him to be quiet, then turned back to me.

'He did when he first came in, yeah. Told me that he was sick of me pissing him about, but he didn't go on about it like he normally did.'

Malik changed the line of questioning. 'Do you know if he ever did anything else for money?'

She said he dealt crack and blow now and again, and occasionally smack, but that was all, as far as she knew.

'Does he, or did he, carry round large sums of money?'

'He always had a few quid on him, yeah, but then he took money off me, and the other girls he had working for him, plus he made money on the gear, so it ain't really surprising, is it?'

Malik then asked whether there were any occasions when Panner had suddenly come into very large sums of cash, but she said she wasn't sure, didn't think so. He looked at me again, and his expression mirrored my thoughts. He wasn't the O'Brien shooter.

'It's important we find Mr Panner,' I said.

'You've found him already, but you let him go. Even though he pulled a gun on me and Jack, and fired it. It don't exactly make us feel safe, does it?'

'I can't comment on that, Miss Ragdale. It wasn't our inquiry. But if we find him this time, it's very unlikely he'll be seeing anything but prison walls for a good few years to come.'

She managed a cynical smile. 'What's he done this time, then?'

'We can't tell you that at the moment, I'm afraid.'

'Thought not.'

'Can you tell us where you think he might be? We've got his bail address.' I reeled it off to her. 'Any other ideas?'

'I ain't had much to do with him these past couple of months, thank God. I know there were another couple of girls working for him. One was called Nicki, and I think another one was Dora. I dunno where they live, though.' She must have seen the disappointment in our expressions, because she tried to justify herself. 'Honest, I'm not trying to protect him. I hate the bastard. If you do ever get hold of him, I hope you throw away the key, but I honestly can't think where he'll be. He moves around a lot. He's got a lot of enemies, people he owes money to, so he's pretty slippery when he wants to be.'

And that was it really. I stood up, and Malik followed suit.

'Thanks for your time, Miss Ragdale. Bye, Jack.'

Jack shouted a very long 'bye' back, and gave me a wide grin.

Malik pulled a card from the pocket of his suit. 'If you do hear from Mr Panner at any point in the future . . .'

'Don't worry,' she said. 'I'll be on the blower like a shot. I don't want that bastard coming anywhere near us.'

She saw us to the door, and as it shut behind us I suddenly felt very depressed. Ever since childhood, I've always wanted justice for people, and by that I mean seeing that they get the fate they deserve. If another kid at school was bullied for no reason, I'd intervene, because it wasn't fair, and I knew that I couldn't just stand by and do nothing. As a copper, I'd spent the last twenty years intervening in the world around me, trying to create an illusion of fairness, but what depressed me now was that I could see no justice here and, worse, I could do nothing about it either. I was leaving behind a young woman and her son to live their lonely existence in a cramped little flat high above the ground, forgotten by the world around them, except when it came calling with threats and violence, and I couldn't help wondering how long it would be before Fiona Ragdale ended up hawking herself for another pimp and escaping reality by sinking back into the dope. And what, then, would happen to Jack? A pimp and a thug in the making? A care-home kid? A street runaway dead by fifteen? Or maybe it would be a story with a happy ending. Such things are always possible, I suppose, but somehow I didn't think so. The thing with me is that I'm a pessimist who's constantly trying to be optimistic, but can't quite manage it. Experience gained through years of policework doesn't allow for that sort of naivety.

I thought about saying something to Malik about how I was feeling, but decided against it. Sometimes these things are best kept to yourself. Perhaps I could buy Jack something, or send them some money. But I knew I was deluding myself. I'd forget about the two of them soon enough, when the next crisis or tragedy came calling.

When we were back on street level, Malik pulled his mobile from his pocket and called the DCS while we made our way through the subway that led under the main road outside the Warwick estate in the direction of Royal Oak Underground station. A watery, early-spring sun fought its way out from behind the clouds as we crossed the wrought-iron bridge that passed over the train tracks heading into Paddington, and I suddenly got that uplifting feeling that the worst of the winter was over and that summer was coming.

We got back to where the car we'd brought was parked at a meter in the somewhat grander ambience of Porchester Square, a few hundred yards and a million miles away from the tower block where we'd just been, and Malik finished talking to Flanagan and hung up. 'He's very pleased with the Panner lead,' he said, as we got in and I started the engine. 'The pressure's beginning to get too much on this one. He's doing a press conference down at Scotland Yard in half an hour, just to keep everyone in the media up to date with our progress. I think he was getting a bit worried about it. Now with this, he's going to tell them that we're following up on several significant leads, which should keep them quiet for a day or two.'

'What's he want us to do?' I said, turning on to the Bishops Bridge Road.

'Get over to Panner's bail address and keep an eye on the place, just until he gets a chance to set up a team from SO11 to put him under surveillance properly. But it's going to take a couple of hours. If he decides to leave the premises, we're to follow him discreetly, see what he gets up to. At the moment, it's only about evidence-gathering. We're not to apprehend him, unless we catch him in the commission of a serious crime.'

'No problem.'

'What the hell's that?'

'What?'

'Over there. Slow down.'

I looked to where Malik was pointing. On the other side of the road, in front of the railings that separated the pavement from the grounds of Paddington's Hallfield estate, a group of four men were fighting. It looked like it was one against the rest, and the one was having a bit of a hard time of it. He took a punch to the head and went down, disappearing behind a parked car, allowing the others to deliver a series of unseen kicks in his direction.

I slammed on the brakes, coming to a skidding halt twenty yards away from the action, and shoved on the hazards. Malik produced his mobile phone and called for back-up, and at the same time we both jumped out of the car. The vehicle behind us did an emergency stop and gave a continuous blast of the horn, but I was already running for the other side of the road, waving my warrant card in all directions, Malik's footsteps sounding close behind.

'Stop, police!' I yelled, unsure what else to say. It's rare these days that I come across a crime actually taking place in front of me, so it's not something I have to practise a lot. I'd almost forgotten the adrenalin rush you get when you suddenly shove yourself in the path of danger.

I was now less than ten yards away and the three men, all eastern European in appearance, turned to face me, their expressions ones of surprise rather than fear. I could see why. One of them was holding a wicked-looking claw hammer in his hand, claw facing outwards, and they also had the numerical advantage. I slowed down, knowing that if they didn't run Malik and I were both in trouble. Neither of us was armed and neither of us was in a position to bring this situation to a swift end, other than through the force of our personalities.

'Police!' I shouted again, still coming forward, speeding up again now, knowing that any obvious hesitation would be fatal. 'You're all under arrest.'

One of them aimed another kick at their unfortunate victim, shouting something in a language I didn't understand, and then, without warning, all three turned and made a dash for it up the road. I ran up onto the pavement, gave a half-hearted five-yard chase – more to make sure they didn't come back than anything else (I'll be straight: there was no way I was tackling a man with a claw hammer when he was hot-footing it in the opposite direction) – then turned in the direction of the victim, who was being pulled to his feet by Malik, one hand covering his face where he'd been kicked.

He looked familiar, but then he would have done: I'd seen his photograph often enough that day, although he was a lot bulkier in the flesh. Malik recognized Robert 'Pretty Boy' Panner at exactly the same time, and took his arm, starting to speak.

Panner might have taken a bit of a beating but he didn't appear too much the worse for wear, and his eyes widened as he realized who we were. Knowing he might make a run for it, I took a step forward to secure his other arm, but before I could reach him he lashed out, hitting Malik in the gut, then swung him bodily against the bonnet of the nearest car. Malik's not the biggest of guys, and he went straight over it. I jumped forward, trying to grab Panner's jacket, but he was a fast mover and did a nice little ballet-style twirl before accelerating away down the pavement in the direction of Paddington station.

I looked over at Malik, saw that he was OK as he clambered up from behind the car, then took off after Panner. He might have been fast, and obviously keen to get away, but I was also very keen to catch him, and now that I'd started going to the gym (albeit erratically) in an effort to get myself fit again and impress Tina, I thought I was in with a chance.

But clearly my fitness regime needed some improving because Panner had the edge and slowly but surely he opened up a gap between us, helped no doubt by the fact that a group of schoolkids across the street were enthusiastically cheering him on. Whatever happened to rooting for the good guys?

As he came to the north-eastern corner of the Hallfield, he turned into Gloucester Terrace. There were ten yards between us now, twelve when I had to dodge an old lady who looked like she was trying to cut me off. Or maybe it was just that I was getting suspicious of everyone. I rounded the corner and saw another schoolkid lying on the pavement where Panner had evidently knocked him over. He was surrounded by a group of his mates who were all staring after the fugitive's rapidly disappearing figure. That bastard could have been a promising athlete if he'd put his mind to it, instead of spending his days pimping, threatening women and children, and getting beaten up. He had a natural swiftness of foot that made it look like there was lead in my brogues. But I was going to get him, I was sure of that.

'Police! Out the way!'

The group scattered, but the kid on the ground sat up and tried to crawl away, and I was forced to jump over him, losing my footing as I landed back on the pavement and stumbling forward onto my hands and knees. Behind me I heard laughter, but I didn't have time to worry about that as I ran on, my breathing getting heavier all the time as the full enormity of my unfitness finally became apparent.

Up ahead – twenty yards away at least, probably more – Panner had stopped by a battered old BMW and was fishing round in his pocket for the key. I made a final burst, ignoring the pain in my lungs, knowing that I'd hardly have the strength to stand up, let alone nick him, by the time we were face to face, but knowing that I couldn't stop. Glory beckoned.

He found the key, opened the door and jumped inside. I was ten yards away now. The engine coughed and roared into life, and he reversed straight into the car behind him, smashing its headlights. Eight yards, six, four . . . He turned the wheel as far as it would go, at the same time moving forward, but a car coming the other way prevented him from pulling out. Two yards, one, and then I was pulling open the door and yelling at him to stop, reaching for the keys.

The other car passed, and Panner slammed his foot on the accelerator and roared out on to the road, with me clinging desperately to the door as my legs were dragged from under me. I had to make a split-second decision, and I made it.

'You fucker!' I screamed at the side of Robert Panner's head, then I let go of the door and tumbled hard onto the road, rolling over and praying that any traffic coming my way would have enough time to stop, all too aware that grabbing hold of speeding cars rarely results in a happy ending.

I heard the shriek of brakes, loud in my ears. A car stopped much too near, and there was the sound of a metallic impact combined with the shattering of lights as another car hit it from behind, shunting it forward. I could smell the heat of the engine, my eyes remaining tight shut, hands covering my head, my shoulder burning where it had struck the tarmac.

Slowly, very slowly, I opened my eyes. The driver's-side tyre of the lead car was a foot from my head. I didn't know whether to laugh or cry.

We were at the scene for more than an hour. Back-up had duly arrived a few minutes later but Panner was long gone, and I hadn't been able to get the registration of the car he was driving. I also had to act as witness in the three-car crash caused by my rolling about in the road, having been rudely ejected from Panner's BMW, and had to give my details to a succession of drivers most of whom didn't seem to understand why I'd felt the need to act like Jackie Chan, all the time rubbing my injured shoulder in a vain attempt to gain even a modicum of sympathy.

In the end, I'd been seen by a doctor at St Mary's who'd put some antiseptic cream on the wound before patching it up, and finally we were in a position to drive back to the station. Now that Panner had committed a serious crime while violently resist-ing arrest, Flanagan had decreed that he should be brought in as soon as he was apprehended. A surveillance team from SO11 would still set up shop outside his bail address but it was thought unlikely he'd head back there now that he was aware the police wanted to talk to him. I only hoped that we hadn't messed up by giving him advance warning of our interest. If he was as slippery as Fiona Ragdale had suggested, then he wasn't going to be easy to find.

'I think we're lovers, not fighters, Asif,' I told Malik as we were heading down the Euston Road in the direction of the station. Traffic was heavy, bordering on ludicrous, and progress predictably slow.

'I prefer to see us as the brains rather than the brawn,' he said with a smile.

I think we both felt vaguely humiliated that we'd been out-fought and outrun by a low-life pimp who'd already taken something of a beating himself, but neither of us said anything. Sometimes that's just the way it goes.

My mobile rang. It was Tina. She was back at the incident room, had heard what had happened and wanted to know how I was. 'I think I'll live,' I told her, and almost let slip that my injuries wouldn't affect my performance in the bedroom before realizing just in time that I had company.

'Panner wasn't driving a Megane by any chance, was he?'

'No, an ancient BMW. Why?'

'I think I might have a lead.'

'Let's hear it.'

'You know I've been going back on HOLMES looking for similar cases to the O'Brien hit? Well, there was an unsolved murder at the beginning of last year in a pub car park in Harrow. The victim was a garage owner called Paul Bailey who owed money to a lot of people. He was shot twice in the head at point-blank range with a .38 revolver, and was dead before he even knew what was happening. A couple coming out of the pub at the same time caught a glimpse of the killer, as did a man walk-ing his dog, and a woman driving past. The descriptions were sketchy but they all tallied with what we've got for the O'Brien killer. Dark hair, late twenties, five ten to six two. I reckon it's got to be the same one.'

'Could well be.'

'But that's not all, John. The man walking his dog was further down the road from the pub. He heard the shots and saw a man hurrying down in his direction on foot. Before the man got to him, he got into a car that was parked up and drove off. The car passed directly by the dog walker and, because he was concerned about the shots, he made a mental note of the model and registration. The plates turned out to be false, but the car was an old-style black Renault Megane coupé, and the investigating team made a list of every black Megane coupé owner in Greater London with that particular model.'

'Christ. How many was that?'

'A lot. Three thousand three hundred and twelve in all, including, I expect, plenty of dark-haired young men, and to be honest, nothing ever came of it. With that many people there were only the resources to speak to those with a criminal record, and in the absence of any other evidence the case finally ground to a halt. But if that list contains our man, and he also comes up on the list we've got of people who bought Desmarches suits, then . . .' She let the sentence trail off, the meaning clear.

'You're on a roll, Tina. Well done.'

'Thanks. It's good to know we're getting somewhere.'

'Changing your mind about retiring, then?'

'That was last week. Things have moved on since then, and anyway, it's a woman's prerogative to change her mind.'

'So, you've spoken to Harrow CID?'

'They're going to fax me over the list.'

'Great. I'll give you a hand going through it when I get back.'

After we'd said our goodbyes, I told Malik what she'd found out.

'The clues are appearing with a bit more frequency now,' he said. 'Which is what we need. I just wonder where they're going to lead.'

I nodded in agreement. 'And to who.'

# 20

Stegs was sitting on the lounge sofa alongside the missus. They were watching *Celebrity Wheelchair Challenge* in which three so-called celebrities, for reasons better known to themselves, travelled across the country in wheelchairs in aid of charity, or something like that anyway. Stegs wasn't really paying much attention. The only reason he was sitting there at all was because he didn't know what else to do. He was suffering from writers' block, having spent three hours that day in a pub in Mill Hill trying to pick up where he'd left off at the beginning of chapter three of *Undercover Cop*. Five pints of Stella, a pack of fags and half a gram of speed later, and he'd written about a page of absolute shit. He'd read somewhere that booze and drugs were meant to get the old creative juices flowing, but whoever was claiming that was either a liar or a crap writer.

He'd got home a couple of hours earlier, somewhat the worse for wear, and had had a stand-up row with the missus, who'd smelt the drink on him and had told him that either he got help or she and Luke were leaving. Promises, promises, he'd thought, but hadn't said anything, recognizing that once again he was the one in the wrong. It annoyed him, because the previous day he'd picked up many a brownie point by taking her and Luke on a trip to Odds Farm, a place out in the country near Beaconsfield where kids could go on tractor rides and feed farm animals. Luke was a bit young for it all really, but it made a nice day out, and the weather had been OK, with the sun putting in its first appearance for as long as he could remember.

In a bid to return to the good books, Stegs had gone out and got fish and chips for them both while she'd put Luke to bed, and had bought her a bunch of flowers from the Co-op at the same time. She'd given him a stern look but had accepted them with the beginnings of a smile, and by the time they'd finished eating he'd even begun to sober up as the effects of the speed had worn off. It had been the last of his stuff as well. He was going to have to get some more.

So now he and the missus were back on an even keel and Stegs was bored. Bored and restless. Wanting to get the next stage of his plan moving. It was a risky one, there was no denying that. And one that could get him into a lot of trouble. But as he sat watching Gaby Roslin in her wheelchair looking very irate as a taxi driver ignored her outstretched hand and drove on by, and wondering where the fuck his life was going, he decided that the risk was more than worth it.

'It does annoy you when they don't stop just because someone's handicapped,' said the missus. 'It's not like they don't charge an arm and a leg for a trip anyway.'

'It's not worth taking a leg off her,' said Stegs, 'not when it's in that condition. That's probably why he's not stopping. That, and the fact that it's Gaby Roslin.'

'I'm serious, Mark. It's not right, and it's not a laughing

matter. If you were handicapped, you wouldn't be laughing.'

Stegs immediately regretted speaking out of turn. It was always best simply to agree with the missus. Start contradicting her pronouncements and you ended up in a bigger quagmire than the Americans in Vietnam. And with about as much chance of victory.

'Yeah, you're right,' he said with suitable vagueness. 'I didn't mean it like that.'

He was saved from further admonishments by the sound of the home phone going. It was on the missus's side of the sofa, and she reached over and answered it, quickly immersing herself in conversation. It was her sister. Stegs knew that because the missus kept saying stuff like 'Don't worry, Linda' and 'It'll be all right, Linda, honestly'. He got up and took the opportunity to go outside for a fag.

When he got back inside a few minutes later, the missus had come off the phone.

'What's happened with Linda?' he asked.

She gave him her wide-eyed expression that signified that some sort of minor drama had occurred. 'Well, Clive's away in Abu Dhabi on business and she's just had a crank call. Some man saying he wants to become a porno star and telling her the size of his you-know?' She lowered her eyes in the direction of her groin, just in case he didn't know what she meant by a 'you-know'.

'That's terrible,' said Stegs. 'How big did he say it was?'

She laughed in spite of herself, and he thought he saw a twinkle in her eye. 'Oh, Mark, I'm serious. She's very worried. You know what Linda's like.'

'He didn't threaten her, though, did he?'

'Apparently not; in fact, he was talking like she was someone else. But she said he got very annoyed when she claimed she didn't know what he was going on about. He even told her to fuck off.'

'She'll be all right. The excitement probably did her good. Especially after a few years married to Clive.'

'At least Clive provides,' she said sternly, her good mood evaporating almost as fast as it arrived.

Stegs couldn't help thinking that where his missus was concerned he was incapable of saying the right thing. She lightened up; he spoke; she darkened again.

'Yeah, well,' he said, sitting down. 'He's got to be good for something.'

The conversation dissolved into sullen silence. *Celebrity Wheelchair Challenge* came to an end and the missus went channel hopping across the whole gamut of Sky's satellite offerings, including such gems as *When Good Pets Go Bad* and *Britain's Worst Plumbers Part 2*, before settling on one of the early editions of *Friends*.

The sound of *Mission Impossible* came from the pocket of Stegs's jeans. The missus sighed theatrically and turned up the volume as Ross tried to justify himself to Rachel about something he'd said to Phoebe which had subsequently been misinterpreted. Stegs had seen variations of this sub-plot a hundred times before on *Friends*. He'd liked the programme once, in the old days before the arrival of Luke, when he and the missus would snuggle up on the sofa and watch it with a bag of popcorn and a bottle of wine. Now it had just gone on too long. Like the relationship, really.

He pulled the phone from his pocket and went out into the hallway. If it was that hound Trevor Murk phoning again to find out what was happening with his reward, then he was going to get a serious ear-bashing. But it wasn't. It was Tino. Stegs walked into the back garden and lit another cigarette.

It was a nice evening, mild for the time of year.

'Hello, Tino. I hope you've got some good news for me.'

'I still do not know what you are trying to do here, man.'

'I'm trying to keep you out of jail. That's what I'm trying to do. Now, have you made contact?'

'*Ja*, I went by her work tonight, the café you told me about. We got talking. She says she will go out with me later. It was pretty easy, man. She was, how you say, very keen. I think she likes me.'

'Well, you're a handsome fellow,' said Stegs, pleased that it had gone smoothly. It hadn't been that easy finding out where Judy Flanagan did her part-time job, but it seemed the effort had been worthwhile.

'Thanks, man. That's a nice compliment.'

'So, you're going to take her back to your room, OK?'

'I think she wants to go out somewhere a bit nicer. She was talking about a bar, maybe a meal.'

Trust Flanagan's flesh and blood to go for a freebie. 'Wine her and dine her a bit, then. But make sure you get her back to the apartment.'

'I don't have a lot of money, Mark. Things are not going so well for me at the moment.'

'Maybe you should flog some of those pills you've got.'

'Flog?'

'Sell. It means sell.'

'Do you know any buyers?'

Stegs was getting tired of this conversation. Tino had got the power to wear out men as well as women, though for very different reasons. 'Listen, there's still three years in jail hanging over your head. Find some money. I'm sure they have credit cards in Holland. But whatever you do, make sure you get her back to your place and keep her there. Understood?'

'For how long? That is the problem, man. How long am I meant to be keeping her for? And why? I still don't understand what this is all about.'

'You don't need to understand. And it isn't going to be for long. A couple of days at most. I'll be round first thing in the morning to let you know what's going to happen next.'

Tino started to say something else but Stegs heard the sound of movement behind him and finished off the conversation by telling the Dutchman to do what he was instructed and leave it at that. He then flicked the phone off and turned to see his missus coming out of the back door. She was holding Luke's baby monitor in one hand, a pack of Silk Cut in the other. Smoking. It remained the missus's only vice. Everything else had been consigned to the dim and distant past, but, like so many people, when it came to the dreaded weed she'd been unable to break the habit.

She put the monitor down on the rickety patio table, then lit one of the cigarettes. Stegs noticed that she was wearing the red clogs she'd bought recently, and he gave an inward cringe. He was obsessed with clogs. To him, they were one of mankind's worst fashion abominations, something that, like Tino, he could never quite forgive the Dutch for. And what was more, it seemed they were now a real clothing accessory among the local brood of mothers with whom the missus seemed to be spending more and more time. Some had even taken to wearing them with socks in what Stegs could only assume was a full-on bid to keep their husbands away from them in the bedroom. He had no doubt that it worked.

'Who was that on the phone?' asked the missus, a suspicious look in her eyes.

'Work,' he answered, taking a lug on his Marlboro Light.

'It didn't sound much like it.'

He wondered how long she'd been listening but didn't let it bother him, retaining his casual stance. 'One of my snouts,' he told her. 'He's setting up a sting for me. It'll go down well on my record.'

She sighed. 'You always tell me how well you're doing, but you're still a DC after all these years, even though you seem to work every hour under the sun. That bloody mobile's never off, Mark. But you've been stuck at the same level for what? How long is it now? Ten years?'

Her criticism hit him hard, not only because it caught him off guard as well as being essentially true, but because it wasn't delivered in her usual whiny rant, but in much more even, pitying tones, as if she no longer felt sorry for herself being stuck with a dead-beat husband, but felt sorry for him instead. Which was far worse. He'd show her. One day, he'd show her that he was more than just a bog-standard copper doing what he was told day in day out for pitiful amounts of cash. For now, though, he needed to keep his mouth shut.

'It's not always going to be like this,' he said, but he could hear the doubt in his own voice.

'Really? What is it going to be like, then? Are you going to go to work one day like Paul Vokerman and not come back? Leave me and Luke on our own with nothing more than a feeble widow's pension to keep us going? Everyone's life's moving forward, Mark, except ours. Is that what you want?' Again her voice was calm, as if she'd been thinking about this for a long time.

'Of course it's not what I want.'

'Or are you just going to keep on going like this? Treating this place like a hotel where you can come in drunk like you did today and put your head down, not putting anything into the relationship, either with me or your son?'

'It's not like that,' he said, his voice a forced whisper in case the neighbours heard them.

'It *is* like that,' she said firmly. 'And how much longer do you want me to put up with it? Something's got to give, Mark. Things just can't carry on like this.'

He felt a pain in the pit of his stomach, a grim realization that she no longer loved him. And the thing was, he'd never even spotted it.

'What are you saying, love?'

'I'm saying, either buck up your ideas and accept your responsibilities or move out. Understand?'

What could he say? Half of him felt like telling her to 'fuck it, he'd walk,' but there was another part – one that had been dormant for a while but which had showed itself briefly the previous day when they'd been at Odds Farm – that thought that maybe having a wife and kid wasn't such a bad way to live after all. And it was that part that was beginning to make its presence felt again now.

'I understand,' he said eventually. 'I'll be better, I promise. I know things have been difficult, and that I haven't been at my best, but there's been a lot of pressure on, especially with what happened with Vokes.'

'I know, but that ought to make you think whether it's all worth it. Because, to be honest with you, Mark, I don't think it is.'

He finished his cigarette, stubbed it underfoot, then put the butt on the table. It was their rule. The butts went on the table, and were then cleared away at the end of the night, and the table wiped. The missus finished hers and repeated the operation. Then she yawned.

'I'm off to bed. I'm shattered. Are you going to sleep in the spare room tonight?'

'Do you want me to?'

'Well, if you're late you can. I don't want to be woken up. At least not by you.'

'OK,' he said, conscious that he sounded sheepish. As if he'd been put in his place.

She said goodnight and disappeared inside. Stegs waited until the light came on upstairs, then he went into the kitchen, pulled a beer from the fridge and went back out to the table with it, lighting another cigarette. He was going to have to do something about his drinking, he knew that. He also knew the missus was right. The job was destroying him.

He wondered at that point whether he still loved her, and concluded that he wasn't sure. Then he wondered whether he hated himself and what he'd become. He took a swig from the beer and wished he had some more speed, even though a good night's sleep would do him the world of good.

No, he thought, I don't hate myself.

It's just all the other bastards.

# 21

It was ten to six by the time we got back to the incident room. Tina had already received the list from Harrow and was going through it. Malik and I got coffees and sat down and helped her. It was a long, boring job, but by seven o'clock when we'd checked and double-checked a dozen times, we were all forced to conclude that none of the registered owners of Meganes appeared on the list of those who'd bought the suits.

Tina was disappointed. 'All that work. For nothing.'

'Life would be too easy without setbacks,' Malik told her, with a reassuring smile.

'I couldn't have put it better myself,' I said. 'Come on, let's get a drink. We've all earned one, and it's Rich Jacobs' leaving do over at the Roving Wolf.'

Rich Jacobs was a DC who'd been at the station for four years and was now emigrating to Australia, where his wife came from. He'd got a job with the police in Perth, and was young enough to make a good go of it. A lot of people at the station were saying that they'd like to have done the same thing, and on my bad days I was inclined to agree with them. Having had a car wheel almost park itself on my head only a few hours earlier, I was counting today as one of the bad ones.

The do had already started by the time Tina and I got over there, Malik having declined our offer to join us ('I can't go to the leaving party of a guy I wouldn't even be able to pick out in an ID parade' being his fairly reasonable excuse), and there were a good twenty CID in the place, including DCI Knox. As I bought us both drinks, and put one in for Rich, I managed to persuade Tina that there was no point getting down about what had happened, and she took me at my word, sinking five G and Ts in the first hour, and sinking her blues with them. For a while I watched her as she immersed herself in various conversations, more often than not the centre of attention within them, then decided that maybe I was being too obvious about gawking at her, and got involved in my own conversations with colleagues I hadn't had much of a chance to talk with in a while.

In the end, it turned out to be a good night, made all the better by the relief I felt at having avoided serious injury during the Panner chase. By half-nine I was drunk and had my arm slung round Rich Jacobs' shoulders as I told him how much I was going to miss him. As I recall, he gave me a look that suggested the feeling might not have been entirely mutual.

'I don't think I've ever seen you hammered, guv,' I vaguely remember him saying.

'Make the most of it,' I told him. 'It's the only time I ever buy the drinks.'

Then, in a moment of madness, I bought him a double Remy.

At quarter to ten, I ate a bowl of chilli at the bar in a vain effort to soak up some of the excess alcohol, but it was way too late for that, and at twenty past I decided to call it a night. Tina and I had hardly spoken all evening, keen as always not to let on that we were lovers, and we'd agreed on our way over that we'd go our separate ways and at different times. I went first, wobbling out the door, leaving her chatting to two young DCs who both looked like they fancied their chances. I felt a pang of jealousy, which was quickly replaced by a need to get home.

In the taxi on the way back to my flat, I remember thinking that, even with all the leads we were picking up, the solution to the case still seemed a long way away.

It never occurred to me that we were already moving rapidly and inexorably towards the endgame.

# Part Three

ENDGAME

# 22

Luke woke up at three a.m., and cried for twenty minutes until Stegs shut him up with a bottle of milk. He then slept all the way through until 7.15, which was late for him and, on that day at least, late for Stegs. As soon as he heard the characteristic hungry cries that always ushered in a new morning, Stegs took a look at the spare room's alarm clock, caught the time, and cursed. He needed to speak to Tino and get the next stage of the plan moving.

In the fog of his newly wakened state, he had a sudden rush of doubt that he was doing the right thing. He could pull out now. It wasn't too late. Pull out and forget the whole thing. But as the conscious world and all its problems invaded his brain, he knew that that was bullshit. It was far too late. The events about to unfold had a sense of inevitability about them, themselves the result of things that had happened and had been said a long time ago. There was no way round that.

He pulled on some smartish clothes, knowing that he had an appointment with the PCA later that morning where he'd be grilled about his part in Wednesday's débâcle, and hunted round for his mobile, finding it on the shelf above the bed. The missus was calling him. Telling him to go and get some milk on for Luke. 'I'm on my way,' he called back, switching on the phone and asking if she wanted a cup of tea. She said she did, and he hurried down the stairs while she went in to coo over her favourite member of the household.

While he prepared the milk, Stegs dialled Tino's number.

The Dutchman took a long time to answer – so long that Stegs was beginning to get worried – but finally he picked up the phone and spoke, his voice a nervous whisper. '*Ja*, hello.'

'Tino,' said Stegs, switching on the kettle. 'Where are you?'

'In the apartment, and there is no need to speak so loudly.'

Stegs smiled to himself, knowing he'd been successful. 'Is she there?'

'*Ja*, she is here. What am I going to do with her?'

'Is she asleep?'

'She is.'

'Did you give her a good dose of the drugs?'

'Two tablets.'

'Blimey. What time was that?'

'About two.'

'Good, she'll be out for a few hours yet.'

'But what am I going to do with her, man? She is going to wake up some time.'

The microwave bleeped, telling him the milk was ready. 'Don't worry about that,' he said, removing the bottle. 'I'm coming over.'

'When?'

'As soon as I can get there. A couple of hours tops.'

'Well, hurry, man. It is important.'

'This is London, Tino, world centre of transporting non-excellence. I'll be as fast as I can, and I'm not coming that far, but don't expect me in ten minutes with croissants.'

'What happens if she wakes up before you get here?'

'With that sort of fucking dose, I'll be pleased if she wakes up at all.'

'Oh shit, man. What are you saying?'

'It's all right, I'm only joking. If she wakes up, give her another dose, but a small one this time.'

'How? She will not trust me again.'

'You're an actor. Improvise.' The kettle boiled and Stegs filled the two cups. 'I'll be over soon.'

He mashed the tea, then took it up with the milk to where the missus sat in their bedroom, cradling an irritated-looking Luke in her arms. Luke had a hungry eye on the missus's tits but there was going to be no luck there for the little man. The missus had stopped breastfeeding three months earlier, her nipples ravaged and torn, but for Luke the happy memories lived on.

The missus smiled at him when he came in. 'Thanks, love,' she said as he handed her the milk and put the tea down on the bed-side table. 'You look in a good mood.'

He grinned at her. 'I've got a feeling today's going to be a new beginning,' he said, and one way or another he knew it was true.

Tino was staying in an apartment he'd rented on a week's let between Baker Street and Marylebone High Street, just north of Oxford Street and the heart of the West End. He'd told Stegs he'd found it on the internet. It was costing £300 for the week, which Tino didn't think was too bad a deal. At least he hadn't thought it a bad deal when he'd first arrived, but then at that time he'd assumed he was soon going to be a few grand richer. Things since then, however, had not turned out quite how he'd expected. And, unbeknownst to Tino, they were about to take a significant turn for the worse.

It was nine o'clock by the time Stegs arrived. Having no desire to pay the congestion charge, he'd driven to High Barnet station and caught the Northern Line followed by the Circle, crammed in with all the commuters, wondering how anyone could ever tolerate battling their way to the office like this every day. His missus wanted him to become like these people, and though he'd felt more sympathetic to her point of view when he'd woken up a couple of hours earlier, by the time he'd got off the train at Baker Street he'd decided that he'd far rather get a divorce than travel like this five days a week. He might have been finished in the police force, but that didn't mean he had to start life as an office drone. Not if things went according to plan, anyway.

Tino's high-rise apartment block was just off Paddington Street, and though it looked all right from the outside, Stegs recognized it as being ex-council. Very cheeky. Some scrote had probably bought the place for about ten grand back when old Ma Thatcher was trying to sell off the public housing stock in order to create a property-owning democracy, and now the lucky bastard was renting it out as a city-break holiday home to Continental holidaymakers for three hundred a week. There is no such thing as justice, and anyone who says different is sadly fucking mistaken.

There was no entry phone, so Stegs walked straight in and took the lifts (which at least didn't smell of piss) up to the third floor and Tino's urban pied-à-terre. He found the right apartment and knocked quietly on the door. This time there was no hesitation. Tino answered near enough immediately, and fair dragged Stegs inside.

'All right, all right, what's the problem?' Stegs hissed as they came into the lounge. Not exactly spacious, but clean and well decorated in various shades of blue.

'I think she may be coming round,' he hissed back.

'I told you, give her another dose. You're either going to have to keep her under for a couple of days, or you're going to have to entertain her and make sure she doesn't phone home or demand to leave. It's up to you. But if she does get out of here, then you're in serious trouble. Even more serious now, especially as you've drugged her with Rohypnol. They call that the date-rape drug over here now, you know.'

Tino looked very worried. Stegs didn't think he had much in the way of backbone, which under the circumstances was no bad thing.

'You are a bad man, Mark,' he said, his voice thick with regret rather than anger. 'I wish I had never met you.'

'You wouldn't be the first person to say that, Tino. Nor, I doubt, will you be the last. Still, at least I don't earn my living fucking girls in the arse.'

'You make it fucking everyone in the arse. At least the ones I fuck get paid for their troubles.'

Stegs ignored the insults. Like threats, they'd always slipped effortlessly off him. It was one of the reasons he was so good at his job. And why he was always prepared to take risks.

'Where have you got Sleeping Beauty?'

'She's in the bedroom.' He pointed to a door in the corner of the room.

Stegs patted Tino on the shoulder. 'Well, lead the way, my friend.'

Tino gave him a look of disgust, then turned and walked over to the door, opening it slowly. After checking that she wasn't awake, he moved out of the way and Stegs peered in.

Judy Flanagan lay on her back in the double bed, her head tilted to one side, long red hair splayed out around her. She was snoring vaguely and he could tell that she was naked under the sheets. The room smelt of sex. Clearly Tino and she had made merry before he'd drugged her. Fair enough, he thought, but it pissed him off too. That smell hadn't been in his bedroom for a long, long time.

He walked slowly up to the bed and peered down at her for several seconds. She lay there peacefully, her breathing regular, air whistling out of the flattened nostrils. Tino was wrong, she wasn't coming round. She had at least a couple of hours in her yet. He put on a pair of plastic scene-of-crime gloves, then took the scissors from his pocket and cut off a sizeable lock of her hair. Then he leant down and removed the silver charm bracelet from her right wrist, noticing as he did so that her nails were impeccably manicured and painted a violet colour. Obviously a girl who looked after herself.

He put the hair and the bracelet into a plastic freezer bag he'd brought with him, placed it in his pocket, then looked around the room, quickly locating her handbag, which was hanging over a chair. Still wearing the gloves, he went over and rifled inside the bag until he found what he was looking for. He switched the phone on and saw she had a message. He recognized the number. Her parents. Probably worried about her. He felt a momentary twinge of regret that it had come to this, but forced it out of his mind. The innocent always suffer. It's the way the world works. He was just doing what he had to do.

He put the phone in the other pocket of his jacket and crept out of the room.

Tino shut the door as he came through and glared at him. 'What is going on here, man? I do not want to hurt her, do you understand that? She is a nice girl. She is, how you say, sweet. If anything happens to her—'

'Nothing's going to happen to her,' replied Stegs calmly, his voice a whisper. 'You're going to look after her for a couple of days, give her a little bit more of the Rohypnol so she doesn't recognize you or give you any hassle, then, when you get the word from me, you're going to let her go.'

'I don't like this.'

'I know you don't. You didn't like it on Saturday either, but that's not my problem. You do as you're told, and everything'll be fine. But do me a favour, eh? Stop fucking moaning about it.'

Tino took a step nearer Stegs. The Dutchman towered above him. If he'd wanted to, he could have made life difficult for Stegs, but Stegs wasn't worried. He had the run of Tino, and he was a good judge of character. This boy had gutless-when-it-came-down-to-it written all over his face.

'Let me tell you something, please, Mark. Do not try to deceive me. I will be very angry if you do.'

Stegs looked him right in the eye and gave him a twinkling smile, the type you give your girlfriend's mother when you meet her for the first time. 'Take a fucking hike, Tino. And don't forget. If she gets out of here, it'll be 2010 by the time you see the outside world again. That's a long time without female flesh.'

He turned and walked away, leaving Tino standing in glowering silence.


Ten minutes later, Stegs went into a phone box on Baker Street and telephoned the Flanagan household. The wife answered, her tone nervous, and, hearing no background noise, Stegs immediately hung up. He then phoned Flanagan's mobile, remaining in the phone box but this time using his daughter's phone. It was picked up quickly.

'Judy, where are you? I told you to phone your mother if you were staying out the night.'

Stegs could tell Flanagan was in a car somewhere. Probably on the way to the O'Brien incident room. He might have been the one who'd overseen the disastrous Operation Surgical Strike, but he'd done a good job of passing the buck to those under him, and had consequently avoided suspension. Which was typical of the bastard.

Stegs put the voice-suppressor to his lips and spoke. 'This isn't your daughter.' The words were high and robotic, not unlike those of a Dalek. He had to stop himself from adding 'Exterminate! Exterminate!'

There was a sharp intake of breath at the other end. Stegs could almost taste the other man's shock. 'Who are you?' said Flanagan, emphasizing the 'are'.

'We have your daughter. She is quite safe. As long as you do what we say, absolutely no harm will befall her and she will be released shortly.'

'What is it you want me to do?' asked Flanagan, his voice calm but strained.

It was, thought Stegs, ironic that the head of Scotland Yard's SO7 unit, which among other things dealt with kidnappings, should be the victim of a crime he himself had soothingly described as extremely rare when he'd appeared on *Crimewatch* a few months earlier. Not rare enough, Flanners, my man. Not rare enough.

'I need you to supply me with a simple piece of information. Your daughter will be released as soon as we have received this information and checked its authenticity.'

'Listen, I can't—'

'Can't's not a word I want to hear. You will supply this information,' he said, emphasizing the 'will'. 'Otherwise your daughter dies.' Exterminate!

'How do I know you have her?' Flanagan was less calm now. Only just keeping a lid on his emotions.

'I have posted a letter to your home address. It is for your attention. Inside it is a lock of your daughter's hair as well as her charm bracelet. The one she wears on her right wrist. She says it was a childhood gift from her mother.'

He was breathing heavily. 'What is it you want?'

Stegs didn't pause. 'I want to know the whereabouts of Jack Merriweather.'

# 23

Tina Boyd watched from the other side of the road as Stegs Jenner came out of the PCA offices in Great George Street. He looked both ways, but didn't see her. She was well hidden in the entrance to one of the imposing buildings that were commonplace this close to the seat of government. She stepped backwards out of sight, ignoring the strange look of a middle-aged woman coming out of the revolving doors, then peered round to watch as Stegs started off in the direction of Parliament Square. When he was about forty yards away, she saw him cross the road and turn and hail a black cab. The cab came to a halt and Stegs leant in the window to talk to the driver.

Breaking cover, Tina came down the steps of the building and hailed a cab of her own, heading in the same direction.

'Where are you going, luv?' asked the driver through the open window.

She bent down quickly. 'Police,' she said, flashing her warrant card before uttering a variation of something she'd wanted to say ever since she'd first seen films on the telly as a kid. 'Follow that cab.' She motioned towards the vehicle carrying Stegs as it indicated and pulled away from the kerb, and jumped in the back. The driver took a quick look over his shoulder and moved off, one car between him and the taxi carrying Stegs.

'I've always wondered whether anyone'd say that to me,' he said, leaning back and inclining his head towards her. He was about fifty-five, with a deeply lined, stubble-covered face and a baseball cap perched on his head that had seen better days. 'To be honest, I never thought anyone would. Especially a bird.' He guffawed throatily, scanning her in the rearview mirror. 'You *are* going to pay us for this, I hope.' He guffawed again. The archetypal cheeky chappie. Tina guessed that he was convinced he was a real comedian.

'I'll tell you what,' she said, 'I'll do you a deal. You keep your eyes on the cab and your opinions to yourself, and you'll get paid. Lose it because you're gawking at me and I'll nick you. Understand?'

'All right, all right. I was only joking.' He gave an exaggerated sigh and fixed his eyes straight ahead.

Tina sat back in the seat as the cab moved down Bridge Street and on to the Embankment, following Stegs to wherever it was he was going. She was convinced of his guilt, as she had been right from the beginning. They taught you, of course, to be very careful in forming your opinions and to follow the evidence rather than your gut instincts, but in this she knew she was right, and slowly but surely the evidence was building up to back her judgement. There'd been something wrong with Operation Surgical Strike from the beginning. Someone had set the whole thing up, and in her mind there could only be one possibility. Now she was determined to prove it, particularly as John had remained sitting on the fence over the last few days, sympathetic to her viewpoint but never quite making the step needed to agree with it. Not that she'd condemn him for that. John liked to take his time over things, mull the possibilities. But even he would have to agree that what she'd already discovered that morning had pushed Stegs Jenner even further into the frame.

She'd got into the incident room early, before eight, coming straight from her flat, eager to continue developing the lead she'd been working on the previous day, despite the fact that (a) it had initially looked like a dead-end, and (b) she was carrying a sore head from the leaving do the previous evening. There might not have been anyone on the Megane list whose name also appeared on the Desmarches suit one, but she hadn't been prepared at that point to throw in the towel. In the past twelve months, there'd been four purchases of the suit made where the list didn't provide the name of the purchaser. Three had been cash buys, and there was nothing that could be done about them. If the killer had paid cash, there was no way the purchase could be traced back to him. The fourth purchase, however, had been made using a stolen credit card in the name of a Mr Bernard Stanbury. It was a long shot to expect that whoever had stolen the card and had subsequently used it would turn out to be their killer, but Tina had decided to follow up on it anyway. She'd called the credit card company, explained who she was, and got the address and telephone number of Stanbury. The address was Barnet. Stegs Jenner's manor. She'd taken a look in the *A to Z* and seen that Stanbury lived less than a mile from her suspect. Another coincidence? She didn't think so.

Bernard Stanbury hadn't been answering his phone, so she'd left a message for him before heading up to Harrow to show the e-fit of the O'Brien suspect to the witnesses in the pub car park shooting. Unfortunately, a long time had passed and none of them could say one way or another whether the picture was of the man they'd seen leaving the scene of the earlier murder. Another dead-end, and a time-consuming one too, and still Stanbury hadn't called back. She'd thought about phoning John and finding out what he thought of this new cloud of suspicion circling round Stegs, but decided to leave it until she had something more. He was busy enough as it was, chasing after Robert Panner, and he'd said he'd phone her when he had a chance. She didn't even bother wondering whether Panner could have been the shooter. At the moment, all she was interested in was the pursuit of the leads she was generating. And the man who appeared to be in the middle of them all.

And this had been what had brought her to the PCA offices that afternoon, knowing that Stegs would be there for his interview. She wasn't meant to be tailing him, and would almost certainly have got her arse kicked if her superiors had known about it, but sometimes you had no choice but to follow your instincts.

Stegs's cab continued along the Embankment, but as the traffic became heavier and more black cabs appeared out of the side streets, Tina was forced to concentrate on his vehicle in particular, not trusting the driver to do the job for her. She could see him sneaking peeks at the pretty young tourists walking along the banks of the Thames, enjoying the first of the spring sunshine.

As they came up to Blackfriars Bridge, Stegs's cab swung sharply into the left-hand lane heading up towards the Farringdon Road. They were three or four vehicles behind it, but the driver was more on the ball than Tina had given him credit for, and he glided smoothly across without breaking pace. The lights were green and the cabs went straight through, turning north in the direction of Holborn.

'Let him get a couple of cars ahead,' she said, leaning forward and wondering why she was speaking so quietly. 'I don't want to make it too obvious we're following him.'

The driver grunted an acknowledgement and fell back a few yards, letting another cab get between them. Traffic on the Farringdon Road was heavy, but still moving. After about five minutes, Stegs's cab turned left into Cross Street, and by the time they'd made the turning themselves it had come to a halt outside an office block. Stegs was already outside, paying the driver.

'Go straight past,' she hissed. 'Quickly.'

'I want to get my money for this, you know,' he moaned, but did as he was told, driving on without changing speed. 'I want to help out the police, course I do, but I ain't a charity. If I was I wouldn't be working here, I can tell you.' He guffawed again.

Tina ignored him and turned round in her seat, watching as Stegs turned away from the cab and started up a side street, moving at a jog.

'All right, stop,' she demanded.

He did a deliberate emergency stop, taking advantage of the lack of traffic to teach her what he hoped was a lesson. It didn't work. Expecting it, she grabbed the handle by the seat and held on tightly, before thrusting a tenner through the hatch.

'Change and receipt, please,' she said, thinking that London's black cabs were as far from a charity as you could possibly get. Much closer to unarmed robbers. He dawdled, so she told him to hurry up or she'd take his number and report him, and he got the message.

She jumped out of the cab and walked quickly down to the spot where Stegs had got out of the cab. She was intrigued. They were a long way from his patch. It could be something completely innocent that explained his presence here – a girlfriend, or a mate he was seeing – but she still felt a flush of excitement.

When she reached the street he'd turned into a good minute

and a half earlier, it was empty. Completely. It was narrow and cobbled, made up of oldish grey-brick buildings that looked to be the offices of small businesses. She hung back and waited a few moments, just to make sure he didn't suddenly reappear, then started to walk up on the left-hand side, checking the name-plates on the doors of the buildings. They were mainly run-of-the-mill companies: graphic designers, specialist printers, photographers, that sort of thing. Halfway up there was an olde-worlde-style wine bar of the kind you get in the financial district, with stone floors, sawdust, bangers and mash, and a wine list to die for. Everything traditional except the astronomical prices. The windows were tinted but the interior was just about visible if you looked hard enough. She did. It was empty, but then again it was close to three o'clock, a dead time of day round these parts.

When she came to the T-junction at the top of the street, she stopped, lit a cigarette, then turned left and started along it, just in case he'd come this far up. Again, nothing stood out. She crossed the street and came back the other way, still not un-covering anything out of the ordinary in any of the signs. By the time she'd got back to the top of the street she'd first come up, Tina was beginning to feel disheartened. Was she reading too much into his movements?

She walked back down on the other side in the direction of the main road, trying to remain as casual as possible, but knowing that she stood out. She might have been in the middle of a city of ten million people but these backstreets were as eerily quiet as they always were, and she was the only person on this particular one.

She stopped. Suddenly. Her eyes fixed on the plate outside a modern tinted-glass door that looked like it was an inch thick. Carroll, Reed and Foster Solicitors. Melvyn Carroll. It had to be him. A smile spread across her face. Bingo.

Then, through the door, she spotted someone's legs coming down the stairs just inside. They were clad in khaki chinos and brogues, and she knew immediately it was Stegs.

'Shit!'

Cursing, she turned and sprinted ten yards before slowing to a casual walk as she heard the door open and close again, hoping he didn't recognize her from the back. She kept walking, and turned into the main road, heading in the direction the taxi had dropped her. She couldn't hear any footsteps behind but kept going for another minute, before finally risking a look over her shoulder.

He was nowhere to be seen.

She breathed a sigh of relief, then broke a long-standing habit by lighting a cigarette less than five minutes after she'd put out her last one.

This was very interesting. Melvyn Carroll was one of the most crooked lawyers in London, which was saying one hell of a lot. More importantly, he acted as counsel for a number of organized crime figures, and for a long time had been the Holtz family brief. As far as Tina was aware, he was also involved in the defence of senior Holtz crimelord Neil Vamen in his upcoming trial. That Stegs was corrupt, she knew. That he'd fed information to the Holtzes in the past, she was sure. And now it seemed he was working for Neil Vamen.

'I'm on to you, Mr Jenner,' she whispered, pleased with her day's work. 'And this time you're not getting out of it.'

# 24

Stegs cursed himself as he watched Tina Boyd. He'd recognized her the minute he'd come out of Carroll's. It was the way her arse waggled effortlessly as she walked, plus he remembered the cream trouser suit. She'd been wearing it the day he first met her. He was observant like that. Particularly with good-looking women, and ones who dressed well. You wouldn't have caught Boyd in a sock-and-clog combination. He'd followed her down to the bottom of the road, then crossed it, heading away from her, before stopping in the doorway of a forlorn-looking antique shop and watching her as she continued up the road. She'd turned round and lit a cigarette, and he'd got his confirmation, as if he'd needed it. Then, after a few seconds, she looked at her watch, took a couple of rapid puffs on the cigarette, and hailed a passing cab.

He really had fucked up here. He'd known they were suspicious of his role in the hotel killings and the O'Brien murder, but hadn't expected them to put him under surveillance.

They were always going on about lack of resources, and he honestly didn't think he was up there at the top of the list of suspects. Still, that was no excuse. He should have prepared for the worst and kept more of an eye out. Now he was in a difficult situation, and one that might have to involve some sort of evasive action.

But one thing about Stegs was that he didn't panic. Yes, he'd made a mistake, but the situation was redeemable. It was always redeemable. He got a momentary twinge of doubt again about his course of action, but forced it back down. This was no time for weakness. This was a time for men with steel in their veins, and whatever else you said about Stegs Jenner, he had plenty of that.

# 25

I'd been carrying a mean hangover all day and I was looking forward to the end of the working part of it. It hadn't been helped by the fact that we hadn't been able to find Robert Panner in any of his possible haunts, and according to the surveillance units he hadn't shown up at his official address either.

Tina, however, had been more successful. By now it was almost seven p.m. and she, Malik and I sat opposite DCS Flanagan in his office adjoining the O'Brien incident room. Flanagan looked the worst of all of us: tired, stressed and irritable all rolled into one. His face had also taken on the unhealthy red pallor it had had in the aftermath of Operation Surgical Strike, and his tie was badly skewed. According to Tina, he'd come in without a word to anyone that morning, his face tight with worry, and had walked straight into his office, shutting the door behind him and not emerging for another hour. It looked like the relentless pressure for a result was getting to him. His fingers drummed a steady, monotonous beat on the table as he stared at Tina for what seemed like an inordinately long time. In fact, I was just about to ask if he was OK, when he finally spoke.

'You're saying that it was Jenner you saw coming out of Melvyn Carroll's office this afternoon? I know we've already been through all this, but I've got to be absolutely sure. This is a serving police officer we're talking about here.'

Tina didn't hesitate. 'I followed him, sir. All the way from the PCA offices in Great George Street. And, before you ask, it was *definitely* Carroll's offices. No question.'

'What were you doing following him?' he asked, with more than a hint of suspicion in his voice. 'I don't recall saying we were going to put him under surveillance.' At the same time, his fingers maintained their steady drumming. Flanagan didn't seem the remotest bit pleased with the lead she'd turned up.

Tina told him what she'd told me earlier, about the fact that the owner of the only stolen credit card used to purchase a jacket identical to the killer's lived in Barnet, just down the road from Stegs. 'It seemed like one coincidence too many, on top of everything else. I knew he was down at the PCA, so I thought I'd watch him for an hour or two, see if something turned up.'

Flanagan nodded, and forced out a constipated smile. It looked like it was the best she was going to get. 'I'm glad you did. What you saw certainly raises a lot of questions.' His fingers stopped drumming and he sat back in his seat, using his hand to wipe the sweat away from his forehead.

Once again, I thought about asking him if he was all right, but decided against it. He might have taken my question the wrong way.

He sighed loudly. 'The question is, where does this leave us? What is Jenner's part in all this?'

Finally, it was my turn to speak. 'This is something Asif and

I were discussing earlier, sir. I think the visit to Carroll, added to what Tina uncovered about possible links he had to the Holtzes in the past, suggests that he's on their payroll somewhere. So, if he was working for the Holtzes, he may well now be working for Neil Vamen.'

'Carroll's Vamen's solicitor,' put in Malik, 'and if he's working for Vamen, we do have a motive for Jenner's role in leaking Surgical Strike.'

'What's that?' asked Flanagan, his interest suddenly very much aroused.

Malik continued. 'Neil Vamen's main rival in the north London underworld, the man who's taken a lot of his old business, is Nicholas Tyndall. The robbery of Stegs and the Colombians last week was carried out by Tyndall's men, including a man who's supposedly one of his closest associates, Ashley Grant. That robbery didn't do Tyndall a lot of good, whether or not he had any part in it. It was such a high-profile failure, in front of so many witnesses, that it was always going to get him serious unwanted attention, as well as upsetting the Colombians. Men he'd be wanting to stay on the right side of.'

'Tyndall's still free, though.'

'That's true,' I said, 'but we've got two of his men in custody facing very long prison sentences who we're trying to get to turn Queen's evidence. It may be that as a result of what happened we can bring a lot of pressure to bear on Tyndall, and even possibly put him behind bars. Which would suit Neil Vamen perfectly.'

'So you're saying Vamen set the whole Heathrow thing up? Using Stegs?'

I nodded. 'It's certainly possible. Likely even. Stegs, for whatever reason, uses O'Brien to provide the robbery tip to Strangleman Grant, either with or without Tyndall's knowledge, and I suspect it was without. Grant, who we know is something of a short-term merchant, sees an opportunity to make some easy money and snatch a few kilos of top-grade coke, takes the bait, not having a clue that he's about to walk into a trap, and bang, it all goes wrong.'

'We were left with O'Brien as the only one aside from Stegs who knew the truth,' continued Malik, 'and who was going to be the most obvious suspect as the source of the leak. So someone else, most likely one of Vamen's people, got rid of him.'

For what seemed like a very long time, there was silence. I could almost hear the cogs whirring as each person picked at the pros and cons of the theory Malik and I had just put forward. Flanagan seemed to be the one concentrating the hardest, his eyes tight shut, the sweat re-forming on his forehead. I could hear his breathing – short and fast, as if he was having a panic attack.

'It's certainly a possibility,' he said at last.

'We know that Vamen's been trying to get at Merriweather in Belmarsh,' said Malik.

Flanagan nodded. 'True, true. I can see the logic in it as a theory. The only thing is there's no evidence backing it up. At the moment, it's nothing but conjecture, and we can't touch Jenner for any of it. I think the important thing's to keep following up on our other leads, particularly Robert Panner. We need to get him to talk.'

'We're pulling out all the stops trying to find him,' I said, 'but he seems to have gone to ground.'

'Well, keep looking. It's urgent we get him in custody. If he is the shooter, he might be able to point the finger at Jenner.'

'What are we going to do about Stegs?' Tina asked.

'Nothing yet. We'll keep an eye on him, but that's all. I don't want to spook him, he's a cunning sod. He made a mistake today, but he's not the sort who makes very many of them. I don't want you to go following him again, Tina, OK? There's plenty of other things that need doing. You can help go through that list of Desmarches suit owners.'

'I'd like to follow up on my stolen card lead if I could, sir?'

'What? The Barnet one? What's there to follow up on? Did they catch the scrote who stole it, then?'

She shook her head. 'No, it's not that. It's my impression of Stanbury, the man who reported it stolen. There's something not right about him. First of all, he didn't phone me back. Then, when I called him again, he became very furtive and sketchy on the details. Apparently the card was taken during a burglary while he was away for the weekend, but he couldn't tell me what else had been stolen. It seemed to me he was hiding something.'

'Like what?' asked Malik.

'I got the idea that perhaps the card hadn't been stolen,' she said, turning in his direction. 'Or maybe that it had been stolen, but that he knew full well who'd stolen it.'

'You think someone paid him so they could use it while he was away?'

She nodded. 'Yes, I do. I checked with the credit card company and the spending on it started on the evening he left for the long weekend and stopped abruptly three days later, two hours before he informed them it had been stolen. There was no other attempt to spend money on it. It sounds very fishy to me.'

'But all it shows is that maybe your man Stanbury isn't the most honest in the world,' I said. 'Even if he can tell us who was actually using it, that person's unlikely to be the killer, is he?'

'I'd like the chance to follow it up though, that's all.'

'Well, you've done pretty well today, Tina,' Flanagan told her, 'so I'm not going to stand in your way. We've got another meeting at eight-thirty tomorrow morning which I'd like everyone to attend. Go and see him after that.'

Tina nodded, and the meeting broke up. I looked at my watch.

Quarter past seven. Time to head home. We left Flanagan sitting in his office looking as if all the troubles of the world were on his shoulders, and it made me think that perhaps running high-profile murder cases wasn't the best career role to aspire to, not if you wanted to live a long and healthy life. After we'd said goodbye to Malik, I told Tina that I was going to buy her a bottle of decent champagne, and she asked me why.

'Because Flanagan may not have shown much enthusiasm for all the hard work you've put in, but you deserve it.'

'He's right, though. We're still a long way from a result.'

'Bullshit. We're getting close. And when we crack this case, it'll be down to a lead that you uncovered, I'd put money on that.'

She smiled. 'You reckon?'

'Definitely. Now, let's go and get this champagne. And keep our fingers crossed that Robert Panner shows up.'

# 26

Robert 'Pretty Boy' Panner was none too pleased with the way Dora Hayes was acting. She was getting way too fucking lippy, telling him she didn't need him now that she'd found a better job, working for those bastard Kosovans from the Hallfield estate. She'd told Panner that they let her keep more of her money, looked after her better and had unlimited access to crack and smack, both of which Dora liked to indulge in. She now operated at the southern end of the Bishops Bridge Road on the other side of Paddington station to the patch off Praed Street where she'd earned money for Panner, and the way the bitch was acting was making it very difficult for him. How was he meant to keep his other girls in line when one of them was so fucking out of order and, worse still, getting away with it? It seemed he was losing them all over the place at the moment. Dora had already set the bastards on him as a warning, and he'd been lucky to escape relatively unscathed the previous day. The next time, she said, they'd kill him. She was living with one of the greasy bastards now. It made him sick the way they took the piss. You help the bastards out by liberating their country and they repay you by coming en masse to yours, taking over your business and acting like they owned the fucking place. Well, they were going to get a shock tonight. Pretty Boy Panner didn't like people stealing his business, and he didn't sit back and take it like a bitch either. He got payback.

He parked his battered old BMW 3 Series, a poor man's pimp-mobile, over on Gloucester Terrace, just down the road from Royal Oak station and only a few hundred yards from Dora's new patch. He hadn't seen her on his drive down the Bishops Bridge Road, and hoped that she was somewhere with a trick and therefore back soon. He didn't fancy waiting around half the night. He'd come here the previous evening, keen to get things sorted before the rebellion spread to the other two girls he looked after, but she hadn't been working. Tonight had better be his lucky night. If it wasn't, he'd cut the bitch to pieces when he finally caught up with her.

The evening was cool and dry, a result of the clear skies. It was even possible to see the odd star among the dull orange glow of the city's lights, but Panner wasn't interested in star-gazing. He was here for one reason, and one reason only. Payback. Justice. And to sort out his livelihood. Even though that was three.

He moved on to the street proper, keeping to the shadows, knowing that he was taking a big risk showing himself on the street with the Old Bill after him, but knowing too that he couldn't just sit back and do nothing. It was 11.15 and traffic was sparse. He spotted a couple of skinny bitches in halter tops and mini-skirts outside the building across the road, but didn't recognize either of them. He kept walking and watching, playing with the razor in his pocket, thinking about what he was going to do to the bitch when he got his hands on her. Make her squeal a bit, and beg for mercy. Let her see the blade, give her a few seconds to ponder what was about to happen, then slash, cut that acned fucking face right across, and listen to her scream. You take my fucking livelihood, I take yours. That's the law of the street. An eye for an eye.

When he got up to Westbourne Terrace, he turned round and walked slowly back the way he'd come. A car – it looked like a Jaguar – pulled up alongside the two bitches. There was a bit of banter as they talked cash, then one of them got in and the Jag pulled away, heading over the Bishops Bridge.

He kept walking up to the bridge, then turned round again. Another car was coming towards him in the opposite direction. A silver Lexus. Sweet. It pulled to a halt, double-parked, about thirty or forty yards away, and the passenger door opened.

A bitch in a fake fur coat and red micro-dress got out. It was a bitch he knew well. It was Dora. A smile like the devil's slithered across Panner's face and he felt himself go hard. She was laughing now and saying her goodbyes, a wad of cash in her hand. She'd done well here. A trick who liked to pay. He bet she'd be feeling real good now, well pleased with herself. Totally unsuspecting. Stupid bitch. Stupid fucking double-crossing bitch. He was going to enjoy this.

The trick's car pulled away, the driver oblivious to Panner's presence as he turned right towards Paddington station, the remnants of a smile on his face. Dora, meanwhile, stood on the pavement, putting the money in her red handbag, giving the occasional suspicious glance in the direction of the bitch on the other side of the street, the one whose mate had got in the Jag.

He was twenty yards away and closing. Walking casually but trying to keep in the shadows of the doorways to avoid attracting her attention. The razor slid out of his pocket, and he opened it, his forefinger stroking the blade. It had a beautiful carved bone handle and was his pride and joy, taken from the unconscious body of a pimp he'd had a run-in with years before. He carried it everywhere, loving the way the blade shone in the darkness, revelling in the fear it infected the girls with whenever he held it up for them to see. And Dora was about to taste the pain it could inflict, the price for being stupid and selfish enough to defy him.

Fifteen yards, ten yards, nearer and nearer. He quickened his pace, the thrill of the hunt making him want to laugh out loud.

Then the skinny bitch across the street screamed a warning and Dora looked up and saw him, her eyes bulging as they caught sight of the blade.

Panner lifted the razor and charged.

With a scream of her own, she turned and ran, only just managing to keep her balance in her heels. She dodged between two cars and stumbled into the road, swinging her handbag round and catching him in the face as he caught up with her. The blow threw him off kilter, and hurt too. It was harder than he'd thought a little crack whore like her capable of. He lashed out with the razor but she was already running again, making for the other side of the street and what she probably thought was safety.

But her heels let her down. She stumbled in them, trying to run too fast, and her legs went from under her. She fell forwards, landing hard on the tarmac, screaming for help with all the power her lungs could muster.

Too late, bitch. Too fucking late. Shouldn't have been so busy counting the money like a greedy, selfish whore.

As she tried to scramble to her feet, he grabbed her by her long hair and pulled her roughly upwards, turning her round so she was facing him. She lashed out desperately, catching him in the shin, and he reflexively let go, yelping in pain. She started running again, but he was on her before she could get two paces, and this time he yanked her back with such force that her head ended up tight against his chest.

'Please!' he heard her cry out. Panner liked that, the terror in her voice. It made it so much better.

Her hand went up to protect the side of her face closest to the razor, and the blade sliced into the fingers as it tried to find the tender flesh of her cheek and mouth and do some real damage. She screamed, this time in pain as the blood poured onto the palm of her hand, and tried to move her head, knowing full well what was going to come next. Even amid the animal fear, she was vividly aware of the implications disfigurement would have on her career and her living situation. Ahmet wouldn't go near her, her daughter would cringe when she looked at the deep, ugly slashes, there for the rest of her life as a testimony to her foolishness for thinking she could ever escape him. The tears were stinging her eyes. She couldn't move. His grip was like iron. She shut them tight and clenched her teeth, waiting for the worst. For the final painful humiliation her life had always been coming to.

But it didn't happen.

Instead, from somewhere behind her Dora heard the sound of footsteps and an angry female shout. 'Leave her alone, you fucking bastard!' There was the tight hiss of aerosol being sprayed, and then it was Panner's turn to cry out.

'You bitch, what you done? My eyes! My muthafucking eyes!'

He let go of Dora and she pulled away, looking down at the blood pumping steadily through the deep cuts on all four of her fingers and splattering loudly on the ground. Panner still had the razor but his hands were pressed against his eyes and he was dancing round in circles, yelling and cussing. Her rescuer, a working girl she knew only as Saph, and who'd been across the road earlier, now kneed him hard in the groin, and he fell to his knees.

'Ohmigod, he's hurt me. The bastard's cut my hand!'

A car was coming down the street. They saw the blue lights on the roof and both recognized what it represented.

'Let's get out of here,' said Saph, grabbing Dora by her good arm, and whistling as she saw the extent of the bleeding. 'I'll get you down to St Mary's. You're going to be all right.'

They ran into the darkness, leaving Panner incapacitated in the middle of the road.

The cop car stopped in front of him and two officers got out.

# 27

Stegs made the call to Flanagan's mobile from the phone box down the road from the One-Eyed Admiral where, as Tam, he'd stopped in earlier for a restful couple of pints, and to get hold of some speed.

Flanagan picked up before the first ring had finished, and Stegs spoke into the voice-suppressor, introducing himself as the man who had his daughter and asking if he had the address Jack Merriweather was residing at. Flanagan told him to hang on, and he heard the DCS's wife's voice in the background asking if it was Judy. She didn't sound unduly concerned, which meant that he'd kept his mouth shut to her about the kidnap. Good. The last thing he needed was panic. Flanagan told her that it wasn't and that he wasn't expecting a call from her for a couple of days yet. His voice was heavily tinged with a forced casualness, and Stegs was surprised that his missus didn't suspect something. Clearly she had her husband's non-talent for detective work.

After a few seconds, Stegs heard the sound of a door shutting.

'All right,' said Flanagan, breathing heavily into the phone. 'Is that you, Jenner?'

Christ, thought Stegs. How the hell had he guessed that? Boyd must have talked. 'Who's Jenner?' he demanded.

'If it's you, I'll have you fucking killed. Now, where's my daughter?'

'I don't know who you think I am, but whoever it is, you're wrong. Now, you change your fucking attitude or I might have to take some unpleasant measures.' That ought to shut him up. Flanagan had never exactly been Braveheart.

It did. 'Look, please, don't do anything to hurt her. She's my only child.'

'At the moment, she's safe and well, I promise you that.'

'I need some guarantee that she's OK. Please?'

'Nothing'll happen to her as long as, number one: you give me that address; number two: it's the right one; and, number three, Merriweather's there when we send our people round to deal with him.'

'Listen, I can't get involved in any of this. You've got to understand, I'm a police officer. I can't condone murder.'

'You will be condoning it if you do nothing,' Stegs told him evenly through the voicebox. 'And it'll be the murder of your daughter.'

The words hit home, just like he knew they would. It was cruel what he was doing. Ruthless. Playing with a father's love for his only daughter. But Stegs took comfort in the fact that, apart from a very bad hangover, Judy wasn't going to suffer as a result of what had happened to her, and certainly wasn't going to die. Still, he thought, Flanagan might. The bastard sounded stressed to the nines, and he wasn't what you'd call the fittest and healthiest of blokes.

'I have the address,' Flanagan said finally, with a loud

sigh, 'but I need some guarantee she's alive. I've told you that.'

'I've got the best guarantee of all: there's no point in killing her if you do what you're told. She's perfectly well, hasn't seen her captors' faces, and does not have a single clue as to who might be behind her abduction. As soon as we have confirmation that the address is correct, and have taken steps to deal with Mr Merriweather, your daughter will be released. If you give me the correct address now, that will be in less than twenty-four hours. You will receive instructions on where to find her.'

Flanagan sighed again. 'Is Neil Vamen behind this?'

'Don't keep asking questions. What's the address?'

'I don't want anyone else hurt. No police officers.'

'How many are there guarding him?'

'There are two men there round the clock. I don't want—'

'I know what you don't want. No-one else'll get hurt, and if they do it'll be their fault, not yours. Now, give me the address.'

Flanagan reeled it out, speaking slowly and painfully as if each word was a sharpened dart hitting him right in the arse. Stegs wrote it down in his spidery handwriting, then asked how to get to it.

'It's off the A22 in Surrey, just south of Blindley Heath.'

'Good. You'll be seeing your daughter shortly.'

Stegs hung up, and called Tino to get an update on how Judy was doing. She was back under again, courtesy of several further doses of the Rohypnol, but Tino was getting worried now. Stegs told him to dose her up one more time when she showed signs of coming round, and said that he'd be there to deal with everything first thing in the morning. 'Hopefully we can just let her go,' he said.

Tino grunted something and Stegs hung up on him, before putting some more coins in the slot and making yet another call.

# 28

DCS Noel Flanagan leant forward in the seat and put his head in his hands, holding the position for several minutes, the pressure in his chest almost unbearable as the terror battered away at him. In all his days as a police officer, he had never felt as helpless as he did at that moment. Suddenly he had absolutely no control over events, events that could indelibly shape his future and that of his family.

His daughter, his beloved daughter, was in grievous danger, and all he could do was obey the instructions he'd been given and, by doing so, break the laws he was paid to uphold, thus putting his colleagues right in the firing line.

Was it that bastard Jenner? Was he behind it? The slippery little fuck had always hated him, ever since that time with Frank Rentners. But that hadn't been his fault; there'd been nothing he could have done about it. Sometimes things just went wrong on an op, even with the best will in the world, and an undercover copper had to be prepared for that, not lash out at his superiors the minute he was put in danger. Jenner hadn't played by the rules and had paid the price, but could he really hate Flanagan so much that he'd resort to kidnapping his daughter? If he had, Flanagan would kill him. Tear the bastard apart for putting him through this.

But what if it wasn't Jenner? What if it was someone else who had Judy? What if they'd killed her? Surely they wouldn't do that. There was no need. He was going to do everything they said. Anything to protect his child.

The terror kept battering away at him, and his heart felt like it was on fire, but he forced himself to calm down, deliberately slowing his breathing until it was normal again. Then he got to his feet, composed himself, and returned to the lounge where his wife was reading the latest Danielle Steel, oblivious to the predicament he was in.

# 29

Stegs arrived at Tino's holiday apartment at six a.m. the following morning, this time by car. He'd driven the back routes through Harlesden and down into Maida Vale before joining the Marylebone Road near Regent's Park, keeping a careful eye out for any sign that he was being followed. He'd already made that mistake once with Boyd, and it had almost cost him everything. He wasn't going to make it again, especially now that Flanagan's suspicions were up.

There was an underground car park beneath the block of flats, constructed several years previously in an effort to flash the place up a little, and Stegs drove up to the entrance. He punched in the code Tino had given him and drove inside as the barrier went up, finding the spot for Tino's pad at the far end on the right, conveniently close to the lift. Not surprisingly, for that time in the morning, there was no-one about and the car park was only half full. Stegs yawned, parked up and got out, making his way to the lift.

The missus had given him serious grief that morning about

waking her up at quarter past five and had demanded to know where he thought he was going. He'd told her it was a new assignment and that it wouldn't be lasting long, and in an effort to placate her had added that he was going to take her advice and leave the Force. 'I don't need this hassle any more,' was his explanation. She'd just mumbled something unpleasant and gone back to sleep, and he'd taken the opportunity to throw on some clothes and leave.

He didn't run into anybody on his short journey through the building to Tino's apartment, which was just as well. They were going to be transporting Judy Flanagan back this way to his car, almost certainly blindfolded, so the last thing they needed was to bump into one or more of the neighbours. Stegs wasn't a hundred per cent sure what to do if they did. He was carrying a replica Browning automatic pistol which had more chance of doing a dance routine than firing a shot, but the sight of it would hopefully put off any would-be heroes. However, it would also draw attention to what was going on, and possibly fuck up the whole thing, and he couldn't have that. He therefore chose to rely on his foolproof method of dealing with all such eventualities: hope they didn't happen and not think about them. It usually worked.

He knocked gently on Tino's door, and a few seconds later the Dutchman answered, wearing his now trademark worried expression. Without speaking, he ushered Stegs inside.

'How's she doing?' whispered Stegs when he'd shut the door.

'I had to put her under again, man. She was coming round, but I can't keep doing this.'

'What's she doing now?'

'Sleeping. What do you think?'

'Don't get fucking cheeky. Have you been giving her plenty of water?'

'Yeah, yeah. She's OK, but she hasn't eaten.'

'Don't worry about that. She's hardly anorexic.'

'You're a very cruel man, Mark,' said Tino, glaring at him with an intensity he'd never displayed in any of his films.

'And you're my wicked accomplice. In fact, you're the one who's held this poor young lady hostage and drugged her, so don't give me any of that shit. Now, get her up. We're going to take her down to my car.'

'And that is it for me then, yes?'

Stegs nodded, as keen to see the back of Tino as Tino was to see the back of him. 'That's right.'

Tino sighed, then turned and went into the bedroom, Stegs following.

Judy Flanagan was asleep in pretty much the same position she had been the other morning, and Stegs had to admit that she was looking very pale and wan. He got a flash of guilt, then pushed it away. Tonight she'd be back in the family seat and all this would be nothing more than a bizarre dream. Judy Flanagan had had more than a passing flirtation with drugs, like so many middle-class girls from good homes, and there was a story going round that she'd been found once by her old man in the parental bed, out of her head on coke, Ecstasy and God knows what else, naked and semi-conscious as she received the attentions of two of the local dealers. A most shocking sight for parents anywhere, particularly when Daddy was senior Old Bill, only a step or two away from an assistant commissioner post. Judy would probably assume that she'd had a bit of a relapse, and had indulged a little bit too much. Either way, she'd be in no position to press charges.

As they stopped to watch her, she stirred, murmuring something.

'I think she's coming round,' said Tino.

'Well, let's get her down quickly then. Throw some clothes on her.'

Tino pulled back the covers, and Stegs couldn't help but take a quick admiring glance at her naked body. She was slim with pale, smooth skin and curves in all the right places. Her pussy was trimmed neatly as well and she was sporting a 'Brazilian', which Stegs thought was a nice touch. The missus, who tended to go for the more unkempt 'Congo' look, could have taken a leaf out of that particular bush.

Judy moaned vaguely and Tino pulled a top over her head while Stegs located her knickers and tugged them on. A couple of minutes later and she was fully clad in the garments she'd been kidnapped in, but her eyes were flickering now and Tino was looking nervous.

'We need something to blindfold her with,' said Stegs, looking around quickly. He spotted one of Tino's socks in the corner, and grabbed it. 'This'll do. It's not nice, but we've got no choice.'

'That's my sock, man.'

'Just get it on her, for fuck's sake.'

Tino lifted her head gently and tied the sock – a sky-blue number with Tweety Pie on it – around her eyes.

'What's going on?'

The voice was an exhausted whisper, but it was enough to scare them both. In a few minutes she'd be getting her faculties back together, and by that time they were going to have her in the car. Stegs looked at his watch. Ten past.

'Don't worry,' he growled in a voice that sounded like a cartoon monster. 'Just go back to sleep. You'll be home soon.'

'Tino . . . Tino . . .'

Stegs gave Tino a shocked glare. 'You gave her your real name?' he hissed.

Tino responded with a helpless look. 'I couldn't think of anyone else,' he whispered back.

'Fuck me, and you're meant to be an actor.'

'I'm an erotic actor.'

'Well, you're a shit one. You'd have trouble acting scared at your own execution.'

'Tino . . . what's happening?'

Judy's hand reached out, pawing uselessly at Stegs's arm, and he suddenly had an urge to burst out laughing. It was all going wrong, the whole thing. It could end up costing him everything: his job, his marriage, his liberty. And the thing was, at that point in time he truly couldn't give a fuck. He was actually enjoying himself for what seemed like the first time in months.

'All right, come on, get her to her feet.'

They lifted her up, and each took an arm to walk her slowly to the door. She stumbled once but quickly regained her footing.

'I can't see,' she said observantly.

'Just keep walking,' growled Stegs in his monster voice. 'Do what we tell you and you'll be home in a couple of hours.'

'I'm frightened.'

Stegs felt like telling her to shut it, but Tino intervened, talking to her soothingly, and without any attempt to disguise his voice. 'It's going to be OK, baby,' he cooed into her ear, as if preparing her for one of his trademark anal assaults. 'There'll be no problem at all. Just come this way down to the car. You're on your way home.'

Stegs pulled open the door, took a quick look in both directions down the corridor and, seeing nothing, led Judy outside. They hurried her to the lift, encountering little resistance, and stepped inside. Stegs pressed the button for the basement.

'Where am I? Please tell me.' The words dripped with fear, but were still delivered quietly enough to suggest that she was going to be sensible. 'I don't feel too good.'

The lift doors shut, and once again Tino whispered sweet nothings of reassurance into her ear. Stegs hoped that she wasn't a porn film connoisseur, otherwise the Dutchman was going to be faced with some very difficult questions. Still, it seemed to do the trick; she even rested her head against Tino's shoulder, as if his very presence made her feel better. Stegs couldn't understand it. If it was him in her position, he'd be well pissed off, but then the psychology of womankind had never been his strong point. Tino put his arm round her and kissed her head. Stegs gave him a look that said, 'Don't get too fucking friendly, we haven't got time for any shenanigans.' Tino glared back at him, and for the first time Stegs thought that the bastard might suddenly decide to give him trouble, which would not be a good thing. Tino had a six-inch height advantage and a couple of stone in weight as well. Plus he looked mighty pissed off. A bookie wouldn't have even bothered taking bets. Still, Tino didn't have a gun.

The doors opened into the car park and Stegs motioned towards his battered red Toyota, a motor that appeared to befit his lowly status in the pecking order of things. They walked over to it, and Stegs unlocked the boot quickly, eager to get out of there as soon as possible.

'Man, she is not going in there,' said Tino.

'Where am I going? Where?' Judy asked.

'It'll just be until I release her. It's only down the road. She'll be in there ten minutes tops, that's all.'

'In where?' she continued.

'In the boot of the car.'

'I don't want to.'

'Look, just get the fuck in.'

All this growling was doing Stegs's throat in, and he was getting impatient. He pulled Judy by the arm, and she gasped loudly, as if he'd just burnt her. She was a lot better actor than Tino.

'I'll scream. I will.'

'Put her in the car, not the boot. It is cruel otherwise.'

'Don't leave me, Tino.'

Stegs half expected her to add 'I love you' and plant a big smacker on his lips. It was that sort of conversation. It made him feel like he was playing fucking gooseberry. It was also highly dangerous, conducting a conversation with an agitated young woman blindfolded with a brightly coloured sock in the middle of a car park that was in regular use. There'd be CCTV cameras in here too, and Stegs didn't want to give the operator an excuse to have a look at them and pick out his grainy mug.

So he pulled the replica Browning, and that did the trick. Tino stiffened and his eyes widened.

'One more fucking word,' said Stegs, pointing the gun at Tino's head, 'and you die. Understand?'

Tino nodded frantically, his bravado deserting him at an alarming rate.

'What's going on?' asked Judy. 'I want this blindfold off.' She reached for the sock, but Stegs pushed the barrel of the gun against her cheek, and she too got the message pretty sharpish.

'Get in the boot now if you want to get home outside of a coffin.'

As soon as Stegs had finished speaking he realized he'd forgotten to growl, but there wasn't a lot he could do about that now. He pushed her inside and she went without complaint, lying down in the foetal position amid the various bits of bric-à-brac, including an empty box that had once contained a baby bottle sterilizer. For some reason, the contrast between the box and Judy made him feel slightly sick.

Tino went for him fast, trying to knock the gun out of his grasp, but he was definitely a lover rather than a fighter. Stegs had been prepared for such an assault and he slammed the boot shut and jumped out of the way, leaving Tino flailing at air. As Tino continued coming after him, keeping low, Stegs brought his knee up hard into the other man's gut, and at the same time smacked him over the head with the gun. Tino kept coming, so Stegs allowed him to grab him round the waist, before turning the gun round in his hand and smacking him with the butt this time. Tino let go and fell to his knees. Stegs took a step back, then kicked him full in the face, knocking him sideways.

Muffled screams came from within the boot, which made Stegs wonder what the fuck Tino thought he was doing. If he wanted to get caught for this, he couldn't have made a better job of it. What was it about people that they suddenly got a burst of morality long after the damage had already been done? Tino had drugged this poor bird up to the eyeballs and kept her prisoner for two days solid, and now, without warning, he was prepared to fight to the death in order to get her the best possible method of transport home. It beggared belief, it really did.

'Tino,' Stegs said, grabbing the Dutchman by the hair and shoving his head into the car next to his, a nice silver-coloured Merc, 'you seem to forget that I'm the one with the fucking gun. Now stay there, and when I've gone, if you know what's good for you, go back to your room, pack and get the fuck out of the country. It doesn't seem to suit you here.'

Stegs couldn't see Tino's face because it was buried in the wheel arch, but it sounded like he was crying.

'My God, what sort of a police officer are you?' he sobbed.

It was a good question, and one that Stegs couldn't readily answer, so he didn't bother trying. Instead, he turned away and got in the driver's side of the car before reversing out of the space. As he did so, he saw a red-faced businessman come out of the lift not more than twenty yards away. Stegs resisted the urge to give him a wave, put the car into first and headed for the exit, ignoring the banging coming from the boot. It was 6.15 a.m., and things were just about going to plan.

# 30

At 8.20 a.m. that morning, Paul Richards – a small-time, north London-based career thug with links to organized crime whose claim to fame was that he'd once bitten another man's ear off in a fight – received the confirmation he was looking for. He'd been standing just inside the tree line for the last three hours, facing a large, modern, white brick bungalow set well back from the road south of the village of Blindley Heath, and he was cold and tired, the early-morning sun having done little to warm his creaking bones. He'd already seen a man in his thirties, dressed in a white rollneck jumper and black leather jacket, come into the kitchen and make a cup of tea an hour earlier, before disappearing again; and then, just as he'd been thinking about going off to find a roadside caff for a much-needed cup of his own, he'd watched, smiling, as Jack Merriweather appeared in the kitchen window wearing a white dressing gown, his shiny bald head still wet from the shower. He too began to make himself a cup of tea.

Bingo. Richards reached into his pocket, pulled out his mobile and made the call his boss had been waiting for.

'Make the most of it, Jackie,' he whispered when he'd finished, watching Merriweather sip his tea and share a joke with the copper in the rollneck who'd come in behind him. 'This is the last morning you're ever going to see.'

# 31

'You had a girlfriend recently, Mr Panner. One of your *bitches*, by the name of Fiona Ragdale.'

It was me speaking. On my right was DI Malik. We'd wanted Flanagan to be in on this interview as well, but he'd phoned in sick this morning, saying that he'd had palpitations in the night. The timing was bad, but there wasn't a lot that could be done about that. The way he'd looked the previous evening, no-one thought he was bullshitting. Across from us sat Robert Panner, along with the duty solicitor, a youngish bloke called Vernon Watson who was often seen skulking round the station and who always appeared to be sweating whatever the weather conditions.

'What about her?' demanded Panner.

'You were arrested in connection with an attack on her at her flat that took place seventeen days ago, on the twenty-seventh of February. You're currently on bail, awaiting charges in connection with it.'

'Yeah?' he answered, seemingly uninterested.

Watson, meanwhile, was staring fascinated at the nails on his pudgy fingers. I felt like telling him to pay attention, but it was probably better for me if he wasn't interested in the proceedings.

'A shot was fired into the ceiling during the course of that assault. Fiona Ragdale claimed that it was fired from a gun you were carrying at the time, and that you were the individual who fired it.'

'I didn't fire no gun. No-one ever found one, did they?'

I shook my head slowly, allowing a thin smile to show itself on my face. I wanted to disconcert him, to let him know that we had something on him, but not what.

'That's right, Mr Panner,' I said after a pause. 'No-one ever found one.'

'Where were you on the afternoon and evening of the eighth of March, that is last Wednesday?' asked Malik. 'Specifically between the hours of midday and eight p.m.'

Panner seemed surprised. So too did Watson, who even managed to look up from his fingernails. 'What's this all about?' he said. Panner said more or less the same thing, but his language was more colourful.

'It was the same day as the Heathrow hotel shooting,' I continued. 'You must have heard about that.'

'Yeah, yeah, I did, but what's this got to do with anything? I ain't done nothing, y'unnerstand? Nothing.'

'Are you refusing to answer the question?' demanded Malik.

'No, no, course not,' said Panner, his demeanour becoming noticeably more nervous. The only thing a criminal likes less than being nicked is being nicked for something he hasn't done, and Panner was doing a very good impression of someone who couldn't understand why the hell he was being asked this. 'I was out and about, y'know. In the day. Seeing some of ma bros. This and that, nuttin' much.' He might have been pushing thirty and

288

white, but Panner liked to talk the ghetto slang so beloved of today's wannabe teenagers, at least when he could remember that that was what he was meant to be doing. He tended to veer in and out of it.

Malik glared at him sceptically. 'That's not really a lot of help, is it? Have you got anyone who can vouch for your whereabouts during that time? Individuals – your bros – who can say that you were with them?'

'I don't know. Why the fuck you asking me anyway? What I meant to have done?'

'What you meant to have done,' said Malik, mimicking Panner's habit of missing words out of his sentences, 'is shoot dead one Robert O'Brien, and his grandmother, Mrs Kitty MacNamara.'

Panner jumped out of his seat, gesticulating wildly. 'No way, man! What the fuck is this? I don't know nuttin' about no shooting!'

'Get back in your seat!' I snapped.

Panner's face dropped and his aggression ran off as quickly as it arrived. He sat down slowly, looking across at his lawyer, who seemed perplexed by the whole thing.

'I thought my client was under arrest for possession of an offensive weapon and resisting arrest,' he said, referring to Panner's interception the previous night.

'And attempted murder of a police officer,' said Malik.

'Fuck that, it weren't my fault he jumped all over my car.'

I smiled. 'So, you're admitting it now? That you attempted to run me over?'

'I didn't,' he whined, knowing he was trapped. 'Fuck this, man. You're setting me up.'

'Who paid you to kill Robert O'Brien and Kitty MacNamara?' demanded Malik coldly, his words designed to shock the pimp.

The fear that spread across the other man's face suggested that they worked.

'No-one did. Dat's truth. I swear, man. I didn't have nuttin' to do wid it. You gotta believe me. I don't even know no fucking Robert O'Brien, or the other one. I never heard them. Y'unnerstand?'

'No, I don't understand.'

'Listen, my client is making it clear he doesn't know anything about this man you keep talking about,' said Watson testily, breaking his self-imposed silence. 'Can you therefore move on?'

Panner took this as a hint to shut up. His fingers drummed steadily on the formica table, and he stared down at them without blinking.

'You're in a lot of trouble, Mr Panner,' I told him. 'At the moment, whether you like it or not, you are our number one suspect in the double murder of Robert O'Brien and Kitty MacNamara, and the evidence against you is irrefutable.' Watson started to say something else but I talked over him, staring straight at Panner. 'We know full well that you fired the gun into Fiona Ragdale's ceiling because not only did she tell us you did, you were also seen by several other witnesses leaving the building directly afterwards.' This last bit was made up, but he wasn't to know that. 'And we also know, without a shadow of a doubt, that it was the same gun that killed two people just over a week later. So, I think it's best if you stop with the boring and repetitive denials and simply admit to us what happened last Wednesday.'

As I spoke, I mentally crossed my fingers. Both Malik and I were almost a hundred per cent certain he wasn't our man, so now it was a matter of hoping that he knew who was, that Catherwood hadn't made a mistake about the bullets, and that Panner felt he was in sufficient trouble that it was worth giving us the information.

Watson leant over and whispered something in his client's ear. After a few seconds, Panner told the lawyer that it was all right. 'I didn't do it, man. I swear,' he said, sounding annoyed that no-one appeared to believe him. Then he turned to me. 'That time with Fi, yeah, I did pull a piece and put bullet in da ceiling, but it wasn't my piece, man.'

'Who did it belong to then, if it wasn't yours? And where is it now?'

'If I help you, will you drop the charges? You know, attempted murder of po-leece man, and all that.'

'If you help us, your case'll be reviewed favourably,' I told him, giving the standard police spiel. 'We'll see what we can do.'

He nodded, seemingly satisfied. 'I got it off a guy a few weeks back. He hires them out, y'know. There was man after me because he said I owed him, and I had to get hold of a piece fast, you know what I'm saying? There's a guy over Acton who rents them out, so I got one off him for a week, just in case this man who said I owed him came calling. Then the bitch, Fi, started giving me grief about something, so I went over there and pulled the piece, just to scare her, y'know? Put bullet in the ceiling, just so she knows the Pretty Boy means business, but she starts screaming, the neighbours start shouting, and I'm outta there. Next day, I got bit worried that po-leece would come a-knocking, so I gave the gun back to man in Acton. I told him I hadn't fired it; y'see I didn't want to lose deposit on piece. If it gets used, then the rule is I have to get rid of it, and I lose the two hundred I had to put down. I needed the money, so I lied.'

'Why didn't he check the gun, this guy from Acton?' I asked. 'He could easily have told if you'd fired it.'

'I borrowed a spare bullet from a friend of mine, put it in there, and he never knew.'

'A spare bullet?' said Malik disbelievingly. 'You borrowed a spare bullet?'

'I swear!' he shouted. 'It's da truth, man. I swear it is. I know it don't sound true, but that's the way it is.'

We all gave him sceptical looks, even Watson. It wasn't that it was outlandish for someone like Panner to go to an armourer if he wanted a gun, particularly if he only wanted it for a matter of days. Because of the UK's relatively draconian gun laws, it wasn't always easy for a criminal to get hold of firearms, and since plenty of the bad guys wanted them, a rental trade in guns had developed, run by individual armourers who typically hired them out to criminals for one-off crimes, or occasionally, as in Panner's alleged case, longer periods of time. The usual way it worked was that a rental price was agreed, and on top of that a deposit put down by the customer as security. If the gun got fired while in the customer's care, he or she not only had to get rid of it themselves, they also forfeited the deposit. That way the supplier didn't lose out. What made Panner's story a lot less believable, of course, was that he was claiming to have given the gun back even though it had been fired. If this was the case, then the supplier clearly wasn't very good at his job, as he should have been able to see that it had been used. And, if Panner didn't have easy access to firearms (and he presumably didn't if he had to use the services of an armourer), then where did he find a spare .38 bullet?

We both glared at him. 'That story's horseshit,' said Malik, with a dismissive snort.

'I'm telling the truth, serious. You can fucking check.'

'All right. What's this guy's name?'

'It won't come from me, right? If I tell you, want it kept quiet I co-operated. I got a rep, y'know.'

'Sure you have,' said Malik sarcastically. 'Now, what's his name?'

'Tony.'

'Tony what?'

'I don't know his last name, man.'

'Then you're going to be spending a long time in prison.'

'He lives in a flat on a place called Haymarket Road over in Acton. Number ten or twelve. If we go over there, I can show you which one it is.'

Malik wrote down the address but didn't let up on the questioning. Neither did I. There was no point. This was a story that reeked of convenience. An armourer owned the gun, so although Panner had been in possession of it once, it was now no longer anything to do with him. Sure.

So we carried on.

What we were trying to do was find inconsistencies in his story and then hit him with them in the hope that he'd tie himself in knots, realize the error of his ways and spill the beans on who the shooter was. Then we could start getting to the bottom of who'd actually organized the hit on O'Brien, and from there bring this whole sorry case to something akin to a satisfactory conclusion.

But Panner wasn't playing ball, and for the next twenty minutes he insisted that the gun he'd fired had belonged to the armourer, and that he'd never seen it since he'd given it back more than a fortnight ago. We tried coming at him from different angles, but nothing seemed to budge him from his story, and eventually we brought the interview to a close. Watson demanded that his client be given bail, but we both laughed at that one, and Panner was taken back to the cells. We had another nine hours before the initial twenty-four were up, so there was no need to worry about letting him go just yet, but it was a concern that he was sending us up what looked like another blind alley, even with a whole host of charges hanging over his head.

# 32

Bernard Stanbury worked as an accountant for a civil engineering firm in Winchmore Hill, a short commute from his Barnet home. At just after ten o'clock that morning, Tina Boyd walked into the firm's cheaply decorated reception area and asked the woman manning the switchboard – the only person in the room – if she could speak to him.

'And whom shall I say is calling?' asked the receptionist in a comically affected voice as she looked Tina up and down with barely concealed suspicion. 'I don't seem to have anything in the appointments book. If you're here to sell anything—'

'Police,' said Tina with a polite smile, removing her warrant card.

'Oh,' the woman said with interest, pausing to hear if there was any further explanation.

There wasn't. Tina simply stared at her, waiting, the smile remaining fixed on her face.

The receptionist got the hint and called Stanbury's number.

'The police are here to see you, Bernard,' she said in hushed, conspiratorial tones. 'A Miss . . . ?'

'Boyd. Detective Sergeant Boyd.'

A few seconds later and she was off the phone. 'Mr Stanbury's office is through those double doors, the second one on the left.'

'Thank you.'

Tina put the warrant card back in her jacket pocket and walked through the double doors. Almost immediately, the second door on the left opened and a smallish man of about forty-five with nondescript glasses and an even more non-descript face stepped out. His expression was a combination of anxious and annoyed.

'Come in, come in.' He ushered her into his small and surprisingly untidy office, swiftly shutting the door behind her. 'What's the problem?' he demanded, returning to his seat, without shaking hands.

Tina smiled and took the seat opposite him, on the other side of the desk. 'I'm DS Boyd. We spoke on the phone yesterday regarding your stolen credit card.' She put out a hand and he took it reluctantly, blinking behind the glasses and avoiding her eyes.

'I know,' he said, 'and I answered everything you asked. There's nothing more I can add, and it was a long time ago. I'm also very busy.'

Tina fixed him with a calm but unflinching gaze. 'It's possible, in fact very likely, that the person who stole your credit card has been involved in a double murder.' Not strictly true, of course – it was still a fairly remote possibility – but there was no point letting Stanbury know that.

'Oh God, no . . .' The words came out like a strangled gasp, and he put his head in his hands.

Tina pressed her advantage. 'The card was stolen from your

house while you were away. The thief gained entry through an unlocked window on the first floor. Two hundred pounds in cash was stolen, as well as your credit card. Nothing else. According to the crime scene report, the burglar didn't leave much of a mess. Why didn't you take your card with you when you went away?'

Stanbury took his head out of his hands. He still looked distraught but was desperately trying to control it. 'I've got another credit card. I took that one instead.'

'Let me level with you, Mr Stanbury. I know that you have money problems. I also know that you owed several thousand pounds on the card you took with you on your trip last August, and that you owed very little on the one that was left behind, the one that was stolen. That's strange in itself. Even more strange is that you leave your card lying around at home with a window unlocked when you're going away for three days. I think what happened is you told someone where your card was and that they stole it and used it with your full knowledge. Presumably they paid you for the privilege. It happens a lot, I'm sad to say.'

'It's not like that, honestly. I didn't—'

'Frankly, I'm not interested in whether you've been involved in anything illegal. And neither will any of my colleagues be. We're far more interested in catching a brutal killer. So, who used your card while you were away?'

'Listen, I had nothing to do with any killings. I swear. I'm not like that. Oh God, why the hell did I ever get involved? This is going to ruin me, you know. What'll my wife say? The kids?'

'It's possible that no-one'll have to know,' Tina lied, knowing that if they were on the right track she'd never be able to keep it quiet. 'Now, who was it?'

Stanbury removed his glasses and rubbed his hands across his face. 'It's a neighbour of mine. He's a friendly enough chap and

I've known him a while, but, to be honest, I wouldn't want to get on the wrong side of him.'

'If he's done what we think he has, then he won't be a threat to anyone. He'll be behind bars, probably for the next thirty years.'

'I was broke, you know, really suffering. He paid me three hundred pounds to let him have the card while I was away. He said it was foolproof. No-one would ever know. He even told me to claim for stolen cash as well on the house insurance. God, why did I get involved? I'm a respectable man, I promise. I've never done anything wrong before.' He gave her a pleading look, desperate for her to believe him.

Tina gave him a reassuring smile. 'This neighbour of yours. What car does he drive?'

'Why do you ask that?'

'Just answer the question, Mr Stanbury.'

'A Megane,' he said. 'A black Renault Megane.'

# 33

Tino lay on the bed in his holiday apartment for a long time, his face and ego badly bruised. He could still smell Judy Flanagan's perfume on the pillow. It was strange, considering that for most of the time she'd been here she'd been asleep, but he genuinely missed her.

That first evening, when she'd still been conscious, they'd had some fun together. He'd started chatting to her in the café where she worked as a waitress, and they'd got on so well that she'd readily agreed to go on a date with him. He'd then taken her to Garfunkel's restaurant in the West End, and a local pub, before heading back to his place for sex. She'd been good, too: enthusiastic, adventurous, admiring of his ample charms. Hygienic and nice-smelling as well, which wasn't always the case with amateurs. In fact, they'd done it for several hours before finally it had been time to do what he'd been ordered, and administer the drugs that bastard police officer Mark had given him.

He'd almost decided not to do it, knowing that he could have been getting himself in a lot more trouble than he was in already (this was, after all, a kidnap), but fear, and the desire to avoid complete humiliation, had driven him on. Perhaps, he'd reasoned, if he did what Mark told him then that would be the end of it, and he could return to Holland and start again, putting the events of the past few days down to experience. But as the hours had turned into days, and he'd given Judy more and more of the drugs, so the realization had dawned on him that, rather than saving him from prison, Mark was making his situation ever more dangerous.

He'd felt guilty, too, awful that he'd got a pretty young girl to trust him and then betrayed her so cruelly, drugging her when she was defenceless. He'd tried to make up for it, talking to her in her sleep, telling her how sorry he was, trying as hard as he could to make her stay with him as comfortable as possible by washing her twice daily, and always making sure she had plenty of water. And now he'd betrayed her again when he'd had the chance to protect her. Who knew where Mark was going to take her now. To her death? It was possible. Why not? He'd lied about everything else. She'd called for him to help her, and when he'd finally tried he'd been beaten like a dog for his troubles. Humiliated, like he'd been back in Holland. Life had once seemed so good. Now it was dealing him a cruel hand.

He continued to lie there, cursing the world. Occasionally weeping, which angered him still more. And with Judy Flanagan never far from his thoughts. Judy, who might be on her way to her death. He couldn't let it happen. For once, it was time to do something good.

He had to find Mark, to stop him. But how could he do that? He was all alone in a city of strangers, all of whom seemed treacherous and keen to do him harm.

One man might know. One man might be able to help him find Mark.

It might save a life. He thought of Judy being choked to death by that vicious little policeman and the thought brought on an angry flush. But still he didn't move. Instead, he debated what to do in his mind, then debated it again. And again.

Finally, when he could stand the guilt and torture no more, he swallowed his principles, rose from the bed and went to phone Trevor Murk.

# 34

Stegs drove the Toyota back out on to the Marylebone Road, and turned west, driving through the still thin early-morning traffic on to the Westway and in the direction of the A40. The A40 became the M40, and from there he turned south at junction 1A on to the M25, officially the busiest stretch of road in Britain. It was quarter to seven, and the commuters of south-east England were waking up and heading out on to the roads like less-than-mobile wildebeeste in their daily ritual of slow torture. Occasionally, he picked up banging coming from the boot, but he knew Judy'd be all right in there. Pissed off, perhaps, possibly very frightened, but all right nevertheless. Such was the dilapidated state of Stegs's vehicle that it had a large hole on the underside beneath where the spare wheel was kept which would provide adequate ventilation for Miss Flanagan. So there was no chance of opening up the boot and discovering a corpse in there, which would have been a little unfortunate.

The traffic on the M25 grew heavier as Stegs approached

Heathrow, and for a while he was slowed down to less than twenty miles per hour, but things picked up again after junction 13, the Staines turn-off.

Stegs was heading away from the crowded, clogged-up roads of Greater London, making his way to quieter, more isolated pastures, where he could release Judy without her being immediately discovered and the alarm being raised. Timing was all-important at this juncture. If her old man was alerted to her freedom too early, then it would fuck up everything.

The M3 takes traffic to Southampton and the towns of the south coast of England, and gives the driver glimpses of the countryside that used to cover that part of the world before it was completely overrun with people and business parks. Stegs had come this way on holiday as a kid. While other kids had headed to France, Spain, the Greek islands and beyond, his family had always favoured the New Forest as a holiday destination. A sizeable national park containing hundreds of acres of unspoilt ancient woodland between Southampton and Bournemouth, it was definitely a nice place, but probably not the best of laughs for a ten-year-old boy. After all, there wasn't exactly a lot to do, other than stroll through trees, and what self-respecting kid wants to do that? Stegs had been an only child, his mum having miscarried twice after him before giving up the idea of a second one as a pointless exercise, and his happy childhood memories were limited where holidays were concerned. If they weren't in the New Forest, they'd be visiting affordable Second World War sites of interest in honour of his old man's obsessions, which basically meant Normandy, and once, for a special treat, Dresden.

It was nine o'clock on a beautiful sunny morning, the sort that makes you feel glad to be alive, when Stegs pulled off the M27 at the turning to Bolderwood, in the heart of the New Forest.

Driving through the thick walls of pine, he had to admit that the place did have a certain serenity about it; he even found himself contemplating bringing the missus and baby Luke down here for a long weekend at some point. He hadn't treated the missus well of late, and it was about time to make a concerted effort to get into her good books. She'd be happy enough soon, when he let her know that they could afford that holiday in France. He might have to be a bit careful about telling her how he'd got hold of the money, but the point was that from now on they were at least not going to have to worry about the Jenner finances quite so much.

He slowed down as he came to a turning off the road he remembered from years back. It was little more than a dirt track which he knew led deeper into the woods. He turned up it and drove for about four hundred yards before parking up and making a cursory check that there was nobody about. Then he opened up the glove compartment and removed a balaclava and a pair of handcuffs he'd bought in a joke shop for a fancy-dress party he and the missus had attended years earlier. The party had had a 'Cowboys and Indians' theme; he'd gone as Sheriff Wyatt Earp, while the missus had dressed up as a Wild West good-time girl, complete with frilly dress, black hold-up stockings and a lady's six-shooter. Them were the days, thought Stegs ruefully. The handcuffs weren't that sturdy, but he was confident they'd hold a girl in Judy's state, and he knew they'd never be traced back to him, even if her old man did decide to risk his career and liberty by making an issue out of it.

He put the balaclava on, then went round to the boot and opened it up. Judy was still in the same position she'd got into when he'd put her in there earlier, and it looked like she'd been asleep. As the wooded half-light seeped into the interior she groaned and turned her face in his direction, Tino's Tweety Pie sock still in place.

'God, where are we?' she said, her voice croaking.

'Your dad'll be coming to collect you soon,' growled Stegs, 'but you're going to have to come with me first.'

'Where's Tino?' she asked.

'He's not here.'

'Did you hurt him?'

'Course I didn't. He's fine.'

'Who are you? And what do you want with me?'

'Enough questions.'

'Tino said he loved me.'

'Eh?'

'He said he loved me. He—'

'All right, all right, that's enough.'

Christ, this was all he needed. She was meant to have been unconscious for the past two days, not conducting some sort of Patti Hearst-style love affair with a small-time porn star. Stegs wondered what on earth else she'd been discussing with Tino. And also, more importantly, how he was going to limit the damage.

He pulled her out of the boot and held her upright, pushing the gun against her chest so she'd know it wasn't worth resisting, then led her slowly into the trees. He could hear her sobbing and he felt duty-bound to tell her it was all going to be OK. Once again, she asked what he wanted with her. He knew he should have just kept quiet, that it wasn't worth getting involved in a dialogue, but he could hear her crying gently against him as they walked and he could tell that she thought this was it, she was going to die, which was too much to expect any person to bear, particularly a young girl whose only crimes were that she liked a shag and had an arsehole for a dad.

'It's not you we want,' Stegs told her, making only a minimal effort at a growl. 'It's some information from your dad. He's given it to us now, so you can go free. I've got to leave you here for a while, but I'm going to phone your dad and tell him where you are, and then he can come and collect you.'

'Honestly?'

'Yeah, honestly.'

She seemed to believe him, and Stegs felt better as he stopped by an oak tree, sat her down and placed one of the handcuffs round a low branch, the other round her wrist, and locked them both. Her arm was stretched, so he put the gun in his pocket and pushed her back against the tree to make it more comfortable. Then he dropped a small bottle of Evian into her lap, stepped to one side, and removed the sock.

Judy blinked rapidly and tried to focus, but Stegs was already turning away, keen to get out of her field of vision before she remembered too many things about him. After all, one thing her old man was going to be doing was trying to work out who'd done this to his daughter, even if he couldn't do much about it, and Stegs didn't want to provide him with any obvious clues, particularly as he was already under some suspicion.

She called out after him, asking when her dad was going to be there, but he ignored her and kept walking the fifty yards or so back to the car, at the same time punching a number into his mobile phone.

# 35

As soon as the Panner interview was wound up, and Panner himself returned to the cells, I headed back to the incident room with
Malik.

'What do you think about his story, John?' he asked as we
walked along. 'All this stuff about hiring a gun, firing it, then
replacing the bullet. I've heard more likely tales from Jeffrey
Archer. I'm actually wondering whether he had anything to do
with the whole thing at all.'

I could see his point, but tried not to think that this entire lead
might be a waste of time. 'Roy Catherwood said it was a ninety-
nine per cent probability that it was one and the same gun. At
the moment, that's good enough for me.'

'Well, then Panner's lying to us.'

'I'll at least check what he's saying,' I said, thinking that his
story was so bizarre I wasn't sure he could have made it up. 'See
if there's anything in it. I know it doesn't sound likely, but you
never know. Stranger things have happened.'

Malik raised his eyebrows. 'Not many.'

And then, ten seconds later, as we stepped inside the incident room, our conversation suddenly became irrelevant. The whole place was a frenzy of activity and it seemed like everyone in there was in the midst of pulling on their jackets, their faces alive with excitement.

'What the hell's happening?' I asked.

From out of the mêlée stepped DCI George Woodham, who was in temporary charge of the case in Flanagan's absence. A big man with an immense walrus moustache, he was wearing a grin that spanned the moustache's entire length as he put an arm through the sleeve of his raincoat. 'We were just coming down to get you both,' he said. 'The bloke you're talking to definitely isn't our man. Your girl Tina's done a good job. She's located the one we're after. He owns a Megane, was in possession of a credit card used to buy one of those suits, and apparently matches the description of the killer perfectly.'

I felt a real surge of pride. Don't ever doubt Tina Boyd. 'It's not the accountant she went to see, is it?' I asked.

'No, it's the guy the accountant lent the card to while he was away. Someone called Trevor Murk. Tina's on her way over to his place now. She's going to wait for us there.'

# 36

Tina turned her car into Milford Avenue, a quiet road of reasonable-sized one- and two-storey semi-detached houses a few hundred yards west of Barnet High Street. It was here that Bernard Stanbury and Trevor Murk lived, four doors away from each other. According to Stanbury, Murk was a friendly young man who didn't appear to work for a living but was never short of money, and could often be found drinking in the Red Lion public house, not far from where they both lived. Stanbury had told Tina that he occasionally popped into the Red Lion for a pint on the way home after work on a Thursday and Friday night, and that was how the two had got to know each other.

One night the previous summer they'd got talking, and somehow Stanbury had opened up more than usual, and had let on that he was heavily in debt. Murk had told him not to worry. 'It's all about playing the system,' he'd explained. 'There's always plenty of money to be had, it's just knowing how to coax it out.' He'd then told the accountant about a scam he had going whereby he would get an acquaintance to rent him one or more of his credit cards which he would then use up to the maximum before giving the nod to the acquaintance, who would then report it or them stolen. Nobody, except the big bad credit companies, lost out. Stanbury had told Murk about a long weekend he was taking with the family, and it was arranged that Murk would have use of one of his cards for the duration for a fee of £300.

Murk, it seemed, had made merry with the card, spending more than three grand on it, and in the process making the mistake that would go a long way towards putting him in the frame for murder.

Tina slowed up as she passed Stanbury's house. At the same time, the front door four houses down opened and a good-looking guy in his late twenties with wavy black hair stepped out, carrying a Nike holdall in his hand.

She carried on driving, keeping an eye on him in her rearview mirror as she looked for somewhere to pull up. There was a space to her left about thirty yards further up the road and she reversed into it, only just managing to get in. She looked in her mirror again but Murk had disappeared temporarily from sight.

Then she saw him on the other side of the road, throwing the holdall into his Renault Megane before getting inside, and she experienced a burst of adrenalin. This was what it was all about. The hours, the days, of mundane statement-taking and hunting for the tiniest clues had finally been rewarded. Tina was proud of herself at that moment, and rightly so. It was her persistence that was going to nail a man who'd killed at least three times, and on each occasion in cold blood. John was going to have to buy her a magnum of champagne now. For the moment, though, it was important to make sure she didn't let Murk out of her sight, or get rid of whatever it was that was in the bag.

He started the engine and pulled into the road, and Tina bowed down in her seat, making out that she was looking for something in her handbag. As he passed, she counted to three, then pulled out after him, pressing redial on the mobile and telling the controller at the other end that the suspect was on the move.

# 37

Neil Vamen knew that many people considered him a violent, murderous criminal of the worst kind, but it wasn't how he saw himself. He was a businessman, an entrepreneur; a man in pursuit of the type of financial rewards and peer respect that plenty of other people pursue every day. Yet he was the one being punished, simply for following a well-worn path. Yes, he'd used violent methods in his business dealings, and a good many people had had their lives cut short on his orders, but it was a hard world out there, and in his line of business – the supply of those goods and services the ruling powers had decreed the populace couldn't have – violence was a necessary prerequisite for getting the job done. Neil Vamen didn't believe that any of the people he'd had executed in the course of his long and colourful career had been wholly innocent. Some, of course, had been less guilty than others, but one way or another all had made their livings in the same nefarious underworld he operated in, and therefore had to be prepared to face the consequences.

It wasn't even as if, by putting him behind bars, the ruling powers – those faceless bastards who made and enforced the laws – actually achieved their goal. If anything, they made the situation worse. Did crime in his manor suddenly stop the day they arrested him and broke up his powerbase? Of course it didn't. It just meant that a dozen other young bucks – more violent because they had something to prove, and less time to prove it in – came looking for the scraps. And none, it seemed, was more violent than Nicholas Tyndall. Vamen knew Tyndall – in passing, anyway. They'd met several times when there'd been talk of a business deal involving Vamen supplying Tyndall with coke, but nothing had ever come of it. Vamen hadn't liked him, hadn't trusted the bastard, although even he was impressed by the way he'd moved in so quickly after the break-up of the Holtzes and his own arrest, and how quickly he'd come to dominate the manor.

In fact, Tyndall could have probably enjoyed a reasonably successful criminal career if it hadn't been for one thing: he was up against the best. Neil Vamen might be in prison, cooped up in a cramped cell deep in the maximum security of Parkhurst, but he still knew how to pull the strings and influence events many thought beyond his control. Already Nicholas Tyndall was paying the price for trying to step into a bigger man's shoes. Soon enough he was going to have the Colombians after him for fucking up their deal. And that was going to be the least of his worries.

As Vamen sat there now, enjoying a Montecristo cigar and a cup of Nicaraguan coffee while peering through the cell window into the morning's spring sunshine, he felt freedom beckoning. The case against him was weak. It rested on one man. One man who so far had avoided the long reach of Vamen's revenge, who'd escaped the attempts on his life carried out in Belmarsh, but who was now about to pay the price for attempting to save his own skin at the expense of others.

Jack Merriweather had hours to live, no more than that. Vamen wouldn't regret his passing. They'd known each other a long time, but disloyalty was a crime more heinous than any other. Grassing to the coppers, giving evidence on their behalf . . . there could only be one punishment. And with Merriweather gone, the case would collapse and he'd be released, his reputation cemented for ever as the man who could do anything.

He'd have to be careful, of course; couldn't get too cocky. The powers-that-be would want him now, and want him badly. He'd be public enemy number one. But it didn't matter. He was too clever for them. Always had been. And he remembered perfectly the old adage: let them hate me, as long as they fear me.

And fear him they would. All of them.

Including Tyndall.

# 38

For twenty-five minutes Tina followed him, first on to the A1, then down the Edgware Road in the direction of the West End. She kept well back, and traffic was heavy enough to allay any suspicion Trevor Murk might have that he was being followed. She kept the mobile on throughout the journey, feeding details of Murk's movements to the control room back at the station, which then relayed them to the armed response vehicles and the members of the O'Brien murder squad as they converged on the route being taken.

As Murk came up to the top end of Baker Street, keeping to the left-hand lane, a message came through to Tina from control advising her that DCI Woodham had given strict orders that she was to remain at a safe distance from the suspect, and not to attempt to apprehend him. Armed officers were being deployed to do that. Tina acknowledged the message and swung into the middle lane, two cars back, only just getting through the Marylebone Road intersection lights as they changed from amber to red.

She acknowledged the message, but she wasn't sure she could obey it. This was her collar. Her perseverance. She wasn't a glory hunter, but she felt she deserved this one, and if she could take him safely and without unnecessary risk to herself, then she would do. There was no way she was letting Trevor Murk go.

She wondered what John would think of her actions. He'd be worried she'd get hurt – she knew how much he cared for her – but she also felt he'd understand that she had to do it. John was a solid guy, someone who preferred caution to jumping right into things, but, at the same time, he wasn't a complete stickler for the rules. He knew when you had to take risks, to put your neck on the line. He'd done it before – had gone alone into a dangerous situation, ended up facing the wrong end of a gun and still come out unscathed and unbeaten, and with an important arrest under his belt – so he'd know why she was doing it. She could have done with him there with her, though. His quiet strength would have done a lot to calm her nerves.

The Megane's left-hand indicator came on and she was forced to do a rapid lane-change, cutting up a white van in the process. Murk turned into Paddington Street and she followed, now only one car behind, conscious that her manoeuvre might have drawn unwanted attention to her. Trevor Murk might have been a cold-blooded murderer, but he was also fairly professional in his dealings, so would be on the look-out for people or vehicles acting suspiciously around him.

But it seemed he hadn't noticed. He indicated again, and pulled into a side street next to a block of flats. Tina had to make a snap decision. Follow him and risk detection or keep on going and risk losing him? She plumped for the latter, carrying on for a few yards before flicking on her indicator and hazard lights and pulling up to the kerb. She cut the engine as the cars behind her beeped their horns, and gave her location to control, before running back towards the side street.

As she got to the corner, she saw the Megane turn into the entrance of an underground car park beneath the block of flats. 'Bingo,' she said, returning to the car and reporting this new information to control.

'ETA for the first ARV is six minutes,' said the voice of Sergeant Colin Brooking, the controller she'd been communicating with for the past half an hour. 'Your orders are to wait until it arrives, Tina.'

'Received and understood,' she said, getting back into the car and performing a dangerous reverse manoeuvre that attracted more blasts of the horn from passing drivers, before turning into the side street and driving down past the entrance to the underground car park.

She parked up on some nearby double yellows and pulled a sign out of the glove compartment advising any over-zealous traffic wardens that she was a police officer on duty. Then, with an audible intake of breath, she got out and headed in the direction of the flats.

# 39

The faint sound of knocking drifted into Tino's trance-like state. He was fantasizing about making love to three clones of Judy on his uncle's boat, all of whom were satisfying him with their tongues and telling him what a good, brave man he was while at the same time, in a perfect combination of his two favourite pastimes, he was fishing for herring off the Friesland coast where he'd grown up. The knocking grew louder, and with his reverie now disturbed, he got up off the bed and walked through the lounge to the front door of the apartment.

'Who is it?' he called out.

'Trevor.'

Without responding, Tino pulled open the door and glared at the man he'd once thought of as a friend. 'Thank you for coming,' he said formally, moving aside to let Murk in, 'but I think it is the least you could do, would you not agree?'

Murk stepped inside. 'Listen, cool it, sweetboy, I can explain. That bastard, Stegsy—'

'Who?'

'Sorry, Mark. The undercover copper. He was blackmailing me, same as you. He made me do it.'

'He said you always did this sort of thing, reporting your friends to the police when they were breaking the law. He said you were a grass.'

'That lying cunt. Don't you believe it, Tino. He's as dodgy as something dodgy. It's his way of sowing the seeds of discontent among the masses. You know what I'm saying?'

'No, Trevor, I do not. But that's not important now. As I told you, we need to find Mark, and quickly. He could have murdered this poor girl, and I don't want her death on my conscience.'

'Very upstanding of you, Tino. I always knew there was more to you than met the eye, and that's saying something. I'm only sorry that Mark put me in a position where I had to cause you this much trouble.'

'Where will Mark be now?'

Murk put the bag he was carrying down on the floor. 'I know a couple of pubs he uses near here. We'll try them, see if he's there. Otherwise I'll have to phone him down at the station.'

'OK,' said Tino, nodding. 'Let's go.'

'You're not going out like that, are you? It's cold out there, you're going to need a coat.'

Tino looked down at his shirt and jeans and decided Murk was right. He wasn't dressed for the English weather, even on a spring day. 'Hold on a minute, I'll go and get one.'

He turned and walked into the bedroom. As he did so, Murk opened the bag and took out a .38 Smith and Wesson and silencer. A rag wrapped round the handle to protect it from fingerprints meant that he didn't have to worry about gloves. He stepped over to the bedroom door and positioned himself to the side of it in a similar spot to the one in which he'd waited for Robbie O'Brien almost exactly a week ago.

When Tino came back through the door, just like Slim Robbie, he didn't have a chance. He must have caught something out of the corner of his eye because he turned towards his killer and his eyes widened dramatically as he saw the barrel of the .38 level with his eyes. Murk pulled the trigger twice and blew the top of Tino's head off, not even bothering to try to catch him as he tumbled messily to the ground with all the dignity of a sack of potatoes, the blood already leaking rapidly from the exit wounds.

Then, satisfied that Tino was dead, Trevor Murk returned the gun to the bag, checked the place over to make sure he hadn't left behind any tell-tale clues, and walked out of there, thinking that he'd earned five grand and it wasn't even lunchtime.

# 40

Tina found the Megane in the underground car park quickly enough. It was parked in the space for apartment 3C. She made a note of the number, then leant down and let down all four of the car's tyres, one by one. Trevor Murk wasn't going anywhere. Not using the method of transport he'd come here in anyway. She tried to inform control of where the car was parked but she'd lost the signal, so she made her way over to the lifts, wondering who it was her suspect was visiting in number 3C, and whether or not it had anything to do with the O'Brien killings.

While she was going up, she tried control again, but although she got a signal it cut out before anyone could answer. A voice inside her head told her that she was heading into extremely dangerous territory, and that with the first ARV only a couple of minutes away there was no point in going on. She'd done her bit, even got Murk's position down to an individual apartment, so why keep going?

'Because,' she told the voice, 'this is my collar, and I do not want him getting away.'

The lift doors opened and Trevor Murk stood there facing her. 'Hello,' he said, with a friendly smile.

Tina managed to conceal her surprise and smile back at him. 'Morning,' she replied, stepping past him, and thinking immediately that his was definitely the sort of face that could charm its way through an old lady's front door. And a young lady's, she thought. He was definitely a looker.

As the doors shut and he disappeared, she tried control again. This time she got through, and was put straight on to Sergeant Brooking. 'He's leaving the building, Colin,' she informed him. 'Via the underground car park. Carrying a black holdall.'

'Keep back from him, Tina, I've told you. Strict orders. He's to be treated as armed and dangerous.'

'I've let down his tyres so he can't get out in his vehicle. He'll probably come out on foot through the car park entrance. Either that or the building's main entrance, wherever that is. Get people to both places. And for God's sake, get them to take him alive. He's got information we badly need.'

Brooking started to say something else but the line was bad and she wasn't really listening.

She found the staircase and started down the steps, taking them two at a time, the adrenalin coursing inside her. Less than a minute later she was coming back down to the basement level. There was a swing-door at the bottom of the stairs that led out into the car park. She took the final three steps in one go, dropping the phone into her pocket, and went to peer through the glass to see whether Murk had discovered her handiwork on the Megane yet.

But as she did so she heard the sound of echoing shouts and the loud clatter of footsteps coming rapidly closer. Then she saw

Trevor Murk's upper body hurtling towards the door. She turned to get out of the way, but before she could he hit it head on with all his weight, knocking her flying into the stairwell.

She landed on her behind on the hard stone floor, and as she went to get to her feet Murk spotted his opportunity and grabbed her by the hair, pulling her upright while at the same time removing the gun from his holdall. He dropped the holdall on the floor and thrust the gun's silencer against the side of Tina's head.

'Sorry about this, my sweet, but I need a hostage. If you don't resist, you won't get hurt. If you do, I'll have to kill you. Hope you understand.' He dragged her over to the swing-door and pushed it open with his shoulder. 'Back off!' he yelled, the acoustics of the car park making it sound so much louder. 'Back off now, or she dies!'

Ahead of them, Tina could see three uniformed officers, one holding an MP5, the other two Walther PPKs, all ready to fire. Behind these three were a number of plainclothes officers and more uniforms running down the entrance ramp in their direction, about thirty yards away. She thought she saw John and Malik, but before she could tell for sure Murk yanked her head back so that her eyes were pointing towards the dank stone ceiling, while increasing the pressure of the gun against her temple. She felt herself panicking inside but used every ounce of her mental strength to focus on remaining calm.

'Armed police, drop your weapon!' instructed the uniform with the MP5. 'Drop your weapon now!'

'Trevor, we can do a deal,' Tina whispered. 'We know you're the shooter in the O'Brien murders. If you turn QE against whoever hired you, the sentence'll be a lot less.'

Mark ignored her. 'I want twenty grand and a helicopter to take me to France!' he demanded, somewhat optimistically.

Tina gave a derisory snort. 'For fuck's sake, Trevor, be serious.

You're not getting out of this one. All you can do is limit the damage by doing what they say and dropping your weapon. Otherwise you're going to end up either dead or doing thirty years.'

'Shut the fuck up!' he snapped. Then, to the uniforms: 'Get back! Get back now!'

John's voice: 'Come on, Trevor, drop the gun. You don't want to do this.'

'I said get back! Do as I say and she doesn't get hurt. Now I told you: I want a helicopter and twenty grand—'

Tina's left arm flew upwards and grabbed the wrist holding the gun, yanking it off to the side. For a split second Murk's resistance disappeared, and she used that second to elbow him in the gut with her right arm and break free from his grip, letting go of the gun at the same time as she tried to run out of the way.

Murk swung round in her direction, pointing the weapon, and that was the moment the shooting started.

# 41

'Come on, Trevor, drop the gun. You don't want to do this.'

I was standing six, maybe seven yards away from him, off to the right of the three armed officers facing him down. Behind me stood Malik and at least a dozen other police, all temporarily helpless in the face of what was going on. I could see the look of tension on Tina's face as she stared wide-eyed at the ceiling, her hair in the painful grip of Trevor Murk, the man we were now sure was the killer of Robbie O'Brien and Kitty MacNamara, and I wanted desperately to do something – anything – to help. My guts were churning, my legs felt numb and useless, and I knew that I was possibly seconds away from losing the woman I loved for the second time in as many years. It was worse, if you can believe it, than the time a gun had been pointed at me, because at least then my destiny had felt like it was in my own hands. Now it was in the process of being irreversibly altered by a man with a frighteningly casual attitude to murder.

'I said get back!' Murk screamed. 'Do as I say and she doesn't get hurt. Now I told you: I want a helicopter and twenty grand—'

Tina made a grab for the gun, pulling it away from her temple, and elbowed him in the gut at the same time. She then broke free of his grip on her hair and started to run. It all happened so suddenly that for a moment I couldn't believe what I was seeing. My heart was in my mouth, and I was rooted to the spot as Murk swung the gun round in her direction, more in an act of desperation than anything else. And then I heard the spit of the bullet passing through the silencer, and suddenly she was stumbling forward, falling hard on one knee, then rolling over.

All three armed uniforms opened up at the same time, hitting Murk repeatedly and sending him dancing wildly in the direction of the swing-door. Even before he hit the ground I knew we'd be getting no answers from him now. There was no way that trained firearms police shooting to kill were going to be unsuccessful from that range.

Instinctively, I ran towards Tina, shoving the uniforms aside in my urgency to get to her, to tell her she was going to be all right, and knowing too amid the adrenalin and the fear that I was finished if she was dead, that I'd never be able to come back from a blow like this. I loved her. I truly loved her. I'd never told her that before because I'd always been so careful not to scare her off, but now I wanted to shout it from the rooftops, because it was so important that she knew before it was too late.

'Get paramedics over here now!' I yelled, crouching down beside her and taking her hand. 'Tina, it's John. You're going to be OK.'

A pool of blood was forming on her right trouser leg just above the knee, her teeth were clenched in pain, but she was still conscious.

'Shit, this hurts,' she gasped, her eyes squeezed tightly shut.

They say it's a grand life if you don't weaken, and for so long I've tried to live my life like that, but at that moment in time, weakness felt so tempting that I almost opened my arms to greet it. Almost.

'We're going to get you to a hospital, don't worry.'

'What about Murk?'

'Don't worry about him.'

'Is he dead?'

'I don't know.'

'We've got to get to the bottom of this,' she whispered, her eyes opening and focusing on me.

At that moment, I felt a burst of hope, elation following close behind. I tried to calm down, not wanting to get too excited, but it seemed that maybe the wound wasn't as serious as I'd first thought, and Murk had intended. Otherwise, surely, there would have been no way she'd be holding a conversation, particularly about how the case was going. I've been with conscious gunshot victims before and, contrary to what you see on the films, they don't chat. They go into shock.

'What's happened with the gun lead?'

'Jesus, Tina, don't think about it. Rest. Conserve your strength.' Then I leant down close to her. 'I love you,' I whispered.

'You're not angry?'

'I'm proud,' I told her, smiling into her blue eyes. 'Really proud.'

At that moment, the paramedics arrived. I continued to hold her hand, whispering soothing words while the paramedics went to work, cutting the trouser leg away to reveal the bloody mess beneath.

'You're going to be OK, luv,' said the older of the two a few moments later, as he wiped away the blood and examined the injury. 'It looks like it's only a flesh wound. A nasty one, but a lot better than it could have been.'

'That's easy for you to say,' she hissed, through gritted teeth.

Five minutes later and Tina was in the back of the ambulance heading towards Charing Cross hospital. She let me hold her hand on the journey, but only after I'd promised that as soon as we got there I'd go back to the station and follow up on the gun lead.

Malik came with me, and after we'd seen her off into the operating theatre he put a hand on my shoulder and gave me a sympathetic smile. 'Are you all right, John? You look like Flanagan did last night.'

I exhaled loudly, still conscious that my heart was thumping hard in my chest. 'That was close, Asif. If Murk's aim had been a little steadier, she'd have been dead.'

He knew then, I'm sure, that the two of us were lovers, but was sensible enough not to comment on it.

'But she's not,' he told me. 'She's not. That's what you've got to remember.'

It wasn't something I was likely to forget.

# 42

Stegs spent lunchtime in the One-Eyed Admiral. A couple of small-time bad boys he knew came in, and the three of them had a good chat about this and that over a few pints. Stegs bought them both double Jamesons when it came to his round and they asked him what he was celebrating.

'Just won a little bit of money on the lottery,' he told them.

'Oh yeah?' said the younger of the two, known to Stegs only as Piko. Piko had a three-inch scar running down his left cheek and very hairy nostrils, and he sometimes sold Stegs speed.

'Not enough to mug me for,' said Stegs, thinking that if they had half a clue how much money he had in the boot of his Toyota they'd have had a knife to his throat in no time.

Piko and his mate left about 2.30. Stegs stayed on for a while and talked at Patrick, the barman, reminding himself that he had to remain sober as his work wasn't yet done. But he was in celebratory mood, and he allowed himself half a gram of whiz in the toilets to keep him from flagging too much. His plan was to have a few more beers that afternoon, then slowly make his way home, buying some chocolate for the missus on the way. He was going to tell her that he'd tendered his resignation, the experience with Vokes having finally proved too much for him. Not that he was going to go and work for that hound, Clive. Instead, he was going to set up his own business, providing security advice to well-heeled firms. He knew a couple of colleagues who'd done that, and it had proved an easy way of making decent money. You just needed a few quid to get you started, and you were away. And now that few quid was no longer going to be a problem.

In fact, everything was going swimmingly for Stegs as he left the Admiral at just after three o'clock. However, ten yards down the street in the direction of his car and booty, that all changed with a suddenness that fate only keeps for those it likes to fuck up big-time.

The mobile rang, the tinny strains of *Mission Impossible* coming up from out of his jeans. He fished it out of his pocket and saw that it was a call from home. He took a deep breath, steadied himself so that he was sounding as sober as possible, then took the call.

'Hello, luv, you all right?'

There was a ferocious hacking sob down the other end of the line, and Stegs initially thought she was having an asthma attack, even though she'd never had asthma before, but then came the recriminations, and he knew she was fine. Physically anyway.

'You bastard!' she spluttered. 'You've been lying to me all this time.'

'Hold on, luv, what is this? What are you talking about?'

'Don't play the fucking innocent with me!' The F-word. The biggest verbal weapon in the missus's armoury. Like an atomic warhead, kept back only for situations of the utmost seriousness. This, then, had to be bad. And it was. 'I've had a reporter on, asking to interview you. He said you'd been suspended since last week. So, what the hell have you been doing, eh? Getting up in the middle of the night and disappearing like some sort of . . .' She couldn't think of the right insult, so instead sobbed loudly again. 'Have you got a girlfriend or something? Is that who you're seeing?'

'No, of course not.'

'And why were you suspended? That's what I want to know. It's the lies, Mark. The way you've lied to me, all this time. I don't think I can ever trust you again. You never talk, you never share anything with me.'

'That's because I can't get a fucking word in edgeways.'

'Don't you dare talk to me like that! Don't you dare! It's you who's in the wrong. You who've been lying. I've had enough, Mark, I really have. Me and Luke don't deserve a selfish bastard like you.'

'Look—'

'How do you expect us to live without any money coming in? It's bad enough as it is, without you being suspended. Oh God! What the hell am I meant to do?'

'I'm suspended on full pay, there's still money coming in. It's all right.'

Her voice suddenly became calm. 'No, it's not. It's not all right. It's over, Mark.'

'What are you saying?' he asked, thinking that that was a really stupid question, since it was pretty fucking obvious what she was saying.

'I'm saying I want you out of our house, and out of our lives. Now. Tonight.'

The full impact of her words hit him then. And something else struck him too. The fact that, when it came down to it, he loved her. He honestly did.

'Please, don't kick me out. For Christ's sake, don't kick me out. I'll change, I promise. But don't do this to me. Not now. Not after my best friend's been killed.'

'It's too late, Mark. I'm sorry.'

'Where am I going to go?'

'You'll think of somewhere. You're a big boy now.'

'I'm leaving the Force. I've been thinking about it for ages. Honestly.'

'You can stay at our house tonight but I want you to pack in the morning and go. You'll still be allowed to see Luke as long as you give me notice. I don't suppose you'll be applying for custody of him, since you hardly give him the time of day, even in those rare moments when you are around.'

'You can't fucking do this to me! You can't!'

Stegs realized he was shouting and that people on the street were looking at him strangely. He also realized, before he could say anything else, that the missus had hung up on him, the first time she'd done that in years.

He put the phone back in his pocket and started walking. He walked and walked, wondering how he hadn't spotted that his missus disliked him that much. He'd win her back, though. When she realized he was going to change, and that he had some money behind him, then she'd come running back. In the end, what was the alternative? Single motherhood. No way. She'd change her mind.

By the time he got to a pub on the Woodhouse Road called the Dog and Badger, he was feeling a lot better. He went inside and ordered a pint of reassuringly expensive Stella.

You can knock Stegs Jenner down. Plenty of people had over the years. But he always got back up again. Always.

# 43

According to the Land Registry, 10 Haymarket Road was registered in the name of a Mr Aptar Singh. A quick search revealed he'd never been in trouble with the police before. Number 12, meanwhile, belonged to a Mr Anthony John Cross. Records showed that he'd owned the property for sixteen years, the first eight jointly with a Mrs Angela Nola Cross, the last eight on his own.

Anthony John Cross. I logged into the database and typed in his name. The long, baleful face of a man in his late fifties, who'd been dyeing his grey hair blond with only mixed success, appeared. No convictions, but he was currently in custody, facing seven charges of possession of a firearm without a certificate, with intent to commit a crime contrary to the 1968 Firearms Act. Date of arrest, 2nd March this year. I found a link to the arrest report. It stated that Cross, a retired career soldier, had been suspected by police of supplying firearms to local criminals either for rental or purchase for some considerable time. It was believed that he'd procured the firearms from various military contacts, and had also been responsible for reactivating replica firearms – a common and easily executable crime – to bolster his collection. Acting on intelligence, officers from Acton CID had raided his home in the early hours of 2 March, arresting Cross and re-covering a total of seven handguns of various calibres. Further, more serious charges of supplying firearms contrary to Section 16 of the Firearms Act were expected to follow.

I sat back in my seat and took a gulp from the cup of coffee on the desk, feeling a lot calmer now that I'd had confirmation from the hospital that the operation on Tina had been successful and that she was going to be all right. Getting back to working on the case was a good way of taking my mind off the tumultuous events of that morning.

So what did this new information tell me? My initial reaction was that it wasn't a great deal of help. Since the gun in the O'Brien slayings had been used only a week ago, it was obviously not one of the seven netted by the local police. Which meant that it had either been hired out or sold by Cross between the time Panner fired it into Fiona Ragdale's ceiling on 27 February and the police raid on his house three days later. Either that or Panner was lying. But how would he have known about Anthony Cross? We were going to need to speak to Cross himself and see if he could provide a link to Murk. Perhaps Murk had been spotted at the premises while it had been under surveillance.

I looked at my watch. It was almost two o'clock. I really needed to eat. My stomach growled and whined, but the hunger simply wasn't there, the morning's drama having played havoc with my appetite. In the end, I got up and bought the last, forlorn-looking cheese sandwich from the canteen and forced it down back at my desk, managing to consume all but a quarter of it. My stomach stopped growling anyway, and it made me feel a little bit better.

The incident room was almost empty that afternoon, and there was a sense that the O'Brien case was as good as solved. Trevor Murk had been pronounced dead at Charing Cross hospital at ten past twelve that afternoon without regaining consciousness, and DCI Woodham had got a number of mugshots of his printed up from his police record (he had two convictions: one for theft, one for receiving stolen goods, neither recent) which murder squad detectives were showing to real and potential witnesses to see if they could get final confirmation that he was the shooter. I didn't think that there would be much doubt that they'd get it, which was a testimony to Tina's detective work. Woodham, meanwhile, was chairing a news conference at Scotland Yard, scheduled for 3.30, in which some of the heat would finally be taken off the team.

As for Flanagan, no-one could get hold of him. According to his wife, he'd gone to see the doctor, and that was all she'd say.

I picked up the phone and called Acton CID. When I got through I introduced myself and was put through to a detective constable called Greg Blake. I told him about the lead that had come up involving the gun Panner had fired, and how it impinged upon our murder investigation. 'I'm interested in talking to someone who was involved in the raid to see if they remember anything about it that could be of help.'

'Well, you're talking to the right bloke,' Blake answered. 'I was there, but I don't know how much I can tell you.'

'I don't know either,' I said truthfully. 'Was there any way anyone could have missed anything?'

'No,' said Blake emphatically. 'No way. We went over the whole place with a fine toothcomb and we videoed the raid too.

We recovered everything there was to recover. It sounds like your man's lying.'

I sighed. 'I'm sure you're right.' And then something else struck me, something I hadn't thought about before. 'Do you remember who else was there from CID on the raid?'

Blake's tone turned suspicious. 'Why do you ask?'

'Because I'm going to need to make a report of this lead, so I've got to cover my arse. You know the score.'

'It was a big op, so it was run by my DCI, Frank Trummer. He was there, so was DC Bradshaw, and me obviously. Half a dozen uniforms and . . .' He paused at this point. 'One of my former colleagues, Paul Vokerman. You might have heard about him. He got killed the other day on that Heathrow thing.'

'Yes,' I said quietly. 'I've heard of him. I was sorry to hear about that.'

'He was a good bloke.'

'It always happens to the best. Look, thanks for that.'

'No problem. Anything else you need to know?'

'No. That'll be fine.'

I hung up and sat staring at the phone for a long time.

So it was Vokes Vokerman who was the traitor. I hadn't been expecting that.

I was still staring at the telephone when Malik came into the incident room with his jacket on, looking like he was in a hurry. 'Heard the latest, John?' he asked me, picking up some papers from his desk. He was obviously going somewhere.

I swivelled round in my seat. 'No, tell me. Then I've got something for you.'

'I don't think it'll be as eye-opening as mine. Trevor Murk . . .'

'Yes?'

'He's a registered informant. Up until very recently, one of his main handlers was none other than Stegs Jenner.' I think I must have looked confused because Malik pulled a face. 'What's wrong? I thought you'd be pleased. Tina will be. She's been convinced he was the source of the leak all along.'

'It's not that,' I said, 'it's just that Panner was telling the truth about that armourer. His name's Anthony Cross. He was raided at the beginning of this month by Acton CID. Paul Vokerman was one of the men on the raid.'

He stared at me aghast. 'You're joking?'

I shook my head. 'I wish I was. I really, genuinely wish I was.'

'You think he lifted the gun on the raid and supplied it to Murk?'

'I don't know,' I said. 'I've been sitting here for the last twenty minutes thinking about it. Someone supplied the information on that deal at the hotel to either Nicholas Tyndall or Strangleman Grant, using O'Brien as a go-between. O'Brien was then shot using a gun we believe was once in the possession of an armourer whose home was raided by one of the undercover officers involved in the Heathrow op. The gun never showed up in the inventory, so, yeah, it seems very likely he lifted it.'

'Where does that leave us? That both of them were involved? Stegs and Vokes? Because Vokes got killed on that op, which is why he's always been above suspicion. If he was behind the robbery, why would he have set it up like that? He was in the room effectively as a hostage. He would have known that when the dealers went to get the gear and Stegs went to get the money that the robbery would occur, as planned, and then his life wouldn't be worth anything. Why would he have done it? It would have been suicidal.'

'But you remember when we were in the control room last week, watching it all unfold, Vokes didn't want to be the one left behind. In fact, he was adamant. He even suggested that it would be best if Stegs was the one who stayed.'

'That doesn't mean he's guilty of anything, though. I wouldn't want to stay in a room with a bunch of armed drug dealers, even if SO19 were next door.'

'Maybe he is innocent, but that still leaves a huge coincidence where that raid on Cross is concerned.'

Malik nodded. 'I know. Two of them. It doesn't bear thinking about. I didn't think even Neil Vamen was capable of that sort of clout.'

'I think we've been underestimating him.'

'I've got to go and see Jack Merriweather this afternoon. We reckon he's got some information on the whereabouts of the body of a thief who's been missing for the last five years. When I talk to him, I'll see if he knows about any involvement Stegs and Vokerman, and even Murk, might have had with the Holtzes or Vamen.'

'We're going to have to bring Stegs in now,' I said. 'His name's coming up far too many times.'

'I spoke to Woodham about ten minutes ago. He's trying to get search and arrest warrants organized for him now.' Malik put the papers he was holding into his briefcase, and locked it. 'Listen, get on to Woodham. He's down at Scotland Yard this afternoon, giving another press conference on the inquiry. Tell him about what we've found out about Vokes. And do me a favour.'

'Your wish is my command, my lord.'

'Sorry, I'm not trying to order you around. I'm just in a hurry, that's all.'

'What's the favour?'

'Can you give me a call and let me know as soon as you've got hold of Stegs? I want to be in on the questioning.'

I nodded. 'Sure. Are you going to see Merriweather now?'

'That's classified information, John,' Malik said, with only the barest hint of a smile.

'Well, if you are, be careful. It strikes me that if Vamen is hoping to be out and about again, then he could do a lot worse than bump Merriweather off. Remember, he's already tried twice.'

'I'm sure he'd send some goons over to Merriweather like a shot if he knew where he was, but that location's even more tightly guarded than the jury's going to be at Vamen's trial. Me, Flanagan and maybe three other people are the only ones who know where he's being kept.'

I laughed. 'Famous last words.'

We said our goodbyes, and I picked up the phone and dialled Woodham's mobile. Although the press conference was still nearly three quarters of an hour away he was already at the New Scotland Yard building where most major Met Police press briefings take place. I told him what I'd found out and what had been discussed with Malik, and he told me he was still awaiting the warrants for Stegs.

'I'll chase them when I've finished the conference. I didn't want to arrest him, particularly as he's a copper, but I don't see we've got much choice. The more we dig up on this case, the more shit there is sticking to him. Vokerman can't talk, but he can.'

'What are we going to do about Vokes? Raid his place too?'

Woodham made some tutting noises down the phone, and for a moment I thought he was admonishing me about something, but then I realized it must be a habit of his when he was thinking hard. 'I don't know. Not for the moment, no. Not until we've talked to Stegs. It won't look too good raiding the home of a recently deceased officer who's had a long and unblemished career. We're going to need to be very sure before we go knocking on his wife's door.'

'But Stegs we can go for?'

'We have to go for him. And the sooner the better. I've got DCs Wrays and Farland keeping an eye on his place at the moment. Apparently, he hasn't shown his face outside all day.'

'Are we sure he's there?'

'No, that's the problem. DCS Flanagan didn't put anyone on him last night so he's only had surveillance since this morning. But from now on, it's twenty-four-seven. When he shows, we'll pull him in and do the search of his house simultaneously.' There was a commotion in the background. 'Listen, I've got to go now. There are a couple of people I need to talk to before the briefing. I'll be in contact later.'

'I'll be on my mobile.'

After the call I sat there for a few moments on my own. Was it possible that both Stegs and Vokes had been corrupt? The evidence seemed to point that way, yet there were still un-answered questions, loose ends amid the theories, and it made me wonder whether or not some of them would ever be answered.

It also made me wonder whether I'd be able to control myself when I came into contact with Stegs Jenner.

# 44

I got to the hospital at ten to six, having fought my way through the tangled and frustrating rush-hour traffic. Tina was in the private room they'd set aside for her, propped up in a half-sitting position. Her leg was heavily bandaged, but otherwise she looked healthy enough considering her ordeal of only a few hours before. Her eyes were shut, but they opened when I came in and she smiled, struggling to get herself more comfortable. I was carrying chocolates and a bunch of flowers I'd picked up on the way, and I put them on the chair before moving in to kiss her softly on the cheek.

'Jesus, you gave me a scare today,' I said, trying hard not to get too emotional in her presence as once again the sense of relief flooded through me.

'It's all right, John,' she whispered in my ear. 'I'm OK.'

I let go and sat down on one of the other chairs, bringing it closer to the bed. I wanted to lecture her about her recklessness that morning, but resisted the urge, knowing that it wasn't what she wanted to hear. Instead, I told her how good her detective work had been. 'You're the toast of the squad at the moment. I think you're going to end up getting used to champagne.'

She smiled, and it was one of the nicest sights I'd seen in a long time. Tina Boyd was a survivor, that was for sure, but only just.

'So, what's the latest news?' she asked with a yawn.

'Something you'll want to hear. We're bringing in Stegs.' I briefly explained his relationship with Trevor Murk.

The smile grew wider. 'I knew, John. What did I tell you? I knew the trail would lead back to him. I think you're going to have to rename me Philip Marlowe.'

'There's more.' I then told her about the gun lead and how it had involved Vokes.

'So there's a possibility both of them were involved?' Tina shook her head. 'I can't see it myself. Vokerman just wasn't the type.'

'It's still very strange, though. And coincidental. And I've never been a one for coincidences. It's going to be very interesting to hear what Stegs has to say.'

'I'd be more interested in kicking him very hard in the nuts. The bastard almost got me killed.'

'He'll get more than a kick in the nuts if he is responsible for everything that's happened. We'll make sure he goes down for the rest of his days, I promise you that.' I shook my head. 'Christ, what a day. I was scared out of my wits when Murk had the gun against your head. How the hell were you feeling?'

'Scared,' she said, thinking about her words. 'But also, I don't know, exhilarated. I can't work out whether this morning was the best few hours of my life or the worst. It just feels strange, like a dream. Even my leg doesn't hurt that much. I just feel very, very tired.'

'Did they say how long you're going to be kept in?'

'Another three or four days so they can check for infections. I can go back to work in about a month if all goes well.'

'You're not going to leave, then?'

She sighed and gave my hand a squeeze. 'Not just yet, no. Why? Do you want me to now?'

'I want you to do what you think is right,' I lied. 'Same as I always have.'

There was silence between us for a few moments. She yawned again, and turned her head away, her eyes starting to close. I took that as a cue to make a move, and I was just about to say my goodbyes when she asked me if I'd meant what I'd said earlier.

'About what?' I felt my heart leaping like it does the first time you ask someone out and they say yes.

'You know exactly what.' She turned her head so she was facing me again, a coy expression on her face.

I grinned. 'Yeah. I did.'

'I think we should maybe take that holiday, don't you?'

'Too right. Safari followed by the Seychelles?'

'I think we deserve it.' She yawned again, a longer one this time. 'Let me know what happens with Stegs, won't you? Straight away.'

I told her I would, but she'd already shut her eyes.

I sat there for a while watching her sleep, thinking that I'd experienced some serious highs and lows that day.

And it wasn't even finished yet.


Outside, in the car park, it was a mild evening. Darkness had just about fallen, and the sky glowed the unhealthy pink of the city at night. The time was twenty to seven, which meant I'd been in the hospital a lot longer than I'd thought. I switched on my mobile and saw that I had a message. It was from DCI Woodham: Stegs Jenner had arrived home; I was to proceed to his address immediately and to wait out of sight of the house if the rest of the team hadn't yet arrived. The message was recorded at 6.38, so I'd only just missed him. I pressed 5 for recall and phoned him back.

# 45

Malik had had just about as much as he could take of Jack Merriweather.

The way the gangster turned informer talked, you'd be forgiven for assuming that he was doing the CPS and the police some sort of favour by testifying in the Vamen trial, rather than simply saving his own skin. Merriweather had been Neil Vamen's right-hand man and a member of the Holtz set-up for at least fifteen years, probably more. It was inconceivable that he hadn't committed murder on their behalf, and, given the evidence against him for more recent crimes, he'd had no choice but to turn against his former allies and employers. Now he was denying any knowledge at all of the whereabouts of Terry Duffy, a small-time thief and thug who'd gone out one morning for some cigarettes and never been seen again. Duffy had left behind a pregnant partner and a two-year-old son. It was known he owed Neil Vamen money over a drug deal and was having difficulty paying him back. In the last week, a potential witness had come forward and claimed that she'd heard Merriweather say he'd been one of those involved in the kidnapping and disposal of the body. The family were desperate for news, even if it was simply the location of the remains, so that they could get some sort of closure on the case. Unsurprisingly, Merriweather was denying any knowledge of the incident.

'I knew the bloke,' he'd told Malik, 'but that's all. I didn't have nothing to do with killing him, and I don't know who did. Or even if he's dead.'

It was bullshit of course, but there wasn't much Malik could do about it, and now it was a quarter to seven and he was finished there. It hadn't been a very satisfactory visit. Merriweather had also never heard of Stegs Jenner, which wasn't going to help the case against the SO10 man, especially since very little had gone on in the Holtz set-up that their chief witness hadn't known about. It left Malik with a flicker of doubt about Stegs's guilt, which was something he could have done without, but he was also aware that Merriweather had never given up the names of any police officers involved with the Holtzes, so either it was an area of the business he'd steered clear of or, for whatever reason, he'd made a conscious decision not to say anything about them. Once again, inconclusive.

But right now, Malik's home and family beckoned. He left Merriweather sitting in the office they'd been using at the back of the house. The discussions had moved on to the upcoming trial, and the ex-gangster was in good cheer, swigging happily from a can of taxpayer-funded Foster's, seemingly unworried about the ordeal ahead. 'Don't you worry about a fucking thing, Asif,' he bellowed after the SO7 man, in a tone of camaraderie that Malik could have done without. 'It'll be a doddle.' Malik lifted a hand to acknowledge that he'd heard Merriweather's boast but kept walking. It had better be a doddle, he thought to himself, because if their star witness didn't come through the case was in a lot of trouble.

Luckily, Merriweather was a resilient character. He had to be, given that less than two weeks before there'd been not one but two attempts on his life, and that, whatever happened in the coming weeks, he was a marked man for the rest of his days. Already his wife had left him, unable to equate the man she knew with the man he'd become, and had taken the kids with her, and it was a possibility that he'd never see any of them again, because to do so would be such a security risk. He was truly on his own (particularly now that his request for visits from his girlfriend had been turned down), which was a lot for a man to live with. But so far Merriweather was managing, and managing remarkably well. In that respect, he was a perfect witness. In every other respect he was an arsehole, and a nasty one at that.

As he walked past the lounge on the way to the front door, Malik waved at the two plainclothes officers who were acting as Merriweather's guards. 'Thanks for that, gents. It's been a pleasure.' He rolled his eyes.

'Take it easy, Asif,' said the younger of the two, Dan Harold, a guy Malik knew vaguely. He didn't know Harold's colleague, Bill Cheek, who simply nodded.

'Fat chance of that,' Malik replied with a chuckle as he opened the door.

His mobile rang, and it made him wonder, not for the first time, what anyone had ever done before the advent of the mobile phone. Had a lot easier time of it, probably. Shutting the door behind him, he put the receiver to his ear.

'Malik.'

The voice that spoke to him was artificial, robotic. Slurred a little. 'Jack Merriweather is in imminent danger. There's a leak within SO7. The leak is DCS Noel Flanagan. He's in the pay of

Neil Vamen and has released Merriweather's current location.' The voice reeled off the address.

Malik froze. It was correct. What the hell was going on? He opened his mouth to say something but the voice continued.

'Neil Vamen has arranged through his solicitor, Melvyn Carroll, for assassins to visit his premises in the very near future to carry out Merriweather's killing. You are advised to act accordingly.'

The phone went dead and Malik was left staring at it, wondering exactly how near the near future was.

# 46

With the worst part of rush hour over, the traffic up to Barnet was less heavy than it had been from the station to Charing Cross hospital, and I turned into Stegs's road at twenty past seven, focused completely now on the job ahead.

I was the first there, and the street was quiet. I could see lights on in the Jenner household but there was no sign of the two officers keeping watch on the place. I hadn't been told how they were conducting their surveillance but presumed they were probably camped in one of the houses opposite in order to make themselves as inconspicuous as possible. If they were here on the street, then they were doing their job very well.

I picked up my mobile and dialled Woodham again.

'We're just coming into the estate now,' he told me. 'ETA one minute. We're going to park outside and go straight in. I'm sending a marked patrol car round to the next street, just in case he tries to escape out the back, but I'm confident he'll come quietly.'

'Let's hope so,' I said, and hung up.

One minute later, the lead car containing Woodham drove straight past me, followed by a second unmarked one – a Ford Orion – with a patrol car bringing up the rear. Woodham's vehicle parked right outside Stegs's house, and the second car managed to squeeze in behind it; the patrol car found a slot about twenty yards further up. Two more figures, whom I recognized as DC Wrays and WDC Farland – the officers watching the place – appeared from the other end of the street and made their way towards the house.

Exhaling loudly, and wondering what we were about to find out, I got out of my own car and crossed the road, catching up with Woodham and four of the other detectives from the squad as they decamped and started up the drive towards Stegs's front door. I remembered then that I'd promised to phone Malik when I'd got any news. I asked Woodham if he'd been in contact with him.

'Not yet,' he answered as he approached the door, hammering on it with a copper's authority. 'He's not answering at the moment.'

A few seconds later the door opened and Mrs Jenner stood there, looking at us all with some apprehension. She spotted me but gave no obvious sign of recognition. 'Yes?' she said with genuine surprise. In the background, a baby started crying. It sounded like the cries were coming from up the stairs.

'Police, Mrs Jenner,' said Woodham gruffly, showing his ID. 'We have a warrant to search these premises. We also have a separate warrant for your husband's arrest. Would you let us in, please?'

Her face seemed to crack under the strain. 'What are you talking about? My husband *is* a police officer.'

Woodham was unmoved. 'You'll see that everything's in order,' he stated without emotion. With his other hand, he produced the warrant and thrust it under her nose, then stepped inside the door. 'Where is your husband, Mrs Jenner? Is he upstairs?'

She moved aside to let him in, her face still a mask of shock. 'No,' she said, with a hint of desperation. 'He isn't here.'

'We have reason to believe he is,' said Woodham evenly as he stepped onto the stairs. Two of the other detectives moved into the hallway and started off in the direction of the kitchen.

'No, honestly, he isn't. He went out about ten minutes ago. We had an argument when he came home. He hadn't told me about his suspension, and now I'm kicking him out.'

Woodham, who wasn't the most diplomatic or tolerant of people, clearly didn't believe her and carried on up the stairs. 'Your baby needs you,' he called down to her, and she pushed past the other detectives on the stairs, her face a picture of humiliation. It looked like, in the life of Mrs Stegs Jenner, things couldn't get much worse.

The rest of us piled into the house. I opened the door into the sitting room. The lights were on, as was the TV, but the room was otherwise empty.

A few seconds later, there was the sound of heavy footfalls on the stairs, and I came back into the hall to see Woodham re-appear looking none too pleased. Mrs Jenner was following him, holding the grizzling baby.

'I told you he wasn't here,' she said.

Woodham glared at Wrays and Farland who'd come in behind me. 'I thought you were meant to be watching the place,' he said accusingly.

'We were,' said Wrays, sounding not unlike a chastised school-boy. 'We must have looked away for a moment and missed him.'

I noticed Farland blushing. Obviously, office romances were all the rage.

'I'm not a liar, you know,' continued Mrs Jenner.

Woodham turned to her angrily, in no mood for pussy-footing around. 'Where the hell do you think he is, then?'

'I don't know,' she snapped, tears in her eyes.

I could understand the DCI's frustration but I didn't think he was going about dealing with it the right way. 'Where's the most likely place you can think of where he'd go if the two of you had an argument, Mrs Jenner?' I asked her.

'The pub probably. That's where he spends most of his time. There's one at the end of the estate on Church Hill that he drinks in now and again. The King's Arms, it's called. Or otherwise, if he's on foot, he might take a walk up to his old school. He goes there sometimes when he wants some peace and quiet. It's just over the back of the houses opposite. There's an entrance at the bottom of the road.' Her gaze moved from me to Woodham. 'What are you arresting him for? He didn't have anything to do with what happened to Paul, did he? Paul Vokerman?'

'We can't discuss it at the moment, I'm afraid,' Woodham told her. 'All right: Wrays, Farland, you get up to the pub. John, you and me'll go up to the school with the uniforms. The rest of you stay here and carry out the search.'

The baby howled loudly and angrily in Woodham's direction, evidently not happy with this man's intrusion on to his territory, and Mrs Jenner finally burst into tears.

Woodham didn't notice. He was already heading for the car, with me following.

# 47

Malik went back inside the house, slamming the front door behind him. The two detectives were still sitting where he'd left them, playing a game of cards. Both had cans of Foster's open. They looked up as he reappeared.

'What's going on?' asked Dan Harold.

'We've got a problem. A big one. Vamen's on to us. He knows Merriweather's at this location.'

'Christ almighty,' he cursed. 'How?'

'I don't know.'

'Who told you?'

'That's the thing, I'm not sure. I just got an anonymous call a few seconds ago.' He didn't add the bit about Flanagan being the alleged leak.

'How do you know it's authentic?' asked Bill Cheek, reaching into his jacket and fingering his shoulder holster nervously.

'He told me the address. It's an authentic call, take my word for it.'

Cheek got to his feet, Harold following.

'What's going on?' called Merriweather from the other side of the house, his voice booming down the hallway. 'Whatchoo doing back, Asif?'

'Let's get all the lights off,' said Cheek, switching off the lamp by the chair he'd been sitting in. 'And pull the curtains. Dan, go down and make sure Merriweather stays put.'

'Do you want me to let him know what's happening?'

'Yes.'

Malik had put the number of DCI Norman Thackston of Crawley Police, the nearest station with armed support, into his mobile a few days earlier, just in case of this eventuality, even though he'd always thought it unlikely in the extreme. He speed-dialled it now, at the same time flicking off the hall light. Thackston wasn't there, but after a dozen or so rings, someone else picked up.

'Thackston's line, DS Kamal speaking.'

Malik strode into the kitchen, switching off the light and pulling the curtains across. As he did so, he told Kamal as rapidly as possible what was happening, and how urgent the situation was, before giving him the address. Twice. 'I need armed response units here immediately. We're going to have to move our man as soon as possible, but I'm not doing anything until you get here. Be quick, for God's sake. We lose the target and heads'll roll, I promise you that.'

He hung up before Kamal had a chance to get a word in edgeways, then headed back into the hall. In the darkness, he could make out Cheek standing there with his gun drawn. It brought home the danger of the situation to him. They were in trouble, serious trouble, and because he was unarmed, having never had the desire to take up firearms training, Malik was going to have to rely on other people to bring him out of the situation alive and unhurt. It wasn't a situation he was either used to, or relished.

'They're on their way,' he told Cheek.

'Good. You need to get down with Merriweather. We'll watch the back and front doors.'

Malik nodded and headed down the hallway in the gloom to the office where he'd spent the last three hours, Cheek following.

Merriweather was in the chair where he'd been sitting all afternoon. He'd lit a cigarette and was still swigging from the can. He didn't appear too concerned. Harold stood next to him, his gun also drawn.

'What's happening then, Asif?' Merriweather asked, trying to sound casually cheery, but not quite achieving it. 'We got trouble or something?'

'You could say that,' said Malik.

'All right, Merriweather,' said Cheek, 'put the fag out. Now. And get on the floor. Dan, you watch the back door, I'll watch the front. Everyone turn their mobiles off. I want it to sound like we're not here. All right?'

Merriweather reluctantly put out his smoke and sat down heavily on the floor. Malik crouched down next to him, and the other two left the room. Now it was simply a matter of waiting.

'How the fuck did they find out where we were?' demanded Merriweather. 'Can't you lot do anything right? I thought it was meant to be a fucking secret.'

'Keep your voice down, Jack. Please.'

The two of them fell silent. Malik reached down and switched off his mobile, wondering what his wife was doing even as he crouched there on the floor of a darkened, silent house, his mouth as dry as a bone as he silently prayed for help to arrive. Probably preparing the dinner or putting the children to bed. Perhaps even reading them a story. The thought comforted him somehow. He looked at his watch. And waited.

A minute became two, then three. Time passed slowly. He could hear Merriweather's heavy breathing.

'I can't believe you've fucked up again,' hissed the other man eventually.

'Shut up, Jack.'

He looked at his watch again, wondering how long it was going to take the ARVs to get up from Crawley. Fifteen minutes probably, even going at breakneck pace. However, their sirens would startle any would-be assassins before then, so time was probably on their side. But it still felt like a long wait.

There was a noise outside the window. A shuffling. Muffled voices. He tensed in the darkness. So did Merriweather, his eyes widening. They were here.

Then the noise was gone, and the dead silence returned, broken only by the faint hiss of traffic in the distance.

'They'll jimmy the door,' said Merriweather quietly, an ominous tone in his voice.

# 48

I saw him standing in the middle of the playing fields, in the shadow of an impressive beech tree, about fifty yards away, his back to me. He was staring straight ahead, facing the school. Several lights burned in the clutch of two- and three-storey buildings in the distance. Beside me by the gate at the playing fields entrance stood DCI Woodham and two uniformed coppers.

'Let me go and speak to him first,' I said. 'I think we might startle him if he hears us all coming, and I don't much fancy a chase round here.'

Woodham nodded. 'All right,' he answered, probably feeling charitable towards me on the basis that my partner (work, to him) had been so recently injured, 'but I don't want to lose him, John. Make sure you bring him back here, and if he starts running, you're in shit.'

'Fair enough,' I said, and started walking.

Stegs heard me when I was about ten yards behind him, and

turned round curiously, but without fear. He was smoking a cigarette, and was about halfway down to the butt. 'Hello, John,' he said. 'I was wondering when you lot'd turn up.'

I stopped beside him and he turned back towards the school. We stood there watching it together for a few moments.

'We've got to bring you in, Stegs. We've got a warrant for your arrest.'

Stegs didn't seem to hear me. 'Five years I spent in this place,' he said, dragging hard on his cigarette. 'And the whole time I couldn't wait to leave. But do you know what? They were the best years of my life. No worries, no fears, no people you trusted fucking you up behind your back. No broken marriages. Just having a laugh with your mates, bunking off, trying to get laid.' He managed a weak smile. 'They were the best years of my life, and I never fucking knew it.'

'I've got to take you in, Stegs. We'll talk down the station.'

'I know what you're thinking,' he continued, still not looking at me. 'You're thinking I was involved in the Heathrow robbery, but I wasn't. I did everything by the book, and that's a promise. Vokes was the one, John. It was him, I swear it. I loved that bloke, you know. He was like a brother to me. We were joined at the fucking hip. We watched each other's backs on ops that would have had most men shitting themselves in fear. But all the time the bastard was bent, and I never knew it. He hid behind this Christian front, made out he was one of the good guys, but all the time I knew him, all those years, he was on the make. Did you know he was working for the Holtzes? Had been for years. Did you know that?'

'If we'd known it, he wouldn't have still been a serving copper.'

'There was a bloke I sometimes used to work with in SO10, a bloke called Jeff Benson. He was good, fucking good. He got into the Holtzes, was getting close to pulling in some real evidence against them, particularly Neil Vamen. He told me about it . . . stupid of him really. Because then one night I went out with Vokes and I'd had a few drinks, which has always been my fucking downfall, and I let slip about it. I didn't even mention him by name, but Vokes had enough info to warn the Holtzes, and they put the frighteners on Benson and scuppered the whole op.'

Stegs sighed and stubbed out the cigarette, immediately lighting another one. I let him do it, making no move to take him back to Woodham and the others. Although none of it was admissible in court, I wanted to hear what he had to say, particularly as he was so talkative. He sounded slightly pissed. Not badly so, but there was definitely an edge to his voice.

'Benson blamed you, didn't he?'

Stegs nodded. 'Yeah. At the time I couldn't understand it, I thought he was being too paranoid, but I suppose he thought only a couple of people in the world knew about it, and I was the likeliest one to have opened my mouth. It didn't occur to me that Vokes could have been the source of the leak. I trusted him so I didn't suspect him. First rule of life, John: trust no-one. It's not fucking worth it.' He waved the cigarette in my direction, trying to emphasize his point, and I saw that he was unsteady on his feet.

It occurred to me too that we wouldn't be able to interview him in this state, and he might be a lot less talkative once he'd sobered up. 'When did you find out about Vokes?' I asked him.

'It was after we did the sting on O'Brien, the one you and Boyd set up. If you remember, he wasn't involved in the first part when we caught O'Brien redhanded.' I remembered. Vokes had been unavailable. 'But he came in for the next stage, the setting up of the sting on Fellano.'

'That's right.'

'When he came in the room and first met O'Brien, I saw

straight away that O'Brien recognized him. I don't think Vokes recognized him back – in fact, I'm sure he didn't – but O'Brien must have seen him with someone else from the Holtzes before. He didn't say anything, but that didn't matter. I saw the look, and I think that's when I knew finally that the bastard was in with them. I should have known a long time back, but I never looked fucking hard enough, because I couldn't see the wood for the trees.' He sighed. 'And do you know the worst part?'

'What?'

'He knew I knew. I've always been a good actor, you've got to be when you're SO10, but my behaviour around him must have changed or something, because he knew that I was on to him. And the cunning bastard, that so-called Christian, he was going to set me up to die in that hotel room, just so he could make sure I kept my mouth shut. I've been thinking about the whole thing a long time, and I've worked it out. The idea of the robbery was to put Tyndall in the spotlight and fuck things up for him. Vokes used O'Brien to set it up, on behalf of Neil Vamen. O'Brien knew that Strangleman Grant, the one who got shot, would go for it because he was such a greedy, short-sighted prick.'

'How do you know he was a greedy, short-sighted prick? You said at Heathrow that you'd never seen him before in your life.'

'I'm theorizing, John. That's all. Anyway, I was meant to be the one staying in that room while the robbery went down. Vokes knew the Colombians would kill me as soon as it happened down in the car park, but he was going to let it happen. Only thing was, it backfired. They wanted him to stay in the room, not me.'

'Why was that?'

Stegs shook his head. 'I don't know,' he said. 'Maybe they didn't trust him either.'

'So, you're the innocent in all this, are you?'

Something about my question – probably the scepticism in it – made him look my way.

'I'm not the best man in the world, John, as my missus'll no doubt tell you. I can be an arsehole, and I can bend the rules, but I promise you this: I had nothing to do with the leak on the Heathrow op.'

I eyed him carefully. 'I hope not, Stegs. I sincerely hope not. For your sake.'

'You don't believe me, do you? But you know Vokes was the one who was working for Vamen. And there are others, too. Try Detective Chief Superintendent Flanagan, for one.'

I put my hand up. 'All right, Stegs, slow down. I know you've had problems with Flanagan in the past, but he is definitely not corrupt. He's the head of SO7, for Christ's sake.'

Stegs opened his mouth to say something but then he stopped and turned. So did I. Hurrying across the field in our direction were Woodham and the two uniforms. Even in the darkness I could see the grave expression on the DCI's face. My heart skipped a beat, and I felt an ominous dread. Something serious had happened.

'Stay where you are,' I told Stegs, stepping forward and putting a hand on his arm.

# 49

DS Bill Cheek was forty-three years old. He'd been a copper all his working life, and as times had changed – more for the worse than the better – he, like many of the other older officers in the Met, was thinking about retirement and the hallowed pension. A life away from the stress of dealing with people who in any other walk of life you'd cross the street to avoid. He and the wife had talked about him quitting next year when his twenty-five years' service came up. She wanted them to retire to France, somewhere in Brittany, where they'd spent so many of their holidays down the years. They'd never had kids so there was nothing to hold them back, and he had to admit, there was something about the idea. They could sell their three-bed semi in Norwood, buy a big place near the sea with land, and still have plenty of money left over.

And now, suddenly, her dream – his too, since effectively she'd won him over to it – was fading as the reality of his situation sunk in. He was crouched back against the hall wall, facing the door twelve feet away, both hands holding the standard-issue Browning in front of him, listening to the scraping of their feet as they came to the front door.

The door was made of wood and looked reasonably sturdy, but Cheek realized now that he'd made a mistake. In the mêlée and confusion, he hadn't been able to find the key to double-lock it, and the chain was too flimsy to act as much of a substitute. If only he'd kept the bloody thing in the door. It was too late now, far too late, and he wondered if it was a mistake that was going to cost him his life. He'd never fired a gun in anger before, even though he'd been a trained firearms officer for close to fifteen years, and had no desire to change that state of affairs now. British police guidelines for opening fire were some of the strictest in the world. If he pulled the trigger, he would face literally hundreds of questions. If he hit anyone, he'd be the subject of a major, and possibly hostile, investigation. There could even be murder or attempted murder charges if he made the wrong decision. It was a bastard of a position to put a man in.

There was a crack as the wood on the door was forced. Cheek's grip on the gun tightened. He tried to force all doubts and fears out of his head, and focus on the few feet of empty space in front of him. But it was hard. Harder than anything he'd ever had to do before. This was it: life or death.

A second, louder crack split the silence, and he heard the door give. His teeth clenched, and he tried to stop his hands from shaking. But they shook anyway, as the fear dragged him deeper into the darkness. The moment of truth, the moment he wished to God he'd never have to face, and it was coming to him as swiftly and unexpectedly as a heart attack. And still he couldn't fire, because he couldn't see his targets, and could not tell for sure whether they were armed or not, even though they had to be, since why else would they be here?

Hold your fire. Pray you can pull the trigger. Pray you've got the strength. Pray they don't fire first.

The door came open slowly, then stopped as the chain went taut. Silence. He thought he heard breathing.

Come on, if you're coming. Come on.

Bang! It flew open like a shot, and then the shadowy figures were there, facing him down from the porch. His chest constricted painfully as he saw they had guns.

'Armed police! Drop your weapons now!'

A stunningly loud burst of automatic gunfire erupted in the hallway as one of the figures opened fire. Cheek pulled the trigger, twice in rapid succession, but then his whole body seemed to burn up, and he felt himself being slammed against the wall as the bullets struck him.

The shooter with the automatic rifle had been hit by Cheek's rounds and he stumbled backwards, still discharging his own weapon in a hail of fire and noise, the bullets tearing into the ceiling. He hit the ground, his magazine empty, and a second figure appeared in his place, opening up in Cheek's direction with a pump-action shotgun.

Cheek lifted his gun arm and tried to squeeze the trigger again, experiencing a tangible and immediate feeling of pride that his training had come through, and that he'd responded appropriately to the armed criminal in front of him, but then the first deafening shotgun blast ripped a huge hole in his chest, and the second took off most of his face. He died within seconds, knowing that he was in the right, and that the PCA had nothing on him.

The assassin with the shotgun now came cautiously over the threshold, reloading as he did so, followed by another man armed with a .38 revolver.

From where they crouched at the other end of the L-shaped

hallway, Malik and Merriweather could see the body of Cheek lying motionless amid the rising smoke. They'd both been deafened by the initial bursts of gunfire, and now realized their complete helplessness in the face of armed opposition.

'Fuck,' hissed Merriweather, crawling into a corner out of sight of the door. 'Never trust a copper.'

Malik moved away to the other side of the door but he knew it was a futile exercise. From his hopelessly exposed position he watched, terrified, as a shotgun appeared round the corner, preceding the powerfully built man holding it. The gunman was dressed in a dark boiler suit and balaclava, giving him the appearance of a medieval executioner of the sort you see in history books. A study in menace.

He started down the corridor in their direction, not having seen them yet, and Malik offered up a silent prayer for salvation, trying desperately to think of a way out of this.

Then, from over the other side of the house, he heard a noise. The gunman turned round towards the lounge, and there was a shout of 'Armed police!', then the sound of shots being fired from a police gun. The shotgun barked angrily in return and the glass in the lounge door shattered. Several other shots also came from somewhere else.

Which was when Malik made a decision. The one with the shotgun had his back to him and was facing the lounge. He took a step forward and fired again, the blast ringing round the bungalow and completely muffling Malik's footsteps as he got to his feet and ran straight at the gunman's back.

He hit him full on, jumping up and wrapping his arms round the other man's neck as he used all his momentum to send them both crashing through the lounge door. Out of the corner of his eye he caught the shadow of another gunman, but didn't have time to react.

As they came into the lounge, with Malik still on the shotgun-wielding assassin's back, he saw the figure of Dan Harold, gun in hand, behind the sofa. Harold fired another two shots towards the door, and the third gunman dived out of sight; then he pointed his weapon in the direction of Malik and the other gunman, who were struggling wildly in the middle of the floor, the shooter desperately trying to dislodge his limpet-like assailant.

The shotgun discharged into the fireplace and Malik let go of his opponent's neck and dropped to the floor. The gunman then straightened up and swung round to shoot at Harold, which was when Harold pulled the trigger again, hitting him in the shoulder and chest and sending him crashing into one of the chairs. A lamp toppled over, followed by the gunman.

A second later, the third gunman reappeared in the lounge doorway. Harold hesitated for a moment, no doubt shocked by the fact that he'd just killed a man, then, realizing that it wasn't over yet, swung round to fire again. But the gunman opened up first, cracking off three shots in quick succession. Harold yelped in pain as one of the bullets grazed his gun-shoulder, at the same time pulling the trigger himself. But he was off balance and the two shots he managed careered aimlessly into the ceiling. The Browning dropped from his hand and he fell back behind the sofa, clutching at his wounded shoulder.

The gunman swung round so he was facing Malik, weapon outstretched in both hands. Malik, still lying on the floor, could do nothing but look up at his would-be executioner, his eyes silently pleading for mercy.

The balaclava-clad gunman simply stared back at him through the near darkness, unmoved and unmoving, and Malik knew that this was it. The end. In the distance, he could make out the sound of sirens. Help was arriving, but it was going to be too late.

Then, suddenly, there was a bellowing roar and the sound of

footsteps charging down the hall. The gunman began to turn round but never made it as he was hit in the upper body by the office chair Merriweather had been sitting on a few minutes earlier. The gunman stumbled but managed to raise his gun in Merriweather's direction and fire off a shot before he was rugby-tackled from the front and sent flying backwards into the room.

Malik tried to get out of the way but he was too late, and the gunman and Merriweather crash-landed on top of him, taking his breath away. Within a second they'd rolled off, and Malik saw that their assailant had lost his gun, which had disappeared off somewhere in the darkness, leaving him unarmed as he struggled to fight off a still roaring Merriweather who was raining blows down on his head and body. He managed to get in a punch that connected with Merriweather's jaw, but the other man, his adrenalin and aggression now at full tempo, hardly seemed to notice it as he launched a flurry of counter blows, rolling round so that he was on top of his opponent. At the same time, Harold had got to his feet, having picked up the Browning in his good arm. He looked in a lot of pain and was moving unsteadily, but it didn't matter now because flashing blue lights were appearing outside the window as the ARVs came screeching to a halt.

'You fucking bastard!' screamed Merriweather as he continued to pummel the third gunman. 'Think you can fucking kill me, eh? Do ya? Come on, you cunt, fight me now!'

There was a lot more noise as the first armed officers came charging through the front door. 'Armed police!' one of them cried out, an MP5 in his hand pointed in the direction of the still fighting Merriweather. 'On the floor, now!'

For a split second, Malik's heart went into his mouth as he saw the officer's finger tensing on the trigger.

'Don't shoot! We're police! Whatever you do, don't shoot!'

'Get on the floor now, or I fire!'

'For God's sake, Jack, leave him alone!'

Knowing he was risking his own neck now, Malik, still winded, sat up and grabbed Merriweather by the shirt with both hands, pulling him away from the now unconscious gunman.

Merriweather turned round, a ferocious expression on his face, and Malik half thought he was going to lash out at him, but then the expression calmed as he finally came to his senses. He lay down on the floor, hands raised above his head.

It was finally all over.

# 50

Woodham and the uniforms stopped in front of the two of us.

'What's happened, sir?' I asked, an irrational fear that it might be something to do with Tina – a relapse of some sort – playing havoc with my imagination.

'There's just been an attempt on Jack Merriweather's life.'

Now I just felt a good, hard jolt of shock. 'What happened?'

'Three gunmen turned up. Two police officers have been shot – not Malik – but thankfully the attempt failed.'

'Fucking hell,' said Stegs evenly.

'How the hell did they find out where he was?'

'We don't know. Only a handful of people knew the location. There's going to have to be a full and thorough investigation.'

'Have they caught the gunmen?' asked Stegs.

Woodham turned to him with a look of suspicion. 'I think one, or possibly more of them, might have been shot, but, yes, they've all been apprehended.'

'Good.'

I let go of Stegs's arm, and watched him carefully. He stared back at me, his expression asking me to believe him, but something in it wasn't right. Something said that he knew much more than he was letting on.

'I'm telling you the truth, John. I promise.'

I wondered how he'd react when I told him we knew about Trevor Murk. Act surprised, and continue to keep to his story, I thought. Stegs Jenner was a born liar. He'd been doing it for a career for the past ten years, and I reckoned he'd been honing his trade for a lot longer before that. I decided then that it wasn't worth mentioning Murk just yet. Best to spring it on him in an interview, where any silence or spluttering denials would be recorded.

But something was bothering me. You see, the thing was, parts of his story made sense. Vokes hadn't been there at the first meeting with O'Brien. He'd also been on the raid from which the murder weapon had almost certainly been lifted. He hadn't wanted to be left in the room back at the hotel, had tried to insist that it wasn't him. Vokes Vokerman could answer a lot of questions.

Except he was dead.

I sighed, continuing to fix my gaze on Stegs Jenner. 'Wherever we go, Stegs, and whatever we uncover, things always seem to keep coming back to you.'

'You're getting paranoid, John,' he said, the beginnings of a smile on his face.

Just that little bit too cocky for my liking.

Which was when all the frustrations and fears of the day got the better of me and I punched him hard in the face. For just one second, it was the most satisfying blow I'd ever landed, and it knocked him spark out.

'I'll pretend I didn't see that,' said Woodham, a faint smile appearing beneath the big moustache.

# Afterwards

Life, it seems, never goes quite the way you want it to go, and what you think might happen often never does. DCS Noel Flanagan, the head of SO7, was uncovered as the leak to Neil Vamen. There'd been some canteen talk in the dim and distant past centring on the fact that he wasn't quite as straight as he'd have the Brass believe, but no one ever expected him to have been responsible for providing information that led to the death of an officer from his own unit, and that came within seconds of collapsing the case he and SO7 had been working on for years. Not only was it out of character, it was always going to be impossible to do without being found out. It was the police equivalent of a suicide note. Rumours abounded as to why he'd done it, and there was even talk that Vamen's operatives had kidnapped his daughter and used her to extract the information from him, but no-one ever knew for sure, and neither father nor daughter ever said a word about it. Neither did we find out who the anonymous caller was who'd given Malik those few minutes' warning that an attack on Jack Merriweather was imminent. Again, rumour suggested it might well have been Flanagan, perhaps suffering a fit of guilt (although it seemed a little strange, him incriminating himself), but no-one ever found out for sure.

Initially, Flanagan was not only suspended but also charged with perverting the course of justice. However, the charges were later quietly dropped due to lack of evidence, and he left the police, having denied any wrongdoing. He now lives in France with his wife, while his daughter continues her studies at university in the UK.

Stegs Jenner also left the Force. He was questioned at length about a number of crimes emanating from the hotel and their aftermath, but he too denied everything and the evidence against him remained weak. When confronted about his relationship with Trevor Murk, who'd been confirmed now as the shooter in the O'Brien/MacNamara killings, Stegs expressed shock. He admitted to having had a long and well-documented relationship with Murk, but claimed to be wholly unaware that his erstwhile informant was also a killer with not only the deaths of O'Brien and MacNamara to his name, but also the earlier murder of the garage owner Paul Bailey, as well as the strange killing of Hans Rieperman, otherwise known as Tino Movali, a small-time Dutch porn actor whose body was found two days later in the same building where Murk had been killed. He'd been shot with the revolver Murk had been carrying when he'd died, and it was surmised that he had been the one responsible. Intriguingly, Stegs admitted to meeting both men in the days leading up to their deaths, but explained that the reason for this was that Murk had introduced him to Rieperman, who was a drug dealer, in order to set him up and claim a financial reward. Stegs said that, even though he'd been suspended at the time, and it went against all the police rules to have unofficial contact with informants, he'd gone along to the meeting out of curiosity. It had, he said, been the last he'd seen of both men. As for his visit to Vamen's solicitor, the reason for this, apparently, was to let Carroll know that Stegs was on to him and his client, and that he was going to make them pay for almost getting him killed at Heathrow.

An unlikely story, but somehow it left me thinking, not for the first time, that some parts of this case will forever be shrouded in mystery. Sadly, that's often the way it goes. Endings in the real world are never usually neat.

One interesting little question that was answered, though, was how Murk had got into the building where he'd murdered O'Brien. We'd assumed that Kitty MacNamara had let him in, but the truth, or the most likely version of it anyway, turned out to be far more interesting. Apparently, he'd had a brief affair in the weeks leading up to the shooting with the married woman living in one of the ground-floor flats. She'd been away on holiday with her husband and young son while the investigation had been going on, but on returning had heard about what had happened, seen Murk's photograph, and approached us discreetly to say that she thought he might have copied her key and used it to gain entrance. The affair, she'd said, had been ended abruptly by him a week before the killings, and she'd been so nervous that he might break in during her absence that she'd left her jewellery in the hands of her mother. Whatever else you said about Murk, he'd been professional to the end.

During the course of this tale, more than one person has alluded to the cunning of Mr Stegs Jenner and whether or not what he was telling us was true (and most of us thought it was far too coincidental to be the truth), but he was sticking to his version of events and, as a result, he was eventually released from police custody without charge. Since then, his wife has sued for divorce, and the last I heard he was dividing his time between London and Spain.

Neil Vamen suffered badly as a result of his attempt to tip the scales of justice in his favour. The Law Society began an investigation into claims that his solicitor, Melvyn Carroll, was acting as his mouthpiece and had had a part in setting up the safe-house attack on Merriweather, and the investigation is still going on. Merriweather himself was moved to another safe house, reputed to be within the British naval base in Gibraltar, where he is guarded round the clock by armed marines and where the chances of anything happening to him range from somewhere between slim and none, but veering towards the latter. As for Vamen himself, such was the public outcry at news that a supposed crime lord could strike so blatantly at those ranged against him that the prime minister himself made a statement claiming that such lawlessness could not, and would not, be tolerated. He sounded like he meant it as well.

Vamen's trial has been put back yet again and he faces new charges as a result of the testimony of twenty-one-year-old Francis Taylor, the only survivor of the three-man assassination team. It's believed that Taylor is going to implicate Melvyn Carroll and Vamen directly. Perhaps this time Vamen might finally get the comeuppance he so richly deserves.

Tina recovered from her injuries quickly and was out of hospital within the week, and back at work within the month. Two weeks after that, we went on safari to Kenya, spending five days in the Masai Mara before flying on to Mahe in the Seychelles where we stayed for another week, soaking up the equatorial sunshine in surroundings that seemed to melt away all the stress and pressures of the daily grind. I even got to take my advanced diving course. The whole trip broke the bank, of course, and for a long time afterwards we were both paying off the debts accrued, but it was worth it. Sometimes you've just got to let go.

In late July, a few weeks after we'd got back from the trip, the two of us (now officially an item at the station) went for a barbecue at the Malik household on a fine, sunny Sunday. Malik's two daughters were eight and five, and Tina played with them like a natural. I even got the idea that she might be getting broody, and funnily enough, it wasn't such a bad thought. An expensive one, perhaps, but not a bad one. We toasted our combined successes on the O'Brien case, and the fact that we were all still here to talk about it, and in the evening, when the kids had gone to bed, Malik raised his glass, and said, 'To the future.' Tina and I, and Malik's wife Kaz, repeated the toast, and I remember that, at that precise moment, I was the happiest I'd been in a long, long time.

To the future. When we left that night, I felt a renewed sense of optimism. Which was ironic really, because I'd never see Asif Malik alive again.

But that's another story. For this one at least, the book was closed.

# Afterwards, part two

The sea front at the resort of Fuengirola on Spain's Costa del Sol is filled with English pubs, and restaurants that offer all-day full English breakfasts. If you want Spanish culture, or even Spanish people, you've come to the wrong place. If you want to blend into a crowd of fellow pasty Englishmen, then it's definitely the right one.

Stegs Jenner took a seat at one of the tables outside a particularly shabby-looking English-style pub, an establishment he remembered being there, and with roughly the same décor, including the tattered San Miguel canopy, when he'd come to Fuengirola on his first lads' holiday in 1990. Other than him, the seating area was empty, which was one of the reasons he'd chosen the place. The food there was apparently renowned for being appalling.

A waiter covered in tattoos who looked like he'd just got out of Wormwood Scrubs, and probably had done, came over with his pen and paper.

'Two pints of San Miguel,' Stegs told him from behind his sun-glasses, and the waiter skulked off again, without writing it down.

A minute later, Nicholas Tyndall slipped under the canopy, looking very suave indeed in a canary-yellow short-sleeved shirt and linen trousers, and took a seat opposite Stegs. He was carrying a black Adidas sports bag, which he placed on the seat between them.

Tyndall smiled, showing gleaming white teeth. 'Lovely day for it again,' he said, relaxing in his seat. Stegs noticed that he was wearing Armani sunglasses. Very nice. You had to give Tyndall top marks for style.

'Always is down here,' said Stegs.

'You need a suntan, my man. You look too . . . English.'

Stegs smiled back. 'I've ordered you a pint of San Miguel. Hope you don't mind.'

'Not at all. It's the only drink to drink down here.'

'To be honest, I didn't expect to see you here. I thought one of your minions would have delivered the goods.'

The beers arrived, and Stegs went for his wallet. Tyndall, however, put a hand up to stop him, and swiftly produced a twenty-euro note that he gave to the waiter. 'Keep the change.'

The waiter grinned. 'Cheers, mate. Just shout when you want another.'

'I wanted to thank you personally,' Tyndall said when he'd gone. 'You've done a lot for me these past few months, and I appreciate it.'

'That's what the money's for.'

'Yeah, but let's just say you went above and beyond the call of duty. You risked your neck on that hotel thing, and I don't forget a thing like that. Know what I mean?'

'It's nice to be appreciated. Thanks.'

'No, thank *you*. Your efforts have put two of my biggest rivals out of business. Vamen's not going to be out now until he's pushing a hundred, and that headcase Strangleman's well out of my hair. You've done well. There's even a little bonus in there for you.'

'You're too kind.'

'I hope we can work together in the future.'

'I don't know how much use I'll be to you now I've left the Force.'

'You've got guts, Stegs. That's always of use to me.'

'We'll see.'

'What's happening with the missus? Back with her yet?'

Stegs shook his head, and took a sip from his pint. 'Nah, I'm enjoying the single life for the moment, and very nice it is too. I can sleep through the nights now.'

'Off the speed?'

'Just about.'

'You should be. Very nasty stuff. Cigarette?' He pulled out a pack of Marlboro Lights.

Stegs took one and let Tyndall light it for him.

'Tell me something,' Stegs said, after he'd taken a drag. 'What the fuck were you doing using Trevor Murk for the O'Brien job? Didn't you know he was a snout of mine?'

'Course I didn't. And anyway, I didn't think he'd get caught.'

'I'm amazed you trusted someone as slack as him to carry it off.'

Tyndall smiled again, this time not showing his teeth. 'Appearances can be deceptive, my friend. Mr Murk was one of the best hitters in south-east England. Very reliable and competitively priced. He must have done ten people down the years, and that's just the ones I've heard about. Look how quickly he took out the Dutch bloke after you phoned me. I get a call from you, I put in a call to him, and that's it – an hour later, the target's dead. Very professional.'

'Except he got tagged.'

Tyndall shrugged. 'That just saved me paying him. Anyway, it's not been a problem to you, has it?'

Stegs shook his head. 'No, I've sorted it. I'm in the clear now.'

'Good. So, what are you going to do with yourself now, then?'

'This and that. I'm thinking of becoming a private eye.' He'd ditched the idea of a security consultancy now. Too boring.

'Well, if ever I want somebody found, I'll give you a call.'

'You do that.'

They finished their beers without saying much else. There wasn't really a lot to say. Finally, Tyndall stood up, winked at Stegs and said he'd see him soon. Stegs nodded, picked up the black holdall and started walking in the other direction, a richer man now than he had been five minutes before, and thinking that he really ought to be feeling guilty for all the crimes he'd committed but not quite being able to make himself. It was the story of his life.

In the end, he couldn't help thinking how clever he'd been. He'd been at it for years, of course, providing the odd piece of information to the Holtz crime family, ever since he'd crossed paths with one of their operatives on an op back in the late nineties, and had even told them about his SO7 partner, Jeff Benson, infiltrating their ranks. He'd always liked old Jeff as well, and almost certainly wouldn't have grassed him up if it hadn't been for the fact that he couldn't risk him finding out from someone in the organization about Stegs's own involvement with them. The problem, though, the one which had led to all this, was that Vamen and co. had treated him shabbily. He'd saved their skins by giving them Benson and they'd paid him a pittance: five measly grand for rescuing a multimillion-pound business empire. He'd tried to get more but Vamen had told him that it was all the info was worth, and that had been the end of it. There'd been nothing that Stegs could do, but he hadn't forgotten either, and the bitterness had festered in him for a long, long time.

However, with the break-up of the Holtzes and the arrest of Vamen he'd been able to let it go, comforting himself with the knowledge that they'd finally all got what they deserved.

Until, that was, he'd been called upon by Islington CID to set up Slim Robbie O'Brien, which was when it had become clear that maybe Vamen wasn't quite as bolloxed as Stegs had believed. The O'Brien set-up had been successful (the former Holtz man having never met him before and therefore unable to pinpoint him as a copper), but then one evening, at a meeting with Stegs and Vokes, Slim Robbie had told them, laughing, after one drink too many that there was no way Vamen was ever going to get convicted. 'He'll get to Merriweather,' he'd said. 'You wait and see. He's got contacts everywhere. He'll even take out that bastard Tyndall, too. Don't ever underestimate Neil Vamen.'

From that moment on, the die had been cast. Stegs had started getting the germ of an idea, an idea for some serious and permanent payback for the man with the contacts everywhere. All his life, people had thought they could put one over on Stegs Jenner. All his life, they'd underestimated him. The missus, his old man, the bosses. And, of course, Neil Vamen. It was time for the tables to be turned.

First of all, he'd approached Slim Robbie and told him that he'd done business himself with the Holtzes before and that perhaps they could work together to help get Vamen free and at the same time use the Colombian bust to set up Tyndall. Slim Robbie had been cautious at first (after all, he'd already been stung once) but, like all true criminals, he couldn't resist the chance to get back in the game.

So Stegs had got him to approach Strangleman Grant – a man Slim Robbie knew from the past – to tell him about a deal he knew going down between a group of Colombians with coke, and local buyers with large sums of cash. For a share of the booty, Robbie offered to give him the time and place of the transaction so that Strangleman could rob the participants, and the Jamaican had gone for it, just like they both knew he would.

The next stage had been to get Vamen involved. Using his solicitor, Melvyn Carroll, as a go-between, Stegs had told the former crime boss that he was in a position to set up Tyndall, and had given him the basic details, quickly gaining his support as well as a fee of ten grand for his troubles, to be paid when the robbery and subsequent arrests had taken place. To whet Vamen's appetite still further, Stegs had told him that he might, with some effort, be able to get hold of the location of Jack Merriweather, if he was removed from prison to a safe house. He felt sure that the new boss of SO11, Noel Flanagan, would have that sort of information and might be susceptible to some sort of blackmail.

And then there'd been the *coup de grâce*.

As the date for Operation Surgical Strike neared, and things fell into place, Stegs had made an approach to Nicholas Tyndall, telling him that Strangleman Grant was planning to rob a drugs deal along with several of his men behind his boss's back, and that the deal was a police set-up. Stegs had again been careful how much detail he'd given out but had told Tyndall he knew roughly when it was going to take place, and had explained that Slim Robbie O'Brien and Neil Vamen were also behind it, hoping to use Strangleman to set up their boss.

Tyndall had been furious, but grateful to Stegs for his help. Knowing that there wasn't much he could do to stop the robbery taking place and, keen to be rid of a loose cannon like

Strangleman who'd evidently long-outlived his usefulness, he'd arranged to be out of the country in the week in which it was to happen. He'd also been keen for revenge on Slim Robbie and, on Stegs's helpful suggestion, had agreed to have him murdered on the day of the robbery. As far as Stegs had been concerned, Slim Robbie was going to have to die anyway, since he was the obvious source of the leak and was the only person who could testify to his own involvement. It had been a pity about the granny having to buy it as well, but that was Trevor Murk for you – a callous hound to the last.

Only one cloud had threatened the success of the operation from Stegs's viewpoint, and that had been Vokes Vokerman. As the weeks had gone by, his colleague had started doing a bit of an Obi Wan Kenobi and had taken to lecturing Stegs about the temptations and dangers of the dark side (a bit late for that, Vokesy old son), and Stegs had become convinced that he knew something about what was going on. Which, unfortunately, meant that he'd now become a dangerous liability.

Stegs had always liked old Vokes, same as he'd always liked Jeff Benson, but he was also aware that sometimes you've got to make sacrifices – even major ones – in pursuit of the greater good, i.e. the enrichment of Stegs Jenner. Plus he was getting something of a taste for skulduggery. So he'd set up Vokes by making sure he was the one left behind in the hotel room when the deal went down, and, just to make sure he actually got dealt with, he'd got Slim Robbie to phone through to the hotel room and tell whoever answered the blower that they were being set up. Slim Robbie's instructions had been simple: Stegs would send him a pre-written text message on a pay-as-you-go mobile he was carrying with him, which would act as the signal to make the call. Robbie had been told to stay away from home while he phoned the hotel room in case technology traced it back to his property, and to get rid of the mobile afterwards. He'd done everything bar the last bit, which might have presented a problem to lesser men, but, since Stegs had already got rid of the mobile he'd used to contact Slim Robbie, nothing was ever traced back to him.

Stegs had always been a lucky sod, particularly where survival was concerned, but that wasn't the whole story. He was also a planner, organizing for every eventuality. Which was why he'd decided to try to incriminate Vokes as well – a particularly naughty thing to do, when you think about it, killing him and then besmirching his Christian memory – but nevertheless something that acted as another useful layer of protection.

Having found out that Vokes and his colleagues from Acton CID were going to raid a local gun dealer, he'd asked Tyndall for help, and had got him to persuade, through threat of serious violence, a small-time pimp who owed him a lot of money to fire the gun that was going to be used in the Slim Robbie hit. The pimp would be let off the money he owed, but should the police ever come calling he was to tell them that he'd rented the gun from the Acton dealer and had given it back before the raid. It might cost him a couple of years inside but, as Tyndall himself had pointed out, the alternative didn't bear thinking about.

And, aside from the odd complication such as the use of Trevor Murk for the Slim Robbie hit, plus Tino's fatal bout of foolishness, the whole thing had worked like a dream. Stegs had made plenty of money and, thanks to his unique ability to double-cross pretty much everyone he dealt with, had completely fucked things up for Vamen, and that bastard Flanagan as well, by phoning Malik to warn him of the impending assassination attempt on Merriweather.

Stegs couldn't deny it; he'd always been a bit of a bad lot. Back at school, he'd even managed to get Barry Growler expelled by setting fire to the chemistry block one night and leaving

Growler's scarf (which he'd stolen that day) at the scene, before phoning the police anonymously and posing, surprisingly successfully, as a householder to report the sighting of a youth matching the Growlster's description running away from the fire.

Treacherous to the last, that was old Stegs. But he was still the one left standing when the rest of them had fallen by the wayside.

To his left, the sea shimmered invitingly; above him, the sky was a deep, unbroken azure; attractive, scantily clad women strolled this way and that. You would have had to say, whatever your views on the world, that it was a good day to be alive.

Vokes, in one of his more crusading moments while posing as Obi Wan, had told Stegs that those with good in their hearts always win through in the end. And that those who harbour evil thoughts and commit evil deeds will always pay the price for their sins.

But then Vokes Vokerman had always been full of shit. It's nothing to do with good or evil, never has been.

When you work the crime trade, it all boils down to how well you play the game.

# Acknowledgements

This book would never have been written without the help of a large number of people within the crime business, the majority of whom would like to remain anonymous for various reasons. However, you know who you are, and I'm very grateful. Thanks too to my agents at Sheil Land and everyone at Transworld. And last, and most definitely not least, my wife, Sally.